THE
HOUSE OF
ROMANCE

THE HOUSE OF ROMANCE · TRIO 11
ISBN 0-88767-012-1
Published April 1977
March 1979 Second Printing
The stories in this volume were originally published as follows:

BACK TO SORRENTO
Copyright ©   Jill Hoyle 1975
First Published in U.K. by Robert Hale & Co. in 1975

SECRETIVE NURSE
Copyright ©   Valerie Scott 1973
First Published in U.K. by Robert Hale & Co. in 1973

A HEART OF SHADOWS
Copyright ©   Robert Hale & Co. 1974
First Published in U.K. by Robert Hale & Co. in 1974

THE HOUSE OF ROMANCE is published by
HOUSE OF ROMANCE PUBLICATIONS INC.,
a NEVASCO CORPORATION, Toronto, Canada.

Printed for PRESTIGE BOOKS INC.
New York, N.Y.

3 Great Romances

Back to Sorrento

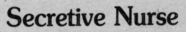

Secretive Nurse

A Heart of Shadows

Back to Sorrento

Jill Hoyle

The one undeniable fact was that I loved Dominic, loved him as I knew I could love no one else. I remembered that evening when we had stood watching the swan fly over against the soft blue English sky. Then, with Rosa's coming, with drama, adventure, the spell had been broken and I had been lost in my own uncertainties ever since.

CHAPTER ONE

"Every day speaks a new scene—the last act crowns the play."
FRANCIS QUARLES.

OUR garden behind The Highwayman in the Cotswold town of Melford is one-third terrace, ornamented by great tubs of brilliant flowers which remind me of Southern Italy, and two-thirds smoothly cut lawns with wide English herbaceous borders.

Seven-foot-high dry stone walling forms a barrier on two sides to a narrow lane which winds round into the market square. On the third, more sheltered side, it separates us from a long, steep-roofed house called Chimneys. If you count them there are certainly more chimneys than there can possibly be fireplaces in use. But they are a picturesque enough asset and, since central heating was installed, haven't needed sweeping.

On this particular evening, the one on which the curtain went up, so to speak, I was idling in my small downstairs office.

When my still-young and pretty mother married Peter Allan, the proprietor of The Highwayman, he had suggested that I might care to take a course in hotel management. I liked Peter and valued his advice. At eighteen I was still dithering over what to do with that long, inviting future which stretched ahead, and the idea had seemed a new and attractive one. From my Italian father I had inherited, oddly enough, certain practical and organising abilities as well as that golden-brown skin which contrasted its perpetual summer warmth with my ash-blonde hair and blue English eyes.

So I took the year's course, learned far more about life in that short time than either my own years or the college syllabus provided and, for the last two years, had settled into my niche at The Highwayman very contentedly.

I was just ruffling through the bills and letters on my desk and had decided to put off dealing with them until the morning, when I heard infantile wails of despair coming from over the wall, across the terrace and through the open door. Distance didn't lessen their volume.

I recognised that wail. Jeremy Crail, Chimneys five-year-old, used it with infinite subtlety as an instrument of blackmail, an expression of unholy wrath and sometimes as a simple outburst of temperament. But I knew Jeremy well enough to recognise it this time as a genuine *cri-de-coeur*, the outbreak of heartbreak and despair.

I ran across the hall and down the short passage where an open door led to the terrace. It was half-an-hour to dinner and some of our more sociably inclined guests were mingling in the bar with the regulars. The doors to the terrace were open and a few of the curious had drifted out to investigate the cause of such heart-rending sounds.

I went over to the wall and could hear Joanna, Jeremy's mother, trying to soothe her offspring.

"Pussy! Pussy Thomas!" I just distinguished the words between sobs. Then Joanna clambered up on to a garden chair, Jeremy in her arms, and sat him on top of the wall.

6

"Look, Pussy Thomas can get down from the tree if he wants to, and when Daddy comes home he will help him anyway." She was pointing towards the top of our three-hundred-year-old tulip tree, with its magnificent trunk and twisting, lavishly leafed branches.

I looked up and saw the trouble-maker himself, Pussy Thomas, who shared first place in Jeremy's heart with a revolting stuffed animal called Lolloppy, bought by Joanna at the last W.I. bring-and-buy sale. The still-kittenish Thomas, a ball of white fur with tortoiseshell trimmings, was perched on a branch three-quarters of the way up the tree, obviously in a paroxysm of height phobia. Occasionally a pathetic "mew" floated down and Jeremy was not believing a word his mother said.

Peter came up from behind us, our two-year-old bull terrier swaggering ahead of him. William looked up towards the faint mewing, recognised that fool of a cat next door and bounced up and down on the steel springs that served him for muscles, full of faith in his ability to deal with the situation if only the right idea would come to him.

"He'll get down sooner or later," said Peter. "I should take Jeremy indoors."

Easier said than done! Jeremy clung to the top of the wall and no persuasions or cajolings could halt his hysterical tears. He was rapidly on the way to making himself sick. I put my arm round him, felt the small body shaken by sobs and looked up at the stranded Thomas in despair.

The branches of the tulip tree sprang out at a low level, forming a thick, impenetrable barrier, and, from the evidence of those fallen boughs which littered the lawn in a high wind, were weakened enough by age to offer uncertain support to any sort of weight put upon them.

Mother appeared and soothingly patted Peter's shoulder and William's back, and Joanna, now on top of the wall herself, looked almost as distraught as her son.

At this moment of impasse, Dominic Lee made his entrance. He came round me to face Jeremy, put one finger under the little boy's chin and turned his tear-stained face upwards. He spoke in that quiet, lazy voice which I only heard occasionally but which was too individual to be easily forgotten.

"Is that your Thomas up there?"

Jeremy nodded and sobbed.

"You keep quiet and watch and you'll see me get him down. Does he scratch?"

"Yes!" said Jeremy, with a gulp and a hiccup.

"If he scratches me I shan't cry, so you must stop crying too. Promise?"

Jeremy nodded again and I spoke, just one word ahead of Peter.

"It's not really safe. The tree's very old and the branches may break."

Dominic looked at me and recognised my existence for the first time.

My year in London and two years in what the police call licensed premises, had given me a defence mechanism, a useful one, against men of all ages. As far as Dominic Lee was concerned it had never been needed at all.

He had come to Melford six months ago and had taken the furnished flat over Peregrine Thorpe's antique shop opposite The Highwayman. He was a writer with two best-selling thrillers to his credit and he was said to be engaged on the third. My office window commanded a clear view of the street and I had grown used to seeing the tall, slim figure bringing the little two-seater from the garage next the shop, sometimes gossiping with Peregrine.

I had been introduced to him in the usual casual fashion of most introductions given in public premises. Just lately he had taken to coming across, borrowing our William and carrying him off for long walks from which even William returned exhausted. Twice I myself had whistled the bull terrier up for him and handed over the lead.

Now, as I spoke, his eyes narrowed and one of his eyebrows slanted upwards in a slightly startled manner.

"I'm not all that heavy," he said. "I'll risk it if you'll promise to bind up the broken limbs."

He turned to Jeremy, smiled down at the small, wondering face on which the tears were drying. Then he stripped off a short light jacket he wore and unceremoniously gave it to me. The fairly close-fitting grey slacks and black polo-necked sweater seemed suitable enough wear for weaving his way through the tree's twisted branches.

"I'll manage. Don't worry," he said. Then, as another cry for help came down from Thomas above, he went into action.

William, of whom those long walks had made an adoring slave, decided to sit and watch approvingly. Jeremy returned to his mother's arms, bravely controlling the occasional sob, and Mother clutched my arm tightly while Peter gave a sigh of resignation and turned

9

to assure the other watchers that all, he hoped, was well. It wasn't until later that I realised my own state of tension. I was clenching my hands until my nails bit into my palms.

There was a trembling in the leaves as the climber moved upwards, the sound of a creaking branch, a stumble and, presumably, a recovery. We heard a voice say, "Oh hell and damnation!" in a singularly good-humoured and relaxed manner. Jeremy, watching fascinated, his mouth open, closed it long enough to repeat a garbled version of the words.

I caught a brief glimpse of a head through the green leaves, copper tints in its mid-brown, the colour of those blooms which, in two months' time would decorate the chrysanthemums in the garden.

There came another ominous crack and a short thick branch broke from the main stem and hurtled down to the lawn.

"My God! I hope he doesn't follow it!" Peter said, and the prayer must have been answered, for he didn't.

A few more tense moments and then a brown hand appeared suddenly, and just as suddenly Thomas vanished from his perch. After that the climber's descent may have been as precarious as the way up, but it was somewhat in the nature of an anti-climax. Dominic dropped to the grass on the far side of the tree and strolled over to the wall, trying to detach Thomas's grip from his sweater.

"Pussy!" Jeremy's hands were outstretched, and the cat, sensing a different sort of danger ahead, leapt from the shoulder to which his sharp little claws were still affixed and streaked across his own lawn to kitchen and supper and safety. Joanna lifted Jeremy down. He ran

10

off in pursuit and, with a hurried thank you to Dominic, she in her turn streaked away after her son.

There was a light clapping from the audience on our terrace, a congratulatory bark from William, and then thirsty drinkers melted away in their chosen directions.

"Well, you saved me a lot of trouble, Dominic. I appreciate it. See you later." Peter went off to his duties as mine host, and Mother, about to follow him, stopped and uttered a cry of sympathy.

"Your hand! What happened? It's bleeding badly."

It certainly was. A long, jagged tear stretched from his wrist up to the base of his little finger and blood was beginning to drip on the lawn. William reached up to give the hand a sympathetic nudge with a wet, black nose. Dominic found his handkerchief and wrapped it round the wound.

"Helen dear, take Mr Lee to your office and give him some first-aid. Mr Lee, you're a hero!" Mother patted his shoulder, gave her own inimitable smile and vanished too.

I looked up into two greenish-grey eyes.

"I slipped when the branch broke and the jagged ends caught my hand."

"Well, come along," I told him brusquely and, accompanied by William, he obediently followed. I was conscious of those observant eyes behind me, so I fell back and we walked in together. It wasn't until we were in the office that I remembered the new books on my desk. Half Melford must have asked for them at the library, but I had bought them the day before when I paid my weekly visit to Oxford. Now I hastily threw the coat which I still carried over them and cleared the middle of my desk for the contents of the first-aid box.

11

"Come over to the staff cloakroom," I told him. "We'll use hot water on that cut."

He followed me once more in silent submissiveness, but as I glanced up I saw his mouth twitch. I bathed the cut, which really was a nasty, jagged tear.

"Please, Nurse, may I wash the other hand?" he asked, and when he came back to my room all traces of his escapade were gone and the cap of coppery brown hair, its sleek cut never obtained in Melford, was smooth again.

"Fa figura," I muttered, using my second language; but I liked that well-groomed look.

So I cut a long strip of Band-aid, or whatever it was the first-aid cupboard provided, and attended to the job in hand. As I finished, John, from the bar, tapped and came in with a tray.

"Mr Allan's compliments and he says you'll need it."

There was a glass of whisky there and a glass of Italian vermouth beside it. Conviviality was being thrust upon me.

I sat down on my desk and took up my glass. Dominic Lee took up his. We looked at each other over our glasses' rims and drank; blue eyes and green eyes caught together for a long time it seemed. Dimly I realised that my treasured defence mechanism was quite out of action.

"Where did you get that colour of yours?" he asked. "You really are a golden girl, aren't you?"

"From my Italian father," I told him. "I am going to Southern Italy on Friday and I shall come back exactly the same, no more, no less."

He made a small grimace. "So soon? But you'll give me just one day before you go?"

William, who had dropped in and was lying nose on

paws in the doorway, thumped his tail absentmindedly.

"But I can't!" I protested. "I must leave things all straight for Mother to take over."

"Just an evening then. What about Stratford? I can pull strings to get tickets. Supper afterwards. *The Merchant* I think it is. Is Venice your home town?"

"No. Sorrento—or near enough. Early school days in Florence, though."

"But you'll come?"

And, eyes caught and held again, I nodded.

He picked up his coat and saw the two books lying underneath.

"I would have liked to give them to you," he said. "Tomorrow then, at five o'clock, destination Stratford." And he was gone.

"My defences are down." I hummed it through under my breath and William gave a small contented snore.

So it was, in a mixture of drama and comedy, the curtain went up on that lovely evening in early May.

CHAPTER TWO

"Pleasures newly found are sweet."—WORDSWORTH.

THE following morning I was up early.

Through my office window I found myself watching the leisurely life of Melford drift by. Dominic's windows were open but his typewriter wasn't competing with the spring chirrup of domestically minded birds. Cleo Patrick, the highlight of Melford Art Club and the inspiration of the Dramatic Society, appeared in Peregrine's antique shop window and began to turn out the contents of his corner cupboard. She picked up a beflowered saucer and examined it closely to see if it were early Victorian as Peregrine claimed or pre-war Woolworth's as she rather suspected. Cleo's pointed nose peered through the hanks of straight hair which hung dismally round her face. That hair was one reason why I had gone to Antoine and let him cut my own into the thick, curving bob which swung bell-like round the nape of my neck.

That morning I had more than enough jobs to do but I couldn't settle to them. My thoughts wandered back to last night, to Dominic Lee and to that instinctively wary attitude I had developed towards most men.

For a girl who, until her twelfth birthday, had attended an Italian school in Florence and had then been transferred to a traditional girls' school in Cheltenham, that year in London had been quite a shattering experience.

Mother had been a little worried at my sudden explosion into the great world, but my reaction was actually the opposite of what she feared. I had left London half-convinced that I was some sort of freak, different from all the rest. I took refuge in a hostel, a very pleasant, easy-going sort of place, only after, unknown to Mother, I had followed up a couple of flat-sharing advertisements from the *Evening Star*.

Two pretty girls they were in that first flat, though they did wear the fashionable jumble-sale look. The flat had two bedrooms. Jane and Judith shared the larger one and I was to have the smaller. That suited me. Then Jane said carelessly, "If one of us has a boy friend for the night you won't mind the other bringing the camp bed in with you, will you, sweetie? You're safely on the Pill yourself, by the way, aren't you?"

Human nature being what it is, I could see myself sharing my room with an occupied camp bed more or less permanently, so, without answering that leading question, I made my excuses and left.

My second investigation at first seemed more promising. The advertiser was an older woman, fortyish, good looking, short, crisply cut hair, elegant shirt and slacks.

"Call me Bobby. My fool parents christened me Barbara," she said. Then I discovered that to Bobby, two girls living together meant inevitably that girls only liked girls. This was going a little too far in the other direction! I liked everyone, male, female and multi-sex. So I said goodbye to Bobby and wished her luck and, as I was pushed for time, took refuge in my hostel.

At the college I made friends easily enough with those young things working desperately hard at being modern. I was fond of most of them, but some comments cropped up with monotonous regularity.

"Duckie, you must be frig.!"

"Darling, you've never even tried!"

"Look, I'll lend you Robin, sweetie, He's an absolute dish and has everything!"

Robin had shoulder-length blond curls, a hairy chest of which he must have been inordinately proud, for he never did his shirt up above the waist, and a string of beads which he said came from a Tibetan monastery and had been prayed over for a thousand years.

I admired the beads but nothing else that Robin possessed.

In the end all my good friends would say affectionately, "Leave Helen alone. She's our vestal virgin."

I ended up as a sort of mascot.

It was a relief to come back to Melford and young farmers and thrusting point-to-pointers, and Peregrine in his antique shop, even to stoutish middle-aged weekenders whom I evaded under the fatherly jurisdiction of Peter. But that defence mechanism of mine was always ready to spring into action.

Now I looked across the street where spring sunshine and May breezes threw dancing shadows across to Dominic's windows and I knew that I had met someone against whom I just couldn't or wouldn't defend myself.

William followed my morning coffee into the room, sensed my away-ness and pushed his black nose into my hand. He was an understanding dog, was William.

16

From then on I had a busy day, too busy to let me look out of the window again. At four o'clock I ran upstairs to my own room. Peter had made me a bed-sitting-room with a luxurious bathroom-cum-dressing-room attached and a big walk-in wardrobe. The olive-green carpet with matching green and daffodil striped curtains and divan cover, the big white rug before the electric fire, the yellow and white cushions in the deep armchairs, and a few bits of elegant Regency furniture found by Peregrine, were all my own choice.

I took a shower and made careful selection of what I should wear. I would dress up to compliment the occasion but not to flatter it. I chose a white dress of Italian silk sprigged with yellow and blue nosegays, full sleeved, high waisted, with an ankle-length skirt of tiny pleats and a scooped-out oval neckline. No jewellery and hair brushed until it shone, little make-up and the well-groomed look that would have dated me had I been fifteen years older.

I looked at myself and approved. Mother met me in the corridor and approved too.

"There's my lovely daughter!" she said.

"Just look at her lovely mother!" I answered, and ran downstairs to see Dominic pulling up at the door in the small black two-seater I'd watched him back into the garage opposite so often. I'd always admired the skill with which that steep incline was mastered.

He smiled as he slipped into the seat beside me and we settled back in the intimacy of the little car. We didn't speak until we reached the top of the hill outside Melford. Then he pulled on to the wide grass verge.

"Let's see the view," he said, and was out of the

17

car and opening my door before I had reached the handle.

We stood looking over the wide field which swept down to a small, twisting river. It was a glorious evening with little white clouds gambolling like fluffy lambs over a blue sky and the breeze throwing silver ribbons across bending grass. There are some things that bring magic with them and one came now—the beat of a swan's wings as the great white bird flew over, darkening the grass with shadow as it passed.

I held my breath and clasped Dominic's arm until the moment was gone, and felt his hand on my waist. Then we were back in the car knowing that we had shared a moment of pure delight. I began to tell him about my coming visit to Italy, that it would be my first since Mother and I had come to England for good. Now I had become completely English, but I still loved Italy for my childhood's and my father's sake.

"How long will you be away?"

"Only a fortnight. An aunt of mine, Mother's sister, is to come for the second week. Aunt Joan is a dear. We shall do things together, and there will be Rosa."

"And who is Rosa?"

"She was at school with me in Florence. We haven't seen each other since we were twelve, when Mother brought me to England, but we've written regularly, Rosa in English, I in Italian. Rosa's father was an American. He was killed in a car crash three months after my father died. Rosa might have gone to America eventually, but when that happened her mother didn't want to leave Italy, of course. So while I became English, Rosa became Italian. We're both of us still bi-lingual though. I am luckier than Rosa because her

18

mother died too, a year ago. I'm longing to see her
again; she was so gay and bright and lovely."

I paused and remembered that letter with the Italian
stamp which had arrived two days ago. I frowned, considering its contents, and Dominic, glancing towards me,
saw the frown.

"What's worrying you, golden girl?" he asked.

"I don't know. Nothing real, I expect. But Rosa
sounded worried herself the last time she wrote. She
has always lived in Sorrento save for school days in
Florence. Her only relative now is an uncle who has
been ill for some time. He is partly paralysed, the long-
term result of a war wound, and now his heart is giving
trouble. Rosa goes to visit him regularly.

"I should have said he *was* her only relative because
a few months ago two more turned up. They are her
father's cousins and she didn't even know they existed.
They'd come over from America for a holiday, I suppose. Rosa was so pleased at first, but the last time she
wrote she said she was worried, that maybe I'd be able
to help her work things out. She was feeling lonely, was
longing to talk to me, and to Mother, about her problems. But she didn't seem sure of what her problems
were."

"Perhaps those new relatives. Maybe she doesn't like
them after all," said Dominic.

"Maybe." I was unconvinced.

"You went to school in Florence, but where was your
home?"

"Not far from Sorrento, at Castellammare di Stabia.
We looked down on a deep blue sea with tall, jagged
rocks reflected in the water. My father was the only one
left of his family and he inherited a cameo factory not

19

far from Pompeii, an old business, one that had survived two world wars. He was building it up and he worked hard. I remember him so gay, full of vitality and charm, but he died from a coronary before he was forty."

Dominic was silent, but he put out his hand and touched mine. Then he said, "I shall have to come to Rome soon to see an English film director out there. They're making a film of that first book of mine and he's doing the Italian sequences."

"Yes, in Florence. I was reading it until one o'clock this morning."

I had read all those biographical details on the book jacket: first-class history degree, lecturing scholarship in the States, work in an advisory capacity for some of the best-known historical TV programmes, then this first thriller with its racy narrative and charm of style.

So we came to Stratford, to the reflection of white swans and golden lights and the shadows of Clopton Bridge in the water, to the tense excitement of a rapt audience and a mercifully un-gimmicky production.

As we drove home through a moonlit night, stage moonlight on the lawns of Belmont was far less real than this moonlight over the Cotswold hills. Yet, when the car slid to its last stop, the latticed windows of The Highwayman, the uneven slate roofs of that stretch of grey stone houses asleep in the moonlight, seemed more like a stage-set than Belmont itself.

Dominic stood by while I unlocked my door. Staff and residents were safely in bed by now; even Mother and Peter should be asleep. We whispered goodnight and I tiptoed in and ran upstairs to watch him drive the car quietly up the steep slope to the garage.

I waited until I saw him unlock his own door and the light shine from his window.

Then I drew my curtains, ready for bed and sleep and the dreams I expected. But my expectations were not to be realised. Far by far the most dramatic event of that long day was yet to come.

CHAPTER THREE

"Fears and Fancies thick upon me came."—WORDSWORTH

I GOT ready for bed in a state of sleepy content. I switched out the main light, turned the bedside one into a warm cosiness and prepared for at least fifteen minutes with Dominic's *Murder at Culloden.*

From the bathroom I had heard a car stop and then drive off again. Between midnight and seven o'clock, Tollgate Street where The Highwayman stands, is usually undisturbed save by the distant chimes of the church clock on the half-hour and the hour.

It struck one-thirty now. Then came a faint tapping sound from below. Our main door stood unlocked all day, wide open in good weather, and it boasted neither bell nor knocker.

How quiet the rambling old house was. Ancient oak floor boards creaking softly, the rustle of falling dust behind the panelling, a spider spinning its web under a dark beam; even these familiar whispers of sound were silenced at this hour.

Then I heard the light tapping again, the faint sound of footsteps on the pavement below. No burglar would tap gently on our door. Perhaps the car I had heard had left some stranded traveller needing a haven for the night. William, after greeting my return, had retired to his cubby-hole behind the reception desk downstairs.

22

He would have leapt up wide awake at the breath of a sound within the building. For anything outside he would have needed an alarm clock. I got out of bed, putting down Dominic's book with a sigh, and slipped on my dressing-gown.

The corridor outside my door stretched long and dark. I switched on a wall light and, as I tiptoed downstairs, remembered a lady resident who had claimed psychic powers. She had wandered about the house in the small hours accompanied by a reluctant William who, like all dogs, she declared, was psychic too. It wasn't until the third night that her antics had been discovered. She had accidentally sent a large copper jug, filled with Mother's gladioli, flying down the main staircase. It scored a hit on Peregrine's favourite warming pan and the resultant clamour and William's barking roused the whole house.

She declared she had twice seen the original highwayman, black masked, booted and spurred, standing in a corner of the hall with his head held at a most unnatural angle. Peter broke it to her that Robert Scarrot, the highwayman of legend, had not ended ill-spent days with neck twisted on the gallows. In fact, ill-gotten gains and natural charm had won the allegiance of the locals and the daughter of a small innkeeper as bride. He had built all our seventeenth-century additions and his name was for ever commemorated in The Highwayman.

However, Mrs Costella had claimed William as a fellow witness to his re-appearance. "Look how the hair down his back rises every time he looks towards that corner!"

It usually did. That corner had once been laid claim

to by the vicar's bad-tempered Chow who had walked in after his master uninvited. William still hoped for a repetition of so glorious an occasion.

Now the tick of two long-case clocks solemnly echoed each other from the entrance hall and from the large lounge. One corner of the hall was assuredly very dark and a tall mahogany cupboard threw grotesque blackness over its shadows.

I shivered and, for a moment, contemplated return to the safety of my room. Then William came tiptoeing to meet me, his whole body vibrant in expectation of adventures to come and I shook off silly fears.

"Quiet, William," I whispered, and he followed me to the door of the long lounge, dimly lit by that single wan street lamp allowed to survive the night. A lazy strand of creeper moved across a window. I stood watching its wavering black fingers. Then a white face was pressed against the latticed panes. It vanished and there came a small scraping sound and silence.

"Come on, William," I said, and he followed me out into the hall and sat obedient as I drew back the bolts. I turned the key and, cautiously pulling the door open, I looked out. To the left was an oak seat flanked by a tub of newly planted geraniums. At its far end sat a girl, feet up, enormous dark eyes staring into mine. For a moment I stared back. Then a smile overspread her face. She was just the same, still as enchantingly pretty as when I last saw her. I held out my arms and we hugged each other as tightly as those two children had hugged each other when they said goodbye nine years ago.

It was Rosa! Rosa here in Melford three days before I should have met her in Sorrento!

We stood apart and looked at each other.

"Helen, dear Helen! I am so glad to see you. So tired I am! I thought I would have to sleep on that very hard seat all the night long!"

"You might have done, too, if I hadn't had a late night myself," I told her. I picked up her case and led her inside. Sweet William, still sitting obediently and showing great self-control, followed us in. When I turned round from re-locking the door they had already made friends and it was with reluctance that William went back to his own bed when I whispered goodnight.

"We'll not talk until we are in my room," I told her, and led the way upstairs, to the glow of the fire, the warmth of the bedside light and Dominic's book open on my pillow. Rosa sank into one of my deep chairs and I saw then how exhausted she was.

"When did you last eat?" I asked her.

"There were little trays on the plane. Helen, it was my first plane flight! I couldn't eat but I drank the coffee."

She drew her feet up into the big chair, pushing off her shoes and looking very small.

"Rest there," I told her. "I'll go to the kitchen and get you something. You'll feel better when you've eaten and then you must sleep."

I turned left from my door and went down the narrow stairs which led to a side entrance and the kitchen, a staircase never used by residents. At the turn I paused. Here two steps led up to a room we usually kept for children. It had its own small bathroom and it was pretty and very quiet, away from the sounds of the house. The bed was always aired and ready and I would put Rosa here.

I slipped in, switched on the fire and drew the curtains over a window which looked across the garden. I took towels from a drawer where they were stored and saw that the bathroom was fully equipped. Then I ran down to the kitchen and, ten minutes later, returned carrying a tray with a bowl of good hot soup, biscuits, butter and cheese, fresh fruit and a glass of milk. I had gone to the bar as well and had added two glasses containing a measure of brandy. We both needed it, I decided.

Rosa was already asleep and I stood for a moment looking at her. Incredibly long black eyelashes curled on her cheeks. I might be a golden girl but Rosa's gold was touched with the rose bloom of a ripe peach. Just now weariness had put dark shadows under her eyes but they would be gone by morning. Her hair, long, black and silky, curled over her shoulders.

I touched her gently and she opened her eyes, then gave a little yawn, looking like a pretty kitten. Within a minute she was eating her soup, making the occasion seem like a midnight feast in a school dormitory.

"Dear, clever Helen," she said. "I was so very hungry!"

"Rosa," I told her, "I am terribly glad to see you and I am longing to know what this is all about. But we are both so tired that I am leaving questions until the morning."

She looked at me, large-eyed.

"I was so frightened and I had to run away. I am ashamed if I must be a nuisance to you, but you and your mother were here and you both seemed so safe. So I came." She blinked tears away, then leaned back and closed her eyes again.

"You'll never be a nuisance, but all the details can

wait. Now you're going to bed." I picked up the un-touched glass of brandy and she followed me to the welcoming little room. I went through to the bathroom and turned on the hot water.

"Pop in and out quickly and you'll feel lots better. Will you need your big case, the one I left downstairs?"

She was already beginning to strip off her clothes and I noticed, tired though she was, how neatly she folded them and put them on a chair.

"No, not tonight, Helen darling. But there are things in the top of the small one. It's not locked because I've lost the keys, but I kept it with me all the time. Could you please bring what I shall want for the night? In one second I shall be in the bath." She vanished through the bathroom door and there was a slight splash and a few words, in ecstatic Italian this time. I went back to my own room.

Her small case was, as she said, unlocked. I lifted it on to a table, not bothering to turn on the centre light. I was so sleepy and the softly shaded lamp made my bed look even more inviting.

I slipped the catch round and the lid opened at once. A blue toilet bag was on top, under it a light silky wrap, a pair of tiny embroidered travelling slippers and a lacy, be-frilled nightdress. I picked them up quickly and, as I threw the nightdress over my arm, it unrolled and a collection of miscellaneous articles fell from it on to the next layer of packing. Something dropped to the floor and I stooped to pick it up, a narrow gold bracelet set with stones that flashed at me in blue fire as I put it on the table.

Rosa must have wrapped her jewellery in her night-dress. I was halfway to her room when the thought struck me that if the bracelet were set with real stones it was worth a great deal.

Rosa was out of her bath and enveloped in a large towel. I tossed the bag and the nightdress to a chair and took the wrap and slippers back to the bedroom. I had barely turned back the sheet and put the brandy on the bedside table before she was there herself.

"Rosa, you had rolled up some jewellery in your nightdress. Shall I bring the case along to you here?"

"Oh, Helen, I did! In so great a hurry I was! The proper box for them is big and heavy. I wanted them safe with me so I emptied it and put it into the suitcase. Would the customs man have thought me a jewel thief if he had unwrapped my nightdress?"

She began to giggle in an overwrought, hysterical fashion, and I remembered how often we had giggled together as schoolgirls. Then, with an effort, she stopped and gave her little yawn again.

"You keep them for tonight, darling. Tomorrow I will tell you everything. If I have been silly you will forgive me?"

"I'll forgive you anything and everything. Now drink this and you will sleep without any dreams." Obediently she drained the glass, gave a little grimace of appreciation and snuggled down on the pillows.

"So comfortable, il letto! Buona notte, cara mia."

I leaned down and kissed her forehead. "Buona notte, carissima," I said, and switched off the light. Back in my own room I moved the tray to the small service table in the corridor and added a scribbled note asking that breakfast should be taken to the "little girl's room" at nine o'clock next morning. I picked up the fallen bracelet to put it back into Rosa's case, and then I stood

like Aladdin transfixed by the glories of his newly discovered cave. This was a dazzling cave in miniature. A
tiara and a deep collar like those diamond ones worn
by queenly heads blazed up at me. I took up bracelets
and necklaces and let them slip through my fingers,
sapphires, emeralds, blood-red rubies.

Then, like Rosa, I began to laugh. These weren't
real—couldn't be. But they would certainly have caused
a minor sensation if a customs official had tipped them
out of their hiding place in Rosa's gossamer lingerie. I
closed the case. I switched off the fire and reluctantly
laid Dominic's book aside. I drank my own brandy
gratefully, turned off the bedside lamp and, as I lay
my head on the pillow, heard the church clock strike
three.

CHAPTER FOUR

"Our Playwright may show in some fifth act what this wild drama means."—TENNYSON.

I DREAMED that Dominic and I, driving back from Stratford, found ourselves in a small square in Sorrento. Shakespeare's Shylock lay fast asleep on a carved wooden seat centrally positioned on a raised terrace before a café. Customers, quite oblivious of his presence, were eating multi-coloured iced concoctions and drinking espresso coffees. We joined them.

Rosa, with a knife between her teeth and dressed in a bikini made of flashing diamonds—which must have been highly inconvenient—came dancing up the steps towards us. A church clock pealed out a tumble of notes, William barked and I woke up. I saw Rosa's case on the table across the room, remembered everything and rang the bell.

It was Mother who brought me my tray and I had already taken a quick shower and was prepared to eat standing up. But she poured out my coffee and made me sit down.

"Now don't get in a flap. It would have done you good to sleep till eleven. Tell me about Stratford; and where did the suitcase left downstairs with Rosa Rossini's name on it come from?"

So I told her that Stratford had been heaven, then gave her a brief account of Rosa's arrival.

"I was afraid we were going to meet the ghost and William was hoping we were. Now I must hurry to say 'Buon'giorno' to her and you must come too and hear what she has to tell us."

I was wondering about my own plans, but they could hardly be changed now. There was Aunt Joan to think about. She had gone back to nursing when Uncle Bill died and had decided to manage a spring break of just seven days. Then a late cancellation had given me the chance of an extra week on my own and I had jumped at it.

"You must go as planned, of course. Rosa shall stay here with me if she cares to," Mother said, and I put on my clothes while she sat looking at and commenting on my Stratford programme.

"I like Dominic Lee so much." She spoke with that inflection which means "Do you?", but I didn't rise to the hidden query. It was too soon to put ideas into a maternal heart and head, so we went along to Rosa's room.

She was sitting up in bed, all signs of strain gone.

"Why, I would have known you at once, my dear!" and it was easy to see that Rosa would be safe and well cherished in Mother's care. I sat at the end of the bed and she settled into a chair.

"Now tell us everything from the beginning," I said.

Rosa began to speak in Italian, then switched back to English, for Mother's Italian had never been as fluent as mine.

"I was so afraid. But I must go right back to the beginning, to what I was doing in Sorrento when the new cousins came. I have told Helen in my letters that my mother left me a little money, so I have been to a school of drama, to learn to speak, to walk, to dance a little. You see, I would be an actress, a film actress perhaps. Already, as a student, I have been given a few small parts—very small. No one has noticed me yet, but one day they will. I shall make them."

"There's no doubt whatever that they'll do that," Mother assured her, and got a radiant smile in response.

"I live, as Helen knows, in a small apartment which I share with another girl, a nice girl. She works in an agency for travel and it is through her that I sometimes get work as a guide. Oh, those women's clubs of America! But this work has helped me and my air passage to England was part of my—what do you say?"

"Perks," I prompted, knowing her passion for English idiom.

"Ah, yes! Because I have worked long enough I have been perked! Oh, those hours and hours in Pompeii with those so earnest ladies! I think I have met every little lizard who lives there!" She made an expressive gesture with her hands and I saw all those little lizards darting in and out of Pompeii's stone walls.

"But I must tell you of my uncle—Vincentio Rossini. It is the name I use now. He was my mother's brother and in Sorrento she was always a Rossini. You know how it is, and it is perhaps easier to say than my father's name of Russell, though it is similar. There were two brothers and my Uncle 'Centio was the older. Guilio was fifteen when the war began and only nineteen when he was killed, during the liberation.

"We of the south were not organised as those farther north, and in Naples there were four days of fighting. Some of those who had always hated the Fascisti died then and Uncle Guilio was one. When the allies came

32

Guilio tried to join the partisans in Naples, but he was betrayed and killed. My Uncle 'Centio survived those days and went on to fight the Germans in Rome and in Florence too. When it was all over he came back to Sorrento.

"My mother, who was a young girl then, told me all this. My uncle lived but he was badly wounded and it is really from that wound he is dying. I hope I have not tired you with all this history, but it is so much part of my uncle, who is a wonderful person."

There was a tap at the door and I picked up Rosa's used tray. Her heavy suitcase had been brought up, too, so I waited while Sheila, our local redhead, brought it in. When she had gone, Rosa went on with her story.

"On his return my uncle reclaimed the family fruit and olive trees. Then later, in Naples, he met my Aunt Tanya, whose mother was in the corps de ballet of a visiting company. The mother, whose name was Anna, had come from Russia during the revolution. Anna was not a great dancer and she did not wish Tanya to be a dancer at all. But I can still remember how slim and graceful my Aunt Tanya was and how different from most Italian girls. Maybe she should have been a dancer. But she met my uncle before she was eighteen and he loved her very much. He still does, though she died twelve years ago."

Rosa paused. "But I cannot go on lying here. I will talk as I get up." She slipped out of bed and sped into the bathroom, and I went to my room and returned with her small case.

A brief splashing under the shower over, she came back wearing briefs and bra and, sitting down before the dressing-table, began to talk again.

"Anna, Aunt Tanya's mother, had a friend who really was a great dancer, who would have become very famous if she had not died when she was only twenty-nine. Her name was Elena Alexyevna, and she had been the mistress of Prince Pontiesky. There was a great love between them. She escaped from Russia, rumour said, with all the jewels the Prince had given her. But Tanya said that was not so. Anna, her mother, knew the truth, for she was with Elena until the end.

"The Prince's family, the Princess and her two daughters, escaped to Paris. But all the Prince's possessions were taken and he was killed by the revolutionaries."

Rosa had put cream on her face with careless but efficient speed. Now she added a dusting of powder, found the keys to her big case and opened it. She began to unpack and hang the dresses and suits in her wardrobe.

"All this you will see why I tell it you later. Tanya died and my uncle has lately grown much worse. The bullet which was near his spine has moved and his legs are increasingly paralysed. His shoulders and arms are strong, but he can walk very little and now his heart is not good."

"Who looks after him?" I asked.

"There is a woman called Teresa Pascati. I think she is not a happy woman. But she has nursed and she is very loyal to my uncle. She has rooms behind a shop which is on the ground floor below my uncle's rooms. She is strong and efficient and my uncle is well content with her services. His rooms are over this shop, a shop for tourists, in the Square S. Vincentio, in the centre of Sorrento about three kilometres from where I live.

"There are private stairs from the courtyard at the back of the shop to my uncle's rooms. He is mostly in his bed now, in the room on to the balcony. I can go straight up the staircase to see him and it is easy. Helen, you will visit him, tell him I am safe?"

"He thought you were in some danger?" Mother spoke quickly.

"No, for I said nothing to him; but he will wonder, will be uneasy, when I do not come.' '

"Why were you so afraid, Rosa?"

"These two new relations, the cousins, came from America about six weeks ago. As you know, my father was an American soldier who came to Italy after the liberation. He met and married my mother and, when the war was over, he found good work with an American business firm in Naples, where he drove each week from Sorrento. And so he died in an accident, on that winding road which is still so dangerous now. My father had very few American relations. He had been left an orphan and an aunt had brought him up as her own. She died soon after he died and, as you would expect, my mother lost touch with America then.' '

"You didn't know of these two who came to Italy?"

"I knew that my father's aunt had a daughter very much older than he was. Of the coming of these two, and the woman was that daughter, she said, I knew nothing until they telephoned me. They have rented a small villa, halfway down to the sea : it is shabby but quiet, on a large piece of ground with two cypress trees and a few fruit and olive trees to give shade. They were pleased to find me and I was so pleased to meet them.

Rosa had emptied her case of clothes and now she sat back on her heels by its open lid, looking at the bottom layer left behind : walking shoes, a silver hand mirror and an oblong parcel wrapped in tissue paper. She looked across at me, her small face distressed.

"They were very friendly, like most Americans. I was ready to like them, but somehow, from the beginning, I did not feel sure. Sophie has once been a good-looking woman. But her eyes are very cold and black and hard, and what she feels is hidden beneath them. Her husband, Myers Cannan, for that is their second name, is thin and short but he looks strong. They both wear dark glasses because their eyes do not like the sun, and they do not go out a great deal which, for Americans, is strange."

Rosa reached across to her other case, opened the lid, picked up a handful of the flashing jewels which had so startled me the night before, and let them drip through her fingers.

My mother gave a gasp, but Rosa, seeming oblivious of what she was doing, began to speak again, letting the glittering handfuls fall in a tumbled heap on the carpet.

"These cousins could not speak Italian of course, so we spoke in English. I would write notes for them to the old woman who came in to clean and who would do some shopping for them. Sophie cooked Italian food very well. They were very interested in me and Sophie told me things of my father when he was a child. They had a snapshot of him taken in his uniform, one he had sent to his aunt in America, they said."

There was a scratching at the door and I opened it to William, overjoyed at finding me. After an all-round greeting he sat down by Rosa and gazed at me. She picked up the collar of diamonds and put it round his neck. It was too small but, like a child, she held it in place for a moment and smiled at the result. William sat looking like some severe and bejewelled dowager duchess. Then she went on with her story.

"Sophie and Myers became more and more interested in me. They found out that Uncle 'Centio was my only living relative and they wanted to know when I visited him and where he lived. Then, always I would find Myers waiting near the courtyard for me when I left. Because I had been working it would be evening and already dark, and he said he did not like a young girl to be alone, which seemed to me to be very silly for an American! But he would make me come back to the villa for supper and then see me to the main road for home. When the drama school ended for me at Easter, and my last job finished, they wanted me to go to stay with them, said they would renew their lease of the villa."

She got up and took down from the wardrobe where she had hung them, a short pleated skirt and a lemon-yellow sweater. "I will soon get to the end," she promised, her voice muffled as she pulled it over her head. She turned to the glass and began to comb her hair, her face expressionless.

"This week, on Tuesday—yes, only yesterday it was —I was free in the daytime at last. So I thought I would go to see my uncle in the sunlight, but first I would call on Sophie and Myers. I would tell them I could not stay with them. I would make some excuse, but I would not go to them."

"Surely they would understand you had your own career to think of," Mother said. "Perhaps they meant you should take a short holiday with them, meant it as a kindness."

Rosa put down her comb with sharp precision and swung round to face us. She was frowning.

"Yes. I know that I seemed to be ungenerous. It worried me. I do not usually dislike people for no reason. I like all people. If I do not like them I do not know them," she added ingenuously. "But these were of my father's family, and though I am become Italian as Helen is English, there are links with America still."

"Rosa, you are sure that they really are your cousins?"

She smiled at me and gave a little shrug.

"I have wondered when you would ask me that. I had no real proof. But what had they to gain by pretending to be of my blood? And they had that photograph and there were things that Sophie knew about the old house where my father grew up. He had told me of the porch where his aunt sat on fine days and of two old apple trees in what he called the yard. Those apple trees are gone now, they said. They had too a letter he had written to his aunt. It told of the position he had found in Naples, of his wife and especially of the little daughter. They showed it to me."

"Did your father ever talk about Sophie?" asked Mother.

"Not to me. Sophie was much older than my father. She got married and left for California when he was just a child. Things were hard then and she was not able to come home though she wrote regularly, she said. My father would be fifty now and she and Myers must be in their sixties. My mother once told me that it was the married daughter who had written to tell her of the aunt's death. But I must get to what caused me really to be afraid.

38

"On Tuesday I got to the villa early. There is a small path from a side entrance which leads through some trees and shrubs to the side of a high terrace in front of the big windows. My shoes made no sound. It was not until I was under the wall of the terrace, about to go round to the steps in its front, that I heard the clink of cups and the sound of voices. It was a late breakfast and suddenly I realised that the voices were those of Sophie and Myers. At first I had not recognised them and now I knew why. They were speaking in fluent Italian, not cultured Italian but with much dialect— Neapolitan, which can be almost a language in itself.

"At first I could not believe it; these American cousins who had not one word of my language! I was bewildered. Then the words became clearer to me and I listened. There was a caged bird singing from a balcony far below, and I heard Sophie say—" Rosa turned to me and talked suddenly in swift, excited Italian. She finished, then sat looking down on small brown hands, clenched tightly on her knee. I turned to Mother, who was looking lost, and translated quickly.

"She heard Sophie say, 'He may have given them to her some time ago, for we are sure she has carried nothing away from him since we have been here.'

"Then Myers said, 'Those jewels are a gamble, for us alone. It is the list for which we have been sent. That will mean much money and we must get it, even if we have to go to him ourselves. But the girl—she is the easiest way. Afterwards—' He stopped and Sophie said, 'She would not be the first pretty girl to disappear. We shall have gone before they look for her.' Go on, Rosa, that is where you stopped," I said.

"I heard the chairs move as they got up. Sophie said,

'The old woman will come soon. We are fools to talk here like this.' Myers said, "It is good to be ourselves sometimes.' If they had come towards the side of the terrace they would have seen me and I was terrified. Quickly I moved from the path, made my way through the trees and into the main road once more. I went to the Square S. Vincentio to see my uncle."

"Did you have any real idea of what they wanted, and why?"

"It meant nothing to me then. I knew of the stage jewellery Elena Alexyevna had given to Tanya's mother, of this list I had never heard. All I myself had was a little money in the bank and a ring my father had given to my mother." She looked down at a small diamond cluster on her finger. "That I wear nearly always. Then, when I got to my uncle's home, though I was longing to tell him all, I could say nothing. Teresa Pascati was waiting at the foot of the courtyard stairs, for my Uncle 'Centio had just had another heart attack and they had sent for his doctor. She told me that I could go to see him but that I must be very quiet.

"He was lying quite still. His lips were blue, but when I leaned over and kissed his forehead, he smiled at me. Usually he could pull himself up with those strong arms of his, but this time he just lay there and whispered to me to take from a deep drawer in the big chest a box which I must take away with me. I found the box and he smiled again and I guessed that it held Elena's jewellery. When Anna died, it had come to Tanya. I had never seen it and I knew that my uncle had treasured it for Tanya's sake.

"His eyes told me what to do and I put it into a large shoulder bag I carried. Then he began to whisper once more, but Teresa Pascati came with the doctor and they sent me away. I telephoned to the shop in the afternoon but they told me he was still ill. He was drugged and must not have visitors for many days. So I found that I might have a passage on a late flight to England and so I came. But I forgot to leave a message for the girl with whom I share my apartment. She is away at her home for a week. So perhaps Helen will see her too and will tell her that I am safe."

Mother gave me a worried look.

Rosa got up and took the paper-wrapped box from her case. She unwrapped it and gave it to me.

"Elena's jewel box. You see with what soft and beautiful leather it is made, covered with fine decoration, as good as the best Italian work. It held the jewels she wore on the stage sometimes, those she valued so much and which her friend Anna and Tanya and my uncle valued too."

The box was indeed a lovely thing. Its soft leather, tooled in gold, covered a hard metal or wooden foundation. On the inside was a lining of patterned and quilted blue satin.

Mother stood up and put an arm round Rosa.

"My darling child, you'll be safe with us here. You must stay as long as you like; for certain until this tangle of events is somehow unravelled."

"Then you do not think me a great coward to have given way to fear so easily?"

"Anyone who was alone as you were would have been afraid," I told her. "You did the only, the sensible thing. We'll make plans for me to help. I'll do some detective work when I get to Sorrento."

I saw Mother's warning glance and avoided it. I had

quite made up my mind to visit both Rosa's friend and
Uncle Vincentio during that first solitary week of mine.
How could there possibly be any danger in that! Now
Mother decided she must get on with her duties as
hostess of The Highwayman. As for my own—well, at
this rate, they would be prolonged until midnight!

I helped Rosa put the heap of jewellery back into its
box and saw her lock it in her dressing-table drawer.
Then we ran downstairs together. I would introduce her
to Peter, who would, in his turn, introduce her to The
Highwayman.

My own world spun round in brilliance again, for
Dominic, who had been chatting to Peter in the hall,
turned to face us. I put my arm round Rosa's waist
and drew her forward. "This is Rosa," I said, and
suddenly the world lost its brightness again, for I
realised that there was no man born who could greet
Rosa for the first time without that expression coming
into his eyes.

"Look after her," I said. "I've got so much work to
do."

I turned away, leaving them both with Peter, and I
did not know whether Dominic's eyes left Rosa to follow
me or no.

CHAPTER FIVE

*"But had I wist before I kissed, that love had been sae ill to win,
I had locked my heart in a case of gowd and pinned it wi' a
siller pin."*—SCOTTISH BALLAD.

FOR the rest of that morning I worked. I drew up the
wages sheets and put the insurance cards with stamps
into their file. I had a tray with sandwiches for my
lunch and Rosa came in to have coffee with me.

"Rosa, shall I leave you in your present room or would
you like to move into Sweetbriar? It's larger and in the
main corridor, but I'm afraid it's next to Colonel Jack-
son, who snores. He's in Forget-me-not, rather appropriate when I come to think of it."

When Peter came to The Highwayman fifteen years
ago, the rooms had already been christened, somewhat
coyly, by the names of wild flowers. He had decided to
leave them unchanged. The staff were used to them and
residents liked the little pictured wooden plaques, remembered them better than numbers which danced rather
wildly along the up-and-down staircases and passages
of the old house. Mother and I had gradually echoed
the room names in the furnishings, with convovulus
entwined curtains or forget-me-not blue bedcovers, so
avoiding the anonymity of more conventional hotel
accommodation.

"Please, I would like to stay where I am if that will

43

be no nuisance. It is near your room and I so like to look at the garden."

"Right! I'll leave you in the little girl's room then."

I picked up my pen and Rosa sensed my preoccupation.

"Helen dear, you are busy and I will go away. When shall I see you to talk more about Sorrento?"

"I'm sorry, Rosa. I have got a lot to do."

But I knew that my detachment was due to some kind of anti-climax, a sort of depression gripping me. Oh, well, what did a brief look in Dominic's eyes when he saw Rosa, when he looked at me even, matter? Are flying swans or one moonlight drive from Stratford of such importance in a world of unromantic realism?

"Rosa, I shall be free of all this by seven o'clock. Then we'll have a drink and dinner with Peter and Mother. Afterwards we'll talk as I start packing. Now, will you be able to amuse yourself for the rest of the day?"

"I am to do the flowers. And later that so very nice Dominic says he will take me driving and show me something of your Cotswolds. Tomorrow he takes me to Oxford, where he must spend some time in a library there. Even I have heard its name, though now I forget it."

"The Bodleian," I supplied mechanically.

"That is it! The Bodleian! I can wander and explore and he will show me where to meet him after his work. Then we shall have our lunch in a village near the river and he will tell me all about the Fair—who?"

Again I prompted, "The Fair Rosamund."

"That is it! Because he said it was my name too, Rose

of the World! She was poisoned by a wicked queen, long long ago."

"Old, unhappy, far-off things," I quoted, and Rosa, all present happiness, ran off to do the flowers.

So, all that afternoon, with William as my more or less silent companion, I concentrated. I did not even look out at the street where leaf shadows danced in sunshine, to the antique shop windows opposite or to the long windows above them.

At seven o'clock I ran upstairs, tidied my hair and washed my hands; then, without bothering to change, I ran downstairs, conscious of signs of hard work and weariness still upon me.

Rosa was in the bar, sitting in the deep window seat, her dark head against a background of latticed windows and branches of yellow forsythia in the garden outside.

A bowl of flowers on the bar counter looked superb; flowers in the hall had greeted me too. Rosa had been as expert in putting them happily together as my clever mother and was evidently going to be very helpful in that direction during the next few weeks.

Then I became conscious of steps behind me and, without turning, I knew who was there. I felt light hands round my waist and Dominic's voice said softly, "How's my golden girl now? What can we get to revive her?"

I saw Rosa look over my shoulder with a brightness of glance from dark eyes and curve of lip. Instinctively I drew myself from the clasp of those gentle but firm hands and went forward to sit by her. When I faced him my eyes were steady and cool. They met the green ones easily. He looked at me for a moment, then moved his glance to Rosa.

"What will you both drink?"

Rosa looked at me. "Please, Helen, what do you drink in England? I do not drink much, only wine, not always very good wine!"

"Try straight Dubonnet," I suggested. "Rather sweet, but it's not too potent. And I'll have the same, thank you, Dominic."

He brought us our drinks and then sat at the far side of the table with a pewter tankard of beer. He was one of Peter's favoured few evidently. Those old tankards were kept for very special customers.

"What is that?" asked Rosa, and the next ten minutes went in discussing the intricacies of beer and the mysteries of brewing. Most of our Highwayman supplies came from a local brewery, one of those few individual concerns not yet swallowed up by vast industrial concerns.

"It is a man's drink?"

"Not always. I often drink beer, especially when I am hot and thirsty."

"Try it," said Dominic, pushing his tankard towards her.

She put it to her lips long enough to take a very small sip. Then, with a little grimace, she said, "It is bitter, is it not? But I shall learn to like it. Helen, by the time you come back I shall be a great beer drinker."

Dominic took the tankard back to his own lips and smiled at her across its rim. "I shall guide you on your alcoholic way," he promised.

I glanced at my watch.

"Rosa, it's nearly seven-thirty and I told Mother we'd eat with them. I'm hungry—only sandwiches for lunch!"

As Dominic stood up a couple of regulars and Jeremy's father and Joanna came in and he raised his hand in salute. We said a light goodbye and left him in conversation with the newcomers.

As we passed the bar after dinner I saw, full though it was, that he was gone. I think I could feel his absence.

Then Rosa and I were girls together again, laughing and chattering whilst I began to pack.

"I love your villages," she told me. "The gardens so neat and yet so full of colour. I love the wide fields. You have space and to spare here whatever your big cities are like. No big mountains pushing you into the sea. I love your little rivers."

"Did you see any swans fly across?" I asked her over my shoulder as I put my favourite bathing dress, a quite discreet sort of bikini, into my case.

"No. They fly too? Those big birds? I have never seen a wild swan. Dominic says he will take me to Stratford one day. Shakespeare is called the Swan of Avon, is he not?"

"Yes, you can call him that. Dominic will tell you all about Shakespeare and Stratford," I told her.

Suddenly I realised what a long day it had been and how very tired I was. I sat down on the divan and put my feet up. Rosa came across, shook up the cushions and put them behind my shoulders in exactly the right position. I caught her hand and put my cheek against it.

"Now tell me how I can help; what you would like me to do when I get to Italy."

"Helen dear, I have talked with your mother and we both think you must do nothing until your aunt is with you. Then take her with you wherever you go and do nothing without letting her know."

"I'll promise to do nothing dangerous," I said.

That promise I certainly meant to keep, and Rosa's face showed relief.

"Then all will be well," she said. "Two of you together will be safe and sensible.

"First of all then, Helen, I would ask you to visit my uncle. Oh, I so much hope he is better again! It has happened like this before, so hope is still left. Tell him I am safe in England. Tell him briefly, without too much detail, that the cousins are not what they say they are. Then will you ask him about Elena's jewels. Tell him they are safe with me here and ask if they can possibly have any value he does not know. He will tell you everything, for I am sure he had more to tell me when the doctor came that morning. That the jewels meant much to Tanya I know; yet somehow I do not feel they meant only money. And will you tell him, Helen carissima, that I love him a great deal."

"I will tell him that; something he knows already."

She gave a deep sigh, then went on.

"If you can, please see my friend, Lisa Pieri, and tell her I am safe and well. Say you have heard from me, that I am sorry that I left so quickly that I did not write her a note. Tell her that I heard suddenly from an agent and am having film tests and try-outs. That there are possibilities for me in Florence, which may indeed be true later, for the dear Dominic, he has said he will do something for me in this film they are making of his book."

Her face was radiant.

"Rosa, that is marvellous!" I said. "I shall finish that first book tonight and pass it on to you."

"Thank you, Helen. Dominic says he will give it to

me, but I would like to read it as soon as possible. About Lisa—I think it safer for her if she does not know exactly where I am. Sophie and Myers knew my address though I never let them visit me there. It was too small, I said, and I was working. But they might find her now and it is better that she should be a little deceived and so deceive them. Do not go to see them yourself, Helen. They are bad people and would do harm to anyone if they could gain by so doing."

"I shall remember all you have said," I told her, but I made no specific promise. "Now draw me a little map of the way to your uncle's home. I think I know the Square S. Vincentio. And write down the address of your own apartment."

When Rosa went off to her little girl's room I was well briefed and I knew that I could keep both her and Mother reasonably happy about my intended movements in Sorrento. Not that they, so far as I could see, would involve me in any personal danger.

I finished Dominic's book that night and took it to place on Rosa's bedside table next morning. The sun, snatching an added gold from the laburnum tree outside, streamed in and she was already dressed in readiness for her trip to Oxford.

"I shall not disgrace him?" she asked.

"You are perfect," I told her.

She was wearing a light, soft blue suit in fine woollen material with a hand-embroidered, beautifully matched silk blouse.

I had never believed there were really black eyes and Rosa's added to my conviction. Though so dark, they were clear and deep, reflecting other colours; like the dark throat inside a mauve iris or the deep blue-violet of gentian.

This time I watched the little car come down its incline from the garage opposite, saw Dominic's smile as he went to meet her. For a moment he glanced towards my office window, said something to Rosa and nodded at her answer. I watched them drive away.

I had broken the pressure of work the day before. I found my thoughts wandering to Rosa, walking in the shade of cool cloisters; to Dominic, looking at old manuscripts in Duke Humphrey's library. I glanced at my watch. Soon, perhaps, they would be meeting under the wise eyes and smooth brows of those newly restored heads round the Sheldonian.

Maybe it was that academic image or the austerity of my own office which made me remember the school-leaving interview, that traditional ordeal I had undergone, with the principal of my Cheltenham school. She was a very wise, far-seeing woman.

"Helen, do you know that you lack self-confidence?" she had told me. "You hesitate to take what is offered you. Try to be more sure of yourself, my dear. Take all that life gives, and take a risk, too, sometimes."

Now I wondered what advice she had given to certain other members of that school-leaving year. Just the opposite, I guessed, in the light of my London experience. But I remembered her warning to me now, though I did not know quite how to adapt it to my present circumstances.

I ran upstairs to get a forgotten handkerchief.

The hum of vacuum cleaners was strident in the corridor. Strange how those instruments, handled by Jean and Sheila, sounded fierce and aggressive. Under

Mother's control, in the days when I came home for holidays, they had always contributed a comfortable, cosy sort of background noise.

I had left my door open and, as the cleaners fell silent, Sheila's voice took up its share in the inevitable duet.

"Them eyelashes of hers, they're lovely! They'm real, too; they weren't lying on her dressing-table when I took her breakfast in."

"Oh, well, I'll give you her eyelashes. Not but that our Miss Helen's got nice ones, too, only hers be gold and don't notice like they dark ones. I thinks I likes 'em better than black. Black 'uns be like them big spiders' legs."

"Well, Mr Lee, 'e likes 'em all right, and all the rest on her too! He's taking her—"

The vacuum cleaners took up their battle-cry again and I took myself downstairs away from it all.

I was already in my room putting the last touches to my packing when Rosa returned, happy and excited.

I was just returning to its place the evening dress I had worn to Stratford. I would have no heart to wear it in Sorrento, so I would leave it here, lonely and abandoned in my wardrobe.

"Darling, I have had a lovely, lovely day. Beautiful Oxford! I think I could love it more than Rome, more than Venice even."

"More than Sorrento?" I asked.

A shadow passed over her face.

"Always I must go back to Sorrento," she said. "It is in my heart. But today . . ." and she smiled again. "There was an inn by a river and we ate delicious fish which they said came out of the river and had been caught early that morning. I saw fish like them swimming when afterwards we had our coffee out of doors, all silver and spotted with gold, and I felt that I was a cannibal!"

"But you enjoyed them before you had any regrets. That is the right order of things." And I wondered if there was some deep meaning in what I said.

I saw Dominic once more that day.

Mother and Peter were talking to us as we all four stood grouped at the foot of the stairs at bedtime. I was preparing for the next day with an early night and Rosa, with her little kitten yawn, said she was sleepy.

He came in through the open main door just as three pairs of eyes were fixed on me, and he must have heard what Mother was saying.

"Now, darling, don't forget. You must wait until Joan comes before you do anything. Rosa and I have talked it over and Peter agrees with us. So promise."

"Mother dear, I will do nothing that is at all foolish or dangerous, I promise you that," I said; and somehow it was into Dominic's eyes that I found myself looking as I said the last few words.

CHAPTER SIX

"Torna a Surriento"—Come back to Sorrento.—NEAPOLITAN SONG.

A HOLIDAY departure from The Highwayman is like the start of a royal progress. Staff pop out one by one to give good wishes and wave goodbye. Faces peer from windows as residents, in varying stages of undress, half-hide behind the curtains. "Nods and becks and wreathed smiles" peep round every corner.

Peter was to drive me to Gatwick, my least favourite airport, and by eight-thirty my luggage was in the car and only Mother, Rosa and a disconsolate William occupied the pathway, the rest of the assembly having melted tactfully away to the making or consuming of breakfast.

Peregrine, in the shop early because he was going to a country house sale, tripped across the road wearing black velvet trousers and jacket with a blue silk shirt matched to a turquoise tie. Peregrine's high forehead seemed to have invaded his scalp, pushing his hair away in its progress. A large, triangular bald patch replaced the straight brown hair which had somehow reappeared as a small pointed beard on his chin.

I liked Peregrine. He was unashamedly himself, never pretended to be anything else, and his knowledge of antiques was acute.

Now he threw his arms round me with girlish fervour

and landed a butterfly kiss on the tip of my nose. He smelled pleasantly though exotically of some lotion. I heard a door bang and saw Dominic leap down the grass slope and run across the road.

"Say goodbye to her," said Peregrine, giving me a friendly push in Dominic's direction. "Have a frabjous holiday, sweetie" (Peregrine was an "Alice" fan). "And give my love to the dear Matterhorn as you go by."

For a moment I stood with Dominic's arms loosely round me and wondered if he would follow Peregrine's example with a kiss rather better directed. But I did not wait to see. I moved away and he held the car door open, leaned down as I settled into my seat and said, very softly, "Come back."

Then he moved to make room for Mother and stood behind Rosa. The last glimpse I caught as Peter drove off was of Rosa leaning towards him, smiling, and of Dominic smiling down at her.

I liked driving with Peter. There was no need to make conversation. It was a good run, a pleasant enough cross-country route. There was a promise of bluebells in woods where the undergrowth was a young green. The ridge of the Hog's Back was drawn across a blue sky in colours of soft violet and blue, the colour of Rosa's eyes.

The road peeled effortlessly away under our wheels and suddenly I realised that Italy, dear sun-warmed Italy, was waiting for me. What did it matter if I left my heart in a Cotswold town? That sounded like a drawing-room ballad and, to Peter's surprise, I began to laugh.

"You sound happy, my dear. I'm glad you're getting this holiday. Don't get sad over old memories though, and Helen, don't get too involved in this queer affair of Rosa's. Wait until your aunt arrives. From her last letter it sounds as though she could do with a holiday too. Not like her to talk about her health, but I expect, like most nurses, she is worked to death. No, this is a strange business of Rosa's."

"D'you think the jewellery is really at the bottom of it?"

"It might be. Of course, one way to straighten that out would be to take the stuff up to Hatton Garden or somewhere and get it valued."

I had considered that possibility myself, but had hesitated to suggest it lest Rosa should think it rather mercenary to try to find out before her uncle had told her all he wanted her to know. The gift's value was so much one of sentiment. Of a second drawback I spoke now to Peter.

"Suppose those jewels are worth an enormous sum of money. They would have belonged to an almost royal family. Suppose Rosa took them to an expert and he discovered that one of those diamonds, for instance, was a star of all the Russias, or something fantastic like that. I once heard a radio programme about fabulous gems that had vanished from circulation, had never been traced, but which could be recognised by a real expert if they turned up again. Where would Rosa and her uncle stand in a case like that? What would be their claim to the jewels? Her Aunt Tanya's claim, even? It wouldn't be an affair that could be hushed up easily, would it? Before she did anything so definite as getting them properly valued, shouldn't she find out what her uncle would want, get legal advice and be prepared to face up to any results?"

Peter looked thoughtful for a quarter of a mile or so. Then he said, "You've got something there, though I doubt whether there's another Koh-i-nor in Rosa's jewel box. She's been telling Dominic the story, from what was said last night."

"Has she now?" I said. But I wasn't surprised.

"Oh, yes. They're getting thick as thieves. He writes those detective books so perhaps he'll have some ideas. You forget it now, and don't try to do anything on your own."

"Well, I hope it can soon all be cleared up. Rosa will want to come back to Italy before long."

"Why?" asked Peter, with male obtuseness. "Perhaps she'll stay in England, settle down and get married. Plenty of men will be after a pretty little thing like her!"

"Rosa's more than pretty. She's beautiful, and she's clever and talented. What's more, she's ambitious. She's got a career ahead of her."

"Oh, I don't know. Now you and your mother have got the sort of looks I really like; and you're the career girl, Helen."

"Oh, Peter! You're flattering, but you're a male chauvinist pig when it comes to pretty girls. It's a good thing I love you," I told him.

"Well, plenty of men would make a grab at you if you'd only give them a chance; go out to meet them like Rosa does. Now Dominic's had a look in his eye lately. I wonder if he wouldn't be a good match for her."

Peter, unhelped by me, was still wondering when we reached Gatwick. He saw my heavy luggage dispatched, bought me the paper and glossy magazines from the bookstall and, when my flight was called, would have walked right to the bitter end of that endlessly winding trail which led to my exit door, if only authority had permitted it.

I returned his hug and kiss as he handed over my light case, knowing that he was my last glimpse of home for two whole weeks; weeks that were to be more desperately eventful than I could possibly imagine. Suddenly I felt very conscious of my solitary state.

It is not until you are airborne that the real moment of departure comes. There is an exhilaration about that feeling of weightlessness, that sensation of soaring power beneath you.

I thought of Rosa's neglected plastic tray as I enjoyed the contents of my own.

I remembered Peregrine's message and gave his love to the Matterhorn as we passed it by—on the left side, of course, since my seat was on the right. I told myself that, on my return, it would be near me; then recollected that queer spaghetti junction of air highways which ensures that all landmarks keep to the same side of the plane on the way back as on the way out. At least, that is how it has always been with me!

So, on the return journey I felt sure, the Matterhorn would still be on my left and my seat on the right and still no more than a glacial white shimmer across an opposite window. But I gave it Peregrine's love nevertheless.

Then came Naples' runway, so like other runways. But here was spring's freshness with summer's warmth. This was Southern Italy. Suddenly I was in my other home again. I was lonely still, but loneliness at home is bearable.

I had almost forgotten Naples with its cacophony of sound, with its crowded wide streets and squares, its passing sight of narrow alleys filled with bulging plastic bags now, instead of over-spilling dustbins. There were glimpses of old tufa stone, worn and discoloured, like decaying teeth; of bright, crude shrines set high in old walls; of vast, modern blocks of flats, even the most luxurious with a flaunting of bed linen thrown over balcony railings to dry and bleach in the hot sun.

Then came the winding coast road to the south. This I remembered so well; on my left mounting terraces with villas and hotels, small individual towns close-neighbouring one another; on my right always the deep blue of the Mediterranean. I saw Castellammare and the high, jagged rocks; a bend in the road and a crescent of rough grass where a few sheep grazed, guarded from the fierce traffic by an old man, a boy and a dog. Olive trees, orange trees, lemon trees—and I knew I was home again, back in Sorrento.

Two hours later I stood on the balcony of my room in the Hotel Risorgimento, unpacked, dressed and ready to go down to dinner. It was a pleasant, quietly modernised hotel, not overflowing in May, its welcome as yet untarnished by a long, hot season.

"It is a good hotel," Rosa had told me in her letters. "Not one of the newest, but better, I think. There is a large and very pretty swimming pool with an orange grove around it; there are single rooms with balcony and bathroom and you will like it. I shall visit you and you will invite me to dinner there. And I shall take you to a trattoria which cooks the best Italian food in Sorrento."

Ah, well, that promise would not be kept this time. Otherwise, she was right.

My room was pleasing. It was a joy to feel the silkiness of the blue tiled floor under my feet instead of the softness of deep carpets. I had forgotten the smoothness of those Italian floors. The bathroom to the left of the little entrance lobby had boiling water, a big bath and an efficient shower.

The balcony was wide, large enough for me to pull that comfortable easy chair on to it if I wished to keep to the seclusion of my own room. The balcony of the next room, which would be Aunt Joan's in a week's time, would allow conversation and a handshake perhaps, but would offer only frustration to any aspiring Romeo and Juliet.

A sort of buttress, supporting the balconies above, swept down and outwards, overhanging the rail of the balconies below and making an effective barrier between them. Looking down, I saw how these small buttresses made a decorative pattern against the façade of the hotel. Some, possibly those from landing windows, bore tubs of flowers, spilling over in great scarlet blossoms.

But Aunt Joan and I would be able to fraternise without any need for balcony climbing. These two rooms were at the end of a corridor, comfortably set back in the slight curve of an inside wall, the furthest from a very efficient and silent lift.

I stood and looked across a lemon grove, darkening in the evening dusk and in the lights of the quiet street below. A deep, harsh bell from a domed cupola away to the left throbbed on a single note. Across a down-plunging outline of trees and roofs I had a clear view to a straight line of sea merging with sky, and that deeply curved bay picked out in starry lights. Far away to my right was the faint grey shadow of Vesuvius, tapering skywards. Here was my Bay of Naples.

CHAPTER SEVEN

"Ca scetato 'o faie sumna"—All my thoughts in wakeful dream.
—NEAPOLITAN SONG.

I STAYED in that world of half-dream, half-reality for five enchanted days.

Each morning I plunged into the hotel swimming pool and lazed afterwards in hot sunshine or the orange trees' shade. The pool was a clear sky blue and the yellow and white tiles round it were as silky under my bare feet as the blue ones in my bedroom.

The high windows of another hotel and those of a block of luxury flats kept their distance beyond the orange grove and a bird sang out its caged heart-break from a balcony. Incongruously sandwiched between hotel and apartments was the back of an unpretentious villa with an outside staircase from the ground to a first-floor room. Vaguely it reminded me of that visit to be paid to Rosa's uncle, some day before Aunt Joan came. Time enough, I thought.

Perhaps the scent of the orange-blossom helped to cast a spell over me. Little tight green buds would fall on the tiles with sharp, sudden impact and I would reach out and pick one up, rolling it between my fingers, drawing the pungent sweetness from it. Over my head hung the pale golden fruit, not yet ready for picking.

I made friends with a tiny green-backed lizard, like some minute prehistoric animal; not a very intimate friendship for, at the flutter of an eyelash, he would flick back into his stone lair, quicker than a falling bud could reach the tiles.

I chatted in voluble Italian to the swimming pool attendant, who took such a pride in the ordered colours of his deckchairs that he stacked them each night with regimental precision, blue by red by green, round the pool.

I made friends with the elderly gardener who, until dusk fell, tended the giant tubs of flowers, marguerites which grew in great blossoming trees, azaleas and scarlet geraniums and carpets of golden red flowers whose name I could not remember. He needed no "Gardeners' Question Time' to tell him the secret of talking to flowers to keep them happy. He seemed to keep up a running flow of conversation with them.

Every afternoon I took a siesta on my balcony, the view spread out before me so beautiful that it seemed unreal. Then I would wander into the town, investigate small shops and drink fruit juice or coffee on a raised terrace, while the tourist and the Italian world milled round me.

I made verbal acquaintance with my kindly neighbours in the dining-room and my occasional fellow-travellers in the lift, but, finding that I was quite at home in Sorrento and was, furthermore, expecting a companion, they happily felt no responsibility for me.

So, when Wednesday came, I visited Castellammare and found that eight years had changed it hardly at all. I climbed the steep hill which bordered our villa. The house was washed over in a clear yellow now instead of its former white, but the big hotel nearby was still a faded pink with scabrous patches left by the touch of last summer's scorching sun. Over the high wall I could see, through the branches of the almond trees, the window of my old room, looking on to the sea and the rocks. The wall-paper had been a soft blue-green then and my curtains primrose yellow, but now the curtains were blue and the wall-paper I could not see.

It was then, suddenly, I realised that throughout these last few days I had walked and talked with an imaginary companion, though not with one of those ghosts from the past. Peter's warning had been unnecessary.

No, this companion of mine was tall and broad-shouldered, his hair a coppery brown, his eyes grey-green. Lying beside me, he too had grown drowsy in the scent of orange-blossom; he had plunged in the clear water of the pool and had watched for my prehistoric lizard to pop his horny little head out into the sun. As I showed him this, my old home, his arm was encircling my waist, my head close to his shoulder. With him beside me my memories held no sadness. And I knew that my need had created his imaginary presence for my comfort. I loved Dominic Lee, knew that I would love him for ever. And at that moment his shadow slipped away from me and I was back in reality again with loneliness as my companion.

When I got back to Sorrento, Giorgio, in reception, handed me two letters, one with an air-mail stamp and mother's writing, the other a square white envelope, unstamped and addressed in what was practically script. I was already opening Mother's letter as I reached my room.

Darling Helen
  We miss you, but we hope you don't miss us too

much. We all send our love and William visits your rooms, upstairs and downstairs, twice a day, hoping against hope to find that you have come home.

The Highwayman goes on as usual, remarkably full for so early in the season and with tables completely booked on Friday and Saturday nights in the restaurant. Rosa is a joy to have around. She does the flowers, has learned to pour out a glass of beer with the correct head on it, and, encouraged by Dominic, is trying to get a taste for it too.

She has discovered Tony's ambition to be thought an Italian waiter and has taught him to say three sentences in a dialect which will stop any respectable Italian talking to him in their own language. Tony is thrilled but Peter has dared him to make use of them on these premises.

Rosa and Dominic took Sweet William for a long walk the other afternoon and, on the way home, they met that wretched Fu Manchu. If Dominic hadn't put William on the lead and used his strong right arm to keep them apart, at the risk of getting bitten too, there would have been a dreadful fight before the vicar got there. He really is a horrid dog! I told the vicar that Fu Manchu had started the feud when William was only a puppy and that he's the only dog in the whole of Melford William hates.

I'm so glad that Aunt Joan will be with you soon. You must be feeling very lonely at times. When she comes you will be able to visit Rosa's uncle.

The child does worry quite a bit, I feel, though she hides it well.

Do take care, my dear. Don't take risks and remember there is safety in numbers.

Thank you for your letter and the postcard which have just arrived.

> *Our love,*
> *Mother.*

I read the letter through twice. I had finished with dreamlike lazy idling. I longed for Aunt Joan's arrival. I would take her to Pompeii, to Amalfi, even up to Vesuvius if so she wanted, but I would get on with the tackling of Rosa's problems at once, alone. I should have done so already. I would do something tomorrow.

I picked up the other letter and frowned at it, at that rather ugly script. I held it with distaste, lightly, and dropped it; premonition, perhaps. I opened it and looked first at the signature. Sophie Cannan. It was addressed to Miss Del Mar. I was so used to being called Miss Allan at The Highwayman—even those who knew I was Peter's step-daughter were inclined to give me his name—that sometimes, when I saw my correct one, I felt as though I had a dual identity.

Well, the first contact had been made for me. I said I would leave this one to chance. Fate was taking a hand.

The letter was brief.

> *Villa Vittorio,*
> *Via Gaelta, Sorrento.*

Dear Miss Del Mar,

Though I feel I want to call you Helen because that is what Rosa calls you when she talks to us about you.

We are worried because she has gone away without telling us where. She was looking forward to seeing you this week so perhaps you have heard where she is. She is the only child of my dear cousin John, who was brought up by my mother and who died here in Italy. We have really gotten fond of the child.

Perhaps you will let us know any news you have. Visit us if you will. We shall be in all day tomorrow and Friday. To see and to talk is better than to telephone especially as these Italian telephones are not like those at home. We shall meet soon then, I hope.

Yours sincerely,
Sophie Cannan.

I walked on to the balcony and stood looking across the trees opposite with their framework of chestnut poles. How far away the trammontana seemed, that harsh winter wind which made the reed covering I remembered seeing as a child, so necessary. Surely this warmth and this sun should last for ever.

A single pale lemon lay on the brown earth under the trees opposite, fruit with a rotten heart, fallen before its time.

Tomorrow I would swim in the pool but I would not laze away the morning in the sunshine. Before Aunt Joan arrived on Friday evening I would have done three things without any risk to myself I felt sure.

I would visit Rosa's Uncle Vincentio, I would find Rosa's friend, Lisa Pieri, and give her Rosa's message, and I would acknowledge this letter and visit the Villa Vittorio to meet Rosa's wicked cousins. That they were wicked I had no doubt, though I could not see in them any danger to myself. However, I was a little uncertain as to what to tell them of Rosa's whereabouts. Certainly not the truth, though for one fantastic moment I thought how madly provocative it would be to declare, "She heard you plotting and giving away your secrets. She knows you are no more American than I am. You are Neapolitans—of the lowest sort, too, from the Bassi. She is far away from you, safe in England. So what will you do now?"

But I put away this imagined temerity, returned to common sense and knew that I would behave in a far more discreet fashion. I would see Lisa and Uncle 'Centio first and probably visit the cousins on the Friday. By that time I might have acquired some extra information and Aunt Joan's arrival would be comfortingly near.

The next morning I woke up still intent on some practical achievement. My morning swim was no preliminary to idling in the sun, watching for my lizard in the lazy scent of orange-blossom.

I decided to visit Rosa's and Lisa's apartment first, leaving after siesta time for her uncle. With a pang of regret for my delay in visiting him, I hoped he was still living.

I stepped purposely down the hotel steps on to the shady pathway. "Dominic, I can manage this without your imaginary presence," I told him defiantly. He must leave my present untouched and I would not trespass on his future.

One of those little gay carriages, carrozzella, passed me, the glossy, high-stepping horse proudly tossing his head in its jaunty hat. The driver raised his whip in enquiring salute, but I shook my head. I would tackle the three kilometres along the coast way on my two feet. I took quieter roads parallel to the main one and discovered a busy market in a small square. I lingered to admire the heaped mounds of fruit, the trays of fish caught only that morning, squid, crayfish, more exotic products of the Mediterranean. There were rolls of coloured silks and cotton. I wished I were an impressionistic painter, to slash paint on to canvas in shouts of exultant colour.

Instead I bought two bright silk scarves, presents for two bright old Melford ladies, and reluctantly took myself onwards.

It was possible, of course, that Lisa might still be away, but Rosa had said she had gone home for the first week of her holiday only. If she were not in the flat I would leave a message, arrange for another meeting.

But I was lucky. The small apartment block was on the far side of the main road, about three steep terraces down towards the sea. I mounted the wide stone staircase and, when I rang the bell of a blue door, to which neatly printed cards bearing the names of Rosa Rossini and Lisa Pieri were attached, a tall, brown-haired girl opened the door to me.

I introduced myself and liked Rosa's friend at once. According to instructions and efficiently, I hoped, I deceived her as to Rosa's whereabouts.

"I am so glad you have found me," she called from the little kitchen where she had gone to make coffee. "I was beginning to be worried about her."

The room where I sat was open to sea and sun-filled air. At one end a bedroom led from it, the half-open door revealing a wardrobe and part of the bed. When Lisa came back, carrying a tray, she closed it tidily.

"It is a pity, perhaps, that I did not know this when Rosa's cousin called yesterday."

"The cousin called here? Sophie?" I was a little startled, though there was really no reason why I should be so. Obviously the Cannans would follow up all traces of Rosa. Yet, for a moment, I felt like the hunted quarry when hounds follow close.

"Yes, she came here. I could tell her nothing, of course, save that Rost was a sensible girl and a good girl. I asked if we should communicate with our police, but she seemed to dislike that idea."

"What was Mrs Cannan like? Did you think her a pleasant person?"

Lisa's face was serious.

"No, I cannot say I liked her. Rosa did not like either of them; she told me so the week before I went home on holiday. They seemed ready enough to care for her, though."

Lisa stopped speaking and looked through the open window to the blue sea. She frowned, turned her glance towards me and seemed to like what she saw, for she smiled and evidently made a decision.

"Something happened that made me like her less. She came only yesterday, the day I returned from home, and within half-an-hour of my arrival. It was late and I hurried straight out to do some necessary shopping, leaving the front door unlatched as we often do. I knew that I should be only five minutes or so.

"She had rung, evidently, and received no answer, and when I came back she was sitting here, in this room. It was strange to come and find a stranger in that chair where Rosa usually sits. It was growing dusk and, for a brief moment, I thought that Rosa had returned. I began to speak, used Rosa's name, before I realised that it was not Rosa."

"To come in here and sit down? That was rather an impertinence, wasn't it?" I said.

Lisa shrugged.

"She is not young and she apologised. But there was something else. I will tell you of it soon. But now she asked me many questions. It is a good thing that my English is fairly fluent, for hers is very American. She asked me, had Rosa a boy friend? Did she 'go steady' with anyone? Did she make dates with many men, strange men, without introduction? I was rather angry at these questions and I answered them with a firm 'No!'"

Lisa twinkled at me. "Not quite true, perhaps, for we both have friends. But we are sensible girls. It is well that Rosa is sensible, for with her looks she has . . . well, we favour only nice men to whom we have been introduced, and we can chaperone each other efficiently."

Italian girls, especially when living alone, must be discreet. They do not enjoy quite the freedom of English and American girls. I am sure that Lisa and Rosa led what to me would be very sedate social lives. Dominic would be introducing Rosa to rather greater freedom now, I thought. Lisa went on.

"Mrs Cannan also asked me about Rosa's uncle, if he gave her presents, family possessions perhaps. His death was so near, she said, that he should make sure that the things he valued, as well as money safely in the bank, should reach the sole remaining member of his family. So often when death comes things of great sentimental value are stolen or lost. Had Rosa been given such things yet? She was very pressing with her questions.

"I tried not to show my resentment. I told her that to my knowledge Rosa had received nothing from her uncle, that she was never mercenary, would never exact gifts. So then she became apologetic and friendly and went. It was afterwards that I made this discovery."

Lisa stood up. "Come and look at Rosa's room. It is off the hall."

I followed her to a little bedroom which looked out across the bay, the same view as that from the sitting-room. It was pretty, spotlessly clean and redolent of Rosa. Hanging on one wall was a picture of The High-wayman, one I had sent to her for Christmas. Cleo Patrick had shown it in a local exhibition and I had been its buyer. I knew that Rosa would enjoy a picture of my English home and Cleo had made a good job of her painting. The house was typically Cotswold and so was inevitably pituresque, but the artist had caught the dappled sunlight which gave warmth to that grey stone, had found more than mere prettiness in her subject.

I looked in through the welcome of the open door, saw the shadowy outline of Peter's favourite clock. Was William lurking round the corner, Dominic on the terrace with Mother and Rosa? Suddenly I felt such a pang of homesickness that I turned quickly back to Lisa.

"When Sophie went I came straight to Rosa's room to see what she had taken in the way of luggage, if she had left any note for me. Rosa and I were good friends.

"Then I felt certain that someone who was not Rosa had been here before me. I remembered too that I had seen no sign of Mrs Cannan when I ran out for my shopping. The road is straight and quite exposed in both directions. You came by side roads and you will have noticed that there are no side turnings into this road close to our house. I was away for only five minutes. In that short time Sophie would have had to walk that distance, climb the stairs, ring the bell and wait for an answer that did not come. How, in that time, could she not only have gone to the sitting-room to wait, but have visited Rosa's room? No, she must have seen me arrive in my car, have watched my departure again as she hid somewhere, behind a tree in the small garden perhaps, and must then have entered through the open door."

"How did you know she had been in this room?"

"She would not have wasted time, of course. She could easily tell which was my room for my luggage was still there, barely opened, nothing put away. And how did I know she had been in here? Well, this room was not as Rosa would have left it. Rosa is immaculately neat, exquisite in everything that surrounds her. Even in great haste I have seen her give that last look round and, with easy swiftness, close every drawer and cupboard on perfect tidiness. In her wardrobe coats and dresses would be on their hangers, perfume sachets on each one. All this would be done automatically. It was second nature to Rosa.

"Now I saw that drawers were left open, their contents in disarray. In the wardrobe there were dresses in heaps on the floor beneath empty hangers. That was not Rosa!"

I remembered how on the night of her arrival at The Highwayman, exhausted though she had been, Rosa had yet shown that same fastidiousness. She had shaken the creases from her coat and dress and had hung them up carefully. As she took off her clothes she had folded them and placed them in a neat pile on their chair.

This room was immaculate now; Lisa had removed all signs of any intrusion.

"Had she taken anything?" I asked.

"I think not. Rosa had no jewellery save her watch and that little ring which belonged to her mother and which she always wore. Otherwise she had only a few bits of valueless costume jewellery such as we all have. Those were mostly still here. Her watch and ring she will be wearing. No, I do not know for what Sophie Cannan was looking. Perhaps she is one of those women who are curious about the affairs of others."

Lisa shrugged again. "I do not like her," she said.

We left the little room and I turned to go.

"I think that tomorrow I shall go to the Villa Vittorio where the Cannans are living. I will tell them what I have told you of Rosa and I do not think they will trouble you again. If they do come, please say you have heard nothing more. It will be better for both you and Rosa, I feel sure. But you need not worry about her at all. I know that she is safe and well."

Perhaps, indirectly, I had told Lisa more than I had meant to. But she was Rosa's good friend and I knew that I could trust her. I thanked her, said I would be in touch with her again and so we parted, newly made friends ourselves.

Halfway home there came the sharp clip-clop of hooves behind me. This time I smiled acknowledgment and stepped up behind the proud driver and his prancing steed. I had chosen one of the most lively and arrived back at the hotel in great style and to Giorgio's amusement.

I was conscious of a well-spent morning behind me.

CHAPTER EIGHT

"Mine own fears . . . dreaming on things to come."—SHAKESPEARE.

I HAD set out that morning in a state of pleasant anticipation. I had wanted to meet Lisa, to give her good
news, and I was interested in seeing where Rosa lived.
I had enjoyed my outing and I had learned something.

Now, at six o'clock, I was not quite so happy.

I changed into a cool, light dress and walked slowly
up to the main square. A network of streets led into
the smaller square, the Square S. Vincentio. I had
walked this way before and, in a dreamy sort of fashion,
had spied out the land. There was an oblong of coarse
grass in the square's centre and a small fountain, its
basin upheld by a stone dolphin deep in flowers. Two
palm trees, green and up-thrusting, adorned each end
of the grass patch.

A row of small shops ran down one side of the square,
a dress shop with an embroidered blouse in its window
like the one Rosa had worn; a shop with a selection of
coloured and gilded Venetian glass; a wine shop, one
window filled with decorative Chianti bottles and, at
the corner of a narrow alley leading into a small courtyard, a shop crammed with typical tourist merchandise.
Even now it was still busy with customers. I joined them
and decided to buy one or two small things and ask my
questions while they were being wrapped.

I selected some leather bookmarks, then saw a rather delightfully carved small musical box which I decided might amuse mother. It tinkled out a few bars of Neapolitan songs, of which, needless to say. *Come Back To Sorrento* was one. When an assistant, free at last, came to me, I startled her by speaking in Italian.

"When will you close?" I asked.

"Late, signorina," she smiled. "When our customers cease to come."

So I paid for my purchases, asked how Signore Rossini was and if he were able to receive visitors, for I was a friend of his niece and she had told me of his illness.

"Ah, he is a little better now," she said, to my great relief. "Rosa telephoned when he had that last bad attack but she has not visited him since. We have wondered if she has been called away, for another lady telephoned me two days ago asking if she had been here. It was not you I know. This one had a different, older voice."

"Was she Italian?" I asked.

"Oh yes, signorina. She spoke with the accent of Naples."

"Then I would not know her," I said. "But Rosa has gone away, to the north. She has a chance in filming and has written to me, but she has not settled in any permanent address yet. I should like to see her uncle to explain why she has not visited him. Will that be possible?"

"I should think so, Signorina, though after each attack Signore Rossini is left very weak. If you go through to the courtyard you will see Signora Pascati's door, just below the outer staircase. If she herself is not there someone will have taken her place, for the signore is never left so that his bell is unanswered when he rings."

She handed me my purchases wtih a courtesy due to one who has spent ten thousand rather than one thousand lire.

I turned into the narrow alley leading to the courtyard. It was quiet here, the bustle of the nearby shops forgotten and far away. The warm air was still and contained within grey stone walls. On two sides the first floor was supported by rough pillars and overhung an enclosed area open to the courtyard. It bore signs of occasional use as a wholesale fruit market. Empty containers, labelled with the producers' names, were stacked neatly under cover, while a bin of rotting fruit gave out a sickly sweet odour in one corner. An arched doorway, surmounted by a weather-worn stone crest, bore witness to former grandeur.

To my right were those premises at the back of the gift shop, with the outside stone staircase mounting to a balcony where wide glass doors stood open. At the foot of the staircase were tubs with flowers dimly blue and white in the subdued light, and beyond, what must have been part of an original lost garden, thick dark bushes and a group of trees, shadowy and secluded, stretching to a grey distance.

It was a melancholy place at this hour, a place of half-lights and half-colours. I remembered Rosa saying that, on the day of his last illness, she had decided to visit her uncle in the sunlight for once. Perhaps, in the morning, with the bustle of buying and selling, when the dull stone would be painted in an extra dimension with the bright gold of oranges, the scarlet and green of peppers and the heaped riches of lemons, peaches and melons, cheerfulness would break in with the intrusive sunshine.

I looked round and saw a door in the shadow of the staircase, flanked by neatly curtained, shining windows, and I knocked gently.

The woman who opened it was short, plump and homely looking, not the Teresa Pascati I had imagined. I found it easy enough to introduce myself, make my request.

"I am sorry, but Signora Pascati is out for a short time," I was told. "I am a neighbour from across the square. I often come to attend the signore." She hesitated. "You say you are a friend of Signorina Rosa?"

I assured her that I was; that I wished to take news of his niece to the signore and that I would be most careful not to disturb him too much.

"Ah, well, I wish Teresa were here to say yes or no. But she is not, and I do not think a short visit would do harm. Wait, I will go and ask the signore if he wishes to see you."

I stood at the bottom of the staircase and heard her heavy footsteps labouring upwards. The waiting silence closed round me, a silence that seemed to quiver on the brink of sudden outcry. I did not like the feel of this place, still and almost threatening as it was.

There was no sound of voices and when, obedient to a beckoning hand from the balcony, I followed her up, I understood why. The wide double doors opened into a large, lofty room which stretched over the whole of the ground floor and part of the shop too. Against the far wall, facing the window, a vast distance away it seemed, was a bed with dark red silk curtains hanging from a carved wooden tester at its head and matching the red coverlet.

I walked across the room. The light was dim, but a small shaded lamp was lit on the bedside table. Vincentio Rossini raised himself up as I came near and I saw Rosa's uncle for the first time.

He was not even a middle-aged man; he must have been in his mid-sixties. He was an ill man, very ill; the pallor of his skin and the blueness of his lips and pinched nostrils showed it. But to an artist he would have been as beautiful in age as he must have been in youth. His eyes were Rosa's eyes; the darkness of his thick, wavy hair was streaked with silver. He had what the Victorians called a noble brow and his profile would have graced any Greek coin.

The smile with which he greeted me lit up his whole face. It was a face that had known hardship and sadness, disillusion and loss, but it was a face that had known love and had learned many lessons.

Now, as the lady from across the square plodded her way down the stairs, he pushed himself up on those strong arms of which Rosa had spoken and held out a thin hand to me. His grip was so hard and firm that I was startled.

"You are Helen, Rosa's friend?"

His voice was low and weak but very clear.

He indicated a chair nearby and I sat and told him yes, that I had come out from England less than a week ago. The difficult part of my story was to come.

"You bring me news of Rosa?" he asked. "She has not been for some time longer than usually passes between her calls on me. I hope the child is well. I have things to tell her, for my illness upset her last visit."

I looked round me. The room was airy and shiningly clean, smelling of some aromatic herbal fragrance. Dark, highly polished furniture made small islands on that vast space of floor. The mirrors of a tall cupboard reflected the room's dim distances to a wavering eternity. The light was shimmering, almost translucent. Velvet-cushioned chairs seemed to float on the surface of that green-tiled floor where white rugs surfaced like water lilies.

For a moment, in this unreal, dreamlike place, I could not order my thoughts. A kind of fear possessed me; some threat from the past and from the future. This sort of panic had caused Rosa's flight. In me it had no rhyme nor reason. I made a conscious effort to possess myself once more, to say what I had come to say.

Vincentio Rossini waited patiently, and at last I collected my thoughts and found words. It would be better to speak briefly, to tell my tale as quickly as possible.

"Signore, Rosa is safely in my home in England, but she does not wish that to be generally known. When she came to you on that last morning she meant to tell you of a discovery she had made. Those two American cousins—they are not American, they cannot be her cousins. They are Neapolitan. They are anxious to obtain something which they think is either in her possession already or soon will be in her possession. She heard them talk of a list which could mean money for them if they could obtain it. They spoke brutally and ruthlessly of Rosa herself.

"She was afraid, for you were so very ill. She was given the opportunity of coming to England and she took it; understandably, for she was so much alone. She is now safe with my mother and my step-father and is well looked after. But she was very unhappy about you and so I am here."

He closed his eyes and the lines on his forehead and round his lips grew deeper. His mouth was drawn into a straight line. I waited. Then he opened the dark Rossini eyes and smiled at me.

"Thank you, Signorina Helen, for coming to me. You have told no one else here of this?"

"No. I have told her friend Lisa and the lady downstairs that Rosa has written to me, since we were to have met in Sorrento this week, that she has the chance of film work in Northern Italy and will be moving round for some time. To you only I am telling the full truth. Rosa has brought the jewels to England, Signore; they are safe. But she is wondering if these two people who are pretending relationship to her have some mistaken idea as to their value."

He lay in silence, for a moment his face twisted in pain. Then he said, his voice weaker than before and the blue shadows round his eyes and mouth spreading, "I am not surprised at what you tell me and I understand what I did not understand before. I had seen that these last few weeks Rosa had been troubled. Now, too, the past is made clearer, I think."

He gave a deep sigh, summoned his breath for more words.

"The answer is in the box itself and in a letter I will give you, one which I should have given to Rosa that morning had the doctor not come, and one which I now must write to her."

His eyes went towards the lowest drawer of a large chest near the bed, but before he could speak again there came the sound of quick steps on the stairway and a tall, strongly built woman came into the room, shutting out what light remained, driving the shadows in before her. She ignored me, spoke to him directly.

"Vincentio, you should not have received a visitor. You are not well enough. It has distressed, exhausted you."

This was the Teresa Pascati of Rosa's description, efficient, practical, materially minded, perhaps, but with a quality Rosa had not realised. Here was jealous devotion, passionate and possessive. Her eyes were fiercely alight with it as she looked at Vincentio Rossini. At me, a stranger, she now glanced with a quick dislike she would not have dared to show openly to Rosa.

Signor Rossini spoke decisively, though I could tell that exhaustion and weakness were close to overcoming him.

"Teresa, this is Rosa's friend who has brought me news that Rosa is 'on location', I think they call it, in Northern Italy. Signorina Helen has come from England and is staying in Sorrento. She is disappointed not to see Rosa, who, however, has written to her, and she has been very kind in bringing us this news."

His voice faltered, died away, and Signora Pascati crossed the room to take a tablet from a small bottle and fill a glass with water.

Feeling guilty for my intrusion, necessary though it was, I stood up. Rosa's uncle held out his hand and I felt that firm grip again. His voice came in a whisper so that only I heard it.

"Please come once more. I must give you the letters for Rosa, tell you of other things." Then, with an effort, he spoke aloud. "Thank you again, Helen."

I pressed his hand and Teresa Pascati, waiting only until she had given him the capsule, followed me to the stair top.

"It was good of you to take trouble, Signorina, but your visit has done harm. If you receive more news you can safely give it to me, but you will not be able to see the signore again for some days. This new medicine the doctor gives him makes him sleep. He must rest."

"I am sorry to have caused trouble, but I had news of Rosa and her letter asked me to visit her uncle. Next time, I hope, I shall see you first. Buono notte, Signora."

Feeling perplexed and disturbed, I went back into the life and colour of the busy streets. In Rosa's uncle I had met a personality who had impressed me greatly, even in that short time. Now I faced the problem of how to make contact with him again, for that I must do somehow.

There was consolation in the thought that by this time tomorrow I should have the comfort of Aunt Joan's presence. She was the next best thing to Mother. I could tell her everything and she would give me physical as well as moral support. I acknowledged ruefully that I was not feeling quite so sure of myself as when I left home.

It was late and I went straight to the dining-room, but I was in no mood for casual conversation. I encouraged my neighbours to venture upon a good local dish, but I had no appetite myself. I decided to go to my room, to an early bed and a session with Dominic's second book. I left the dining-room for the lift intent on losing myself in its pages.

The reception desk was empty as I crossed the hall.

Then Giorgio appeared from a small room behind the counter and, with relief on his face, hurried towards me.

"Signorina Del Mar, good! No delay over finding you now! There is a telephone call from England. Come!"

My heart turned over. I thought of Mother, of some accident. I was in the small office picking up the receiver before I could think again. It was Mother's voice, thank God! Thin and far away, but it was Mother, and she was safe and well.

"Helen dear, can you hear me? The line is shocking."

"Just about—but not well. What is it?"

There was an intermittent buzzing and then the words again.

"—not to worry. They operated at once, late last night. Poor Joan! Appendicitis, at this last moment!"

I began to speak again but my words were drowned in the English Channel, lost in the fields of France, scrambled by the Alps and by Peregrine's dear, damnable Matterhorn!

Mother's voice came once more, like the odd, lost refrain of a very new and modern symphony.

"—hope not lonely, dear—bring her to The Highwayman to recuperate. All send their love."

I managed, I hope, to get across an assurance that I'd be okay and to send my love back to everyone in return. Then the Matterhorn must have collapsed right across the line. There was a thud, a rattle and a click, and I knew I was cut off for good.

"I heard enough," I told Giorgio, who was looking at me with apologetic concern for the failure of E.E.C. telephonic communications.

CHAPTER NINE

I READ *The King's Men* until after midnight, keeping depression at bay with its infective vitality. It dropped from my hand as I fell asleep.

When I awoke and walked out on to my balcony there was a blue mist over the distant curve of the bay and Vesuvius tapered up into a heat haze. I was looking at a spectacular stage set. Perhaps, I thought, I had a role in the drama to be enacted there.

During the last week I had seen little of my neighbour. That room would be vacated today but no Aunt Joan would be moving in. I realised again how much I had been looking forward to her company.

I decided to leave my call at the Villa Vittorio until mid-afternoon. Let Sophie Cannan offer me a good cup of tea, something the Risorgimento did not provide, even though its pride in those little tea bags floating in hot water was so excessive that the recipient would always smile bravely and drink courageously rather than tell the truth and hurt the waiter's feelings.

I studied a map and found that the Via Gaelta was about fifteen minutes' walk, dropping downhill towards the sea.

After breakfast I bathed and settled in the company

of my lizard, the orange blossom and what remained of Dominic's book. Regretfully I closed it at last. I wondered if there were a proper bookshop in Sorrento where I could buy Italian paperbacks or magazines. I had not seen one so far.

In mid-afternoon I went upstairs and saw, from my balcony, a small group of children on their way home from school, the little girls in spotless white overalls with blue bows, the small boys in bright blue with red bows; traditional wear preserved in modern nylon. They looked very sweet and decorous until some squabble began and a free-for-all started, satchels wildly swinging in grievous intent to inflict bodily harm. I was amused to see that the girls were winning, when a young priest in a black cassock came striding along. A few words from him and peace was restored, evidently with honour, for the group went on its homeward way quite amicably.

How Aunt Joan would have enjoyed the performance! She loved children and always regretted having none of her own. I decided to visit Pompeii next week as I would have visited it with her. No guided parties for me, though. I would find my own transport. I remembered enough and had read enough to wander in the past and meet the ghosts alone.

The Via Gaelta was easy to find; the villa a little more difficult, in a short turning down a steeply twisting hill. I deliberately passed the gate that led to the front and found the side entrance used by Rosa on that last morning. I saw the path wandering through almond trees and could guess at the side of the terrace hidden in green undergrowth.

I retraced my steps and made my way to the front of a small pink-washed building, once the unpretentious dwelling of an owner who had worked long hours to wrest a living from his harvest of small black olives and his scattered orange and lemon trees. It had probably been modernised adequately but it was still a mean sort of place, though its status had been raised for tourist attraction when it was re-christened a villa.

The door stood open on to the usual square tiled hall. I knocked and a harsh American voice called, "C-ome," spliting the invitation into two syllables.

I walked through to a room running the length of the building. Long windows opened to the terrace which overlooked a sea of olive green and a blue stretch of Mediterranean far below. Then, from a chair in the corner behind me, the owner of the voice stood up, a short, stout woman, wearing a bright blue dress, sleeveless over thick red arms, and tight-skirted above short, muscular legs.

At first sight she was unprepossessing; at a second look, interesting, maybe. As Rosa had said, one could still see in her face the better features of youth. Her eyes were intensely black. So I had found out at last that black eyes really did exist. Hers were "blacker than ash buds in the front of March", an opaque, dull black which, as Rosa had said too, hid thoughts below their surface. The face was strong, the brows thick and well marked, the lips full and sensual. Take her years and the heavy weight of years away and Sophie Cannan would have been a woman of considerable animal attraction.

And what is more, with the help of my foreknowledge perhaps, to me she looked typically Italian. She had aged in a typically Italian peasant fashion. If, instead of being backcombed and waved round the large head, her chestnut-dyed hair had been left dark and streaked with grey and drawn smoothly back to a heavy knot, she would have been the exact image of her Neapolitan grandmother.

Later I was to find that the American accent sounded authentic enough. Perhaps it was foreknowledge again that made me aware of those Italian inflections which showed in rapid conversation. I would be more conscious of this than Rosa, whose own English, in a way probably not realised by herself, revealed her Italian heritage in a quite charming fashion.

"You'll be Helen Del Mar then? I sure am pleased to meet you." Sophie Cannan's welcome couldn't have been warmer. Snatching up an outsize pair of dark glasses, she hid behind them as she ushered me out to the terrace. Her husband, small, wiry, muscular, got up to meet me. He was thin-faced, sharp-boned and dark-complexioned. I have seen Americans like him, Italians too. He was less talkative than his wife. After a few minutes Sophie left us to make that "real English" cup of tea and the interval before her return was spent in talk of the view, the weather, the wilderness of a garden. When she came back bearing a tray with tea-cups, tea and small, sweet biscuits, it was a passable product, but I felt that Sophie would have achieved better coffee.

"Now, have you got news of that cute little cousin of ours?" she began. "Take another cookie, honey. We've gotten real fond of her and can't think what can have happened."

I told them the same story I had told Lisa and Teresa Pascati. In essence it was true, after all.

"And you say you don't know her address?" she asked, sharply.

"The first stages of film-making are a bit unsettled," I said wildly, hoping they knew even less about film-making than I did. "Rosa gave me no definite address. You can be sure she's safe, though. This may be a fine opportunity for her."

"And what about this uncle of hers?" Sophie's eyes watched me keenly from behind those dark screens. "How did he take this sudden departure?"

"I've seen him once and told him all I knew of Rosa's whereabouts. He is very ill, you know."

"Yes, very ill. Rosa told us that. We'd like you to tell him that if he has anything he wants to send her, any special bequest or message, we can undertake it for him. After all, we're her only relations on her father's side, not mere friends or acquaintances."

I stood up. I was irritated and did not care if she knew it.

"Perhaps you could try to get in touch with him yourselves. I can't very well be a go-between," I said.

Sophie glanced at her husband, a sharp glance of communication. Then she turned to me with a deprecatory smile.

"Of course you can't, honey. I was just thinking aloud. That's what we could do, of course. But Rosa will be writing to us and to her uncle soon, and she'll be back, I'm sure."

She led the way into the shadowy sitting-room again.

"You wait here while I fetch that photo of Rosa's father—and the letter he wrote to my mother."

She went out and I heard her heavy step on the stairs. I looked back to the terrace and saw Myers going down the flight of steps to the garden. He walked quickly and lightly, with the speed of a younger man.

I watched him cross the grass and vanish under the olives.

I looked round the room, at its gimcrack, flimsy furniture. I didn't want to sit and so establish a longer stay, and I walked over to a small bookcase in a dark corner. Books, of whatever sort, are always a magnet to me. Most of these, in the main paperback thrillers, had been left by former tenants : Simonen in French, Agatha Christie and James Bonds in English, the rest Italian with some school books which must have belonged to the former owner's children.

An old-fashioned volume in sun-faded red caught my eye. I read its Italian title, translated it, *A Story of Famous Jewels, Lost and Found*, by an unknown author, Giovanni Marcello. I heard the sound of Sophie's return, looked at my fairly large handbag and, for the first time in my life, contemplated small-scale pilfering. But no, I decided. When Sophie Cannan came back into the room I was standing with the book in my hand, turning over its pages. Her eyes slid to it and, quickly, I spoke.

"I'm sorry, but I just can't resist bookshelves. I finished a book by Dominic Lee this morning and was wondering where I could find something else to read. Have you come across his two books?" This was hardly the time to indulge in talk of Dominic, but the chance was irresistible. Her eyes still on the book in my hand, Sophie said, "Yes, I've read his first book. Did you like it?"

For a few moments I enjoyed myself. Then I looked at the book I still held. "I can't remember a bookshop in Sorrento. My school books came from Naples. Is there one?"

Sophie shrugged. "Haven't seen one, honey. Why? D'you want a book?"

"I'll be lost without something to read. I wonder—" I hesitated, looked down at the book in my hand. "I wonder if you could possibly lend me one? I'd bring it back before I go."

"Sure! Help yourself. They're not ours—just rubbish left by other tenants, I guess. There's some in English there. You wouldn't like that one." She realised her slip and covered it quickly. "Those hardbacks are all in Italian. I've looked through those shelves to find one I can read often enough."

"I've read most of the thrillers and nothing in that line will seem up to Dominic Lee for a bit. Besides, you forget I'm half-Italian. I haven't let my father's language go." I looked at the book I held again. "May I take this? I think it might be interesting."

Sophie shrugged. "Sure, you take it. What's it about? A nice romance?"

"Oh, no! Far more interesting. It's the story of famous jewels, the 'Star of India' and that sort of thing. I heard a radio feature on the subject once, found it fascinating. This looks a bit old fashioned, but that will be good for my Italian grammar."

Again the shrug. Sophie really should have rid herself of that gesture. "Sounds dull to me. Can't work up any feeling for jewellery myself. Never having had any, I suppose."

"Thank you. I'll bring it back next week," I promised, wondering if, by then, I should have learned any more to throw light on this intriguing pair.

Sophie held out a small photograph and an envelope. "Take a look at this—Rosa's father. I found it in my mother's album and pulled it out to bring, thinking Rosa would be interested. And you can read the letter."

A young American soldier looked up at me. There was little of Rosa in the likeness save a smile that had gaiety and sweetness combined, the sort of smile she could inherit from her uncle, too, I thought. I took the letter from its envelope and read it through, an affectionate letter that any foster mother would have been proud to receive. It ended—"I hope I'll be visiting you soon, with Marguerita, my dear wife, and our lovely daughter, Rosa. Gee! But she's beautiful!"

Rosa had been ten when that was written and John Russell had been killed in the car crash only two years later.

I sighed and gave it back into Sophie's outstretched hands. I tucked my borrowed book firmly under my arm and said goodbye. Myers was still away under the olive trees and I left him my farewell message without any regret. My visit had certainly offered me no danger and had been reasonably profitable, I thought.

CHAPTER TEN

"A casement ope at night . . . to let the warm love in."—KEATS.

I GOT back to my room, threw my book on the bed and was immediately overcome by dull depression again. If only Aunt Joan could have come as we planned, we should be together, in and out of each other's rooms, catching up on Highwayman and hospital anecdotes, making plans for the coming week, Pompeii, Amalfi, Capri, even grim disillusionment on the summit of Vesuvius.

It wasn't that I disliked my own company, always needed people around me. I usually enjoyed solitude, in fact. But now I was restless, expectant of something, knowing I could expect nothing. I changed and went down to dinner. I met the assistant manager on my way, small, dapper, bright eyed.

"I am sorry, signorina, that you will not have a lady companion for the rest of your stay. The room will not be vacant though. You will have a neighbour—"

Giorgio signalled to him from reception and he went off with an apologetic gesture. I talked of Capri and San Michele and Gracie Fields to my neighbours, then sat idly leafing through old magazines in the lounge, gossiped again and went early to my room.

I re-opened my balcony window, always so considerately shut by the chambermaid, and stood there, looking at that dark strip of bay, the few lamps in the street below which lit up the little pale ovals of lemons on the trees across the way, the twinkling stars of light edging the uneven shore and studding the dark, leafy terraces which leapt upwards from the sea.

There was no sound or sign of life from the hidden door on to the next balcony.

I looked down over the strip of drive to the hotel entrance. A small, beetle-shaped car pulled into a space at the side where the cars of residents could park, very elegant cars they usually were, too. This one had a kind of impudence, rather engaging; a left-hand drive, so Italian, presumably. I didn't recognise the make.

A pair of long legs unfolded as their owner extricated himself. Then my heart jumped wildly, beat again in an unaccustomed excited rhythm. I was looking down on a smooth, shining head of coppery brown hair. Could it be? Instinct said yes, common sense said no.

Before I knew what I was doing I was out of my room, waiting impatiently for the lift. Downstairs I turned the corner, had full view of the entrance hall, and it was true! Dominic was at the reception desk, talking to Giorgio.

Perhaps my eyes touched him with a kind of electric contact. At any rate, he turned in the middle of a sentence and came towards me, his hands outstretched as I held out mine to him.

Realisation came suddenly. I had rushed to meet him like the adoring fan of a pop star idol. Giorgio's smile was both sympathetic and humiliating. I dropped my hands, managed a well-controlled greeting and recognised that twitch at the corner of his mouth, that uplift of eyebrows.

"Helen!" he said, looking at me for a long moment. "Still golden, no more, no less, as you said. Well, will I make an adequate substitute for Aunt Joan?"

Speechless, I nodded, as Giorgio spoke. "Signore, we will take your case to your room and I will get your telephone number as soon as possible. Could you perhaps stay in the lounge so that we may let you know when the call comes through without delay."

Giorgio smiled at me again in congratulatory pleasure and, with Dominic's hand on my arm, I went before him to a deserted table near the door.

"Vermouth, campari?" he asked, and left me to get drinks at the small bar which led from the lounge and gave on to the terrace round the pool, on to the scent of orange-blossom and the coolness of water.

Bother the telephone call, I thought. I realised how, each evening when I had gone primly to bed, I had longed to wander with that scent around me and Dominic at my side. He came back with our glasses. I watched him, then lowered my eyes lest they should show my thoughts.

"Tell me, how did this happen? Why did you come?" I asked.

"Need you ask?" He paused, looked at me for a moment, then continued. "I knew I'd have to come to Rome sooner or later, to see Joe Hendrick. He's in Florence now, but, with luck, should be in Rome by Sunday. If not, I'll have to go to Florence, because see him I must. I'd planned for next month, but this seemed an opportunity I could take, so I took it. I want to fix that part for Rosa, too, before he gets someone else."

So that was his real reason for coming—Rosa and the

93

film. Suddenly the lamps in the lounge were too dim, the red tiles and flower-patterned rugs no longer gay. The voices round us were flat, without warmth or brightness.

I heard him say, "I managed to hire rather a jolly little car in Naples which might speed things up."

"When must you go? How long will you be away?" I spoke with my eyes on my glass.

"With bad luck, if it's Florence, I'll have to go tomorrow, be back on Wednesday as early as possible. With good luck, reach Rome Sunday night, back here Tuesday."

I worked out the time left in Sorrento and contemplated, at the worst, just one full day here with him. This was bitter disappointment after the delight of his coming.

"Look," he was saying, "When can I do something with you about Rosa's problem?"

"There's no need for you to worry. I've coped so far." My voice sounded cold and detached. "I've visited Rosa's uncle, seen her friend and called on the Cannans."

There was a silence and I looked up to find his eyes fixed on me with an expression I could not interpret.

"Well, tell me what happened and your impression of what's going on," he said.

So I told him of Vincentio Rossini and my interrupted conversation with him and of my visit to the Villa Vittorio.

"Helen, somehow I shall get back here, even if it's only for one day. Please wait and let me come with you next time you go to Rosa's uncle. He must have something to tell which these so-called Americans want to know.

If you find out what it is the knowledge may be dangerous for you. As for the jewels—I told Rosa it would be easy enough to discover their true value, but she prefers to hear the full family story from her uncle if possible. She is really very sweet."

There was so much affection in his voice at that moment that surely, I thought, it indicated a deeper emotion. I looked at my watch—after eleven o'clock— and I stood up.

"I think I'll go to bed. I'm tired," I said. "Your telephone call will come through soon, I hope, and I expect you will be glad to end your long day, too."

Again I got that enigmatic look, but I knew I must be alone. I was afraid of giving away my own feelings, of embarrassing him as well as myself.

"Goodnight," I said. "I'm sure to see you before you go."

I sat on my bed, the room lit only by the lamps in the street and the lights from the hotel, chequered and wavering in the breeze which stirred the leaves of the trees.

With considerable inefficiency I played the amateur psychiatrist and tried to analyse by own emotions. The one undeniable fact was that I loved Dominic, loved him as I knew I could love no one else. I remembered that evening when we had stood watching the swan fly over against the soft blue English sky; the enchantment of Stratford, the drive home through sleepy villages. Then, with Rosa's coming, with drama, adventure, the spell had been broken and I had been lost in my own uncertainties ever since.

To what a state of muddled confusion had my foolishness brought me! In an upsurge of misery and bewilderment, I wept, my head buried in my pillow.

Long after, it seemed, I sat up, damp, depressed and miserable. I heard a low whistle from the direction of the window. I thought at first that it came from the drive below.

"Helen, come here." It was Dominic's voice and he must be standing on the neighbouring balcony. "Come out here, please," he called again softly.

"I can't," I called back, and lied, "I'm ready for bed."

"Well, put on a dressing-gown. You're safe. I can't rape you from here, you know."

"No, Dominic. I'll see you tomorrow."

How could I let him see me now? Even the light from the street would show signs of my tears.

"All right! Have it your own way."

He sounded impatient and annoyed. I didn't blame him. I'd asked for it. I had behaved like a spoiled child. How could he possibly imagine that turmoil of emotion in my heart. For one infantile moment I longed for my mother, for her to comfort me, to tell me she understood. I gulped down a sob and felt like Jeremy.

There came another sound from outside. I sat frozen as I saw a pair of hands on the balcony railings, a head just level with it. A dark shadow sprang upwards with swift agility and Dominic stood outside my window.

His eyes must have seen in the dark, for he took one step forward, then came quickly across the room, straight towards me. I stood up to face him and his arms were round me, holding me close.

"What's the matter, Helen my darling, my golden girl? Don't you know I've come because I can't be without you, even if I only get you for a day? I've told your mother, I've told Rosa, I've told everyone, I think, save you! Are you really trying to say no to me? I thought you felt the same way."

"I do, oh, I do!" I said, and he kissed me as no one else would ever kiss. Then he put a finger under my chin and turned my face up towards him. "Have you been crying?"

I made a last attempt to restore my lost pride, but I held him to me as though I would never let him go.

"Aunt Joan couldn't come and I was lonely. I thought you'd not really come to be with me. I've been homesick. I've missed Mother and The Highwayman and—and William."

Dominic threw back his head and laughed aloud.

"Sweet William is missing you almost as much as I did if that's any consolation. But how much have you missed me?"

There was an interval while I told him. Then his words came through to me again, close to my ear.

"When are you going to marry me? Because you will, you know. Nothing else will do."

Wouldn't it? For him as well as for me? I wasn't a freak. I wasn't the vestal virgin. I was Dominic's!

"Swans flying over?" I heard him whisper.

But at last we came back more or less to reality.

"First, it's good news," he told me. "Joe will be in Rome by Sunday. I'll drive up to see him and be back here on Tuesday night at the latest. I'll have to come over again in a few months' time. Darling, we'll make that visit part of our honeymoon, shall we? Of course, you could come up to Rome with me on Sunday, but I'll be in Joe's flat talking half the night. I'd rather rush things through and get back here."

"We'll do something lovely tomorrow," I promised.

Dominic drew me towards my balcony. We stood together looking over to that perfect view which so far had been only mine.

"Darling, if I don't go now I never shall," he said.

"Not that way!" I exclaimed in horror, drawing back.

"Then which way?" He laughed. "If you think I'm going down to reception at—" he checked his watch. "At one o'clock, an hour after I came up, to tell them I locked my key inside while I was visiting you—!"

He stifled my objections, for indeed, looking down on that drop made me shudder. Before I could say another word he had swung over the rail, his feet at its base. His fingers gripped the railing top. He reached each foot down, first left, then right as he felt for the support of those small buttresses which projected over the window below. His hands and feet groped carefully along both railings and supports. He was level with his own balcony; then, hardest of all, he brought his left foot up to its base, his right foot following. One more effort and he swung his legs across his own railing and stood there triumphantly.

I breathed once more and my heart beat normally again.

"Well, I've learned the way it's done, step by step, in easy stages," I told him.

"Don't you dare try it," he said and, at that moment, to try such a thing was far beyond any possible stretch of my imagination.

CHAPTER ELEVEN

"E te vonno tantu bene."—"Chanting tender songs of love."
NEAPOLITAN SONG.

We were to have three complete days in Sorrento and I shall never forget a moment of that first perfect and unspoiled one. I looked across at Dominic as we sat over our breakfast table, cool, lean and relaxed in dark blue slacks and white sweater, and remembered my make-believe companion of those days of solitude. I touched the hand he held out in response to my glance.

We swam in the pool together and lazed under the orange trees. I introduced Dominic to my lizard. A tightly wrapped bud fell on to the tiles and our miniature monster did not stir. Soundlessly I stretched out my hand and he vanished in half an indrawn breath. I crushed the blossom in my fingers, smelt its sweetness and dropped it into the pocket of Dominic's jacket, where it lay over a chair. "You'll find that again some day and remember this morning," I told him.

We decided to go to Pompeii in that friendly little car he had hired. We stopped at Castellammare and I showed him our old villa and we had lunch down by the sea at the restaurant where Mother had treated me to luscious ice-creams during the holidays.

We stopped too at the cameo factory, which I scarcely remembered. Queer to think that this place was, in a way, part of me; that, as I grew interested, I should have been shown round it by my father. I felt a kind of sadness but no bitterness.

And so we went on to Pompeii, that resurrected ghost of a town. We avoided the groups of tourists as we wandered, hand in hand, where other lovers had wandered too, had lost each other in fear and terror. I was pleased with my ability to guide Dominic through those reclaimed streets, where the voices of distant tourist parties sounded far away and unreal, as though they echoed through dead centuries.

We gave Rosa's best wishes to all those little lizard acquaintances of hers and, for the time being, said goodbye to Pompeii. Then, half-laughing at our conventional route, we went on to Vesuvius, meeting returning coaches on those intricate hairpin bends.

"All Southern Italians can sing," I told Dominic as the music of one of the couriers entertaining his flock in Neapolitan love songs floated back to us, his voice transformed by distance into that of another Caruso.

We parked the car near the stalls where they sold orange juice at inflated prices, near the cafés and gift and postcard counters. We sent off a lurid picture of Vesuvius to The Highwayman. Then we swung across the sparsely green valley beneath that tapering grey peak which looks so beautiful from across the bay.

Am I the only girl to have been kissed in a chair lift for two on the passage to Vesuvius, I wonder?

But even with Dominic the summit of the volcano had no glamour for me. That grey, ashy expanse with its small puffs of steamy smoke was heavy and laden with foreboding. Retreating, we brushed its dust from our shoes and Dominic restored normality by calling upon me to choose the colour I liked best from those strangely shaped pieces of what had once been molten lava, they told us. Whether this were true or no, their shapes and colours were beautiful and this was Dominic's first present to me.

I chose a piece in smoky blue-green, "The colour of my true love's eyes," I told him. "And it's the first of our household gods," he said. "When I infuriate you by getting too immersed in a difficult chapter, you will hurl it at me in a volcanic eruption of your own. Then I shall sing *Come Back To Sorrento* and you'll forgive me at once."

So, as the evening grew cooler, we drove home along the small, less frequented roads we could find running parallel to the sea. We parked the little car, went upstairs and kissed outside our doors for a twenty-minute separation before dinner. A perfect, perfect day!

When Sunday came, with its temporary parting to be faced, other things intervened.

I caught sight, on my bedside table, of the book I had borrowed from Sophie Cannan and had almost forgotten. I took it with me when I went to join Dominic, already lying under the tree we had claimed as our own.

"*Jewels Lost and Found*—borrowed from the Villa Vittorio itself!" I boasted, and got a rather doubtful look as reward.

"I've only turned the pages over so far, but I think—" I turned them over again. "The Star of South Africa," "The Colenso Diamond"—I found the chapter I was looking for, headed "The Three Stars of Georgia". The book was written in a stilted, pedantic style which, as

I had told Sophie, though it would be good for my grammar would do little for my colloquial Italian. I offered it to Dominic.

"You translate it for me. I can stumble along, but it's hard work. Besides, I like your voice." So I began to translate the appropriate passages aloud.

" " The three stars of Georgia were three magnificent diamonds which came into the possession of the Pontiesky family during the seventeenth century. The gems were cut in a six-sided fashion which was, at that time, thought to bring good luck to their owner, and legend has it that without them good fortune would leave the Pontiesky family. Certainly, with very few adventures by the way, they remained with their rightful owners until they vanished during the revolution of 1917. They have never been seen since."

"Here's a long piece about the evils of Tsarist Russia, Dominic, for which, I gather, neither the Tsar nor the Pontiesky family were in any way responsible! The last Prince was a real do-gooder, it seems."

I turned over a few pages.

"Oh, here we are again, back at the diamonds. 'Until the beginning of the nineteenth century the three stones had formed a beautiful pendant, but at that time they were put into a small diadem, three central ornaments in a gold circlet. The last Princess wore them rarely, on state occasions only.

" 'The Pontiesky marriage was, as were so many at that time, an alliance of convenience, and the Prince had formed a liaison elsewhere, with a young ballet dancer, Elena Alexyevna. There were rumours that the Prince had given Elena the diamonds, but the truth or otherwise of that story will never be known.

" 'When the revolution came, the Princess and her two daughters managed to escape from Russia, and it is a fact that the Princess took none of the Pontiesky jewels with her. She lived in a style not ostentatious but suitable to her station, in Paris, and her daughters married into the French aristocracy.

" 'The Prince, who refused to leave his country estate in Georgia, was murdered by the advancing revolutionaries. When later, under Kerensky's brief period of well-intentioned leadership, the Pontiesky estate was seized, they found the great house largely destroyed with no jewels or any personal possessions remaining in its vast, empty rooms!'

"Shall I go on, darling? It's very pompous!"

"Go on, go on, my love. Be pompous—I like it," said Dominic dreamily, his head on my knee.

"All right, more about Elena then. 'Meanwhile the heartbroken Elena managed to get out of Russia. With a life-long friend, another dancer, she eventually joined the rest of the company in Paris. Her death, in Italy, ten years later, at the early age of twenty-nine, came when she was reaching the height of her fame. Whether she ever possessed the three stars of Georgia is not known, but what is most likely is that they were stolen at the time of the Prince's death, were smuggled out of Russia into the hand of some Swiss receiver and cut up into smaller stones with but a fraction of the originals' beauty or value.'

"The chapter finishes on a dramatic note, Dominic." And I declaimed, " 'So, hidden in the past, unlikely to be revealed by the future, rests the fate of those magnificent three Stars of Georgia!' "

I closed the book and looked down into Dominic's

face. One week ago and he was just the shadowy creation of my longing for him. Now—he took my hand and held it to his lips.

"I did listen, in spite of certain distractions. Well, our Neapolitan friends have undoubtedly read that and got it by heart."

"There's plenty to think about in it."

"You know, Helen, Rosa showed me that stage jewellery which belonged to Elena. The thing I liked most was that little sapphire bracelet. It had a personal touch, a charm about it."

"I liked it too. Diamonds have never appealed much to me."

I got the quizzical look which made my heart turn over.

"That's a relief, my golden girl," he said. Then he selected a finger from my left hand, which he still held. "But you won't mind if I put a diamond on this one, will you? Maybe we can add a sapphire or so to make it acceptable."

There was only one group by the pool, at the far end, and the interlude that followed was quite unperceived. I told Dominic he could put a chip of blue lava from Vesuvius on that finger and it would still be everything in the world to me, but he insisted on settling for the more conventional symbol. Discussion of that purchase interrupted stories of jewels of the past.

When we came back to the present Dominic took up his comment on Elena's jewellery where he had left off.

"We noticed something that Rosa had not noticed before. After all, she hadn't had much time for a close inspection. That coronet affair was built up to a point in front, each row decreasing to the crowning brilliance of three large stones. And those three showed signs of once having been broken off and repaired. You can see the mark of the fracture on both sides, a neat but fairly amateurish sort of job—like this."

He sat up, reached for a pencil from his pocket, found a used envelope from the same source and sketched a little picture of Rosa's tiara. The bottom row of stones encircled the wearer's head. The front rose to a graceful point crowned by those three large gems. The setting was very simple, the side pieces, where Dominic marked the signs of a break, almost like curved wire.

He handed me his finished drawing.

"Good Lord! That looks a bit like a wedding cake," he said, adding a few lines in improvement. "Must be my subconscious taking over. I never could draw, anyway, but you get the idea?"

"I get it," I said. "Did you see if those three stones were cut in any special way, and what was the setting like?"

"Oh, a sort of gold, I suppose. Paste and pinchbeck : wasn't that the recipe for less expensive Victorian jewellery? Actually this workmanship didn't look too good. You could have bent those end pieces as if they were wire.

"I got Peregrine waffling on about Victorian jewellery and from what he said I should think those stones are in an ordinary enough claw setting, nothing like so craftsmanlike as those in a pendant he showed me.

"The stones themselves had facets which made them glitter, but I couldn't give you any details, hexagonal or octagonal prisms or what-have-you. My bet is that, always with the possibility of those three stones excepted of course, the tiara is in quite good paste set in rolled gold. In stage lighting and at a distance, the thing must be quite something!"

"Ah, well!" I folded Dominic's wedding cake sketch and put it into my white shoulder bag. "We've learned something about Elena Alexyevna and about the Pontiesky family too. Uncle Vincentio said, 'The answer is in the box'. That can only mean the jewel case. Then he added, 'And in the papers I will give you.' Oh, Dominic, I do so want you to see Rosa's uncle. Even now, ill as he is, he's got the most marvellous personality."

"I will, my darling, when I come back from Rome."

We had lunch, sat on my balcony for the hour that remained, then said "Goodbye" in my room, "Arrivederici" in his.

Down in the drive he slid into the little car, then reached out and took my hand.

"Sweetheart, I'll give you two things to think about while I'm away. Firstly, as soon as you can manage it, I want to take you down to Sussex to meet my people. Father's the sort of country town family solicitor who'll never retire, and Mother's always busy, but never too busy. And there's an older sister married to a farmer, with a small boy named John, rather like Jeremy. You'll be the answer to a mother's prayer and they'll all love you.

"And secondly, Charles and Joanna have definitely decided to leave Chimneys, taking Jeremy and cat Thomas with them. He's got promotion to elsewhere. D'you like the idea of buying the house from them? I'd be near my favourite mother-in-law and you'd have your Sweet William as a neighbour. Think about it! Charles has promised not to sell to anyone else until we give him the word. You see how I've taken things for granted! Are you cross?"

"No, oh, no!" I said. He kissed my fingers then turned neatly in the drive and in a moment was gone from my sight, but not from my heart.

I went back into the hotel, my mind full of his suggestions—another family to meet and Chimneys and Dominic and me.

I handed in his key, then realised that I had left my own upstairs. Giorgio saw my little grimace of annoyance and I had to explain its cause.

"There won't be a chambermaid around now, I suppose?" I asked, feeling like Public Nuisance Number One. "I'm sorry!"

"It is nothing, Signorina." Giorgio's courtesy was equal to any resident's carelessness. He turned to the pigeon holes behind him and produced another key with my number on it. "Here are two spares for such an occasion. Return it at your convenience." I thanked him and went straight to my room.

The hours stretched ahead till bedtime. I settled on my balcony with the view to delight in and thoughts of Dominic and myself and Chimneys in my head.

CHAPTER TWELVE

"Oh what a tangled web we weave!"—SCOTT.

I WAS a problem to myself for the whole of the next day. I had no desire to swim. I sat under the orange trees and read a bulky letter that had arrived by the morning's post. Mother gave me the latest report on Aunt Joan.

> *"We telephoned and had a talk with the Matron. Joan narrowly escaped peritonitis, she said. She had been feeling under the weather for some time, nothing that she hadn't thought a holiday and the sun would put right. Then on Wednesday night she became desperately ill and they operated at once, quite successfully.*
>
> *"I spoke to Joan on the bedside telephone and she sounded wonderfully cheerful and is going on well. Peter and I will go down towards the end of next week and bring her back with us to convalesce. Everything's straightforward and, thank goodness, they don't keep you in bed three weeks now. The Highwayman will be a poor substitute for Sorrento, but we'll do our best."*

There was a note from Rosa in the same envelope. Mother had asked me to give Dominic her love and had said how glad she was to send him to me. She hadn't any news from me yet and was being cautious, but Rosa was more girlishly forthcoming.

"Dear Helen,
*   I am so glad that the dear Dominic is with you.*
Indeed, his heart has been in Sorrento all this last
week. He has made each sentence end in talk of you!
Please love him as he loves you or I too shall be
desolate!"

She went on:

"I am glad you have seen my uncle and that you
found him all I told you. But you did not keep the
promise which I now realise you did not really give.
Next time you see Uncle Vincentio you will be with
Dominic and you will, I hope, bring back the letters
he will give you. You are doing for me what I should
have done for myself before I left Sorrento. Give dear
Uncle 'Centio my love."

I wrote a return letter at once, the lizard a silent witness. What I said to Mother would dispose of all further need for discretion over Dominic, and I gave Rosa the reassurance she wanted. "The dear Dominic is my dearest and most dearly loved, and you are our very dear Rosa. Stay in England long enough to be my bridesmaid," I told her.

A lean white and ginger cat crept cautiously to the edge of the pool and drank its artificially blue water thirstily. I thought of that ball of fur, Pussy Thomas, who had, after all, brought about my first real introduction to Dominic. This cat would have to get herself out of any predicament she might get into. I spoke to her in the usual cat language, but perhaps she only knew some feline Italian dialect. She wove her way back through the undergrowth with a mistrustful glance over her shoulder.

I addressed, sealed and stamped my letter ready to leave it at the reception desk for posting. I had brought *Jewels Lost and Found* down with me and I glanced through the apposite chapters again, fixing all the details in my mind. That six-sided cut supposed to bring good fortune to its owners intrigued me. Possession of the diamonds would have been important to the Pontiesky family, would have meant far more than their monetary value. Could those three brilliant jewels crowning Elena's tiara possibly be the Three Stars of Georgia?

Suddenly I decided to take the book back to the Villa Vittorio that morning. By doing so I could avoid having to call there later in the week. Those two precious days here with Dominic were becoming more and more important to me. I put the book into my capacious shoulder bag and set out—shopping first, then I would take the Villa Vittorio in on my way back for lunch.

I wandered round the shops in those narrow streets linking up squares and markets. I bought Mother a silk embroidered blouse and myself the most exquisite and delicately hand-made lingerie for my wedding day. I found a soft leather belt, small enough for Rosa's waist, and for Peter a leather tobacco pouch. I knew enough to choose one that would be airtight. What could I give to Dominic as a memento? In the end I selected a pair of gold cuff links chased in a cleverly intricate pattern which, on closer inspection, proved to be the curve of the bay and the peak of Vesuvius.

Then, with a brightly coloured Italian shopping bag

full, and deciding that homeward-bound luggage would carry no more, I went to the gift shop in the Square S. Vincentio and found two small dolls, perfectly dressed as Neapolitan tarantella dancers, for the collections of Sheila and Jean, one with Elizabeth Taylor eyes and one a gorgeous redhead, like Sheila herself.

I asked how Signor Rossini was.

"Better, Signorina," I was told. "Very much better. The doctor is pleased. By tomorrow he should have visitors again." Good news indeed!

I looked at my watch and found that I had timed the morning's occupations well. I started off on my path to the Via Gaelta.

The villa from the front, even in this bright sunshine, was shabby and depressing. Two cypresses stood, funereal sentinels, on either side of the door. Rough patches of plaster on the walls looked like patches of decay. The door stood half-open and, at my knock, Myers came from the room at the back. I would have avoided going in but he turned from me and led the way, leaving me no option but to follow. The house was cool when compared with the outdoor heat, and perhaps that is why I gave an involuntary shiver. He threw me a quick, darting glance, swift as the lizard on his stone.

"Sophie will be back from marketing any moment," he told me. "Come through to the garden."

I explained that I had brought back the borrowed book since I should be leaving Sorrento on Friday or even earlier, and might not be able to call again.

I took it from my bag and gave it him and he looked at the title, gave no sign of having understood its meaning.

111

"You enjoyed it?" he asked.

I shrugged. "I skipped through it. It passed the time and exercised my Italian. The subject didn't really interest me."

He nodded and placed it back in the bookcase. I was preparing to go but he repeated, "Come out into the sun. You must wait and say goodbye to my wife."

So, gladly enough, I left my bags on a chair and followed him out of that depressing room. He did not stop on the terrace but went down the steps and the sloped grass to a group of olive trees, grey-green, gnarled, some of them a good age. I remembered the story of the olive tree told in Corfu. An old couple lived their long life together, making a precarious living from their grove of olives. Their only wish had been to die together as they had lived together and to be buried under the shade of one of their olive trees. Their wish was granted and, ever since, each olive tree has grown up with two main stems, single yet divided.

I looked at the trees around me, two trunks intertwined at their roots, branching out into mingled, leafy boughs at their summits; buried symbolically beneath them so many Romeos and Juliets, so many Dominics and Helens. I put my hand on one of the rough old trees and stroked it, smiling at my thoughts; then realised that Myers Cannan was looking at me appraisingly from behind those dark glasses he wore. I shivered again. I looked at the dark, crumbling softness of the earth beneath the trees and remembered Rosa's story.

"She will not be the first pretty girl to run away, to disappear. No one will come to question us. We have been careful." Sophie's words.

Was I walking on the planned site for Rosa's grave?

For a moment I was shattered by that thought. Then I realised that Myers Cannan was speaking.

"I've brought you down here to show you the outlook. It's real good from beyond the trees."

From this flat piece of bare ground the view stretched clear to the shore. We were far nearer the sea and could watch the white frilled waves curling up on to a rocky beach. I could see the bright awnings over café tables. But it was a view of no particular pretensions, no more lovely than most of the views to be seen in Sorrento.

I gave it dutiful appreciation, however, then turned to go back through the trees to the house, glad to leave behind that silent, dark place of shadows, Myers followed me, light-footed, catlike.

In the sitting-room I went across to the chair where I had left my things. As I reached it Sophie came in at the door wearing sun glasses and a large, shady hat. She exclaimed in surprise at seeing me.

"I've just come in and have been unloading my goods in the kitchen," she said. "Our twice-weekly woman usually does the marketing, but I had a few things I wanted to get for myself. I sure miss those little notes Rosa would write in Italian. Now, have you heard from that girl of ours? We've had no mail yet."

I told her no and said that perhaps I'd find another letter waiting for me when I got back to England. She was taking off her hat and pushing up her sleeked-down hair before the mirror and I saw her mouth twitch curiously.

"When d'you go?" she asked.

"I'm not sure," I said, for some obscure reason not wishing to commit myself. "I should leave on Friday but I've met a friend with a car and we may leave here earlier but get home later. We can drive back, linger in Switzerland and France and cross the Channel by ferry."

I rather amazed myself by this sudden flight of fancy. I felt compulsion to leave them both uncertain as to my exact movements.

"Are you going to see Rosa's uncle again?" Sophie asked.

Again I prevaricated.

"He isn't really well enough for visitors. I asked in the shop below his apartment this morning. Meeting this friend has changed my plans. We'd rather like to go down the coast towards Calabria, too." I tried to sound careless, involved in my own plans. I shrugged. "After all, I did give Signore Rossini all the news I had."

Sophie glanced across at Myers.

"Well, I hope you have a swell time with your—boyfriend—is it?"

I smiled an assent and, picking up my shopping, showed her the two dolls I had bought for Jean and Sheila. I said goodbye and added, "Give my love to Rosa when you do see her and tell her to write again soon."

I went off feeling rather elated by my efforts. Deception improves with practice.

At lunchtime a nice English family, father, mother and a boy of fifteen or so, invited me to join them in hiring a car next day for a trip to Salerno and Amalfi. I agreed gladly. There was most of tomorrow disposed of!

Then, after dinner, came a telephone call from Rome, no Swiss Alps and no Matterhorn to interrupt this time, just Dominic's voice, close to my ear.

114

"Sweetheart, if I'm not back before seven, it means an important meeting will have been postponed till afternoon and I shall have to be late, after midnight perhaps. So go to bed and sleep and when you wake on Wednesday morning I shall be there. I shall call you from the balcony."

"Call me from the balcony when you come back, however late," I told him.

"Whatever happens I shall come straight down the autostrade from Rome like—"

"Like the careful, competent driver you are, darling!" I finished for him. "Come safely, please."

He sounded so close as we whispered goodbye. I went to sleep still hearing the sound of his voice.

CHAPTER THIRTEEN

"I seemed to move among a world of ghosts
And feel myself the shadow of a dream."
—TENNYSON.

I WOKE up in a state of complete happiness, convinced that Dominic would leave Rome early, that we should be together for dinner tonight.

Meanwhile there was that pleasant expedition down the coast. I made contact with my friendly English trio and ran upstairs after breakfast to collect what I needed for the trip. The sun shone gloriously and there was a heat haze over the bay. Even the lemons on the trees across the road seemed to glow more gold than on the day of my arrival.

I decided to take my big, useful shoulder bag and began to turn out the debris it had collected : the bills for some of the goods I had bought yesterday, an unused picture postcard, Mother's letter with Rosa's enclosure and an old envelope addressed to Dominic. Ah, yes! His wedding-cake sketch of Rosa's tiara. He had added a small round face with corkscrew curls and it looked more like what it was supposed to be. I smiled and put it with my letter into my writing case. Then I had a sudden moment of recollection and uneasiness.

Yesterday I had left my bag with these things in it at the Villa Vittorio while I walked down through the olive trees with Myers. That had been careless of me!

Suppose Sophie had been elsewhere in the house when I arrived. But no, my things on the chair were undisturbed. Sophie's start of surprise when she saw me had seemed real enough and she still wore that shady hat in which she had been shopping. If she had opened my bag, what would she have discovered? That Rosa was in England at my own home, that my "boy-friend" was also a friend of my family and of Rosa too, and that we were both expecting to see Vincentio Rossini and receive from him something to take back to Rosa.

Ah, well! This was all highly unlikely and I put away thoughts panic gave rise to. I picked up my key, then remembered the second one Giorgio had given me and which I had not returned yet. I had an idea that I had dropped it into this bag of mine. I burrowed through the contents again, investigated each small compartment, but with no results. I must look through the drawer of the dressing table where I had probably put it along with the scarves, belts and other odds and ends. Or maybe I'd left it on the table itself and the chambermaid, thinking I had locked myself out, had taken it down to reception for my return. I'd sort it out later, for I had no time now. I picked up my things, hurried to the lift and joined my waiting friends in the hall.

It was after half-past six that evening when we got back to the Risorgimento. We had all four enjoyed every minute of the day; every minute as the day went by brought me closer to Dominic.

I parted from my companions and, as I collected my key, asked if Mr Lee were back yet. I had glanced up at the balcony high above as we came in, almost expecting to see him there; then had imagined him waiting in the hall.

Now Giorgio told me, "No, Signorina, he is not back, but this morning an American lady telephoned to ask if you were in. I told her no, you had gone out by car for the day and would possibly be back very late tonight." Giorgio gave me a conspiratorial grin. "You see, Signorina, I thought that if the Signore came back early you would want no other."

I smiled at him and wished him an enjoyable evening himself. Giorgio was about to go off duty and his private life was just beginning. He must know all about 'wanting no other'.

I went slowly up to my room and wondered why Sophie Cannan had telephoned. Was she checking up on me? I remembered the bag left in her sitting-room again, and felt a return of uneasiness.

I walked through to my balcony. Dominic had said he would be back before seven if things went well. I stood there looking out at the dusk softly closing in. That harsh, deep bell sounded again from the little domed church. It was queer how everything seemed to echo the sights and sounds of my first evening, a strange, unreal, dreamy repetition. I felt that I too was part of a dream. I stood there for some time as the air grew cooler, sweet and scented.

Then, quickly, I showered, pulled on a jersey outfit, slacks of a soft, misty amethyst colour with a low-cut sleeveless blouse interwoven with silver thread, decorative enough. I knew by now that Dominic would be late. I was restless, and if I wanted to speed away the time to his return by going up to the square for a liqueur and coffee, I could put on the cardigan which built this affair up into a three-piece and be warm enough.

My English family were almost nodding over their dinner. The sun and the air and sight-seeing had overwhelmed them and they said goodnight and went off to bed while I was still finishing my meal.

I was wider awake than I had been all day, half-frustrated, half-excited, yet still with that strange feeling of being in a dream, a dream in which I waited for something to happen, something dramatic and of immense importance. I never want to experience that feeling again. At the time I was conscious of no fear at all, merely an alert anticipation.

I said no to coffee and ran upstairs to slip on my cardigan. I re-opened the long window to the balcony to let in the coolness of the outside air. My bed had been turned down, my nightdress elegantly laid out. The Risorgimento chambermaids were as well trained as Sheila and Jean, and I made a note that these little niceties were well worth while for the feeling of luxury they gave the recipient, the nearest that any ordinary woman would ever get to the cossetting of a personal maid. Our pair got a great deal of fun out of it themselves.

"You should just see Bluebell's! All lace and ever so see-through! Think they're on their honeymoon?"

"Not like Buttercup's, then. Them 'Cuddly 'Jamas' she's got. Been married too long to expect any other sort of cuddle, I guess."

Oh, dear!

I looked out at the gold-spangled dark of sea and sky. I must just aim at making the four hours or so until midnight go quickly. I slipped my key into the pocket of my slacks and added a couple of hundred lire notes, plenty for my needs. I could have joined a party for a night club, watched the Tarantella, but that would mean too many drinks, too much sitting around in a stuffy atmosphere, I decided.

I ran downstairs, saw a stranger in Giorgio's place in reception and went up the five hundred yards or so of curving pavement to the square. I sat on the café terrace at a corner table and ordered black coffee and a small brandy. I had the feeling that in my dark, closely fitting clothes, I was half invisible. People walked the pavements before the brightly lit shops, talking, gesticulating, vivid as tropical birds in an aviary.

The striped blue and white umbrella over my head swayed in the breeze. In a corner of the square a couple of the horses, their drivers hanging on in hopes of a last-minute fare, tossed their heads and stamped their feet, impatient for home.

I looked across to the far corner where a maze of streets led through to the Square S. Vincentio and suddenly, I made up my mind.

I would go and knock on Teresa Pascati's door, arrange to go with Dominic next morning to visit Rosa's uncle. I would ask her to warn him of our coming so that he might be prepared, be able to give us any message, those letters he wanted us to take to Rosa. In the shop they had said he was better. If I made my request firmly enough, Signora Pascati could hardly refuse me.

I paid my bill and wove my way between the dwindling groups on the pavement. I walked quickly, still with that strange sense of invisibility.

The gift shop was as busy as it had been on that

evening of my first visit, but the courtyard behind was dark and patterned with black shadows. The bushes at the foot of the outside staircase rustled as the breeze stirred them. I swerved away like a shying horse, in aversion to the touch of their dusty fingers. I could see no light through Teresa's windows under the stairway. The drawn curtains stirred slightly and were still.

The sound of the iron knocker, shaped into an ornate ring, echoed back from the grey walls surrounding me. I knocked again and again, but there came no answer to my knocking.

CHAPTER FOURTEEN

"Murder most foul, as in the best it is,
But this most foul, strange and unnatural."
—SHAKESPEARE.

I STOOD still in the silence that followed as I let my hand fall. Sounds from the street echoed dimly back through the high walls of the narrow passage. I was puzzled. Vincentio Rossini was never left so that the sound of his bell could not be heard.

I stepped out from the shadow of the staircase and looked upwards. My eyes were accustomed to the dark by now. I could see that the door to the balcony stood open, and yes, through it a dull light shone. I did not think of what I was doing, I braved the thought of Signora Pascati's forbidding presence, went to the staircase foot and lightly, quickly, mounted the stairs. I stood in the open door and looked at that wide, shadowy room again.

The pale, watery green floor, with its rugs like floating water lilies, was the same, the shining dark furniture seemed to stare back at me. But everything was in mad, chaotic disorder. Cupboard doors stood wide open, drawers were in disarray, their contents turned out on to the floor.

I took three steps into the room, towards the crimson-covered bed with its heavily carved tester and then I saw what still seems unreal to me, still like part of some horrible nightmare.

Vincentio Rossini lay back on his pillow, his chin pointing upwards, his mouth stretched wide and his lips drawn back in a fixed, macabre smile. The light from the red-shaded lamp painted his face in a grim semblance of life. But he was dead. I had never seen death before, but this was death I knew.

And I saw that it was not only Vincentio Rossini who lay there. Those thin, strong hands of his were still round the throat of the man who had died with him. The body of Myers Cannan lay across that of his killer.

His head rested in a travesty of affection against Rossini's shoulder. His face, turned towards me, was darkly livid, swollen and distorted. The crimson silk of the coverlet was twisted in tangled, imprisoning folds round the lower part of his body.

I stood for an endless moment on a floor that swayed beneath me, my hand across my mouth stifling any sound. Then, dazed, my head swimming, I turned to escape, nearly tripped over a small packet tied with red thread lying by the foot of the bed, near the open drawer of the large chest.

Unseeing, I picked it up, stumbled on to the balcony, down the stairs and out from the black shadows of the courtyard, running blindly back to the colour and bustle of the pavements again. Unseeing, still with my imagined cloak of invisibility round me, I sped through the network of streets. All I could think of was the refuge of my room, the haven of Dominic's arms.

The entrance hall of the hotel was full of people coming and going. I passed through unnoticed, ran up the three deserted flights of stairs, fumbled for my key and at last, at last, closed my door behind me. I went through to the balcony, stood leaning up against the window, drawing in deep breaths of cool air, scented with the fragrance of the lemon trees opposite.

How long I stood there I do not know, but at last my senses began to return and I could see and hear and think again. I looked down on the ground below, on the trees and bushes and tubs of flowers and on the short drive up which, in a few hours' time, Dominic would drive that blessed little car of his. I could hold off the terrors of memory until then.

A few residents were still drifting in and out. The lovely evening was too good to waste indoors. As I looked down, a short, squat figure, crowned by a large brimmed hat, suddenly stood out from the rest. As she put her foot on the first step of the wide flight to the entrance door, she glanced upwards, her face grotesquely foreshortened, her eyes hidden by dark glasses. It was Sophie Cannan.

I felt the blood drain from my face, my heart thud mercilessly. But I could refuse to see her if they rang me from reception. If she slid by unannounced and tapped on my door, I would not let her in. She could not know my room number anyway. She had no key. She had no key! The words shouted themselves at me. That second key—the one I had not found in my bag, the bag I had left unguarded in the room at the Villa Vittorrio. My mind stumbled, stopped and, as I struggled to regain control, I heard the sound of a key in the outer door.

Panic, wild, unreasoning panic, gripped me. I would not, could not face her. The evil I had seen that night, met with for the first time in my life, had made me a shivering coward. I could not face it again.

I still held the packet of letters. I pushed it down the front of my blouse. Then, hands gripping the rail of my balcony, I swung myself over, toes, in soft sandals, feeling for foothold between the rails.

For a moment I tried to squirm my way along without that downward fumble for the buttress supports, but the barrier between the balconies thrust too low, too far forward. So, groping for those narrow, unseen footholds, first the left foot, then the right, I found them. My hand barely reached the railing and I was standing on tiptoe, for I was a good seven inches shorter than Dominic. Thank God I was not Rosa's height!

My fingers tight on the railings, I began to edge along towards Dominic's balcony. Suddenly I was conscious of the inner door to my bedroom opening, of a dim light from the small entrance hall where the bathroom was. So she had fumbled her way in the dark, had found one light switch.

Oh, my God! If she saw my white hands moving on the rail! I thought of a knife slashed across my knuckles; of any weapon, my hairbrush even, snatched up and beaten down upon my hands; the fall to the ground below.

I had learned that climb from Dominic in easy stages. Now I moved in panic, soundlessly swift, and I was level with his windows. How I managed the last movements I do not know; that long reach up to the bottom of his balcony, first my left, then my right foot. Somehow I did it. I balanced precariously, was conscious of a couple of heedless people chattering far below, then I swung one leg over and suddenly stood on firm ground again, in safety.

For a moment I cowered in one corner, I heard

footsteps in my room, saw another light spring up. A faint breeze shook the window near me and I realised that the glass door was unbolted. Silently I put my fingers to the crack and pulled the door open. I stepped in, closed it behind me and, shaking uncontrollably, shot the bolt along. I pulled the cord which closed the long brocade curtains.

Then, at last, I knew that I was safe. In a moment I was across the room, lying on Dominic's bed, shaking from head to foot in a paroxysm of terror and relief.

Slowly, slowly, I pulled myself together, sat up and listened. There was no sound from the next room, but in any case the closed windows would shut out all noises.

Dominic's pyjamas, smooth and silky, were lying across his bed. I gathered them up in my arms, held them close to me. Then, my cheek against their softness, I put my head down on his pillow and drifted into the sleep of nervous exhaustion, restless, uneasy and full of nightmarish dreams.

CHAPTER FIFTEEN

"Safe shall be my going . . . Safe where men fall."
—RUPERT BROOKE.

FROM a queer, indeterminate half-world between sleep and waking, I struggled to escape. I was balanced precariously on a precipice edge; I was invisible, yet fierce lights flushed me out from the sheltering dark; my lips were sealed and speechless yet discordant sound deafened me.

I heard a key grate in a lock, a door opening, and I sat up, my eyes wide with terror as a bright light blinded me.

Then I was wide awake again. Dominic stood looking at me. I was kneeling up on his bed with its tumbled pillows and tossed sheets; and then his arms held me to the blessed warmth of his heart beating under my cheek.

"Darling, what is it? What is it?" he said, over and over again, and I began to speak, my voice muffled against him while I poured out the whole story.

"He was dead, Dominic, quite dead, and Myers Cannan lay across the bed, dead too. Vincentio's hands were round his throat. I ran back through the streets. Then, from my balcony, I saw Sophie Cannan come into the hotel. She must have stolen my second key, the one Giorgio gave me. I took that book back yesterday and I left my bag in the room while I followed Myers to the olive grove. She was out then, but she came back, and Rosa's letter was there too, and your drawing of the tiara."

My words tumbled one over another in a wild torrent.

"Hush, sweetheart! It's all over now and I'm here. How did you get into my room?"

"I heard her come in. I was on the balcony and I climbed—" I began to laugh with silly, hysterical giggles— "in easy stages."

Dominic, his fingers stroking my hair, pulled my head back and looked down at me.

"Oh, my God!" he said, and what I saw in his face made me myself again.

"Darling, darling, it's all right now. I"m not afraid any more. It's over." I pulled his face down to mine and kissed him.

He gave a deep sigh and held me closely. Then in his normal voice, half-laughing, he said, "Why are you clutching my pyjamas like that? Put them down and be content with what goes inside them."

I smiled weakly and obeyed.

"And what makes you go snap, crackle, pop like a breakfast cereal? What's this sort of breastplate you're wearing?"

"This "breastplate" was that packet of letters I had brought from the Square S. Vincentio hardly knowing what I did; that I had pushed down the front of my blouse when I escaped to Dominic's room. Thank heaven for that more or less automatic action. I had left nothing behind me to tell Sophie more than she already knew.

I retrieved the package as I explained to Dominic. We sat on his bed and looked down at the neatly tied parcel, its cover one large envelope with the name "Rosa" written blackly across it in a bold, large hand, deeply underlined.

"I wonder what secrets this will reveal," I said, and we put it away in the briefcase Dominic had brought back with him, locked it safely away.

Briefly he told me that things had gone well in Rome. He and Joe Hendrick were kindred spirits.

"He says he'll give Rosa a test as soon as she can get over. If she's as good as I say, and I'm sure she will be, we'll blow up the part to a size I'd like anyway, so that she'll get a real first chance.

"And, Helen, I've said I'll come over for three days or so in two months' time. Darling, can you make it? Wedding in early July and three weeks' wandering wherever we want to go. We'll bring the car and those days in Rome will be fun, I promise you. Will you?"

I would; oh, I would!

"Peter has contacts," I told him. "Someone experienced can take over my Highwayman job by then."

"And Chimneys will be waiting for us," he promised.

Somehow he had got me away from nightmarish horrors and I was the first to come back with sanity to the present. I stood up and re-made the bed I had disordered.

Dominic opened his balcony door and went out.

"There's still a light, but the curtains are drawn," he told me. "Wait here while I go to see if your door is locked."

I stood and watched as he walked towards his own

door. Then, suddenly afraid to be alone again and unwilling to watch him go, I followed him, stood by his side as he tried my door.

It was not locked. It gave as he pushed and we went in together. The only light was the bedside one and the room was empty. Sophie was gone. But the disorder she had left was like that I had seen in the room above the courtyard. I shivered again.

Every drawer was open, the contents on the floor. Even my dresses were torn from their hangers, my shoes thrown round in confusion. This was how she had left Rosa's room for Lisa to find.

Silently I began to pick up, fold and restore everything to its place. Dominic helped me, hanging clothes up once more, collecting shoes and slippers. Nothing was missing. Two keys, my original and the stolen one, were thrown together on the dressing-table top. The contents of my bag were tipped out on the bedside table. The letters from home, Mother's and Rosa's enclosure, were torn into minute fragments and scattered over the table top.

As I dropped the pieces into the waste-paper basket, I saw the nightdress which, earlier in the evening, I had noticed laid out so neatly.

It was ripped again and again from neck to hem, the pretty fragile silk torn into a dozen frayed and ragged strips.

Dominic saw it at the same time and his lips tightened and his eyes had a new hardness. But he picked up the fragments and folded them.

"I'm taking these as a memento," he said, and put the small bundle into his pocket. I opened a drawer and took out another nightdress.

"I'm glad she hadn't time to do all the damage she evidently wanted to do," I said.

Dominic stood looking at me. There were lines on his face I had never seen before, lines of anger and exhaustion.

"You've got a smudge on your nose, my sweet," he told me and kissed it.

I looked at my hands, grimy from the dust on the balcony railings; at my trousers, ripped, I couldn't remember how, across one knee; at my cardigan, snagged and pulled in several places.

"I hope you've got more pyjamas than those crumpled up ones I slept with," I told him. "I need a bath and you need bed."

"We both need both. Since we can't take them together, I'll beat you to the balcony to say goodnight, my darling."

He gave me the old wicked grin and was gone.

When I came through from the bathroom, clean and fresh again, my mind almost free of shadows, he waited for me.

The chill of dawn was creeping up from the sea. It was four o'clock. I shivered, but welcomed the cold, clear air, like an iced drink when you are thirsty.

So we said our goodnight and, in a matter of moments, I was in a deep, untroubled sleep, while Dominic dreamed peacefully next door.

CHAPTER SIXTEEN

"Port after stormy seas"—SPENCER.

FROM the time when Dominic's soft whistle from his
balcony woke me, until nearly midday, we did not even
mention those events of that past night. We swam, we
relaxed, we talked in the shade of the orange trees, and
gradually everything slipped into place again.

We made plans for our future, we talked of our past,
family things, personal things.

"Why did you change so that morning after Stratford?" Dominic asked. "Because you did, you know.
That first night I felt we understood every single thing
about each other, that words weren't necessary. Why
did you go so far away, try to hold me off at arm's
length?"

"I can hardly understand why myself now," I told
him. "It was all mixed up with Rosa's coming, somehow. Everything was so dramatic. The whole background seemed to change, like the atmosphere of a play
when the principal actor comes on stage. She is so lovely
and so lovable, and, Dominic, you really did look at her
as though you thought so too!"

He sat up and looked down at me. Then he threw
back his head and laughed and gave my hair a little
tug.

"When I don't look at a pretty girl like that, oh,

my prettiest of all girls, I shan't be of much use to you!"

"Oh, Dominic!" And then I told him of my year in London, of that muddled sort of existence with which I had made brief contact, of my built-up, so-called defence mechanism.

"And you thought you'd need it against me? That I'd try to seduce you? Get you to take me on as the first instalment of your love life?"

"No, oh, no! I couldn't really think that. I knew you weren't like Robin and his crowd. But I do lack self-confidence, Dominic. My head mistress once told me so."

"And she must be right?"

He was laughing at me, but I could laugh too.

He picked up my hand and wove his fingers through mine.

"Listen, sweetheart, you and I, we're right out of this permissive world. I like the idea of a good old-fashioned marriage—bridesmaids and Handel and happy tears in the vicar's vestry and all. I really want you to make an honest man of me."

He looked at me with an expression in his eyes that I knew no other girl, however pretty, would ever see in them.

"D'you know your hair is almost silver in the sunshine?" But all I knew was that I could never get lost from him again and suddenly matters of immediate urgency became important once more.

"Dominic, I'm worried. I ran away last night. Ought I to have got help, contacted the police somehow?"

"No." He spoke with decision. "How could you? You'd have done no good. You knew it would all be discovered sooner or later, and what did it matter if it were later? There is still no need for you, or Rosa, for that matter, to be involved. It was fortunate you rescued those letters though."

"It was just a reflex action on my part. Providence threw them there and I nearly tripped over them. I can hardly wait to find out what they say. Dominic, I do so wish you could have met Vincentio Rossini. He must have been a wonderful person. It seems terrible that he should have killed Myers Cannan that way and have died himself doing so. Was that really possible?"

"There seems no other explanation." Dominic spoke slowly.

"His hands were very strong," and I shuddered.

"I wonder why there was no answer when you knocked on Teresa Pascati's door."

"When I ran upstairs I thought she would be up there, that she'd be angry with me. It all seems so strange. Couldn't we go to the Square S. Vincentio again? Try to find out more?"

"I think we must, but tomorrow rather than today. Give things a chance to get sorted out. Today I'd like to go to the Villa Vittorio, come face to face with Sophie if she's there. Could you do that?"

"With you, yes. But I don't think we shall find her there."

"Maybe not. She must be pretty desperate by now."

"She's quite alone," I said. For one moment she was the trapped animal, the one for whom I felt pity.

Dominic saw it in my face, jumped up and pulled me to my feet.

"My darling, she'd have felt no pity for you or Rosa."

"Perhaps she loved him though," I said, with my new understanding.

"Perhaps," and for a moment there was pity in Dominic's face too.

However, neither pity nor anger were needed for Sophie that day, for we found the Villa Vittorio deserted.

Late in the afternoon we went to it via the main square and the network of streets, the path I had once taken before.

The gift shop in the Square S. Vincentio was crowded and we did not go in. The glimpse of the courtyard through that narrow passage was serene and peaceful with no sign of life. A soft golden mist of sunlight gave warmth to the flat shadows of those grey walls. We walked quickly past, did not linger.

The villa, when we reached it, was empty and forsaken, shabby and neglected as always. The front door stood closed and there was no answer to our knock. We took the path Rosa had taken to the side of the terrace and walked round to its front. The windows were shut, the room inside deserted.

Dominic took a slim penknife from his pocket. He did some rather intricate manoeuvring with it and suddenly the lock gave and the door opened when he turned the handle.

"Only possible with a simple lock," he explained. "I wouldn't let my hero, Iain Macdonald, do it until I'd learned how it could be done myself—with this knife." And he laughed when I said, "Perfectionist!"

"Frustrated burglar, I guess! I'm going in. Are you coming, Helen?"

I shook my head, stood waiting, looking over the olive

trees to the deep blue of the sea. He was gone for a very short time; the villa was small enough.

When he came back he shrugged and carefully closed the door, making it secure again.

"There's nothing left. They must have brought very little with them. There are some old grey slacks, a pair of what the Americans call sneakers and a summer-weight jacket, a grey one, hanging in a small wardrobe. All that's left of Myers Cannan. Sophie has probably taken the first flight back to America."

"You really think we shall hear no more of her?"

My voice was uncertain and Dominic looked at me thoughtfully.

"I wish I could believe that," I told him.

I turned and looked through the window once more. I could see the bookcase in the corner, even discern the red bound copy of *Jewels Lost and Found* where Myers had carelessly pushed it into an empty space.

Suddenly I remembered that livid, distorted face, the red light of the small lamp, the disorder of the room, and this place, where I had followed Myers Cannan down to the olive grove, seemed haunted, a place of ghosts.

Dominic sensed the urgency with which I turned away, put his arm round my waist and, in that closeness, we went back up the narrow path to the main road.

That evening we spent with Lisa. I rang her at her place of work and suggested that we take her out to dinner.

She agreed happily. "Let's go to Rosa's favourite place, Toni Fenelli's trattoria, down near the sea," she suggested. "She had meant to take Helen there."

So that is where we went, to a decor of gay scarlet and white awnings and napery, brightly vivid Italian crockery and perfectly cooked, delicious Italian food.

It was too short a drive there for much talk. Not until we were settled over our aperitifs did Lisa drop her bombshell.

"Did you know that Rosa's uncle has died? No, you would not. It happened only last night. A girl who works in our office during the afternoon lives in the Square S. Vincentio. Her mother has sometimes relieved Signora Pascati when she must go out."

I looked across the table at Dominic. He held my glance with one of caution. Lisa continued.

"Signore Rossini must have died quietly in his sleep. The Signora went up about seven o'clock this morning as usual, and found him there. Rosa will be glad to hear how peaceful the end was. Signora Pascati said he had a smile on his face and all signs of pain and illness were gone."

There was a silence. Then, "That will make the news easier for Rosa," Dominic said firmly, and I murmured agreement.

"It is a pity we cannot let Rosa know," said Lisa, giving me a thoughtful look. "But perhaps it is not good for women to go to funerals in any case. Signore Rossini had many friends, comrades of his own age. They are of the war, of the time of the liberation."

"We'll drink to all those who survived," said Dominic. We raised our glasses and the moment passed.

It was a pleasant evening. Rosa's trattoria was all she had promised and the only thing missing was Rosa herself.

We dropped Lisa at her apartment, then covered the

short distance to our hotel without speaking. But our thoughts were following the same pattern. Dominic pulled up in the drive and turned to look at me.

"What do you make of it?" I asked him.

He shook his head.

"I know nothing about the methods of the Italian police, of course, but I hardly think they would hold back the news of murder for any reason. The answer must lie elsewhere. Darling, we meant to see Teresa Pascati anyway. Shall we go in the morning?"

"Yes. We can tell her we've heard of Vincentio's death from Lisa, would like to know more details so that when we are in touch with Rosa again we can tell her everything. Dominic, I'd like to telephone The Highwayman tonight."

"We'll do our best. We might be luckier than The Highwayman was in telephoning you!" Dominic had heard an account of that disastrous call from Mother.

And this time we were lucky. A thunder storm or so to contend with perhaps, but far better results than those of last Thursday which had left me in such a state of loneliness and frustration.

Now Dominic's shoulder was close, his arm round my waist.

Peter took the news, promised that he and Mother would pass it on gently to Rosa.

"At the moment she's in the bar, spinning out half-a-pint and surrounded by an eager crowd of the Y.F.U." Then to me, "You're a dark horse, aren't you!" But I gathered that Peter was delighted that I had gone out to meet someone at last, and that that someone was Dominic.

Mother's voice seemed very close.

"Darling, you know I love you both," she said. "Peter and I won't be there to welcome you the minute you arrive back on Friday. We'll be bringing Joan back —travelling in easy stages. We'll give her a good rest in the morning and start back in the afternoon. But we'll be home in time for all of us to have a celebration dinner. Can you hear William snoring?"

I listened and I could, faint and far away but distinct. I could see him stretched out on his rug near the desk, his head on the blue velvet cushion to which he had taken a fancy and which, in the end, tired of his sneaking off with it, I had given him.

I put down the phone and smiled at Dominic.

"Well, even William's snoring by-passed the old Matterhorn that time," I said triumphantly.

CHAPTER SEVENTEEN

"I tell you, hopeless grief is passionless."—E. B. BROWNING.

WE WERE not late the next morning. It was to be our last day in Sorrento and our plan to go to the Square S. Vincentio was a barrier to be surmounted. After that the rest of the day would be ours.

As we crossed the hall Giorgio waved a large white envelope at me from reception and Dominic went to collect it.

"It is a lady has brought," Giorgio called and, for a moment, my heart leapt into uneven beats. Then Dominic put it into my hand and I saw it was not addressed in the ugly black script of that other letter, but in the old-fashioned, careful calligraphy still taught in some Italian schools, the sort I had learned myself in Florence and which I had shaken off at my more tolerant English school where I had reverted to that upright, rounded style natural to me.

We settled at our table to coffee, hot rolls and cherry jam, and I opened the letter. It was in Italian.

Dear Miss Del Mar,
You are soon leaving Sorrento. I think you should see me before you go. I shall be in my own home each day this week.

Teresa Pascati.

I handed it over to Dominic.

"Well, the invitation makes things easier," he said. "I imagine she wants you to pass on to Rosa the news of Rossini's peaceful death."

I sighed. How complicated life was! When was truth desirable? Dominic's face reflected my uncertainty.

"Helen, you'll just have to wait and see; play it off the cuff, and it won't be easy. You do want me to come with you?"

"Oh, Dominic, yes! Signora Pascati will just have to accept you. Let's go early, before we do anything else. Then the rest of the day will be ours."

"Every minute of every day is ours now."

He smiled at me and no other truth mattered.

In the courtyard behind the Square S. Vincentio the long door to the balcony was closed, the red curtains drawn. I thought of the cold silence behind that door and shivered.

"Vincentio Rossini died peacefully in his sleep, a smile on his lips, all signs of pain and stress gone."

Could one ever get used to the sight of death—its stillness, its emptiness?

The curtains were drawn over the downstairs windows too. Across the courtyard, under the shade of its deserted upper storey, a certain amount of market trade was going on. A small van had been backed in through the narrow passage, crates of oranges and apples loaded up, and we watched it driven precariously out through the alley into the colour and warmth of the square again. A small, swarthy man with a handcart had taken on a load of vegetables, the dull earthiness of potatoes, the

141

silver-misted purple of cabbages decorated by the scarlet
and green of peppers.

Voluble talk was going on between buyer and seller,
but it was muted, lacking the usual ribald coarseness of
such exchange. Market talk, whether in Sorrento or
Billingsgate, is not all that different. But here was
restraint imposed by a deep peasant respect for the dead
man lying nearby. The couple of traders would be as
glad to leave their bartering and the little courtyard this
morning as I should be to take my own departure.

I looked at Dominic and saw that he waited my signal
to knock. I nodded and he dropped the heavy iron ring.
Even its echo, so ominous and loud that other evening,
seemed muffled now.

The door was opened at once.

Teresa Pascati, erect, wearing a dark dress with a
small white collar, stood looking down at me. She was
almost as tall as Dominic. Now she stared at him with
ill-concealed distrust and I intervened.

"Signora, Mr Lee is my companion for the rest of
my stay here. He is also my affianced husband. Anything that concerns me concerns him. If he were not
here I should tell him everything later."

Without answering, she stood back and ushered us
in, into a small square hall. She looked at Dominic
again, gave him a grudging acceptance.

The room leading from the entrance was a central
one, red tiled with a dark patterned carpet and heavy,
threatening furniture. The shadow from the outside
staircase shut out nearly all sunlight and made it gloomy
and dark. From each side wall a door opened, one leading to a kitchen, for she closed that door as we entered,
the other, presumably, to a bedroom. A filled-in door

in the long wall facing the entrance had once obviously communicated with the gift shop.

Perhaps it was because of its gloom, perhaps because there was only one real exit from the place, perhaps because of my knowledge of what lay in the room above, that I felt claustrophobic heaviness weigh down on me.

Signora Pascati took another glass from a cupboard to add to the couple already on a table in the room's centre. She gestured towards two red upholstered chairs which stood near, and, after she had filled the three glasses from a bottle of the rough local wine which stood near them, she herself sat in a hard, upright chair with her back to the curtained window.

We raised our glasses and took token sips. Teresa Pascati drank off the contents of her own and refilled it.

Dominic crossed long legs negligently and I admired his ability to look completely at ease in any situation. I gripped my own hands together. My palms were damp, not very steady. I was too close to that remembered horror of just one night ago. Dominic moved his chair a little nearer, put his hand on the arm of my chair. I looked down at the strong brown fingers, then into those steady grey-green eyes, and felt safe again. I sighed and relaxed.

I saw Teresa's mouth twitch in an expression I could not interpret. She lifted her glass and drank again. Then she began to talk in Italian, but clearly and concisely. Afterwards, I found, Dominic had understood most of what she said.

"Signorina, I saw you when you came here on Tuesday night, when you knocked at my door and then went up to Vincentio's room. I saw you go, carrying the letters, and I did not grudge them to your care, for

'Centio said they were for Rosa and I know you will take them to her. I knew by your face that you had seen what had shocked, had stupefied you. I knew that you would run to safety; that later, when your English common sense returned, it would tell you not to get involved, would send you home to England without speaking of what you had seen. I was right. That is still what you mean to do."

There was a kind of bitterness in her voice. As she looked across at me I noticed the dark circles in which her eyes were sunk. Those dark eyes were dull and expressionless now, had none of the fiery devotion with which she had looked at Rossini on the night I met him.

"Yes, you are right," I acknowledged. "I did not see how my running away could stop justice taking its course."

"And you find that you have prevented it? That justice has not been done?"

"I don't know. I only know the news that Rosa's friend has given to us." My voice was uncertain and Dominic's hand moved to take mine. I spoke again, firmly and more sure of myself. "I think that true justice may have been done after all. Can you tell me?"

"I know you have seen Lisa Pieri, that she will have told you what she learned from Maria, who works with her. You met Maria's mother when you first came here. Well, I will tell you the whole story. That I owe to Vincentio. He loved Rosa and he would want you to know and to tell her all.

"But first, after you had gone that night he died, I saw that other one come out from the shadow of the bushes where she had watched for him, her husband. I had not seen her for many years, but him I had seen

144

when he waited for Rosa after her visits. I did not speak of him to Vincentio. There was no need to trouble his heart with more."

She turned and stared through a gap in the curtains where a pale gleam of sunlight filtered in, wishing to turn her face away rather than to see the dusty bushes and the skeleton stairway. Then she began to speak again.

"She looked after you but did not follow. You were running swiftly. She went up to that room. I waited, let her come down again and depart, her face shadowed by that large hat she wore. She carried nothing and I knew she could have found nothing. And by that time I was strong again, strong enough to do what had to be done."

"Then when I first knocked you already knew what had happened? You were hiding here?"

I looked round the room in which we sat. So, still and dark though it had been that night, it had not been empty. The echo of that iron knocker had been heard by two listeners, by Teresa Pascati hidden here and by Sophie Cannan lurking in those dusty branches by the stairway. I remembered how I had flinched away from their touch and shivered again.

Teresa's mouth twisted in the ghost of a smile.

"Yes, I was here. I will tell you how it came about."

She stood up and poured more wine into her glass, offered a replenishment of ours and accepted refusal.

"That night 'Centio was stronger than he had been for some time. I should have been happy, for the promise of even a few weeks, a few days, should have meant much to me. But that night I was fearful and uneasy.

145

"I heard no sign, had no warning of that man's approach. I was in the kitchen there when the sound of Vincentio's bell came to me rung once, sharply, with urgency, but once only. It is down here where I can— could always hear it." She nodded towards one of the corners.

"The bell push, on a cord, was under his pillow. One of his friends fixed it for him. So now I ran upstairs, almost I flew. And then I saw what had happened, what was still happening.

"Michaele Battista, for that had once been his name, had already opened drawers and cupboards, looking for what he did not find. All was in confusion. Vincentio had awakened, had seen him and had recognised him. Did you, Signorina, see the knife on the floor beside the bed, where it had fallen from his right hand?"

I shook my head. "No, I saw no knife," I told her. I could see every detail of that scene, but no, not the knife. I had stood motionless in that one place until I turned to fly.

"No, nor did she, for she did not take it with her. I may keep it as a remembrance." Teresa laughed shortly. "When I entered the room was in the disorder that you saw; Battista was at the bed, the knife in his hand. 'Centio had raised himself from the pillows. His hands, in self-defence, had seized that other by the throat, had dragged him across his own body. They were still strong hands, but their hold was weakening. I came in time. I twisted the coverlet round Battista's legs, like a rope tightly binding them. He tried to free himself in vain."

"Yes, I remember that. I thought his struggles must have entangled him that way."

She smiled again. "His struggles helped," she said. "Then I put my own hands over Vincentio's. They are the hands of a woman who has always worked, strong hands."

She held them out, thick and powerful, and flexed her fingers.

"And I pressed, pressed hard, my hands working still, for Vincentio Rossini, for Guilio Rossini and for all those who were betrayed in the old days, when the Germans and the Americans came to us. Battista's knife fell from his hand to the floor. How long the rest took I cannot say. It was the first time I have killed. But when I thought that it was over, when I looked down at Vincentio, then I knew that it was all over indeed, for me was finished for ever. I came down here to get back my own strength, for my own brief time of weeping. You came and she followed and I let you both go.

"Then, when my strength was returned, I ran to his friend, to Maria's father. They came, four of his comrades of the old days, and they took away the body of that traitor, the real murderer. No one will ever find it, for it lies weighed down and rotting, far out at sea where no tide can bring it ashore.

"And in the room above this one I made order out of chaos. I laid Vincentio into an easy rest. It is true he had a smile on his face. All signs of his pain were gone. Perhaps he is with his Tanya, for he loved her dearly."

She laughed softly, but her laughter was more like the soft sound of grief.

"For her he would be as beautiful as he was when I first saw him. But, as God is my witness, I never thought of his love. I was a faithful and loving wife to

my good husband. To Vincentio, I thought only of the
services I might give."

Her voice died away. I think she had forgotten us.
There was pity in Dominic's face, great pity in my own
heart.

'Any man's death diminishes me.'

Now, with this new awareness of mine, I shall share
in the sadness of every lost and tragic love for the rest
of my life, I thought.

"Signora, at the end you were able to give him peace
and dignity, and he had comradeship in death," I said.

She stood up and we rose to go.

"You will tell Rosa," she said. "She is a good girl,
though sometimes I may have grudged her Vincentio's
affection. Tell her I will keep things here until she
comes. For your patience, I thank you, Signorina Del
Mar, and you, Signore. May you be happy."

We left the shadowy courtyard behind us, wandered
back through the sunlight of the busy streets, drank
campari on our terraced café. I told Dominic of my
dream on that Stratford night, of Shylock on his couch,
of Rosa in her diamond bikini. We drifted into our
world of dreams that were real.

Late that night, our cases locked for the morning, the
sadness of our departure already upon us, we went out
for a last goodbye.

We crossed the road and, for the first time, found a
small path, its entry crowned by an arched gateway,
gateless now. It led through the lemon grove and the
olive trees I had so often looked at from my window.

I told Dominic the legend of the olive tree.

The path turned into a track which led round to the

main square, but opposite was the garden of another hotel, one terraced drop nearer the sea than ours. That familiar sweetness of blossom filled the cool air and Dominic, his arm round my waist, began to sing softly.

"Breathing orange-perfumed greeting. . . ."

Then he hummed a wordless accompaniment as I joined in with the Neapolitan words of the old romantic tune.

> "No prufumo accussi fino
> Dinto'o core se ne va . . ."

And we both finished together, his deep, soft voice and my own contralto well joined.

> "Ma nun me lassa
> Nun darme stu turmiento . . .
> Torna a Surriento. . . ."

Come back to Sorrento! Wherever our future life might lead us, always, together we must come back to Sorrento.

CHAPTER EIGHTEEN

"An English home . . . Softer than sleep . . . All things in order stored . . . A haunt of ancient Peace."—TENNYSON.

THE promise of bluebells had been fulfilled. They lay under the fresh green of budding trees in swathes of silky blue. A shower of rain had fallen and crystal drops danced from the leaves in sunshine.

Dominic's own car had been parked at the airport. We were in good time and, without losing much more, kept away from the main roads as far as was possible. The smell of damp, mossy earth came in through our open windows.

"We've stepped back into spring again. 'Oh, England, my England!'" I said.

It was four o'clock when we dropped down from the Friday traffic of the main road into the sleepy calm of Tollgate Street, and the picture postcard welcome of The Highwayman. As Dominic began to get my luggage from the boot, Peregrine fluttered across the road like a discreetly coloured butterfly, shades of crimson and brown this time.

"Duckie, how super to get you back! You look just marvellous!" He seized both my hands enthusiastically. "I've got a new arrival, a lacquer corner cupboard! It's all woodworm and dry rot and deathwatch beetle and what-have-you inside. But six of the most fantastic butterfly hinges holding it all together! You must come over and worship the very first minute you can spare. They're worth travelling miles to see, honestly, dearie!"

"Like Katisha's right—or was it left?—elbow," I murmured, and Dominic, from behind me, said severely, "You leave my girl alone, Perry. One of your own is running wild in the Waterford glass over there while your back's turned."

With a scream of dismay, Peregrine fled back to his own premises. Old Mrs Lambden, reputed to leave behind her trails of chipped rims and cracked cups, had slipped in unobserved and was going through Peregrine's stock with spring-cleaning fervour.

I laughed at Dominic reprovingly and went through the open door to the onslaught of a white whirlwind with a black eye patch; just Sweet William telling me he'd never forgotten me, no, not for a moment; he alone had kept the whole place going and here it was, given back to me on a plate and in perfect condition.

And so, as far as I could see, it was. We were back on the stage where the action of the play had begun; where it must end, too.

"I'll park the car, take my stuff in and be across in twenty minutes," Dominic said. "Then will you give me a cup of tea?"

I watched him go and turned to reception, where one of our oldest members of staff, dear, dependable Mrs Ellison, waited to greet me.

"Your mother and Mr Allan were so sorry not to be here. But they'll be back by seven for certain and Frederick has planned a wonderful dinner for you. We're all so pleased about the news. Everyone says that Mr Lee's the only one good enough for you!"

I found myself blushing in approved style. Then I

151

asked, "Is Miss Rossini in her room?" for I was surprised that Rosa hadn't appeared yet.

"No. She isn't back yet so she must have missed her first train. But the next one should get her here quite soon and she'll manage a taxi. We didn't book her one in case this did happen. London can be so unpredictable."

"London? Is that where she's gone?"

"Oh, didn't you know? Of course not though. It was rather last minute, after your telephone call. She went up with Mr and Mrs Allan but said she'd make her own way back and try to get here before you arrived. She had some business in town she wanted to see to before she has to go back to Italy. But she says she'll be back here for the wedding and she did the flowers before she left yesterday."

Indeed, those flowers I could see, flowering cherry and white tulips in a blue and white jar, looked bridal and beautiful.

"House full?" I asked.

"Yes, practically. Mrs Allan's sister is to have Primrose because of its big bathroom. I'm afraid we've had to put an American lady in Bryony."

Bryony was the only room which invaded my corridor and, for that reason and because it had no private bathroom and was some distance from a communal one, it was left empty whenever possible.

"An American lady." A description that held no appeal for me at the moment. A ghost walked over my grave and I shivered. William, as close to my knee as though he were chained there, gave me a nudge to remind me of his presence and I stooped to tickle his head.

This would be one of Rosa's club women, of course. But alone? I turned to the book, to the entry against Bryony. We kept these records for our own future reference as well.

"Irene Palmer-Chicago," written in a square, ugly script. Script often looked ugly anyway, in one hand very similar to another, I told myself. I looked down and recognised some names, old friends many of them.

"Good! You've managed Wild Rose for Mr and Mrs Ransom, their favourite room," I said, then added, "The American, when did she come?"

"Late last night. Toni booked her in because I'd already gone off. We didn't expect anyone else. This poor thing had a migraine. She had no breakfast this morning and rang down to have just soup sent up for lunch. Jean said she was still in bed with the curtains drawn when she went in, so she couldn't do the room properly. She said the light hurt her eyes, but she was feeling better and asked lots of questions about the hotel. I expect she'll come down later and perhaps make a good dinner."

"Let's hope so," I said, and turned to follow my cases which were being taken upstairs by our handyman-porter. William followed us.

Tom carried my things through to the walk-in clothes cupboard.

"Mr Lee will be coming over soon," I told him, and got a broad smile in response. "I'll ask for tea then; and perhaps Miss Rossini will be back too."

"When you be away us misses all on 'ee," he said.

I was home again, home from Sorrento.

My room looked fresh and pretty. Rosa, I guessed, had put a posy of late blue and white violets on my bookcase, gathered from the grass bank which sloped up to the dividing wall between us and Chimneys, where Dominic planned to put, so he said, a gate for William. Their faint, earthy fragrance came to me as I crossed the room.

I unlocked my case and began, in a desultory way, to hang up a few things. I saw the dress I had worn to Stratford and that I had left behind in such a confusion of emotion. I'd wear it tonight, I decided.

Somehow I couldn't relax. That door with the Bryony plaque had been shut when I passed it.

I was pretty sure why Rosa had gone to London. Both Peter and Dominic had told her of the jewel experts of Hatton Garden. Finding herself with two days alone in which to wait for our return, facing the news of her uncle's death, she must have made up her mind to take the first step in solving the mystery of Elena's jewels. She knew I would probably be bringing her letters, but not what would be in them. Moreover she would soon have to return to Italy to settle up Vincentio's small estate and to take her own film tests. Rosa's quick, alert mind would not wait easily.

Well, I could make sure of this one thing, anyway. William at my heels, I went down the corridor and up the few stairs to the little girl's room.

It was sweet and fragrant and smelled of Rosa. William wagged his tail in appreciation. The long drawer of the dressing table was unlocked. I opened it and, as I expected, it was empty.

Then I heard the sound behind me. I turned quickly to face the door and William gave a short bark as he looked up at me enquiringly.

The dark, squat shadow came before her and,

foolishly, I stepped back and gripped the edge of the table behind me for support. William, with that extra sense dogs have, knew that something was wrong here. He laid his ears back and I saw the muscles of his legs quiver as he made ready, at the given word, to spring.

Sophie Cannan stood in the doorway, something in her hand. That she was recovering from a migraine I could well believe. Her face, always sallow, was colourless. Deep lines were etched from nose to chin, black eyes sunk in their sockets.

"Why, she is mad!" I told myself as, in horror, I saw what she held. I know nothing of revolvers save what I have learned through television and the films, but this one looked deadly and vicious.

"Where is it? Tell me where it is!" she demanded, her voice harsh, barely audible.

The clarity of my own voice in contrast, surprised me. It came cool and detached, sounding far away.

"What are you talking about? And what right have you to come here?"

"No rights for me, nor wrongs either, and you know well enough what I mean. The packet of letters, that list—and the diamonds too. If you don't tell me I shall shoot. I've found this one useful before." She laughed and I saw the hairs on William's back rise. "It's quiet enough, less than a car back-firing."

"Don't be a fool! D'you think you could shoot me and get away with it?"

She made an ugly sound, the distortion of a laugh again.

"Shoot you, honey? No, not you, not yet, anyway. I think I'll shoot the dog. He looks dangerous and, after all, I've a right to defend myself. There's no one else left to do it. Pity! He seems fond of you. Now, tell me quick. I've no time to waste. Where are they?"

For a moment I couldn't speak. I could hardly breathe. She saw what she had done, spoke again.

"Perhaps I'll not have to kill him, just break a leg maybe?"

She saw me lift my hand towards the bedroom telephone, almost within reach, and snapped out, "No! Or he'll get it!"

I heard William's low growl, was terrified lest he should move in on her without command.

"Quiet! Stay, William!" I said, and he looked up at me, obedience overriding his better judgment. I went on pouring out words, anything, anything to stop her doing what she threatened.

"The jewels aren't here. Rosa's taken them to London, to Hatton Garden to get them valued—"

As I saw the shadow moving slowly across the wall behind her, moving forward, I went on talking, talking, promising wildly, anything so that time won could turn that shadow into reality.

"She will be bringing them back, at any moment now. Her train was late. I promise you that you shall have what you want. Don't hurt the dog—"

I babbled on, one fear in my heart, that this advancing shadow, cautious, light-footed, might be Rosa herself. I prayed and, as I saw my prayer answered, I managed to keep that flood of relief from showing in my face. For it was Dominic who stood behind her, Dominic's arm that, in one swift movement, reached out and grasped her wrist, twisted it cruelly so that she screamed and dropped the weapon.

William, with an excited bark, was almost the first to

get to it. I had visions of an infuriated bull terrier, pistol between his teeth, shooting it up, wild-west fashion, all over The Highwayman.

"No!" I shouted and he stood back, looking at me with injured innocence as I gingerly retrieved it. "Wot, me?" said his ears. Then he stared up at Sophie and gave that low growl again.

"Put it in my pocket, sweetheart," said Dominic. I dropped it in and then, on my knees by William, threw my arms round his neck and called him all the endearing names he knew.

I stood up. Dominic still held Sophie's arm in that merciless grip. She tried to move away but his tightened grasp brought another cry of pain from her.

"I'm sorry, Helen. These aren't my usual tactics. Where? To your room?"

We walked the few yards, Sophie's head sunk on her shoulders, her steps dragging.

Dominic pushed her, gently enough, into a chair in the far corner. He closed the door and stood before it, then took the small weapon from his pocket. He looked down at it, looked more closely. Then, with a shout of laughter, he tossed it up and caught it as it came down again. He walked across to Sophie, who stared boldly up at him.

"Why, you wicked old—"; he left his sentence unfinished. She gave a derisory sniff, tossing her head, and grinned after him as he came back to me and held out his hand with the revolver in it.

"See, one of those clever little dummies about to be baned we hope—an invitation to crime with a built-in precaution. Lock it up, darling. We'll drown it in the river where it can tempt no one again."

All that wasted emotion of mine! I felt a fool and wished that William had bitten her! As I took the wicked little toy, Sophie held out her hand.

"You give it me! We never liked guns, noisy things! But Myers bought that for me in New York. He said, 'With this you'll be able to scare off those American "ruffianos" in Central Park.' So I always kept it in my handbag—knew it'd come in useful some day. Give it back to me! If you take it that's stealing!"

I was fascinated by Sophie's logic, but I shook my head and locked it into a drawer of my desk.

"Rosa has gone to London," I told Dominic. "She took the jewels with her."

"Rosa has come back. She is saying hullo to everyone and is coming straight up here after she has ordered tea."

As he spoke there were light steps outside and Rosa's voice. "Helen carissima, may I come in or are you in a passionate embrace?"

Dominic opened the door and she stood there, small and beautiful, gay and exquisite.

It was a dramatic moment but William, as usual, occupied the stage. One can do nothing with William save let rapture take its course.

I went across and put my arms round her. She held me tightly for a moment. Then she crossed the room to stand before Sophie.

"So, you have even followed me here. You want them so badly? Well, here they are."

She swung the large leather bag she carried over her shoulder on to the desk, took from it Elena's jewel case, unlocked it with a key she took from her handbag and tipped out all Elena's jewels on to the desk top.

As the flashing medley of colour spilled out, Sophie,

hunched in her chair, leaned forward, one hand greedily stretched towards it.

"This was what you wanted, wasn't it?" Rosa picked up the tiara, let it swing from one finger. "The three at the top. Those are the ones, I think." She dropped it on to Sophie's lap. "Look, you can see the break where the originals were."

Sophie, who had clutched the sparkling thing to her breast, straightened and looked down at it.

"They are worth no more than any good paste jewellery set in—pinchbeck—they call it. Maybe they were never worth any more than that. Maybe that mark is the result of no more than an accidental breakage, a routine repair. On the other hand, there could once have been an exchange and one day, perhaps, I shall know what really happened."

Sophie let the thing fall from her lap on to the carpet. William leapt forward but Rosa restrained him. For a moment she held it over his head as she had held the collar round his neck on that morning which seemed so very long ago. Then she laughed and put it back with the others.

She took up the sapphire bracelet.

"These are the only genuine stones in the whole collection," she said. "And even they would not be enough to satisfy your demands. In any case, you shall not have them. I shall always prize and treasure them even if I never know what they stand for."

Opportunely, for I think we needed it, one of the waitresses came up from the kitchen with our tea. Rosa hastily threw her coat over that dazzling collection on my little desk. When the door closed again I began to pour out.

"Take this to Sophie first," I told Dominic, for indeed she looked on the verge of collapse. He moved a small table and gently placed the cup near her hand, then took across a plate with sandwiches and biscuits. She drank greedily and began to eat.

Rosa took her cup, perched on the edge of the desk to drink it. Dominic and I, finding we were a cup short, shared the same one. We remembered Rosa's introduction to beer via his tankard and he winked at me over the cup's rim.

I heard the grandfather clock in the hall strike five. All this to have happened in so short a time, I thought.

Then I stood up.

"Rosa, I have brought something back which may answer your questions," I said, and I went to my dressing-room, took the small package from my case and gave it to her.

CHAPTER NINETEEN

"Oh Memory! Thou soul of joy and pain."—R. SAVAGE.

"I FOUND them the night your uncle died," I told her. "Dominic was in Rome and I went along to the room behind the Square S. Vincentio. Myers Cannan, or Michaele Battista, as I believe his real name was—" I was conscious of a sudden quiet movement from the corner, but I went on, "He had been there too. He had climbed the outside staircase and, in the dusk, had got into Vincentio's room unnoticed.

"Later, when I came and knocked on the door below, there was no answer, so I went up myself. I found the room in chaos. Your uncle had woken and Battista had gone over to him with a knife.

"But, Rosa, as you have always said, Vincentio's arms and hands were strong. When I came both of them were dead. Your uncle had died naturally, but that other—" I broke off and began again. "Rosa, Vincentio died quickly, easily, I think. There was a smile on his face."

Rosa passed her hands across her eyes, was very still. I could not tell her of Teresa Pascati's share of those deaths with Sophie listening. I turned to look at that figure in the corner.

"Were you hiding in the bushes the whole time that was happening?"

"No. I followed Myers, alone. I came just before you came. I watched you go up, thought that Myers would deal with you easily enough. I was only waiting for him.

161

Then, when you came down again, running with that look of terror on your face, I went up into the room, to find out what had happened there. I saw, and then I followed you. But you were hidden somewhere, those letters still with you. Perhaps that was as well for you." Her voice cracked. "Tell me, where is his body?"

I knew what she meant. Had there been a kind of loving there? For a moment a kind of pity was in my own heart. I told her.

"It is deep in the sea, where no tide will throw it back against the rocks. It is safe."

There was silence. Then, "We were Neapolitans," she said. "The sea was always near. We came further south later, for the olive picking, for fishing, for any work at first. He knew the sea. The sea will keep him."

Rosa was looking at me again.

"I will tell you everything later," I said. "When I ran away I nearly tripped over that packet and, because your uncle had told me he had letters for you, I picked them up. They are the right ones."

Rosa looked down at the packet in her hand, her fingers tugging at the knot which held them, and she began to speak to Sophie in Italian.

She talked rapidly, with angry vehemence, poured out the whole story of how she had discovered the truth, had decided to leave Sorrento taking with her the jewels that Vincentio had given to her that same morning.

Sophie nodded her head with the slow, tired movement of an old woman. Then suddenly she said, speaking in that Neapolitan dialect she and Myers had used between themselves:

"But once I saved Vincentio Rossini's life. He did not know it, but for that he could have thanked me."

She gave a short laugh as she caught Rosa's glance of incredulity.

"Oh, yes! Michaele and I were on the winning side, we thought. But we had to give good return for our privileges. That night two parties were to get through to Naples, your Uncle Vincentio leading one, your young Uncle Guilio with the other. It was I who took the message to the German captain. I told him only of one party. Later they thought he had blundered. But it was I who chose that Guilio should die and that Vincentio should have the chance to live. I was a woman who liked men." A grin flashed up over her ravaged face as she looked across at Dominic. "Still do, if they're real men. Always my own man was first though. But Rossini, eh, he had something always. Any woman would have spared him, and I did. At my own risk it was, but I was lucky. So you lost only one of your uncles, Rosa, and which one was my decision."

She shrugged. How often I had seen that movement.

"Michaele was a good husband to me. Always he stood by me. But Vincentio was a man in a thousand."

She gave a sigh, her heavy eyelids hooding those dull black eyes.

Dominic still stood behind my chair, before the door. As Rosa slid the string from the stout envelope I leaned my head back against him. He put his hand on my shoulder and I turned my cheek against it, a warm, brief contact.

Rosa took out three crisp, thin sheets of paper, covered closely in a pointed artistic hand, the ink brown and faded. A smaller sheet holding only a dozen or so lines in boldly black, masculine writing, fell unnoticed by her to the carpet.

Rosa began to read in silence, three pairs of eyes watching her. Halfway down the second page she stopped, looked up, her face wondering.

"Helen, Dominic, I will go back, I will read in English. She there shall know too where those gems are gone and how they went. Oh, yes, they still exist, but I think we may never see them."

In a clear, low voice, slowly she began to read.

" '*My darling, my little daughter Tanya,*

For when you read this you will know that I am your mother, I Elena Alexyevna. My dear friend Anna will take my place when I am gone. Though I think you have loved us both equally, you have always thought of her as your real mother. That you should do so we thought would be better for us all. But now I know that I must soon die and I wish you to know the real story when you are old enough to understand. But love Anna always, my darling, for my sake as well as your own.' "

Rosa paused, hesitated and looked up.

"Helen, you understand that this letter is written in Italian. Elena had settled in Naples with Anna for the few months before she died. That I knew. She realised that Tanya would forget most of her Russian, perhaps guessed she might marry an Italian. So, fortunately, she writes in our language. I translate into English as clear as I can make it." She went on :

" '*Now, as I write, you are still too young for the story I tell you. You shall read it when you are seventeen, when you are given the jewels in my jewel box.*
164

They are not real, they will never bring you wealth, but they are part of me, of me as a dancer.

" 'You will never be a dancer yourself, for it is a hard life and we do not wish it for you. But these jewels you will cherish in my memory and there is one memory you must cherish above all.

" 'My darling, can you go back to that very first time you came to the theatre, saw me dance? It was on your sixth birthday. The ballet was "The Sleeping Beauty" and often, at your bedtime, I would tell you that old story. And so you knew what my dancing meant. You had a new dress to wear, a pretty, gauzy white dress of which you were very proud.

" 'Do you remember, Tanya, how happy and excited you were when they brought you round to my dressing-room? How a lady came there, too, a tall, rather haughty lady, not light-hearted and gay and laughing as I so often seemed to be. Do you remember how my jewels lay on my dressing table, how, so clumsily, I knocked down that diamond crown? You picked it up and gave it back to me, but three of the stones broke off in my fingers and fell to the floor again. This time, as you stooped, the lady put out her hand and took them from you. Then she smiled and kept them.

" 'When she went, almost at once, she took from her arm a narrow gold bracelet with six sapphires and put it on your wrist. It was too big for you then. But she bent and kissed you and said, "They are Siberian sapphires and they come from your own country. It is in memory of one who would have loved you." Then she turned to me. "She is very like him," she said.

165

" 'That lady was the Princess Pontiesky, Tanya, and Nicholas, the Prince, my Prince, was your father. He gave me great happiness and it was because of your coming that we parted. But at those two stolen meetings we had before he was murdered, we planned how I might bring those three diamonds, the Three Stars of Georgia, which brought good fortune to his family, out of Russia. There was a craftsman in Nicholas' service who substituted them for the three pieces of paste in that crown of mine. Nicholas put them, with all my other jewels, in that beautiful box of soft Russian leather which will now be yours. Our plan was successful. Unnoticed, secretly, I was able to leave Russia, taking them with me.

" 'And so, that night in Paris, you were able to restore to the Pontiesky family those jewels which had been their pride for four centuries, without which, it is said, good fortune will leave them.

" 'One day, perhaps, when the Three Stars of Georgia have become a legend, a forgotten mystery, they will be worn once more and their story told.

" 'Never forget your share in it, my darling, and always treasure the bracelet you were given, a gift from Imperial Russia. It is a sign that I kept faith with your father as well as the love he would have had for you.

" 'Goodbye, my little Tanya. May you find a love as great as the love that found me; but, pray God, one blessed by the peace and security of a marriage the world will recognise.

" 'Do not forget me, Tanya. Your mother,
                    Elena Alexyevna.' "

The room semed very quiet as Rosa's voice died away. She folded the thin sheets of paper before she spoke again.

"So my Aunt Tanya was the daughter of Elena, the great ballerina. Perhaps that is why to see her walk was to hear music. And the diamonds? Well, the daughters of the Princess Pontiesky married noblemen. Perhaps that is when good fortune returned to them and I am glad they still possess the family treasure. One day, perhaps, their descendants will wear those Stars of Georgia again. That will be good. But I shall always keep and treasure this little sapphire bracelet." And she touched it lovingly.

A hoarse laugh came from Sophie's corner.

"More fool you then, honey," she said. "If that Elena had used her chances, made them pay well, you could have been a wealthy woman. Oh, you good women make me sick! Your father's aunt was a fool too. She talked too much, trusted too much for her own good. It was easy enough to find out her secrets. Here, you'd better add this to your treasures."

She rummaged in the handbag she carried with her and threw a square envelope across. As Rosa caught it, opened it and took out that photograph of her father and his letter, I saw Sophie's foot move, try slyly to cover the square of paper which Rosa had dropped unnoticed.

"Rosa! Don't forget that other paper. Pick it up and read it."

As I spoke Sophie's eyes flashed into real fire and William, head on paws, uttered his low growl. Sophie was as good as another Fu Manchu to him. The hot tea and food had restored her usual self-confidence amazingly well, I thought. She moved angrily in her chair as Rosa retrieved the paper, read it and passed it to me and Dominic, who read it over my shoulder. The writing was clear and bold.

"Little Rosa,

You will find the list. Tear it into a thousand fragments. Thirty years ago I began to compile it and, when I wrote that first name, I hated deeply. But Tanya's love for me and my love for her have taught me much and now my hatred is gone.

Fifteen years ago she hid that list for me where no one could easily find it, knowing that one day I would have the will to destroy it. If I had not been ill, you and I, Rosa, would have destroyed it together.

Some of the names there are those of men who have buried their misdeeds in the past. Let them do so. Many of them have wives and children and I would not harm those who are innocent. I am near death and death will not be the end, it is never the answer.

A man whose name is on that list came seeking it, hoping to gain much by blackmailing those who had once been his fellows. He lost his life, for he was a Sicilian and his own brothers took their revenge.

So, Rosa, destroy it for me, lest others should come seeking it again.

Dear little Rosa, may life be good to you.

Vincentio Rossini."

I looked up from the letter to Rosa. Her eyes were moist and bright.

"Dear Uncle 'Centio!" she said. "Helen, where is

this list now? Do you know? Is it in the jewel box?"

"The list?" Sophie's voice from her corner startled us. "It will mean nothing to you. I can explain it. Show it to me."

"Now do you really think you would be the right interpreter?" asked Dominic mildly. He was leaning nonchalantly against the door, a formidable enough guard for our prisoner.

I went across to my desk and took up the empty jewel case. I held it, rather hopelessly, upside down and shook it. Then, putting it down, I explored that satin lining with my fingers.

Yes, here it was! Hard, almost impossible to see because of that patterned and quilted padding, a very fine, delicately stitched seam. I thought of Tanya's small fingers, neatly and firmly making those minute stitches, hoping that she was hiding away, for ever perhaps, that record of shame and betrayal.

I took a small pair of scissors from a drawer and carefully unpicked the stitches. The silk was old and fading. As I slipped my fingers inside and drew out two sheets of paper, closely written and folded several times, its edges frayed and split and a fine silky dust fell on to the folds of paper.

I recognised the clear bold script of Vincentio Rossini's letter and I handed the papers over to Rosa.

CHAPTER TWENTY

"This is the true beginning."—SHAKESPEARE.

WE WATCHED Rosa as she unfolded the two sheets.
Thick black lines boldly divided each piece of paper
into three columns. Rosa held them out towards me so
that I could see what was written on them; two columns
of names, thirty or more in all, I think. Heading them
all, in thick black lettering, were the names of Sophia
and Michaele Battista. That entry I read in detail.

The second column beside their names had been left
blank. So Sophie and Myers Cannan had managed to
keep the secret of their new identity. But in the third
column against them was the date November 1943, and
the one name, Guilio. That name stood out clearly, but
there were other names, other dates there too. The
Battistas had betrayed others than Guilio.

Entries below that first one of all followed the same
pattern, but in most cases there were newly adopted
names in the second column and always, in the third,
records of past treacheries and past betrayals. Even I
was able to recognise in that second column the names
of some men now well known and respected in the new
worlds they had found, the new lives they had made
for themselves.

Now they might have wives, children, grandchildren,
innocent of their past. But here long buried deeds were

faithfully recorded; deeds that were shameful, deeds to invite blackmail and to demand revenge.

Sophie Cannan's yellow claw snatched suddenly at the papers Rosa held. There was a fantastic pleasure in the vigour with which I struck the hands down. Sophie's curse, in vituperative Italian, was expressive, even though it was a new one to me.

I caught Dominic's low laugh, then laughed aloud myself, for Rosa had already ripped the pages across again and again. She tipped the paper clips and drawing pins from a square brass tray and dropped the fragments on to it. I took a match from a highly decorative matchbox and set light to them.

Sophie crouched back in her chair again, dead black eyes fixed on the charred pieces. I opened the window wider to let out the smell of burned paper.

"Well, Cousin Sophie, there go your last hopes of making a fortune," said Rosa. "The idea was blackmail, I suppose?"

I am not fond of spiders. Usually I cope by persuading them somehow into a tumbler and dropping them from a window. Sheila and Jean hate them and, with broom, duster or mop, give them very short shrift. I had seen the way those dark, swiftly moving creatures could shrivel up and wither away into almost nothing.

That is what Sophie Cannan looked like now, a small, withered, black spider, ugly and harmless.

Rosa spoke to her again.

"What will you do now? Where will you go?"

There was silence; then the slow, tired travesty of that usual shrug.

"Will you go back to America?"

The answer was not much more than a hoarse whisper.

"Chance would be a fine thing. I've got no cash left, honey. Spent the lot to get here." The shrug again.

"Would you manage if you were back there?"

"I'd be okay. There are plenty I could go to. I've lost Myers and they'd do something. There's always South America, houses I could run well enough." She gave a coarse laugh. "Places where you might have finished up if the luck had been ours and not yours, honey."

Was she talking about white slave traffic in these days, with Rosa? Hold-ups with dummy weapons, blackmail of men in high places! This was melodrama indeed.

Then I remembered Myers Cannan's dead face, the soft dark earth under the olive trees, and I shuddered.

Rosa stood up.

"Helen dear, what is the true meaning of a blood tie? There is none between us, Helen, yet you—you are my sister, Dominic is my brother. Your mother and Peter, it is as though they are my parents too. Elena Alexyevna is not really of my family, yet, because of my Aunt Tanya, she is a part of me. My Uncle Vincentio, my own mother, they would have been yours too.

"Somehow this woman has bound herself to me, she has worked her way into my life. Though she must always be in my past, I will not have her in my future. Wherever she goes she will be evil. Let her go back to the country of her choice."

She took a notecase from her handbag, extracted a thick wad of notes; more than half of what was there, I realised.

I felt Dominic make a quick movement behind me. I

looked upwards at him. This must be Rosa's private affair, a matter of her own self-respect. His return look at me showed that he understood.

"There will be a little more waiting for me in Italy and I can make my own life. In this way, too, my uncle would have rid himself of her, with dignity. Already she is at the end and there is nothing ahead of her save death."

She held out the money to Sophie.

"Here, take this. Leave this country, where there is nothing for you. You dare not return to Italy, our Italy. Go away from here, back to your own world, out of all our lives."

The clawlike hand grasped the money greedily, pushed it deep into a large handbag. Sophie looked straight into Rosa's face.

"You know, I'm beginning to get kinda fond of you, honey," she said.

The silence that followed this statement could only be described as pregnant. Our thoughts were too deep for words, I suppose. I broke it.

"I'll take you to where you can catch a bus to Oxford station," I told her. "You can be in London by eight o'clock, get a flight tomorrow, with luck."

Sophie stood up. Some of that brash assurance and self-confidence had come back, but still she was an old, woman.

Dominic moved.

"I'll drive her—" he began, but I shook my head.

"No, she must go the way I say. Mother and Peter and Aunt Joan will be here very soon. We will not have our lovely evening spoiled by her. She shan't touch it. I can get her a taxi if she wants one."

Sophie Cannan and I walked up Tollgate Street and round to the square and, as we reached it, the long red bus swung in.

Old George Tooley, sitting on the wooden bench and sucking his empty pipe in the sunshine, called out to its driver.

"Well, Bill, be'st on time for once then?"

And Bill called back, "Come along to The Pigeons tonight, you old varmint, and I'll give 'ee a pint to celebrate."

I gave Bill Sophie's case and watched her climb heavily up the steps.

"Be sure you put her down at the station," I told Bill.

I felt a hand on my arm.

Dominic stood there, William beside him, two pairs of eyes, black and grey-green, on my face.

The grey-green smiled at me and suddenly I was home from my wandering.

"Where were you, my darling? Come back to me now, back for always."

Then, just at that moment, over his shoulder, I caught sight of a familiar figure—the vicar, ambling along in his absent-minded way up the middle of the road, Fu Manchu beside him, sans lead, sans collar, sans everything save the will to do battle.

I looked down at our William, equally well equipped.

"Run! Run before they see each other!" I cried, and with old George Tooley's chuckle following, with William bouncing and barking wildly around us, hand in hand we raced back to The Highwayman, to the end—or could it be the beginning?—of my story.

Secretive Nurse

Valerie Scott

Secretive Nurse

Valerie Scott

"The Harleys have been rather a strange lot, but there's never been any suggestion that a woman wouldn't be safe amongst them. If you have any doubts then you should quit the case, Clare."

"That's the strange thing about it, Amanda. I can't quite put my finger on what is causing the disquiet I'm feeling. I'm sure its just my imagination and yet there's the fact that David warned me."

ONE

CLARE CRAWFORD attempted to read, but it was impossible to forget the situation. This was her first day back at the London flat since her last patient died, and she had become so very involved in the case that she felt the loss personally, although Mrs. Anson had been in her eighties. The fact that she was now on holiday for a fortnight made no difference to her feelings. She had been looking forward to her holiday for months, and now August was here and she wished it was December, when the pain and anguish of this last case would be faded along with all the memories of the other cases she'd handled.

She threw down the book and got to her feet, a tall slim blonde with troubled blue eyes, and at twenty-six she was beginning to think that she had made a mistake in entering nursing. She always became too involved with her patients! It was a golden rule that one remained detached, for the good of the patient as well as for the good of the nurse, but she wasn't made like that, and her heart ached at times.

The telephone rang and she sighed as she got up to answer. She hoped it wasn't the Bureau. It wouldn't be the first time she'd started a holiday, only to be called by the Bureau and asked to take an emergency case. But this time she wouldn't do it. She couldn't take any more strain upon her emotions until after a long rest.

There was a frown upon her smooth brow as she lifted the receiver and gave her name. She was all alone in the world. She knew utter loneliness because her parents were dead, and she had never been one to force her company upon relatives who had their own lives to lead. She had found a certain amount of satisfaction in nursing, because it had enabled her to give some of her suppressed love to people who really needed helping. But some of the cases she'd handled lately had been rather distressing, and she longed to get a normal one where the patient might be recovering from an illness instead of languishing into death.

"Hello, this is Clare Crawford," she said, and there was a tension inside her because one day she knew that when she answered the telephone Tim Millard was going to answer in his usual flippant way, but with that background menace in his voice which always sent a shudder through her.

"Clare, this is Grant Laverne. Do you remember me?"

"Grant!" She spoke the name while her mind set her memory into action, and a series of quick pictures showed upon the screen of her mind. Grant Laverne had been a houseman at the hospital where she had trained to be a nurse. He'd left just before she'd departed to become a freelance nurse on the books of Medical Aid Bureau. They hadn't been in love, but he had been attracted to her because she had always seemed to be forlorn and lonely, and they'd gone out together a number of times. But they had parted and gone their different ways, and she had often wondered what became of him. "How did you know where to find me?" she asked.

"I got in touch with some of our old friends and they told me you were on the books of the Bureau. They gave me your telephone number when I explained who I am, and so here I am. I understand you're on holiday at the moment."

"Well they call it a holiday, but I'm not going away anywhere. I just feel that I ought to try and set my mind to rights. I've just come off a particularly bad case, and I don't know how I feel, really."

"I can imagine how you do feel," he said, and she imagined his rugged face and piercing brown eyes. "Look, you sound as if you need a complete change of scenery and a good rest. Why don't you come out to where I'm in general practice? I'm married now; been married almost a year, and I'd like to see you again."

"Married!" She could not keep the surprise out of her tones. "I always thought you weren't the marrying kind! But congratulations. I hope you're very happy."

"Thank you, we are happy! I thought I wasn't the marrying kind either, but when the right person comes along, that's it! I don't suppose there's anyone in your life, is there?"

"No!" She didn't sigh, but wasn't far from making some recognition to the fact that she was still lonely. "What's behind this surprising invitation, Grant?"

He chuckled, and she found herself recalling those days when they had worked together. It was strange how a sound could take one's mind back.

"You're as sharp as ever, aren't you?" He was still chuckling. "Look, I've got a very difficult case on my hands and I need a nurse for it. If something isn't done soon then the patient will probably die, and that would be a great pity because she's only four years old."

"It's a child!" Clare caught her breath. "I was about to turn you down out of hand, because I've had more than my share of difficult cases lately. But what's wrong with her?"

"Her parents were both killed a month ago. It was a particularly nasty road accident, and the child was in the back of the car. She's recovering well from the injuries she sustained, but it's her mental outlook that's the problem. But why don't you come to Chippenbury and stay with us for a week and I can fill you in on all the details?"

She was silent for a moment, thinking over her immediate future, and the two weeks she had planned for herself. Remaining at home to catch up on odd jobs and some reading, didn't appeal half as much as the prospect of getting away from everything familiar. "Am I obliged to take the case if I come?" she demanded.

" Certainly not. But if you don't take it you might be able to put me on to someone who would. I must have a reliable person. The child's uncles and grandfather have a girl acting as housekeeper, but although she may be able to perform those duties well enough, she certainly isn't capable of taking care of this child."

" What's the address?" Clare demanded. " I'll come tomorrow."

" Good girl!" There was a world of relief in his voice. " Have you got a pencil handy?"

Clare took the address, and learned that the village was near the town of Devizes in Wiltshire. She couldn't help feeling that this was one of the little acts that Fate was sometimes guilty of when it felt that a person was too set in her ways. She felt greatly relieved for some unknown reason as she said goodbye to Grant Laverne.

Her depression seemed to have evaporated already. Now she had something definite to look forward to instead of a fortnight acting like a recluse. She decided to pack immediately, and went through to her bedroom to get out the battered case she always used. It had travelled a great deal with her, and she regarded it with mixed feelings, knowing it was a link with the past but being too sentimental to want to dispose of it.

As she was selecting the clothes she wanted to take with her she came upon a photograph lying face down in the bottom drawer, and a chill feeling spread through her as she turned it over and looked into the narrowed, cruel eyes of Tim Millard. Even a mere photograph of his likeness made her feel scared, and she felt like a rabbit under the cruel observation of a preying stoat. Her throat constricted and her mouth dried. A sigh escaped her and she shook her head slowly.

She had been a girl who always relied upon her instincts when it came to making friends, but her instincts had let her down very badly in this case. She had fallen under Tim Millard's spell—she wouldn't call it love—probably because he had paid so much attention to her when she had been so lonely. They had been around together for a number of weeks, until she felt that he was the only man in the world who really mattered. Then the police had picked him up and he'd been found guilty of robbery! She would never forget the anguish she'd felt when he'd pleaded guilty in court, despite his fervent protestations of innocence to her, and been sentenced to five years imprisonment. That was when she left the hospital where she'd been a staff nurse and gone free-lance. She'd had to get away from everyone who knew her.

It was about time Tim Millard was released from prison, she knew, if he'd earned full remission for good behaviour, and that thought had been nagging in her subconscious mind for quite some time. She never wanted to see him again, and she'd made that quite clear to the friends of his who had called upon her from time to time in the early days after his trial. Then she had changed her address several times and completely separated herself from all her old acquaintances. Now she felt fairly safe from the past, and it didn't seem likely to be able to catch up with her.

But Grant Laverne had found her easily enough! She froze as the thought came home to her. He'd mentioned calling old mutual friends and discovering her whereabouts! She sighed slowly and heavily as she considered. A really determined person could always trace someone such as she! But surely Tim wouldn't want to see her after so long. He would probably swing straight back into his old ways of life and wouldn't give her a second thought.

The next morning she felt almost happy as she caught the train that would take her into Devizes. Her depression had gone and she was looking forward to meeting Grant Laverne again. They had been very good friends, and she'd often wondered what had happened to him. Before leaving the flat she had called the Bureau to inform them of the situation, and they asked to be notified if she decided to postpone her holiday and take the case.

The journey was relaxing, she found, and having notified Grant of her time of arrival, she expected to be met by him and taken by car to the village of Chippenbury where he lived and had his practice. When she arrived at the station she felt a little disappointed that she couldn't see Grant anywhere, but as she passed through the ticket barrier a tall, slim, dark-haired girl confronted her, a smile on her face.

" Are you Miss Crawford?" she demanded pleasantly.

" Why, yes!" Clare paused, looking a little surprised.

" I'm Mrs. Laverne, Amanda Laverne, Grant's wife. He's so sorry he couldn't get to meet you, but he's been called out on a case, so I've come in my car to pick you up."

" Thank you!" Clare smiled. " You're very kind. I do hope my visit isn't going to inconvenience you."

" Not at all." The other smiled, and she had nice brown eyes that showed genuine friendliness. " I'm always pleased to meet anyone who knew Grant before I did, and from what he's said about you at different times I'd say you and he were very good friends."

" We were. Grant was a decent sort, and he knew I was

very lonely and intense. I was so very pleased to hear from him yesterday."

They began to walk towards the exit, and Clare could see that Amanda Laverne was studying her intently. To Clare, the woman seemed exactly the type she would have expected Grant to marry, and she felt pleased that Grant had done so well for himself.

"Did Grant say much to you about the case he hopes you'll take on?" Amanda Laverne paused at the kerbside to unlock a grey Rover.

"He didn't say much about it over the telephone, but I understand he's very worried. He mentioned that the patient is a four year old girl."

"Sue Harley! Poor little girl!" There was heavy sympathy in Amanda's voice. "I knew her parents quite well. The Harleys run a very large farm—Oakapple Farm —which is just outside the village. In fact they own most of the land around that locality. There's Cornelius Harvey, Sue's grandfather, and three sons, her uncles. A girl is housekeeper at the farm, but Sue is due out of hospital in a day or two and Grant thinks a trained nurse should be brought in for the first month at least. The child is still dreadfully upset by the accident which killed her parents, and shock has robbed her of her speech."

"Oh Lord! It does sound as if she needs help." Clare's professional instincts were instantly aroused. They got into the car, and Clare relaxed while Amanda began driving through the town.

"It was a stroke of luck that you're between cases," Amanda said, "although I understand this is your holiday."

"I wouldn't call it that. It was going to be two weeks of sheer misery."

They exchanged glances, and Clare saw sympathy in the other's eyes.

" Grant has told me about you, so I think I understand. But you're feeling upset about your last case, aren't you?"

" I'll get over it. I've been a fool in that I've always felt too close to my patients. I expect you know a great deal about that side of it, being married to a doctor."

" I've learned a lot in the past year, but I was a secretary before I married Grant. However I can see the problems that exist for someone as naturally sympathetic as you."

They lapsed into silence for some time, and Amanda concentrated on her driving. They soon left town and drove through the bright countryside, and Clare felt her spirits rising still more as she gazed around at strange views. This was the best part of her work. She managed to get around the countryside. She met so many people! Looking at Amanda, she felt that she could like the woman, and when Amanda glanced at her and smiled, Clare felt a warmth begin to fill her.

" I'll drive by Oakapple Farm so you can see what it looks like," Amanda said. " But don't think that I'm going to try and put any pressure on you because I wouldn't even think of it. Grant would be pleased if you could take over there, and the Harley family are desperate for someone. But don't let us influence you in any way!"

" All right!" Clare smiled. " After talking to me like that my professional feelings are aroused, so you won't have to influence me. But have you any idea how long I'd be needed here if I took the case?"

" It's difficult to tell, so Grant says. It depends upon the child."

Clare nodded her agreement, and soon they were approaching the village of Chippenbury. She could see a church tower in the distance, and a thrill of anticipation began shooting through her.

" All these fields you see now belong to the Harleys," Amanda told her. " There's a lane on the left that leads to the home buildings, and we'll stop the car and I'll show you the place. The old man, Cornelius Harley, was a Brigadier, but his family have been farming here for generations. Cornelius has three sons, now, with Sue's father having been killed in the road accident. Adam is the eldest at forty, then there's Owen, who's thirty-five, and David, the nicest one, is about twenty-six. None of them is married, and the only woman on the place is Betty Smithers. She's a sort of housekeeper-cum-everything else. Personally, I think she would like to marry one of the Harley men, but which one I wouldn't even guess at. Perhaps she wouldn't mind any of them. I'm not just gossiping, Clare, don't think that. I'm trying to give you some background details in case you take the job."

Clare nodded, becoming interested as she listened. Presently Amanda stopped the car just past a narrow lane, and when they alighted and stood on a grassy bank Clare could see across the meadow. There was a magnificent square old house in the distance, surrounded by trees and looking very pastoral and peaceful in the strong sunlight.

"What a beautiful place!" Clare was enraptured by the view. To the right of the houses there was the glint of water, and she caught her breath as she imagined the pleasant sensations of picnicking by a lake at this time of the year.

"It is lovely! When Grant has had occasion to call at Oakapple Farm I've always tried to be in the car, so that I can just sit and look around while he's visiting his patients. Cornelius Harley is a bit bronchial in the colder months of the year, so Grant has to call quite often."

A car appeared at the entrance of the lane, and a horn sounded raucously, throwing harsh echoes across the meadow and making a flock of birds rise up out of some nearby trees and go wheeling away through the bright air.

"That's a damned silly place to park a car!" The driver had his side window down, and he stuck out his head and glowered at them.

Clare looked intently at him, sensing this was one of the Harley men, and she saw a rugged face that was dark and weatherbeaten with a thick black moustache to add to the sombre appearance that was presented.

"Owen Harley," Amanda said in an aside to Clare. "He's never very sweet tempered."

Clare was watching the man, and she saw his face soften a little as he recognised Amanda.

"Oh, Mrs. Laverne!" he said in slightly mollified tones. "I'm sorry! I thought you were just a couple of sightseers." His dark eyes came to study Clare's face, and she watched him closely as he got out of his car and came forward.

Amanda introduced them, and Clare was a little surprised when he held out his hand. But she shook hands gravely, and as Amanda explained why Clare had come, Clare saw immediate interest show in his dark eyes.

"Sue will be coming out of hospital tomorrow," he said. "We've been most worried about her. There's no one at home to take care of her."

"Well I haven't decided about the case yet," Clare said slowly.

"I see!" He spoke acidly, and seemed to breathe hostility. He had a very heavy manner that slightly overwhelmed Clare, and she watched him closely as he gazed into Amanda's serene face. "I thought the Doctor said it was all fixed."

Amanda glanced at Clare, and she was slightly embarrassed. Clare smiled.

"I wouldn't worry about it," she said instantly. "No doubt Grant said he might be able to persuade me to take the case, and I expect he'll be able to talk me into it."

" Why should you need persuading?" Owen Harley demanded. He shrugged his heavy shoulders. " You're a nurse, aren't you? If we have someone who is ill and you are available then what is there to think over?"

Clare nodded slowly. " Of course you're perfectly right," she said slowly. " What is there to think over?"

" Nurse Crawford is on holiday at the moment, after finishing a serious and exacting case," Amanda said.

" Is that so?" His dark eyes studied her face for a moment. " I must say you do look sort of strained. Of course you must make up your own mind to what you want to do, but we have to have someone in a hurry. Sue comes out of hospital tomorrow morning."

" Then I'll take the case," Clare said.

For a moment approval shone in his dark eyes, and he almost smiled, but he seemed to be the kind of man who was under constant internal pressure. He nodded slowly.

" Thank you for such a quick decision. Would you care to come up to the farm and meet my father? He's the boss in all things."

" I'll bring her along this afternoon if I may," Amanda said quickly. " Would two-thirty be all right?"

" Fine! I'll warn Father to expect you." Owen Harley nodded again and turned away. He paused after moving a few steps and glanced back. " It's a pleasure meeting you, Nurse," he said in a kind of afterthought, and then he departed.

" He's a strange man," Clare commented as she and Amanda returned to the Rover.

" They're all strange men," Amanda said, and Clare frowned as she glanced quickly at the girl, catching her eye.

" What have you and Grant let me in for then?" she demanded.

"They're not that bad." Amanda shook her head. "It's just that they seem to have no time for women at Oakapple Farm.

"But I shan't be going there as a woman," Clare asserted. "I shall be going there in my capacity as a nurse."

"That's very true." Amanda started the car and glanced into the rear view mirror before pulling away from the verge. Her brown eyes were very serious. "But you are a woman beneath the uniform, remember, and they'll see you as such."

"Now you're trying to put me off the case, after I've as good as accepted," Clare said.

"No. I'm just trying to give you the right impressions," came the steady reply. "But I'll always be around to keep an eye open for you, Clare, and Grant won't let them bully you at the farm."

"I don't think I would permit that myself," Clare said with some spirit."

They drove into the village and Clare looked around with great interest. There was a green in the centre of the village, with a duck pond in one corner, and most of the houses and cottages were around the green. Trees grew in profusion, giving plenty of shade, and the one main street was quiet and still. The church was in the background, it's tower rising up above the trees, gaunt and square and very solid.

"This is a beautiful place!" Clare said softly, her blue eyes gleaming as she looked around. "It's certainly the place to come for peacefulness."

"It's not everyone who can take the silence," Amanda said, glancing at her as she brought the car to a halt at the kerb in front of a large, red-brick house. "But you look like the kind of girl who would be very happy in these surroundings," Amanda added.

TWO

WHEN GRANT LAVERNE arrived home for lunch, Clare was really pleased to meet him again, and she smiled with genuine warmth as they shook hands. The doctor was medium sized, stocky and very strongly built, with keen brown eyes that showed a shrewdness and attentiveness one looked for in a medical practitioner. His whole manner seemed to exude confidence, and one was immediately at ease in his company. He gripped Clare's hand tightly as he looked into her blue eyes, and a wide smile showed on his weatherbeaten face.

" Clare, it is nice to see you again. I'm so happy you decided to come. You're looking a bit strained, but I'm sure you'll not regret staying here if you decide to take this case."

" I've already decided to take it, Grant," Clare replied. She smiled as Amanda described their meeting with Owen Harley.

" Well if you've met Owen then you've got nothing to worry about. He is the worst one among the Harleys as far as temperament goes." There was a smile on Grant Laverne's fleshy, good-natured face, but Clare saw indecision in his dark eyes.

" I don't know so much about that," Amanda said teasingly. " If you think of some of the things Adam has done in his time!"

" Now don't start putting impressions into Clare's mind," Grant said, shaking his head. " You have nothing to worry about because you'll be going to Oakapple Farm to help the Harleys. They do think the world of little Sue, and if you can help the child then the Harleys, all of them, will be your friends for life. In any case, David Harley is a fine chap, and I'm sure he wouldn't stand by and let the others push you around, Clare."

" What do you mean by push me around?" Clare demanded. " Are they a violent family?"

" Boisterous is a better word to describe them," Amanda said. " But the way they'd work on you is mentally rather than physically."

Grant was silent as he parked the car in front of the solid old farmhouse, and Clare was sure he would be able to hear the beating of her heart! They alighted from the car and she waited for him to join her, but the large front door was opened before they reached it, and Clare saw a tall, thin, fair-haired woman standing before them.

" Good afternoon, Doctor," the woman greeted in thin tones, but her eyes were on Clare, and there seemed to be hostility in their pale, unblinking depths.

" Good afternoon, Miss Smithers!" Grant glanced at Clare as he greeted the woman, and she could tell by his expression that he was warning her about this woman. " I want you to meet Nurse Crawford. I believe Mr. Cornelius is expecting her this afternoon."

" Yes, Doctor!" The woman moved back from the doorway, not greeting Clare in any way. " Please come in."

Clare glanced around curiously, and the house seemed faded to her keen mind. The interior decoration was drab and old, and it seemed that the whole house could do with repainting. But this was just an impression she gained as she steeled herself for what she imagined would be an ordeal. From what she had been told about the Harley family she didn't know quite what to expect, but she was

ready for just about anything as Miss Smithers pushed open
a door on the right and stalked into a long, wide sitting
room and announced Grant's presence.

There were three men in the room, and they were standing by one of the tall windows, watching the door as if
they didn't know what to expect at the doctor's entrance.
Clare recognised Owen Harley immediately, and an older
edition stood at his brother's side, looking darker and
more powerful. It would be Adam Harley, the oldest of
the three brothers, Clare decided, and she turned her
attention to the old man who stood a little apart from
his sons. Cornelius Harley was in his late sixties, a tall,
thin, greying man who had once been every bit as dark
and powerful as his sons, and it was Cornelius who came
forward as Clare entered the room at Grant's invitation.

" Oh, Doctor, we weren't expecting to see you!" It
was difficult to say if there was pleasure or regret in the
old man's tones. "I was under the impression that your good
wife was bringing the nurse."

" I felt it was my place to be here, Mr. Harley," Grant
said lightly, and introduced Clare to the men.

She found she had assumed rightly who they were, and
shook hands gravely with each of them. She found Owen
Harley slightly hostile, while Adam, taking her hand in
a large and powerful hand, subjected her to a close scrutiny.
She couldn't tell what passed through his mind, but he
didn't seem too prepossessing. He was about forty, and
middle age was beginning to add flesh to his face, but
she imagined he had been a very attractive man in
his youth.

Cornelius Harley made quite an impression upon her,
Clare found as she shook hands with him, and she was
pleasantly surprised when he smiled gently at her. She
had been expecting hostility, such as was showing slightly
in Owen Harley's face. Not that it would have personal

connotations. No doubt they didn't like the idea of their very masculine situation being invaded by a female who would have a great deal of responsibility, if only for a short period.

" I'm very pleased to meet you, Nurse Crawford," Cornelius Harley said. " I'm sure you'll be satisfactory because Doctor Laverne selected you, and I do hope you'll be happy while you're here with us. No doubt the doctor has told you about Sue, and we can all see that the child will need skilled nursing for some considerable time." He glanced at his sons as if to dare them to contradict his words, and Clare got the impression that there had been long and heated discussion over the subject of employing a private nurse. But commonsense had obviously held sway, and she was here.

" I'll take Nurse Crawford into town for this evening's visit at the hospital," Grant said. " I'll introduce her to Sue, then I'll bring her here in the morning so she'll be waiting when Sue comes home."

" That sounds like a good idea," Cornelius said, nodding eagerly. " We have everything here prepared, and I hope you'll like the room we've selected for you, Nurse. I'll get Miss Smithers to take you up to see it before you leave. Sue's room is right next door, and you'll need to be near the child all the time, won't you?"

" Of course!" Clare nodded. " Doctor Laverne will instruct me in my duties, the methods of nursing to be used, and I'll carry out his orders implicitly."

" That settles it then," Cornelius said. " I do hope you will be happy here!"

His tones seemed to carry some kind of a warning to his sons, and Clare saw a harsh expression cross Owen Harley's face as she glanced at him. Adam Harley moved his feet unconsciously, as if taking up a fighting attitude, and she wondered exactly what had been said about the employment of a nurse for Sue Harley. These seemed to be men of deep passions, and no doubt there had been a number of altercations between them before final decision came.

" I'll bring Nurse Crawford back at about ten in the morning," Grant said. " If you'd like to see the room now, Clare, then Miss Smithers will show you. I expect she's waiting in the hall. I'll have a word with Mr. Harley and his sons until you return."

There was something in his tones which seemed to give Clare orders to leave the room, and she nodded and turned away. There was relief in her heart as she opened the door and departed, but she found the housekeeper standing by, and could not help wondering if the woman had been listening at the door.

" Mr. Harley said you'd show me the room I shall have when I arrive tomorrow," Clare said.

" Certainly. If you'll follow me I'll take you up." Betty Smithers let her expression show nothing as she nodded and turned away to lead on up the stairs.

" This is a beautiful old house!" Clare said brightly, wanting to create a friendly atmosphere between them. In a house that consisted of male members, she wanted the only other female to be on good terms with her, but she felt that she would have to work hard at being friends with this woman. Betty Smithers resented a professional nurse and clearly showed it.

" The house is all right," came the short answer, and Clare firmed her lips as they continued.

" Have you been housekeeping here long?" she persisted.

"Since my husband was killed five years ago!"

" I always wanted to be a nurse," came the surprising admission. " But I got married at seventeen and that put paid to all my ambitions. My husband worked here on the farm, and his tractor overturned and crushed him to death." Betty Smithers turned to open the door of a room.

" It's like stumbling unexpectedly upon an oasis in a desert!"

"Sue's room has been redone as well. They'll do anything for that child! It's good to see how they have taken to her now her parents are dead. The poor little thing will need all the love and understanding she can get. I know what it's like to lose a loved one! But Sue has lost both her parents, and no one will ever be able to completely fill the spaces their loss leave in her life."

" I understand," Clare said, nodding.

" I think you do!" Betty Smithers looked into Clare's face for a moment, and Clare sensed that the woman's instinctive hostility was evaporating. " Well if you look after Sue all right then you have nothing to worry about."

" How do you mean?" There was a frown on Clare's face as she looked at the housekeeper.

" They're very serious-minded in this house, and they'll soon let you know if you're not doing the right thing. Many's the time I've cried myself to sleep after Owen has bullied me over some housekeeping failure. But they're good men underneath all the toughness. I don't think you need to worry. In any case, the doctor is on your side, and they respect him."

" Well that's a relief." Clare smiled to show that she was not really worried. She had a job to do and that was all that mattered to her.

" Would you like to see Sue's room?"

"Yes please!" Clare nodded, and she felt easier as she followed Betty Smithers out of the room. They went along next door and Clare was pleased at the sight which awaited her in the child's room. Here again no expense had been spared to make the room comfortable, and Clare began to feel that she had nothing to worry about from people who could love a child so much. The great contrast in the rooms for Sue Harley and her new nurse and the rest of the house was so marked that Clare could not help but notice it.

" Have you seen Sue yet?" the housekeeper demanded, and she was becoming friendlier by the minute.

" Doctor Laverne is taking me into the hospital this evening to see her. I hope she's quite recovered from her injuries now."

" She wasn't so badly injured, and that seems to be a miracle to me, considering that her parents were both killed. Her father, Frank Harley, was the old man's favourite son, and although it doesn't show much on the surface, the master feels Frank's death very keenly. I don't know if you're aware of it, but Doctor Laverne said he thought of you for this post because you're so like Sue's mother to look at. The doctor said he thought it would help if we found someone who looked as much like Sue's mother as possible!"

" I didn't know!" Clare shook her head slowly as she considered. Was that the significant fact she had been looking for since her arrival? There had to be some reason why there was such a heavy atmosphere here at Oakapple Farm! Was it because she looked so much like Sue's mother? Was she bringing a dead woman back to life in the minds of these hard men? She could understand Grant's reasons in selecting her, and appreciated his intelligence in thinking of it, but what was medically right was not always socially right, and humans had a strange way of reacting against what was done in their interests.

" I don't know how Sue is going to take to you, and I can't help thinking that it won't help her to see someone like you who will remind her constantly of her dead mother."

" Am I that much like her?" Clare demanded.

" You're the same height and colouring, obviously, but

there is more to it than that. You do have a lot of the child's mother in your face. It's uncanny, but the doctor knew what he was talking about when he said everyone had a double in the world. But your double is dead now! She was Sue's mother!"

" We'll soon see what effect I have upon Sue," Clare said. "If it doesn't seem to be working then I'll leave immediately, of course."

" Wouldn't that worry you? Having to go off abruptly, I mean!"

" Not if it was in the best interest of my patient," Clare retorted.

" You must lead a hard life!"

" Why do you say that?"

" Because you have to steel yourself against human feelings and view your work objectively."

" You're quite perceptive. That's exactly what a nurse must do. But I've been guilty of failure lately and I've let my personal feelings enter into some of my cases. Consequently I've been suffering for it."

" Then this isn't the right kind of a case for you!" Betty Smithers shook her head slowly. " Little Sue will tug at your heart-strings. I've been to hospital to visit her, and she just lies there like a doll. She can't talk, and she had such a lovely little tongue. She was so forward it was almost unbelievable to hear her."

" The shock of what's happened will wear off and she'll get better," Clare said, nodding slowly. " But she may have a bad time getting back to rights, and that's why I've been called in. I shall need your help in the first days, telling me the child's likes and dislikes and that sort of thing. But once I get to know her I'll be able to handle her."

" She's such a little one! She's only just over the four years mark. Before the accident she could talk of nothing

but going to school. But her tender years are going to
be overshadowed, without a doubt."

" Does she know what's happened to her parents?"

" Yes. It was thought better to tell her when it was
discovered that she wasn't seriously injured."

" And was she dumb before they told her?"

" Yes! She hasn't spoken a word, to our knowledge,
since the day of the accident. That was about five weeks
ago!" Miss Smithers was beginning to talk animatedly,
and Clare could tell that she had won her over. She felt
a great deal of satisfaction as they left the child's room and
started down the stairs. Already the atmosphere seemed
less heavy!

Betty Smithers showed Clare back into the big sitting
room, and Grant looked around with a smile. He was seated
by the table, and got to his feet at her entrance. Clare looked
around and felt a little bit relieved when she saw that
Adam and Owen Harley had departed in her absence. Old
Cornelius got to his feet and seemed to bow slightly.

" I hope you liked your room," the old man said, and
his dark eyes seemed like polished ebony in his weatherbeaten, craggy face.

" It's beautiful!" There was pleasure in Clare's tones
and she made no effort to disguise it. " And Sue's room
is just perfect. I'm sure she'll be quite happy with
it."

" Good!" Cornelius nodded happily, and relief showed
for a moment on his ageing face. " The doctor and I have
been discussing ways and means of taking care of Sue.
But I'll leave it to him to work out something that will
help the child. Between you, the girl will be in very good
hands."

" We'll soon put her back to where she was before the
accident," Grant said cheerfully.

" But you won't be able to bring back her parents, and

they're the ones she is going to miss," the old man said
softly.

Clare was watching the old face closely, and she knew
the child was not the only one suffering. But she could feel
the deep sense of sympathy in the atmosphere
more keenly now, and she knew everything was going to be
all right. This family loved little Sue so much that they
had been jolted out of their habitual manner and forced
to accept swift changes in their household. It was nearly
always the case where a nurse was brought in, Clare
knew, and she was relieved to find herself believing that
Oakapple Farm would prove to be no different to other
cases.

" I must be on my way now," Grant said, glancing at his
watch. " I have some calls to make, and I'm standing
in for Dr. Betts. I shall be taking Nurse Crawford to the
hospital this evening so she can meet Sue, and there's
little more we can do until we see how the child accepts
her."

" That's true." The old man nodded. His dark eyes
lifted to Clare's intent face, and she watched him steadily.
"You accept that if the child does not take to you then your
case will be over before it starts!" he asked with some concern.

" Of course!" Clare smiled as she nodded. " The patient
comes first! Don't worry about anything, Mr. Harley.
Sue will be all right. She'll want for nothing, and we'll
soon have her back to normal."

" Thank you. If you can help her at all then I shall be
eternally grateful to you, Nurse. Perhaps we'd better talk
about your times of duty and that sort of thing! I don't
exactly know how you will work because we've never had
a nurse in the house before."

" Don't worry about that side of it!" Clare told him

instantly. " I shall be at Sue's side all the time she may need me, especially in the first days."

Grant was moving towards the door, and there was an easy expression on his face.

" I'll bring Nurse Crawford back here in the morning, Brigadier! She'll be here when Sue arrives from the hospital."

" Thank you!" The old man came across the room and ushered Clare to the door behind Grant. " I'm sure everything will be all right. This is a worrying time for us all, and I hope you'll forgive my sons for being human if they do seem a little hard and upset at the moment."

" I understand!" Clare said. " I shall slip into the routine of the house with no trouble at all. I shall always be in the background, and after a day or two no one will really notice me."

She was pleased as she departed with Grant, and when they were seated in his car he glanced at her with a grin on his face.

" Well?" he demanded as he started the engine.

" Well what?" she countered. " Was there supposed to be a great deal of difference here at the farm than in any of the other places I've been? I thought the family very nice, and not at all like the people I'd been told to expect to meet."

" They're all still rather shocked by the accident and the death of their brother Frank," Grant said. " But that will wear off in time!"

She nodded, but she was more than satisfied with what she had found awaiting her at Oakapple Farm. Betty Smithers was on her side, and would prove to be a good ally if needed in future. But the future was one thing that Clare never worried about. In her work she could only live in the present, and her world was a familiar one of nursing. Nothing would ever go wrong with that!

THREE

THAT SAME evening proved to be the most testing time that Clare experienced. Grant took her to the hospital, and they went along to the Children's ward, where they found Sue Harley lying in a bed in a corner. The first thing that Clare noticed about the child were the large brown eyes that stared lifelessly at her as they approached the bed. Grant bent over the girl and spoke to her in gentle tones, but there was no response, and Clare watched intently as Grant tried everything in his experience to get the girl to respond. At first he made no reference to Clare's presence, but eventually he turned and glanced at her, then looked back at the child.

"This is Nurse Crawford, Sue," he said. "She will be at the farm when you go home tomorrow. She's going to stay with you until you're really better."

The child looked up at Clare, but made no effort to speak, and her eyes seemed filled with the unspeakable horror which she had suffered in the accident.

"Hello, Sue," Clare said gently, moving to the side of the bed. "I expect you'll be very pleased to leave the hospital and go back to the farm."

Sue made no reply, but there seemed a brightness in her expressive eyes, and Clare smiled encouragingly. She felt touched by the sight of the slight figure under the bedcovers. The child was lost in a world of fear and grief, and it would not be simple to reach inside her mind and put matters right. It would need care and understanding and plenty of time to effect the right process that would lead to her cure. Clare knew she could do what was required of her but she had to have patience from the outset if she would hold any hope of doing the right thing.

" We'd better be going now, Sue," Grant said at length. " When they take you from here in the morning it will be to fetch you back to Oakapple Farm, so don't worry about being moved, will you? And Nurse Crawford will be at the farm waiting for you. She's going to be a great friend of yours in the days ahead, and when you feel like going out again you'll have her for company. Will you say goodbye now?"

Clare watched intently. The child turned her head slowly and looked at her, but made no effort to move her lips, and Clare smiled and reached out a gentle hand to stroke the girl's forehead.

" I shall see you tomorrow, Sue," she said. " You have a nice room at the farm, and it's next to mine. We'll have a lot of fun when you're really better. Goodbye, now!"

She turned away from the bed, smiling a farewell, and she saw the child blink a little before returning her eyes to Grant's intent face. Waiting for Grant at the door to the ward, Clare looked back and watched the scene that was being enacted in the corner. She saw Grant stroke the girl's forehead, and then he turned away and came towards Clare. He nodded slowly as he reached her side.

" I think you've made a good impression," he commented as he took her arm and led her from the ward. " She began to show some animation, although she made no effort to speak. I still don't know for certain if she's lost her power to speak or if she's deliberately witholding the ability in a psychological protest at what has happened to her world. But you'll find out, Clare, in the days ahead. I feel optimistic about this now." He broke off as a tall, powerfully built man came along the corridor towards them.

Clare, looking ahead, saw for herself that the newcomer was in a great hurry. " This is David Harley," Grant went on. " He's the youngest of the Harley boys, and the best of them, I think."

Clare felt her interest sharpen, and she looked at the newcomer with keen gaze. She could tell he was a Harley. He had the same dark, intense eyes and complexion, but his features seemed finer than his brother's and he smiled cheerfully when he saw Grant.

" Hello, Doctor!" he greeted. " I'm sorry I missed you at the farm this afternoon, but someone has to visit Sue each day." His eyes came to study Clare as he spoke, and she felt her pulses quicken slightly as his dark eyes took in all the details about her.

Grant introduced them, and Clare felt her hand being grasped and shaken. She smiled in answer, and murmured some conventional greeting.

" I didn't come in too early this evening because I knew you were bringing Nurse Crawford to see Sue," David Harley went on, still watching Clare's face. " I do hope you're going to like being at the farm, Nurse. I fixed up your room as best I could."

" It's very nice!" Clare smiled as she acknowledged his words. She was telling herself that life wouldn't be so bad at the farm after all, if her instincts were correct in their first impressions of this man.

" How is Sue?" Harley went on. " Did she speak?"

" No! You mustn't expect too much, David. Give the child time to get over her shock. You haven't got over it yet, have you?"

" I certainly haven't, and it will take me a long, long time to do so. But it isn't so bad for us! We can take it. Poor Sue is just a child, little more than a baby, and she's so helpless." His tones quivered with emotion, and Clare felt a pang go through her at the sound of it. She caught and held her breath for a moment, and then let it go in a long, silent sigh.

"You'd better go in and see Sue before the visiting period comes to an end," Grant said. "I shall be dropping Nurse Crawford off at the farm in the morning about ten."

"I'll see you then!" David Harley looked once more into Clare's blue eyes, and he nodded. He was friendly and completely lacking the strained manner of his two older brothers. "I'm so pleased you're coming to take care of Sue. She really needs someone like you. I must say you do look a lot like Sue's mother!"

Grant reached out and patted David Harley's shoulder. "See you in the morning, David," he said.

Harley nodded, and smiled at Clare, then went on his way, and Clare could not help turning to watch his departure. When she looked back at Grant she found his eyes upon her, and he nodded slowly as he took her arm and led her from the hospital.

"I've been banking on David Harley helping to make your life easy at the farm," he said. "David and his father are all for your presence in their home, but Owen and Adam Harley were bitterly against it."

"Why?"

"I don't know! They all think the world of the child and want the best done for her. But Adam is a woman-hater and Owen is too bad tempered to find anyone interested enough to want to know him permanently."

"Adam is a woman-hater!" Clare ejaculated.

"Well he had an unfortunate experience with a girl, and that put him against women completely. He was engaged to be married at one time, before I came into the district, and she went off and married another man. He never got over it, and seems to have crawled back into his shell since the incident. Owen you know about, and David seems to be the only one who is quite normal."

"What happened to their mother?" Clare demanded.

"She was knocked down and killed one night on the main road near the farm. They say she didn't have a very good life with Cornelius. He was always a bit too regimental for a woman, and the boys take after him. But since that day the only woman who's been permitted to stay at the farm is Betty Smithers, and she's there because her husband was killed in an accident at the farm and they felt they owed her something."

"They are not strangers to grief then!" Clare observed. "No wonder they feel bitter about what's happened to Sue's parents. It seems as if tragedy is marking them down!"

"No doubt that's the way they look at it too!" Grant opened a car door for Clare and she got into her seat. He walked around the car and got in behind the wheel, and for a moment he sat motionless, thinking over the situation.

Clare narrowed her eyes and peered into the bright sunlight of the evening. Her thoughts were racing, piecing together all the items of information and all the impressions she had gained from the day's experiences. Through the many veils of fact that clung to her mind, Sue Harley's face came clearest, and Clare found herself suffering for the child in her tragic loss. She knew they would be very close together in the future, and she hoped and prayed that she would be able to justify her presence, that she would be able to help the child.

"I don't think there's much else I can tell you, Clare," Grant said as he started the car and drove from the park, heading in the direction of the village. "You're a cool, level-headed girl and you know what your duties are. I don't suppose you'll be able to get away from the Farm very often in the first week or two, but don't try to overdo things, will you?"

" I certainly did the right thing by getting in touch with you, didn't I?" he demanded.

" You were a godsend!" she replied.

Amanda appeared in the doorway, and a shadow crossed Grant's face as he turned and saw her.

" Don't tell me you've got a call for me!" he said sharply.

"I'm afraid it's Mr. Jefferson!" his wife replied.

" Well I was afraid they would have to send for me when I saw him this morning. He hasn't much longer to live and there's nothing I can do for him except drug him to make him a little more comfortable. When did you get the call, Mandy?"

" About thirty minutes ago."

" I ought to have called you from the hospital," he retorted. " I'll be on my way now. See you later!" He grinned at Clare. " I expect Mandy will make you a cup of tea, and I'd like one when I get back. I'll be about thirty minutes."

They stood and watched him depart, and then Clare looked into Amanda's brown eyes and found the girl studying her.

" How did you get on at the hospital?" Amanda demanded.

" I don't think there will be much trouble with Sue when I get her home! Poor child! She looked so pathetic!"

" Did you see David Harley?"

" Yes! He came in as we were leaving. He seemed a very nice person to me; not at all like his brothers."

" David is the best one of the three!" Amanda smiled as she led the way into the house. " That doesn't sound too pleasant, does it? But the other two are rather surly, and David has a nice way about him. He runs the accounts on the farm, and doesn't get out into the fields like Adam does. He's the real farming type, and isn't happy unless he's out there in all weathers, getting dirt on his hands."

" And what about Owen? He doesn't strike me as being the type to dirty his hands."

" He doesn't! From what I've seen of him I'd say he lives the life of a gentleman. You'll often see him riding his horse across the fields, but he isn't keen on working."

Clare nodded, and she was thoughtful as they went into the little kitchen and Amanda made tea. There was a picture of David Harley in her mind, and she found herself thinking that he would be a good friend to have. She let her thoughts run away with her until Amanda set the tea tray on the table before her.

" Grant is taking me to the farm at around ten in the morning, so I'll be there when Sue arrives from hospital!" Clare looked into the girl's eyes. Amanda was smiling. " It's good of you to put me up for the night!"

" Nonsense! It's good of you to interrupt your holiday and take the case," came the swift reply. " You're all that Grant says you are, Clare. Before I met you I was a little jealous of you, making my husband admire you the way he so obviously does. But now I've met you I can understand why he enthuses about you, and I'm not feeling jealous in any way. You're a good person, and I do hope that one day you'll find happiness such as I know with Grant."

" Do I look as if I need someone to make me happy?" Clare asked softly, and she saw the girl nod briefly.

" You're not completely happy, are you?" Amanda demanded.

" No! I've been putting it down to the cases I've been handling lately, but I don't think they are totally to blame. There's something much deeper that's affecting me and I can't get to the bottom of it."

" Perhaps it is the subconscious knowledge that you

need someone to love!" Amanda was quite serious as she stared at Clare.

"I wouldn't like to let that thought take root in my mind," Clare said slowly. She was thinking of Tim Millard as she spoke, and a shudder rippled through her. He had been the only man in the world ever to get close to her, and he'd let her down pretty badly. After that episode she had been shy of making personal contacts, and had thrown herself all the harder into her work. Perhaps that was why she had been getting more hurt lately! She was giving everything to her duties and getting nothing in return. There had to be a fine balance in all things, and it seemed that she was sadly out of balance emotionally.

"You've been unlucky in a love affair, haven't you?" Amanda asked softly as she poured their tea. "It isn't any of my business, Clare, but you have all the earmarks of that particular disaster."

"I thought perhaps I'd be over it by now," Clare replied, smiling. "It wasn't so much a broken love affair either, because I wasn't that much emotionally involved. But I got quite a shock, and that did take some getting over."

"It happens to all of us at one time or another. But you were alone as well, and it's always more difficult to take such blows if there isn't a mother somewhere in the background."

"That's why I feel so for Sue Harley!" Clare spoke softly, and there was a trembling inside her which hurt. "The poor child has no one to turn to now."

"She has," Amanda said softly. "She's got you now, Clare."

"I'll do as a stand-in! But it isn't like having a real mother on hand." Clare spoke from experience, and knew what she was talking about. She sighed as her past flashed through her mind.

Clare nodded thoughtfully. She was aware of the true situation, and she knew the next few days would be highly critical and vital to little Sue Harley. She pictured the child's elfin face, and a cold hand seemed to grasp at her heart with poignant fingers.

"I think we'll manage," she said confidently. "Unless my instincts are all wrong in this case, I think we're going to succeed, and quickly."

"I think it will be quickly or not at all!" Grant studied her face for a moment. "It depends what the Harleys want!"

"How do you mean?" Clare frowned as she met his gaze. "They want the child to get well, don't they? Sue Harley is all they've got left of their son Frank and his wife."

"Frank they miss, yes," Grant said. "But they hated the very ground his wife walked upon. They never made her welcome at Oakapple Farm, and the poor girl must have regretted the day she married into the family."

"I don't understand!" Clare said.

"There's a lot I don't understand, Clare, and I've lived around here all my life!" Amanda spoke slowly, but her voice was low and intense. "However you'll get a first rate chance to study the Harleys at close quarters, and don't forget that we're at the other end of a telephone wire, if you should need us."

"There you go again," Clare said. "Before I went to Oakapple Farm this afternoon you were both warning me against the Harleys, but when I met them they seemed quite ordinary people to me. I really don't think there is anything to be careful about. If you do know anything specific about any of the brothers then I wish you would tell me about it. Should I be on my guard for some unknown reason?"

"I don't know for certain, but there can be no harm

in being prepared," Grant said easily. " I am responsible for your coming here, Clare, and I'd be a fool not to take all precautions possible."

" What do you think could happen to me at Oakapple Farm?" Clare demanded.

He shook his head, and Clare looked at Amanda, who shook her head slowly.

" There are a lot of rumours about the Harleys," Amanda said. " It doesn't pay to repeat any of them, but one cannot help hearing them, and it's only natural to think there cannot be fire without smoke. So be careful, Clare, please!"

" All right! But what do I guard against, and how?" Clare shook her head in wonderment.

" Look, we're probably putting thoughts into your mind which have no right to be there," Grant said. " Let's call a halt to this. You'll have to play it by ear. Don't forget my telephone number."

" I'll agree to that!" Clare nodded slowly, but she was more than a little puzzled by what had been said, and there was a frown on her face as she tried to reason out what had caused Grant and Amanda to talk in such a fashion.

She was still puzzling when it was time to retire, and she went up to her room with their words of warning still pounding in her mind. But her main thoughts were for the child still in hospital, and Clare did her best not to let wrong impressions take root in her thoughts. She wanted nothing to complicate the relationship which she had to strike between herself and her patient, and it didn't matter to her what the situation at Oakapple Farm was. Betty Smithers was there and seemed to be happy enough in the employ of the Harleys, and a nurse would not overburden the household.

FOUR

PROMPTLY AT ten Clare stepped out of Grant's car in front of the big farmhouse, and Betty Smithers appeared in the doorway of the house so quickly that Clare was certain the woman had been watching for her arrival.

"I'll be in touch," Grant said, taking Clare's suitcase from the back of the car. "Sue will be home in about thirty minutes, so it will give you a chance to settle in here before she arrives. Keep her quiet for a day or so, but if she feels like moving around then let her do so."

Clare nodded, and she walked at his side to the big front door, where Betty greeted her warmly and took the suitcase from Grant.

"I'll leave her in your hands, Miss Smithers," Grant said. "I'll be in touch, Clare. Can't stop any longer. See you later."

"Goodbye, Grant," Clare said, and she stood on the step and watched him depart with mixed feelings. She couldn't help feeling uncomfortable after the warnings she had received, but in the bright light of day those warnings just didn't seem real. She sighed a little as Grant drove away, then turned to find Betty Smithers watching her. "There is one thing," Clare said slowly. "Grant called you Miss Smithers!"

"That's right. I took my maiden name again after my husband died. I didn't want people to hear me being called Mrs. and have them wondering about my husband."

Clare nodded. She would have been sensitive like that,

she told herself, and she liked Betty Smithers a little more because the woman showed the same kind of weaknesses that Clare herself suffered.

"I'll take you up to your room and you can sort out your clothes before Sue arrives. Will you be wearing your uniform while on duty?"

"I ought to have asked Mr. Harley about that!" Clare considered for a moment. "Usually I wear uniform all the time when I'm nursing an adult, but with Sue it might be better not to in order to help her forget about hospitals and that sort of thing."

"I agree with you!" Betty nodded emphatically and led the way into the hall. She set down Clare's suitcase and faced her. "I'll go and have a word with Mr. Cornelius. He's in his study. Wait a moment and we'll hear what his views on the subject are."

Clare nodded and the housekeeper went off, leaving her alone, and silence descended abruptly and seemed to close in about Clare. Again she sensed the heaviness in the atmosphere, and recalled that strange houses seemed to hold hostility until one became accustomed to them.

A door banged somewhere, and then footsteps sounded in the hall at her back. Clare turned slowly, to find David Harley coming towards her. He was smiling, and she felt relieved to see him.

"Good morning!" he greeted. "Glad to see you here! Sue will be home soon. Is someone taking care of you?"

"Yes thank you!" Clare smiled. She explained the situation, and he glanced down at a sheaf of papers in his hand.

"Betty will take good care of you. It will be great to have Sue back with us! I've been waiting for this day."

Clare felt no intuitive reservations about him, she realised. He seemed perfectly normal and straightforward.

His brothers seemed to create tension inside her, and she wondered if that was the result of the impressions she had gained from what had been said by Grant and Amanda. But she could face this man without thought of what had been said. She sensed there was nothing shadowy in his background.

Betty Smithers came back from her visit to Cornelius Harley's study, and she smiled in friendly fashion.

" The Brigadier says it will be all right for you not to wear uniform while you're on duty," the woman said. She barely glanced at David. " I'll take your case up to your room for you."

" Is my father in his study, Betty?" David demanded.

" Yes, Mr. David. You'll find him there."

" Then I'll see you later, Nurse!" He smiled at Clare and moved away, and Clare nodded in acknowledgement.

She followed the housekeeper up the stairs and into her room. Betty Smithers seemed to have changed her manner now, and was in an uncommunicative mood.

" I'll give you a call when Sue arrives," the woman said softly as she departed, and Clare thanked her and turned to unpack her suitcase as the door closed.

The window of the room was opened slightly, but the interior was still warm. Clare walked to the window and pushed it wide. She leaned on the sill and looked out over the small garden. When she thought of the glinting water she had seen when Amanda showed her Oakapple Farm for the first time she felt a strange yearning to be by the water's edge, and she smiled faintly as she straightened and returned to her unpacking.

She was feeling a little bit strange, but that was always the case in a new position. It would wear off after a few days. But there seemed to be more in the atmosphere than she cared to admit, and she wondered about it as she finished her unpacking.

She heard the car approaching that brought Sue Harley home, and Clare was a little surprised when she looked from her window to see Owen Harley driving it. The car stopped before the front door and Owen alighted, coming around to open the nearside door. Clare watched, smiling a little when Sue Harley appeared, hugging a big doll.

Moving away from the window, Clare was about to go down to meet her charge when she paused as a thought struck her. No doubt the family would want the child to themselves for a few moments. Betty Smithers had said she would come for Clare when she was needed. She sat down on the foot of her bed to await the summons.

It was only a few moments later when there was a tap at the door, and Clare got to her feet as she called out an invitation to enter. She was surprised, when the door opened, to see David Harley standing there, and he smiled as he met her sharp gaze.

" I'm sorry. I thought Betty was coming up for me," Clare said.

" She's got Sue with her, and the child won't go with anyone else," he replied. " Would you come down and take charge?"

" Certainly. I expect we'll find Sue a bit bewildered by this sudden change from hospital. This is her first time out since the accident."

" I agree with you. I think you ought to have gone to the hospital to collect her. I talked of you last night after you and Doctor Laverne had gone."

" Did you? That's a good thing! It will help me get closer to her more quickly." Clare looked up into his face as they walked to the stairs. He was darkly handsome, she was thinking, and tried to tear her mind from the thought. She had to concentrate upon her duty!

" I don't think you'll have any problems with Sue. She

has recovered from the injuries she received in the accident."

" Her physical injuries," Clare said.

He nodded, and she saw his face harden a little. " Of course! Mental scars can be worse than physical injuries, can't they?"

" In a case like this. But we must hope for the best."

They descended the stairs and Clare was conscious of a tension seeping into her. David led the way into a sitting-room, and Clare paused on the threshold when she saw Cornelius Harley and Owen standing over Betty Smithers, who was holding Sue on her lap. The men moved away as Clare approached, and Owen caught Clare's eye for a moment. There was a sharp expression on his face, and she saw him glance at his brother David.

" Here's the nurse, Sue," Betty Smithers said in gentle tones. " You met her last night, didn't you?"

Clare looked into the child's face and smiled. She could see tension in the dark eyes, and the small hands were clutched tightly around the neck of a big doll. Clare moved to a seat beside the housekeeper and reached out and touched the doll.

" That's a lovely doll you have, Sue," she said. " What's her name?"

A silence followed the question, and Clare could sense that all attention was focused upon her. She sensed that these men expected her to work some kind of miracle with this child. They didn't know that time itself was needed to unlock the girl's mind.

" Would you like to see your room?" Clare continued, talking softly to the child. " It's very nice. It's next to mine."

Without hesitation Sue Harley turned to Clare and lifted her arms to her, letting the doll fall to the ground. Clare got to her feet and took hold of the child, smiling as the tiny arms locked around her neck and the small body pressed hard against her. Betty picked up the doll as Clare turned to survey the three men watching her.

" I'll take her up to her room now," Clare said. " She must be kept very quiet for the first day or two."

" I can see that you're going to be able to handle her very well," Cornelius Harley said in heavy tones. " I'm very glad that you're here, Nurse."

Clare nodded and started to the door, and David Harley went with her, opening the door for her and following her into the hall. He closed the door behind them and escorted her to the stairs. Clare could hardly breathe because Sue was clinging to her so tightly, but she was relieved that the child had taken to her, and she held the girl gently as they ascended the stairs.

" Is she heavy?" David demanded, and he placed a supporting hand under Clare's elbow.

The child seemed to cringe away from him, and he noticed and moved away again.

" You're not afraid of me, are you, Sue?" he asked gently, and put a hand upon the girl's head. There was silence, and Clare looked down into the child's face. Dark eyes looked up appealingly at her.

" You're not afraid of anyone, are you, Sue?" Clare said, and fancied the girl shook her head ever so slightly.

When they reached the girl's room, David opened the door, and he looked into Clare's face as she passed him in the doorway.

" If there's anything at any time that you want then just call me," he said. " I'm usually in the house all day, and you know where my office is, don't you?"

Clare nodded and he departed. She closed the door of the room and took Sue across to the bed, sitting down on the foot of it and holding the child on her lap.

" Isn't this a nice room, Sue?" she demanded lightly.

" Look at the lovely wallpaper! All giraffes and bears and animals from the zoo. Have you ever been to a zoo?"

The child looked at her silently, and Clare waited for some sort of a response, but there was nothing, and Clare went on to talk about other things. She wouldn't push the girl. There was time enough later to try and get her to act normally.

" Are you feeling tired? This is your first day out of hospital, and you will feel strange until you've settled down here again. When you are accustomed to being home we'll go out for walks. It will do you good to get out into the sunshine."

Sue did not try to answer, but she crawled off Clare's lap and lay down on the bed. Clare stood up and moved to the window.

" You can see the water from here. We'll have to go along there when you feel better and see if there are any fish."

There was a tap at the door and when it opened Betty Smithers appeared, carrying some linen over one arm. She smiled at Clare and stood looking down at Sue, who closed her eyes and lay as if asleep.

" She'll be all right!" Betty said.

" I'm sure she will!" Clare nodded. " After a few days we shall see some improvement."

" They're all very pleased with the way Sue took to you," the housekeeper said. " Even Owen admitted that it was right a nurse should be here."

" He didn't think so before my arrival?" Clare queried.

Betty smiled slowly. " There were a lot of harsh words said about employing a nurse," she said. " David was for it, but then he always agrees with his father. Adam didn't think it would be a good idea, and Owen was positively against it."

Clare nodded slowly. That was how she had summed

up the situation. She glanced down at the now sleeping child and nodded slowly. There was nothing to worry about here. She had her patient to care for, and everyone was concerned about her welfare.

" You'll be taking your meals with Sue," Betty went on, and it was evident to Clare that matters had been discussed since she had brought Sue to her room. " The Brigadier thinks it would be better if Sue was kept isolated for a few days until she gets used to being here. Then you'll have your meals with the family. You have to become part of the family in order to give Sue the proper attention she needs."

" They want me to be a mother to the child," Clare said. " I don't know if that would be a good thing or not."

" It can only help her!" Betty's blue eyes were steady as she looked at Clare.

" At the outset, I agree. But what happens when it is time for me to leave here? Sue is going to be so attached to me that it might put her back to lose me!"

" That angle hasn't been considered!" Betty pulled a face as she considered. " You think it would be better if you maintained a nurse and patient relationship with Sue?"

" Certainly! Of course she won't miss out on affection and care, but there must be this gulf between us or I'll never be able to terminate the case successfully."

" I'm inclined to agree with you!" Betty glanced down at the child's immobile face, and there was sympathy showing in every line of her countenance. " I suggest you carry on as you think fit. No one here knows much about your business, and you should know what's best."

" I'll always do what I think is best for the patient," Clare said.

" I'm glad you're here. I don't mind telling you that I was against your coming when I first heard the decision to employ a nurse. I thought I could give Sue everything she needed. But I can see now that I was wrong, and I'm pleased you're here."

"Thank you!" Clare sensed that the woman was genuine. "I'm happy to know that you feel this way now."

"But watch out for Adam and Owen!" Betty lowered her tones as if she suspected that the two men were eavesdropping at the door. "I don't see what they can do about you now you're here and installed, but they don't want you here and they might try to make your life intolerable."

"I don't think they'll go that far!" Clare smiled slowly. "I believe they want nothing but Sue's complete recovery, so they'll be on my side."

"I hope you're right!" Concern tinged the woman's tones. "I don't think Adam would go too far, although he's deep and moody at times. But Owen has such a violent temper that sometimes I'm afraid of him."

"Really! Has he ever threatened violence towards you?"

"No!" Betty shook her head. "It's what he makes you think he might do that causes most of the fear. I've seen him in some frightful rages, and even his father can't control him when he gets like that."

"That sounds bad. Has Sue ever seen him like that?"

"No! She was hardly ever here before the accident. Her mother wasn't too highly thought of here so she didn't come unless it was strictly necessary."

"So Sue is as strange to this house as I am!" Clare nodded slowly. She was trying to form a picture of the situation.

"Her father used to bring her here on his own, more often than not. His wife was never welcomed."

"I find that difficult to understand!"

"A lot of people might agree with you, but none from around here."

" But you stay here!" Clare watched the woman's face closely, and she saw Betty smile thinly.

" They feel guilty about me. It wasn't entirely an accident when my husband was killed!"

" Not an accident?" Clare felt horror start through her, and she stared at Betty with a frown on her face.

" I didn't mean that entirely as it sounded. What I really meant was that the accident was partly due to negligence on Owen's part."

" Oh!" Clare was not certain what Betty meant, but she felt it better not to pursue the subject. The woman moved away, and she was smiling thinly as she departed. But she paused in the doorway of the room and glanced back at Clare. " I'll call you in time for lunch. Will you have it up here in this room, or come down with Sue?"

" I'll let you know at the time. I don't know how long she'll sleep!" Clare glanced at the child, her face softening a little as she did so. " She must get plenty of rest while she can."

Betty nodded and went off, and Clare turned with a sigh when she was alone. She watched the child's face for some moments, and could hear the gentle, regular breathing. She nodded slowly as she considered. The house was silent and for the first time there was not that sense of heavy foreboding which she had found so noticeable before. Now there was a child here, and that seemed to make all the difference.

Sue slept for two hours, and Clare was on hand when the child returned to her senses. She had been standing by the window, lost in thought, when she heard a movement on the bed, and when she turned quickly she saw the child sitting up and rubbing her eyes.

" Hello, Sue," she greeted cheerfully, going to the bedside. " You have slept for a long time. Do you feel all the better for it?"

The girl looked up at her, and Clare stared into the dark eyes, looking for some sign of emotion, but there was nothing, and she sat down on the foot of the bed and took hold of the child's hand.

" Are you hungry? Shall we go down and see what we can get for lunch?"

Sue looked up into her face, then reached out with her small arms, and she encircled Clare's neck and clung tightly to her. Clare stood up and carried the child from the room, descending the stairs and walking along the corridor to the kitchen. She found Betty in the kitchen, and the woman exclaimed heartily at sight of them.

" My, you have had a long sleep! I'll bet you're hungry right now. What shall we do for you? Do you like lettuce?" The woman glanced at Clare. " I don't know what she likes, but I thought a salad would suffice.' '

" I'm sure she'll like that!" Clare nodded. " We'll sit in here, shall we?"

" The family have eaten. They all believe in an early lunch. Adam came in from the fields and went on out again as soon as he'd eaten. I don't know where Owen went off to, but he went out in his car. David is busy in his study. He has a lot of paperwork to do."

Clare listened to Betty's idle chatter as she and Sue had their lunch, and afterwards the housekeeper sat down at the child's side and took hold of Sue's hand. But Sue looked towards Clare, who smiled reassuringly.

" You did eat a lot," Betty said. " I'm glad, Sue. It is a pointer in the right direction. But what are you going to do this afternoon?"

" What would Sue like to do?" Clare asked. She did not pause because she knew the child would not answer. " Would you like to go outside for a walk?"

There was a slight nod from Sue, and Clare smiled as she got to her feet.

" We'll wash your face and hands and then go out and look around the gardens," she said.

Sue slid off her seat and took hold of Clare's hand. Betty opened the kitchen door for them.

" I'm happy now she's home," the housekeeper remarked. " She is what's needed around here to lighten the gloom that's fallen over this house. An innocent child has the power to put right what has slowly been going wrong for a long time."

Clare said nothing to that, and she led Sue from the kitchen. When they reached the bottom of the stairs Sue paused and held up her arms to be picked up. Clare swung the child from the ground and held her tightly, and as they began to ascend the stairs, David Harley called from the passage that led towards his study.

" What are your plans for this afternoon?" he demanded.

Clare paused on the bottom stair and turned to look at him.

" I thought I'd take Sue out into the grounds," she said. " I'd like to look at the lake myself. It's such a hot day, and I'm sure Sue would like some fresh air."

" May I come out with you?" he asked. " I feel stifled myself."

" I'd be pleased to have your company," Clare responded immediately. " I'm just taking Sue upstairs to wash her face and hands."

" I'll wait down here for you then," he said.

When they went out into the grounds, Clare carried Sue in her arms. The child was small for her age, and she clung to Clare in silence, her dark eyes wide and expressive as they walked through the flower gardens to one side of the house. Clare said nothing at first, feeling a little awkward in David's company, and he didn't say much beyond commenting upon the weather and the scenery.

Sue saw the lake and pointed to it, and Clare turned her feet in that direction. David saw the child's action and nodded slowly.

"We'll have to keep her away from the water," he said. "She was a terror for getting down there when she was younger. She fell in once and my brother only just managed to fish her out." There was a thin smile on his face as he spoke, and he nodded slowly. "I can't help thinking there must be a curse upon this household," he went on. "The things that have happened to my family in the past!"

Clare watched his profile as he stared at the lake, and there were shadows in his dark eyes. She held Sue tightly when they reached the waterside, and the child clung to her, narrowing her eyes against the sun's reflected glare from the placid surface.

"It would be nice to have a boat on the lake," Clare commented.

"We have one in the boathouse that's just around the bend from here," he replied. "Adam uses it for fishing in the centre of the lake. I'll take you out in it one day if you'd really like to go, but you'd have to keep hold of Sue all the time." He turned and smiled at the child, coming close to stroke her dark cheek, and Sue stared into his eyes and remained motionless. "Is she ever going to talk again?" he demanded shortly.

"I should think so. Her condition is caused by shock, of course, so there's no way of knowing how long she'll stay like this, but as time goes on she will recover. I'm sure of it."

"Poor little mite!" His voice was husky. "What will become of her?"

"She'll be all right. She's young and she'll forget as she grows older. Soon all of this will be just a dream, and that will lessen as the years pass."

" We're the ones who suffer the most," he went on softly, staring down at the bright surface of the lake, and his dark brows were drawn together, his teeth clenched. His voice wavered slightly as he went on. " Frank went out in a temper the night they were killed. He should never have driven a car. He was like Owen in that respect. They both have wicked tempers. But I can't help thinking that Frank would be alive now if he hadn't lost his temper."

" Do you want to tell me what happened?" she asked softly, and Sue clutched her more tightly around the neck.

" I don't want to talk about it. Frank was the brother I cared most about. It wasn't that he was my favourite, but we seemed to be closer together than any of the others. There seemed to be a bond between us! I can't explain it, but now he's dead, and it's hard to accept the fact that I'll never see him again."

Clare remained silent, for there was nothing she could say that would help. Time took care of these things, and Time could not be hurried. But she felt great sympathy for him. He was the only one who showed that he was human, she thought, and her mind began dwelling upon the family generally. That was one of the things she could not understand, she told herself. Owen had his bad temper, but Adam was almost emotionless. Apart from that none of them seemed really human. They were lacking something, and Clare thought she knew what that something was. She felt that they were insensitive to everything outside their own particular circle. They didn't want to know about the rest of the world. They couldn't care less about outsiders.

But David wasn't like that, and she sensed that he was a very lonely man. He was the one who had visited Sue in hospital!

FIVE

THE AFTERNOON seemed never ending, and Sue didn't once complain either by expression or gesture of the brightness and the heat. They sat by the water's edge and enjoyed the scenery and the peacefulness. David talked a lot about the past, but didn't really say much about his family, and Clare listened attentively, hoping to learn as much as possible.

Sue eventually fell asleep on her lap, resting her dark little head against Clare's shoulder, and a breeze came and ruffled the child's hair.

" I suppose we'd better go back to the house," David said at length, and Sue stirred uneasily at his words and then lifted her head to peer around. She looked into Clare's face and clung to her in relief.

" Did you think I wouldn't be here?" Clare demanded gently, and hugged the girl.

" You've certainly got a way with children," David commented. " I'm greatly relieved that you're here." He sighed heavily and shook his head. " There was quite a row when it was decided to get in a nurse."

" So I gather. But what were the main reasons against the idea? It must have been agreed that the child's health came first."

" That's true. There were no arguments about that, but the fact that a woman would have to be admitted to the house didn't sit well with either Adam or Owen."

" Don't they like women?" Clare watched his face for

expression as she asked the question. " You're all bachelors, aren't you?"

" Frank was the only one who married, and now he's dead!"

" That's a strange thing to say! Surely you don't blame his death upon his marriage!"

" Did it sound like that?" His lips twisted a little as he spoke. " In a way it could be put like that. After Frank married he seemed to become an outsider in the family. It was something that Owen had said that night which made Frank lose his temper and go off in such a rage."

" Something about Frank's wife, or women generally?" Clare asked.

" Owen was always making remarks about Frank's wife!" David spoke in low, intense tones. " He made it sound as if he were joking, but I knew he wasn't, and so did Frank."

Clare pictured Owen's dark features and nodded slowly. He seemed the kind of man who could become aroused. But she couldn't for the life of her imagine why he didn't like women. Girls must have found him attractive! It was Adam who had been let down by a girl, and Adam was the quiet one. But there had to be a reason for Owen's manner.

" I think we'd better get back to the house now!" David got to his feet and held out his hands to Sue. " Shall I carry you back?" he asked.

The girl turned away from him and put her arms around Clare's neck. He stared down at them for some moments, then took Clare's elbow and helped her up.

" You've worked your charm on Sue," he remarked as they walked along the path that led to the house. " It's a relief to know that she will be taken care of. I didn't feel like leaving her to Betty." He glanced at Clare as he spoke. " I didn't mean that exactly how it sounded. Betty is all right! But Sue was always a little bit afraid of her before the accident."

"We're going to be great friends aren't we, Sue?" Clare demanded, looking down at the girl.

Sue did not reply, but she looked into Clare's eyes unblinkingly, and Clare smiled fondly at her, showing her concern and feelings. It was the only way the child could gain confidence. Sue would begin to respond when she felt the need to, and until that day Clare would have to wait and hope, just watching for signals.

When they reached the house David excused himself and went off around to the rear, leaving Clare to enter alone with Sue. Clare was thoughtful as she took her charge to the kitchen. She had learned something this afternoon about the Harley family, but could not say exactly what it was she had discovered. Owen seemed to be the one to watch out for, and she reminded herself to stay well out of his way at all times.

Betty was in the kitchen preparing tea, and she turned with a smile as they entered.

"I'll bet you can do with a nice cup of tea, eh?" she demanded. "Where have you been all afternoon?"

Clare explained as she sat Sue down at the table, and she saw a shadow cross Betty's face.

"Have I said something wrong?" she demanded.

"No! It will be a good thing for you to make friends with David. But Owen won't like it. He was talking about the stresses that a woman coming here could impose upon them."

"Really? What's wrong with him that he can't take a woman's presence in his stride? It was Adam who was jilted, wasn't it?"

"Did David tell you about that?" Betty demanded.

"No!" Clare shook her head. "Are you interested in David, Betty?"

"Why do you ask?"

"You sounded as if the last thing you wanted me to do was get to know David." Clare felt that she could talk plainly to the woman.

"It isn't that! David would never look at the likes of me!" Betty smiled thinly and shook her head. "I'm thirty-four now. I'm a widow. No one would look at me."

"You're wrong there, surely! Aren't you interested in meeting anyone else?"

"No. There were times when I thought I might, but after I came here to work I had only to mention to any-one living locally that I was the housekeeper and I was left quite alone. No other man wants to know me."

"Why not? Because you are the housekeeper here, or because they fear the Harley men?" Clare was still striving to discover exactly what the situation was here. There were glimpses for her, but not enough to give her facts. David had said several things that sounded significant, but the complete picture eluded her still, and she looked at the housekeeper and wondered what lay at the bottom of all the passions and emotions that seemed to have built up into a high and wide barrier between this family and the rest of the world.

"Don't get the wrong idea about this place," Betty said. "I know I've been warning you; not in so many words but trying to get you to read things between the lines, so to speak. But you'll be all right here, Clare, if you don't start falling in love with one or another of the men in this family."

"I'm not likely to do that!" Clare smiled at the thought. "I have a golden rule, Betty, that I never break. I never become involved with the family of my patient."

"That sounds like commonsense." The housekeeper

smiled and turned away. " Now what about some tea, Sue?"

Clare looked down at the child. She had almost forgotten her presence because she didn't speak. But Sue was looking at her with a kind of appeal in her dark eyes.

" Is there something you want, Sue?" she demanded.

.The girl pointed to a chair opposite, and Clare smiled as she moved around the table and sat down.

The kitchen door opened abruptly and Clare looked up to see Owen Harley peering in. There was a scowl on his dark face, and her heart seemed to miss a beat as she caught his eye. He stared at her for a moment, then closed the door again, and she heard his feet departing along the corridor. Betty turned from the stove, a boiling kettle in her hand.

" Who was that?" she demanded.

" Owen, and he seemed in a bad mood." Clare forced herself to speak lightly, but she was aware that her hands were trembling and she clasped them tightly as she returned her attention to Sue.

" He's hardly ever in a good mood," Betty said. " I don't know what's wrong with him, I'm sure. You'd think with his position and wealth he'd be the happiest man alive."

" Money isn't everything," Clare retorted.

" Perhaps not, but it goes a long way towards helping make a person happy."

Clare was nervous while they had tea. She half expected Owen Harley to return to the kitchen and start shouting at her for some unknown reason. But they were not disturbed, and when Sue had eaten her fill, Clare decided to take the child up to her room. Sue was looking sleepy, and this was her first full day out of a hospital bed. She needed a good rest.

" Come along, Sue!" Clare held out her arms to the

child and Sue got off her chair and hurried to her. " Let's go and have a nap, shall we? "

She swept the child up into her arms and smiled at Betty as she moved to the door.

" See you later," the woman said. " Come down and have a chat with me if you can find the time. I'm always here."

Clare agreed, and carried Sue into the hall. She frowned when she heard the sound of raised voices somewhere in one of the rooms, and saw a half open door that led into David's study. She paused as she reached the foot of the stairs, and could not help overhearing what was being said. It was Owen who was talking loudly, and in anger-filled tones.

" I tell you we can't have her staying here. She'll have to go. I'm not going to accept any responsibility, David, and you know you can't. I was against her coming here in the first place, but you and Father were against me. Sue would be all right with Betty, and we don't have to worry about Betty. But this girl will have to go. We can't have her wandering around the house. It isn't right."

" I'll keep a close eye on her," David replied stoutly. " As soon as Sue recovers her speech then the nurse will go."

" That's not the point and you know it. We've been over all this before and there's no use beating over old ground. She should never have been permitted to come here, and I want to see her out of the house as soon as possible."

The door was shut loudly then, and Clare started nervously and began to ascend the stairs. There was a frown on her lovely face, and she clasped Sue tighter as they reached the girl's room. The words she had overheard were heavy in her mind, and she felt a little bit hurt that her presence should cause so much upset in this family.

She had begun to see David as the only one she could look to for support. He had seemed friendly from the outset, whereas the others were strangely resentful of her presence. But she realised that she was not going to get any support from David. Owen wanted her to leave, and by his tones she accepted that he would never change his mind.

But it struck her that there was a deeper reason than just resentment behind Owen's desire to have her out of the house. She recalled the conversation she'd overheard word by word, and a frown came to her forehead as she considered it.

Why didn't they want her wandering around the house? Those were Owen's exact words. What responsibility was there to be accepted? Clare shook her head slowly when she failed to make any sense out of what she'd heard. They wanted Sue nursed back to full health. There was no doubt about that! But they didn't want a woman in the house! Were Adam and Owen such woman-haters?

There was a tap at the door and Clare started nervously, so deeply was she lost in thought. But she went in answer, to open the door to David. Having been thinking about him, she was a little surprised to see him, and she coloured a little as she felt his dark gaze upon her.

" Is Sue asleep?" he demanded.

" Yes!" Clare nodded. " I've just left her."

" May I come in? I'd like to talk to you."

" Certainly!" She opened the door wide and he entered passing her closely. When she closed the door he turned to face her, and she could read nothing in his impassive stare. He smiled faintly, and she felt relieved as she walked towards him.

" Now you've taken up your duties we'd better talk about your off-duty periods. You're not expected to be on duty with Sue twenty-four hours a day, seven days a week, are you?"

" No!" She shook her head and smiled, dismissing the

sombre thoughts that had entered her mind. " I should have a complete day off, and a half day twice a week, but I won't insist upon them until Sue has had the chance to get used to me."

" She's taking to you quite well." His dark brows drew together for a moment, and a shadow seemed to cross his face. " I was expecting a lot of trouble, but you seem to have the knack of gaining a child's confidence quickly."

" A child needs to know comfort," she said. " I nursed Sue for a few moments before she went to sleep and she'll be all right. We have become friends already, and that's a good thing."

" I doubt if a male nurse would have worked!" His eyes were narrowed for a moment. " I asked Doctor Laverne about having a male nurse, but he wouldn't agree to it. He said Sue needed a woman's company."

" And I quite agree with him!" Clare stiffened herself mentally as she felt the urge to question him about the situation existing in the house. " Why is everyone here so against having a woman at Oakapple Farm?" she paused, watching him intently. " Or isn't it any of my business?"

" You sensed that a woman is not welcomed here?"

" It was plain to see. It is none of my business, of course. I'm here to do a job and that's all I'm concerned with, but if there is an atmosphere in the house then I can't help noticing it."

" Don't let it worry you." He spoke through stiff lips. " It has nothing to do with you, whatever you may think. I expect this is going to prove a bit difficult for you because Owen isn't a very pleasant chap, and he was against having you here. But he has agreed that we need a woman here with Sue, so you won't experience any unpleasantness with him."

" And what about your other brother?"

" Adam?" He moistened his lips. " Adam won't even speak to you unless you speak to him. He won't bother you." He spoke forcefully, and Clare saw a glitter in his dark brown eyes. " But I'd like to get back to discussing your day off and the rest. Is there any particular day you'd prefer?"

" No. Whenever it's convenient will be all right with me." She smiled, seeing that he was trying desperately to introduce a light note into their conversation. " I expect Betty will have Sue when I'm off duty, so there's no problem about which day. However I feel I should stay with Sue all the time for a week at least. If I go off for a day now she might get upset. In any case, if I had a day off there's nowhere for me to go."

He nodded slowly. " We are rather remote here. But I'd drive you into town any time you'd like to spend some time there."

" I'm not one for wanting to trudge the streets," she said. " I have nothing to do outside my duties, and if I went into town for the day I'd be happier to take Sue with me."

" It's refreshing to see someone like you," he said. " These days it's more customary for people to want to know what they can get out of a job rather than what they can put into it."

" Well this is no ordinary job. I'm dealing with a child's life and future happiness. I'd be a poor nurse if I counted the cost to me."

He nodded. " The more I listen to you the happier I am that Father agreed to have you in to take care of Sue. How long a job do you think it will be?"

" I'm afraid it's impossible to say! One can't tell with cases like this. Even the doctor wouldn't be able to forecast an ending."

" That's what I'm afraid of! But there's little doubt that she will get better, is there?"

" No doubt at all in my mind, if she gets the proper treatment and nursing now."

He nodded, and moved slowly to the door, and Clare was sorry that he was leaving. But he paused and looked down at the door, and she frowned when he glanced sideways at her.

" There's a bolt on the inside of this door," he said. "I'd feel better if you used it at night."

She stared at him for a moment, not wanting to believe she had heard him right. A pulse began hammering in her throat, and she felt nervousness seize hold of her.

" Why on earth?" she began, but he cut her short.

" There's no need to question what I've said." His tones were sharp and clipped. " Just push home the bolt before getting into bed each night."

She held his gaze although he was unwilling to look into her eyes, and she was making a desperate attempt to remain outwardly casual.

" Do you have sleepwalkers in the house?" she demanded.

" That could very well be. Look, I've made myself responsible for you, and I want to take all precautions possible. It's a little thing I ask you to do. Just push home the bolt before retiring every night."

" And if Sue should need me?" she countered.

" Sue can't call, so you wouldn't hear her crying. She would get out of bed and come to your door. She would knock. So if your door is bolted or not makes not the slightest difference to that situation."

Clare nodded. " Very well! I'll do as you say, and I won't ask questions."

He nodded abruptly and departed, and she stood motionless, listening to his fading footsteps. Her imagination was afire with speculation as she crossed to the door and slid home the bolt, and she tried the door, finding it securely locked. Her lips were compressed, her throat dry as she considered, and then she took a quick breath and sighed heavily.

What possible reason could he have for insisting that she bolt the door? She shook her head slowly as she un-bolted it and went out into the passage. She went to peer into Sue's room, and satisfied herself that the child was sleeping peacefully, and some of her tension fled as she looked down into the immobile face of the girl. But she could not keep her thoughts from what David Harley had said, and she left the room silently and slowed her steps as she made for the stairs. She felt in need of a chat with Betty, and went down to the kitchen, tensing a little as she passed through the hall, but she didn't see any of the family, and a sigh of relief gusted through her as she tapped at the kitchen door.

Entering, she found Betty alone, and the woman smiled at her and got up from the table, where she had been reading a magazine.

" Hello, is Sue asleep already?" the housekeeper de-manded.

" Yes. She's been asleep for quite some time. I expect the exercise and the excitements of the day have tired her out. She'll probably sleep right through the night."

" That would be a good thing!" A strange note had attached itself to Betty's tones. " Are you a nervous type, Clare?"

" Not really. Why?"

" Well this is an old house, and there have been reports of unusual things happening at night."

" Ghosts?" Clare smiled despite the cold hand that seemed to clutch at her throat. " I don't believe in them."

" I know several intelligent people in the neighbourhood

who wouldn't spend the night here. I've been intending to talk to you about it, Clare. You're a sensible girl, but I think you should lock your door at night."

Clare stared at her, wondering what to say. Two people had given her advice on the same subject within the space of a few moments.

" You're joking, of course! " she said lightly.

" I'm not! I bolt my door every night, and I check it before getting into bed." Betty spoke firmly, and her face was set in harsh lines as she stared at Clare. " I wasn't going to let you go to bed tonight without mentioning it."

" David gave me the same advice a short time ago," Clare admitted slowly.

" Did he? " Relief showed in the woman's face. " I'm glad to hear that."

" What exactly am I supposed to be bolting out of my room? "

" I wouldn't know. I've never heard or seen anything suspicious, but I never fail to bolt my door."

Clare drew a sharp breath, but did not pursue the matter. She studied the woman's face but could derive no information from Betty's expression. She felt it would be better to drop the subject, but there was a tight knot of worry in her breast which no amount of instruction would disperse. She was beginning to feel decidedly nervous for some inexplicable reason, and she made herself think of the child placed in her care. If she needed strong nerves if only for the girl's sake, then she would find the necessary strength to subdue her fears. But she couldn't help wondering what was behind the frightening order to bolt her door at night. She couldn't help thinking there was more to it than talk of ghosts!

SIX

WHEN SHE went to bed that night Clare was a little apprehensive. She checked Sue and found the girl sleeping peacefully, and then she went into her own room. She paused with the door closed and stared at the bolt. It went against the grain bolting the door against possible calls from her patient, but two people had warned her to do so, and she slid home the bolt, feeling a little bit guilty when she thought of the child sleeping next door, with her door unbolted.

But she checked that the bolt was securely home before getting into bed, and then she lay trying to induce slumber. But her thoughts were rampaging through her mind like a mountain torrent, and she sighed heavily as she tried to relax.

This was a strange house and there was no way to get over the fact. Each house had its own characteristics, she knew, and she listened to strange creaking sounds that made her wonder if someone was outside in the corridor. She could feel her nerves beginning to weaken under the strain imposed upon them, and had to think hard about Sue in order to revitalise her determination. Then she slipped into sleep and knew no more . . .

When she awoke next morning, Clare lay for some moments just thinking about the situation, and she stared around the room as if expecting to find something changed. There was no outward evidence of anything having gone wrong during the night, and she hurriedly got out of bed and put on her dressing-gown. Her first thoughts were for Sue, and she crossed to the door and unbolted it, pausing for a moment to look at the bolt. Then she went out into the corridor. Sue's door was closed and Clare opened it softly and peered into the room. She felt relieved when she found the girl still asleep in her bed.

She went back to her own room and prepared to dress. She could not keep her thoughts from the warning she had received the night before, and her imagination seemed to have coloured her attitude towards the house and its occupants. But Sue suddenly came tapping at the door, and Clare forgot herself in the minutes that followed.

" And how is Sue this morning?" she demanded as she opened the door to the girl. " Did you have a good sleep?"

Sue nodded, and she took Clare's hand. Clare smiled and sat down on the foot of the bed, taking the child on her lap, and they looked into one another's eyes for some moments.

" You're looking a lot better today, Sue. What would you like to do after breakfast?"

The girl shrugged one small shoulder, and Clare laughed.

" We'll wait a bit before deciding, shall we? But you'd like to go out for a walk, wouldn't you? It looks another lovely day out there, and there's so much to see."

Sue nodded, and Clare hoped for a moment that the girl would say something. She was half convinced that Sue hadn't lost the power of speech but was deliberately withholding her words. Shock had a way of affecting young people in that way, and probably the child didn't realise that she had only to make the effort in order to speak. But the shadow of shock still showed in the young brown eyes, and Clare knew she would have to control her impatience. She might do more harm than good in trying to rush the girl.

When they were ready they went down to the kitchen,

and were on the stairs when David Harley appeared from his office. The door had been left open, and Clare believed he had been waiting for her appearance.

" How did you sleep?" he demanded gravely.

" Fine." She smiled slowly. " I didn't see or hear anything after I closed my eyes."

" That's good." He looked as if he hadn't slept at all and Clare could not help noticing how gaunt he looked. " What about Sue?" He looked down at the girl in Clare's arms, and placed a gentle hand upon her dark head. Sue looked up at him, and Clare saw the child smile faintly.

" Did you sleep well, Sue?" he demanded.

A slight nod rewarded him, and he stroked the girl's cheek.

" You're going to have breakfast now, aren't you? I haven't eaten yet, so why don't you come into the breakfast-room with me? Father won't be up yet, and the other two will be about their business by now. Look, go along to that room there; the third door on the left, and I'll go and tell Betty to serve your breakfast with mine."

Clare did not argue, and she thanked him before turning to obey him. He went off in the direction of the kitchen, and Clare watched him for a moment before walking along the hall. Sue slid down out of her arms and walked at her side, their feet echoing on the polished wooden blocks, and when Clare opened the door of the breakfast-room the child ran in eagerly ahead of her.

Clare paused on the threshold of the room and stared at the figure seated at the long table. Owen Harley had finished his breakfast, but he was reading a newspaper, and he looked up ferociously at their interruption.

" I'm sorry," Clare said instantly. " I was given to understand that the room would be empty."

" Well don't back out now you're here. Come in. If you're working in the house then we must expect to see you around occasionally. I've finished breakfast and I'm about to leave, anyway." He glanced at his watch, his set face showing intensity.

Clare was recalling the words she had overheard him speak to David the evening before, and she didn't have to wonder why he had said them. He was looking at her now as if she had become his worst enemy, and she entered the room slowly and took hold of Sue's hand as he got to his feet and folded his newspaper.

" David said he wanted to have Sue at the table with him during breakfast," she volunteered.

" So you're calling him David already, are you?" He seemed to sneer. " It doesn't take you long to make yourself at home, does it? But then you must be used to entering strange houses and settling down."

" That's all part of my work, I'm afraid," Clare retorted coolly. " And I meet all kinds of people. Some are very nice, but others are extremely rude, as if I were trespassing. They want me on hand because of the patient, but the fact that I don't sit by the sick bed twenty-four hours a day, seven days a week, seems to annoy them. Of course I make myself as unobtrusive as possible, but sometimes my presence is noticed."

He came around the table, his dark eyes on her face, and she imagined his thick black moustache was bristling with anger. She moved out of the doorway and he paused at her side, looking down into her face. He was tall and heavily built, and she felt dwarfed by him.

" What are you going to do with Sue today?" he demanded, and Clare was faintly surprised by his change of subject.

" I don't know yet! We haven't decided."

He glanced down at Sue, who was looking up at him.

" Well I'm going into the village later this morning if you'd care for a lift."

" That's very kind of you. But if we go into the village how do we get back again? It's too far for Sue to walk."

" I'll be staying about two hours. I'll bring you back in time for lunch."

" Thank you. We'll see how Sue feels after breakfast, shall we?"

He nodded. " You'll find me in the library until a quarter past ten. If you want to go out for the morning then let me know before I leave."

" Thank you!" Clare nodded slowly, and he departed.

She put Sue at the table and sat down at the girl's side, and a moment later David appeared. He was smiling, looking perfectly normal and at ease, and Clare could not help wondering what was in his mind. Compared with him Owen was not normal, she considered, and she just didn't know what to make of Adam.

" Breakfast will be along in a moment," he said, seating himself opposite, and he leaned back in his chair and grinned at Sue. " I expect you're hungry, Sue," he remarked. " Growing girls are always hungry."

Sue looked at him, then glanced up at Clare, who took the child's hand and held it tightly.

" You like everything, don't you, Sue?" she demanded.

There was a slight nod, and Clare glanced across the table to find David's eyes upon her. There was a serious expression on his face.

" I'm going into town this afternoon," he said, moistening his lips. " Would Sue like a trip all the way?"

Clare told him about Owen's offer for the morning, and he seemed surprised.

" What are you going to do?" he asked.

" I think I'll accept." She didn't give her reasons for wanting to do so, but she was hoping that spending some time in Owen's company might mellow him towards her a little. "Would that be all right?" she demanded.

"Why not? If you can stand Owen's bad temper and his impatience then of course it's all right. Why shouldn't it be all right?"

The door opened then and Betty appeared with a breakfast trolley. Clare was glad the conversation was ended, and she busied herself attending to Sue. They had almost finished the meal when the telephone rang in the hall. A moment later Betty opened the door and peered in.

"It's Doctor Laverne for you, Clare," the housekeeper said.

"Thank you, I'll be right there," Clare said, getting to her feet. She glanced at David, who was still watching her closely. "Would you keep an eye on Sue until I get back please?" she asked.

"Certainly." He smiled and turned his attention to the girl.

Clare went out into the hall and took up the telephone receiver. She was pleased to hear Grant's voice, and he asked the inevitable question.

"I'm settling in quite well,'" she responded, "and Sue has taken to me. I have her confidence and we're great friends already."

"I shall be passing through in about thirty minutes, Clare. I want to call in and have a look at Sue. Will you be in?"

"Yes, although we shall be out for most of the day later."

"I see. Well get the child out as much as possible. In a week we'll consider if she's made any progress, and if she hasn't then I shall consult a specialist. Amanda sends her best wishes. I'll see you very shortly. Sorry I can't stay longer, but I have an emergency call to answer before coming to Oakapple Farm."

" We'll be here," Clare responded, and she was smiling as she replaced the receiver.

When she went back into the breakfast room she found Sue had left her seat and gone around the table to David, who was holding the girl on his lap. He was telling her a story, and Sue was listening with great interest. Clare said nothing, but she sat at the table and waited for the story to end.

" Now I must go back to work," David said when he finished the tale. " Is the doctor coming today to see Sue?"

" He'll be here very shortly." Clare told him what Grant had said, and he nodded slowly.

" She may need specialist treatment at that! Well she'll have everything that money can buy, I'll see to that." He looked at the girl with sudden longing and wistfulness showing in his eyes and expression. " Shall we go into town this afternoon and buy you a present, Sue?"

The girl smiled, and Clare watched closely. Already Sue was beginning to show slight changes in her manner. She had seemed inwardly frozen yesterday when she arrived from the hospital, but now she was beginning to settle in, and she knew that the people around her were friends.

" What would you like?" David pursued. " Would you rather have a doll, or a soft toy?"

" She brought home a lovely doll yesterday," Clare said. " I think it would be better if she looked around the shops and let her fancy do the selecting."

" That's a good idea." He was suddenly eager, and Clare watched him as he formulated some plans. " Shall we leave here at about two? Owen will have brought you back from the village by then. We don't have to hurry, do we?"

" No. Sue will be all right for the afternoon. If she feels sleepy then she can have a nap while you're driving into town."

" Good. I'd better get a start on my work or I'll never

get done in time." He was smiling easily now, and the tension seemed to have left him. He ruffled Sue's hair and went to the door. "See you later!"

When he had gone, Clare took hold of Sue's hand. "Do you like your Uncle David?" she demanded.

Sue opened her mouth as if to speak, but no words came, and she didn't even make a sound. Her dark eyes widened a little, as if she couldn't understand why she was unable to talk, and fear came into her gaze to mar the brightness of her eyes.

"Don't worry about it, Sue," Clare went on, bending to get closer to the girl. "You can understand what I'm saying even if you can't reply, and you'll be able to talk again soon. Your voice will come back. It was just frightened because you had to go into hospital. But now that you're home again it will return."

Sue seemed to understand what Clare said, for she nodded and smiled, and Clare led her from the room. They went along to the kitchen where Betty was busy, and Clare informed the housekeeper of her intentions for the day.

"I'm surprised Owen agreed to take you into the village," Betty said. "But David is all right, and he thinks the world of Sue. I was talking with him just before breakfast, asking him what was going to happen when Sue is better and you've gone on to another case."

"Although it won't affect me because I shan't be here, I am interested in Sue's future," Clare said. "What is going to happen to her?"

"That's exactly what I asked. The child needs a woman around her! David said something about probably sending her to a girl's boarding school when she's old enough. But I don't think that will be a satisfactory answer. The child needs a lot of individual attention and plenty of loving, after what she's been through."

Clare nodded. But there would be time enough to discuss Sue's future when the child had completely recovered from the effects of the accident.

"I'm glad they're beginning to accept you, Clare," Betty went on. "I was pleased to hear that David wanted you at the breakfast table. But it wouldn't please Owen if he knew."

Clare told the woman about seeing Owen in the breakfast room, and Betty shook her head.

"I just don't know what's coming over him, and that's the truth," she said. "He does seem to get worse and worse. I keep telling myself that there must be a limit to his tempers, but he certainly hasn't reached that limit yet."

"Does he ever get violent?" Clare demanded, still wondering about the instructions she'd received to bolt her door at night.

"He has been involved in some incidents in the area," came the steady reply. "No sooner the word than the blow with Owen Harley."

Clare was thoughtful, and she took Sue up to her room to prepare the girl for the morning's outing. When they were ready they went out into the garden to enjoy the sunlight until it was time to leave with Owen, and they romped around the lawns until Grant arrived.

The first she knew of his presence was when he spoke to her, and Clare looked up to find him standing there, a smile on his face.

"I didn't like to interrupt, seeing how absorbed you both were," he said. "But I don't have much time to spare this morning and I must get on."

"Hello, Grant," she said. "We're going into Chippenbury shortly with Owen, and Sue's just letting off a little steam."

" How are things here?" He came to her side as she straightened, and Sue took hold of Clare's hand as if she were afraid that Grant had come to take her away.

" It couldn't be better," Clare responded brightly. " Sue and I are becoming very good friends, and the family are doing all they can to make things easy."

" Good!" Grant seemed relieved, and Clare studied his face for a moment. She felt a twinge of intuition, and held his gaze as he looked at her.

" Are you keeping something from me, Grant?" she demanded.

" How do you mean?" She saw him come alert, and his eyes seemed to narrow a little.

" Perhaps you know how I mean! Is there something about this place or this family that I don't know about?"

" I don't follow you!"

" You're not usually so slow!" She told him about being warned to lock her door at night. " Betty said it is because the house might be haunted in some way, but you and Amanda warned me to be careful, although you didn't put it into so many words. What is the situation here? If there is something wrong then I feel I ought to know about it."

" What could be wrong?" He shook his head firmly. " You don't think I'd send for you out of the blue and put you into a position of danger, do you?"

" No!" She spoke hesitantly, trying to get her intuition working properly. It was trying to tell her something. " But I can't help feeling there's something wrong somewhere. It's in the atmosphere, and nothing I can really put my finger on. It may be that I'm using my imagination. I don't know! But there is something that's not quite right."

His face had hardened a little, and he stared openly into her blue eyes. Then he looked down at Sue, who was staring up at them both with mute appeal in her dark face.

" I honestly don't know what could be at fault here," he said. " Of course I have heard rumours, but they don't amount to anything, and one should always ignore them."

" What sort of rumours?" she persisted.

" I wouldn't like to repeat them," he countered evasively.

" Well you brought me here and stuck me in the middle of this family. I'm ready to do everything possible for my patient, but I think I ought to have full knowledge of the situation, and of anything that may affect me while I'm here."

" Clare, I can only repeat that I don't know anything. I certainly wouldn't have brought you here if I felt there was the slightest risk in any way to you. I know the Harleys don't have a good name in these parts. I haven't lived here all my life so I don't know them very well, but from what I've seen of them I think they are much maligned by the locals, and they couldn't possibly have done everything they're accused of. People find them unfriendly, I suppose, and that has counted against them. They don't work for a living like most of their neighbours. They have this huge farm and all the work is done for them. Cornelius Harley is a gentleman farmer who has never soiled his hands."

" But that can't account for the atmosphere that seems to exist here," Clare protested.

" I wouldn't let anything happen to you, Clare," he insisted.

" You wouldn't be in any position to help me when I'd need help most," she retorted. " That's at night."

" I'll have a word with David about his instruction to lock your door at night," he said instantly. " Perhaps he'll tell me what he had in mind when he spoke to you."

" He didn't want to elaborate on it to me," she said.

For a moment there was worry showing plainly on her face, but she fought it and won and the expression fled. Sue was tugging at her hand, and she looked down at the child. The girl was pointing across the lawn, and Clare turned to look in the direction indicated and saw Owen Harley walking towards the garages at the rear of the house. " Is there anything you want to ask about Sue?" she continued. " Owen is fetching his car. He doesn't seem to be the type who would want to wait around for me."

" No." Grant shook his head, and Clare heard a sigh escape him. " Sue looks all right to me. She's recovered completely from the slight injuries she received in the accident. Her mental state is going to get better as time goes on. It's easy to see that. You're doing a good job with her, Clare."

" Thanks! But she took to me, so there isn't much I've got to do but take care of her. I'm glad she's on the road to recovery."

" Well you run along and have a nice time today. I'll go into the house and have a chat with David. I want to get to the bottom of this business you've mentioned. I'll let you know what he tells me."

" I'll be interested to hear an explanation," she replied, smiling faintly. " When shall we see you again, Grant?"

They turned and walked towards the house, and Sue clung to Clare's hand.

" I think I'll continue calling once a day, around about this time," he said at once. " Not so much to see Sue but to find out what's happening."

" That sounds as if you're not sure yourself that something won't happen," she said.

" I just want to check that you're all right," he retorted. " I am responsible for you, Clare."

" I don't expect anything to go wrong," she said as they reached the drive, and she could hear the sound of a car starting at the rear of the house. " But I can sense that everything isn't quite as it should be, and it is disconcerting to know that intuition can make one feel uncomfortable."

" I'll have another chat with Amanda when I go home," he promised. " I'll try and get some truth out of those rumours I've heard. She has lived in this area all her life, and she should know what's what. If there is any suspicion at all that you're in a bad position then you'll leave at a moment's notice."

" I couldn't do that now," she retorted quickly. " I've taken on Sue and I'll stay here until my services are no longer required."

" I knew you'd say that, so I'll do what I can do ensure your safety."

" That sounds bad, doesn't it?" she queried.

" Well you brought this up, and from what you've said I'd say you fear for your safety in some way." He looked at her obliquely, his brown eyes alert.

" I don't know!" She spoke slowly, trying to clear her mind of conjecture to get at the sharp facts. Something bothered her inwardly with great persistence, and she had to know what it was. Until she discovered what was causing her unrest she would never be able to settle down to do her duty properly.

" Well leave it with me and I'll see what kind of an assurance I can get from David. You're quite happy about him, aren't you, Clare?"

" I think so," she replied, nodding, and she pictured David's face. " Yes. I think he's all right. In fact I sense that he's the best one of the brothers here."

" That bears out my own judgement." He smiled and patted her shoulder. " See you some time tomorrow morning. Now here comes Owen, and you mustn't keep him waiting."

She smiled and nodded.

SEVEN

OWEN HAD little to say on the drive to Chippenbury, and Clare sat stiffly at his side for the most part, too conscious that some sort of mystery existed at Oakapple Farm. If Sue had been able to talk the child's chatter might have broken the ice between them, but the child was as silent as ever, and Clare sighed deeply as she wondered what to say. Owen seemed to be so reserved, and yet she could not overlook the words she had overheard him saying to David. He certainly didn't want her at Oakapple Farm, and there seemed to be a serious reason for his attitude.

"It's a beautiful day!" she commented at last.

"Eh?" He seemed startled as he glanced at her. "Oh, yes! It is beautiful. What are you going to do with yourself in the village? There's nothing much for you to pass the time on."

"I'll take Sue around. It's really a matter of getting her out into the sunlight." She saw the church tower looming, and knew the trip was coming to an end. "I hope I'm not upsetting your normal routine too much."

He looked at her, but made no comment as he returned his attention to his driving. She glanced at his profile, and dearly wished she could have divined what was passing through his mind.

"You don't upset me at all," he said shortly. "I rather fancy your presence at the farm will give David more to think about. He runs the place, and I just live there. I don't take any active part in the administration."

It wasn't quite what Clare meant, and she could not for her life think how her presence could affect the running of the farm, but she said nothing more. Owen so obviously didn't want to talk, that she remained silent and let her thoughts have full sway.

When they entered the village Owen parked the car near the green, and he turned to her before alighting.

" I'll be ready to go back to the farm at about twelve-thirty," he said, his dark eyes watching her intently. " Don't be late, because I have to go out again this afternoon."

" I'll be here in good time," she promised.

They left the car and Sue took hold of her hand as they crossed the green to the pond. Ducks were quacking in the distance, and Sue became excited as they approached. But Clare glanced back, and she saw Owen standing on the road and watching their progress. When he saw her looking at him he turned carelessly away and went off.

Clare wondered about him as they reached the pond, but Sue soon took her mind off her thoughts. The child was excited to see the ducks swimming and feeding on the smooth surface of the wide pond, and Clare watched the child for some moments, hoping her excitement would bring back her speech, but Sue was silently appreciative of the scene, and her dark eyes shone as she watched the waterfowl.

A voice hailed them from across the green, and Clare turned quickly, to see Amanda Laverne coming towards them, a smile on her face.

" Hello," she said, panting a little as she reached them. " I saw you from the window. How are you making out? Have you seen Grant this morning?"

" I was bringing Sue to see you after she'd seen the ducks," Clare said. " Yes, I've seen Grant. Everything's all right." She looked into Amanda's brown eyes and wondered if there was anything the woman could tell her about Oakapple Farm. But she resisted the impulse to ask. Grant would find out for her, and she didn't want to start enquiries which might go on and on and completely ruin her stay in this area. Sometimes it was better to let sleeping dogs lie.

" How did you get into the village?" Amanda asked, and seemed a little surprised when Clare explained. " Well that's something. Owen is coming out of his shell at last. You'll have to be careful, Clare, or you'll have those bachelors falling over themselves to get to know you."

" I don't think I have to worry about that sort of thing where Owen in particular is concerned," Clare said with a laugh. " Both he and Adam seem to be born women-haters. I'd like to know what's wrong with them. Not that I've seen much of Adam. He works on the farm like any farm worker, so I hear. David takes care of the administration side of the business, but Owen seems to do nothing at all."

" He's always fancied himself as a gentleman," Amanda said. " I never did know what to make of him. He's got a dreadful manner, hasn't he?"

" I don't suppose I shall see much of him!" Clare didn't let her thoughts influence her tones in any way. " If I keep out of his way then not much can go wrong. But he's very fond of Sue, and he wouldn't do anything that might hurt her in any way." Again Sue tugged at Clare's hand, and when she looked down at the child, Clare found her pointing to the road. When they looked in that direction, Clare saw Owen Harley walking in the opposite direction, and there was a woman with him.

" There's Owen," Amanda said sharply. " What's he doing with Mary Hacon?"

" Who's Mary Hacon?"

" She's the woman Adam Harley almost married!"

" Oh!" A thrill ran through Clare as she watched the two figures walking along the road. " Why did she refuse Adam in the end?"

" It's difficult to say. There was talk that she went off to marry another man, but when she returned to the village after all the fuss had died down she didn't have another man with her and she hadn't been married."

" Adam took it badly then!"

" That's putting it mildly. My father was the doctor here before Grant came. He told me Adam was almost out of his mind because of what happened."

" Until I arrived yesterday then no other woman has been at Oakapple Farm!" Clare spoke quietly, but her eyes were glinting with curiosity.

" They wouldn't have a woman on the place after what happened to Adam! That is, a woman interested in the men. There was talk that Cornelius actually forbade his sons to come into contact with women."

" And that's why there was such an argument when it was found that a nurse was needed for Sue!" Clare nodded slowly. " I'm beginning to see daylight now. But that still doesn't account for the atmosphere I found at Oakapple Farm."

Amanda studied her face for a moment, and Clare shook her head, wanting nothing more to be said about the situation, whatever it might be.

" They are a strange family," Amanda said. " But you're all right there, Clare."

" Oh yes!" Clare nodded. " I'm perfectly all right."

" Will you come across to the house for a cup of tea?" Amanda seemed keen to change the subject now, and Clare was thoughtful as they turned and walked back to the road. Sue clutched at her hand, and the pressure of the child's tiny fingers was all that seemed real at that moment.

They talked generally until they reached the house, and Clare sat Sue on her lap when they went into the kitchen for tea. Amanda busied herself, and they sat at the table with a tray before them. The house was quiet and cool, and reminded Clare of Oakapple Farm.

" I'm not sorry I came here," Clare said thoughtfully, " but I wish I knew more about the Farm."

" Is there anything I can help with?" Amanda demanded.

" I spoke to Grant this morning but he seemed to put it all down to my imagination, although he's going to have a chat with David Harley."

" Has something happened then?" Amanda narrowed her brown eyes as she looked at Clare.

" Would you be surprised if I said yes to that?" Clare countered.

"Why, I don't know!"

" Well nothing has happened, but I'm not quite happy about the general situation." Clare explained all that she'd told Grant, and Amanda shook her head.

" I really can't throw any light on this," she said at length. " Of course we wouldn't have brought you in if there had been any doubt about the way you might be treated at Oakapple Farm. The Harleys have been rather a strange lot, but there's never been any suggestion that a woman wouldn't be safe amongst them. If you have any doubts then you should quit the case, Clare."

" I wouldn't dream of doing that, but I can't help thinking. I don't know how to explain it, but I have a feeling that all is not as it should be."

" David is all right. He's the one who told you to lock your door at night! Is it Owen or Adam that's set you wondering?"

" Neither as far as it goes! That's the strange thing about it. I can't put my finger on what it is causing the disquiet I'm feeling. I'm sure it is just my imagination, and yet there's the fact that David warned me."

"What does Grant say about it?"

"He thinks like you, but he's going to try and get to the bottom of it."

"Are you really worried about it?"

"No! How could I be when nothing has happened?"

"If it does happen then it will be too late to worry. That's it, isn't it?"

"Exactly!"

Amanda nodded. "I don't think I'd like to stay there under these circumstances."

"There's nothing I can do about that now!" Clare glanced down at Sue, who was looking up at her, and she smiled reassuringly and stroked the girl's hair. "I think we'll go for a walk, shall we, Sue? I haven't had the chance to see the village yet."

"I'd come with you if I had the time, and I have to be on hand in case there are any calls for Grant."

"That's all right. Sue is good company. We'll come and see you again, Amanda, if we may."

"Please do. I'm always glad to see visitors. It's rather lonely here. And perhaps I can come and see you at the Farm sometimes, or pick you up and take you for a drive. There's no reason why you should be tied to the place, is there?"

"No reason at all. I have to keep Sue happy and free from worry. It does her good to get a change of scenery."

"Then we'll make arrangements later." Amanda was smiling, and Clare felt that she had nothing to worry about because Grant and his wife didn't seem to think there was any cause for alarm. Grant was her friend, and he wouldn't have let her enter into this case if he'd any suspicion that things might not be all that they ought.

Clare took her leave of Amanda, and Sue waved as they walked from the house. Amanda was pleased and kept waving, and Clare watched the child as Sue waved repeatedly. These were signs that Sue was making a return to normal, and surely it wouldn't be long before the girl's mind was able to relax sufficiently for her to regain the use of her speech.

They sauntered around the village, and Clare bought some lemonade for the girl, and then some ice cream. The child seemed to be enjoying herself immensely, and when it was time for them to go back to Owen's car, Clare felt that she had been over-dramatising the situation which she felt had arisen. If only David Harley hadn't told her to lock her bedroom door. That was what had started her off on this long bout of worrying.

Owen was seated in his car when they reached it, and Clare caught her breath as she saw him behind the wheel. His face was expressionless, but she knew he would be angry if she had kept him waiting. She dared not glance at her watch to see if they were late because it would be so pointed in front of him. But he leaned sideways and opened the car door for her, and Clare thanked him as she slid into the front seat beside him. Sue clung tightly to her, and Clare glanced at him.

" I hope we haven't kept you waiting," she said.

" Not really! I got back to the car a bit early." His tones were gentle, without that harsh background she had come to know. But he didn't look at her as she settled herself with Sue on her lap. He started the car and drove quickly from the village. Sue laid her head against Clare's shoulder and went to sleep. After a few moments Owen spoke again. " Did you have a nice morning?" he asked.

" Very nice, thank you! I think poor Sue tired herself out completely. But she enjoyed herself, and that's the main thing."

" Of course. The patient comes first, doesn't she?"

" Every time!" She glanced at him overtly, and saw

that he was looking at her. She looked away again, unable to take his heavy stare.

" I suppose you've been to a great many patients, going to live in their homes as you've come to Oakapple Farm."

" Yes! A great many."

" No doubt you meet a variety of people. But I expect you get along quite well with all of them, don't you?"

" I usually manage to get along with even the most disagreeable people," she ventured.

" I'm sorry you are having such a tough time with me!" He smiled briefly as she caught his eye. " I know I'm not very agreeable, but my family have got used to me. You're a stranger among us, and I was thinking this morning that you must be finding me a bit hard to take. I've seen it in your expression. Well I'm sorry, and I'd like to apologise for making you feel unwelcome at Oakapple Farm. You have come to do us a favour, and we all want Sue to get better. You need me on your side, not against you, and in future I'll do all I can to help you and make your stay with us more comfortable."

" Does that mean you've changed your mind about wanting to get me out of the house?" she asked.

His face hardened for a moment, and he stared at her, holding the car steady on the road.

" Did David say something to you?" he demanded brusquely.

" No!" She explained how she had overheard him talking to David, and he nodded briefly.

" I see!" He seemed to relax a little. " Well I'm sorry for that. As I said, you came here to do us a favour, and I've been treating you as if you were an intruder. It's nothing personal! I didn't even know you."

"That makes it a little better!"

Their eyes met again, and she saw that the tension had left his mouth. His lips were no longer habitually compressed, and she could not help wondering what had happened to him that morning to make him change his mind about the situation. Could it have been the influence of the woman he'd met; his brother's ex-fiancée?

She still puzzled over his apparent change of attitude when they reached the farm, and when he brought the car to a halt before the front door he reached across Clare to open the door for her. Sue was asleep on her lap, and he smiled thinly as he looked into the girl's serene face.

"Poor child," he said. "I'm glad she's got someone like you to take care of her. Shall I carry her in for you?"

"No. It might disturb her as we transferred her from me to you. I'll take her up to her room and try to get her settled on her bed."

"I'll open the door for you!" He got out of the car as she alighted, and hurried before her to open the door of the house. When she passed him in the doorway he took hold of her elbow. "Is she very heavy?" he demanded.

"I can manage," she replied.

But he followed her to the stairs and ascended at her side, opening the door of Sue's room for her. He watched while she gently put the child down on the bed, and when she turned from the bed she found him still standing in the doorway and watching her.

"You've got a nice way with children," he said as she walked towards him. He kept his voice low for fear of disturbing the sleeping girl, and Clare found his dark eyes compelling her to look at him. He was a totally different man without his bullying, bad tempered manner.

"It comes with practice and experience," she replied with a smile.

" The same as handling or winning over bad tempered people." His eyes seemed to become depthless, and he nodded slowly. " I am sorry for the way I welcomed you here."

" You still haven't told me your reason for bitterly opposing my arrival," she said.

" Well that doesn't matter now. But tell me, what are your plans for the rest of the day?"

" David said he would drive me into town this afternoon. But I rather fancy Sue has had enough exercise for today, and if we repeated the formula this afternoon we might overtire her."

" Trust David to get in first," he retorted coolly. " But I'll tell him you won't be going with him this afternoon. If you like I'll take you and Sue out on the lake in the boat. You told David you'd like to go out on the water, didn't you?"

" Are there no secrets between you and your brothers?" she queried.

" Not if we can help it." He seemed bolder now, and sure of himself. Clare was trying to sum up his attitude, and was wondering what lay behind the apparent change. " I'd like to get to know you better. Sue might get well suddenly and then you'd be gone, wouldn't you?"

" I shall leave immediately my services become no longer necessary. And I think you ought to know that I have a golden rule. I never permit myself to become involved with any member of my patient's family."

" I'm Sue's uncle, not her father," he retorted.

" That makes no difference." Her voice was firm and determined.

" I expect a lovely girl like you has a boy friend somewhere!"

" I don't have anyone!"

" That's a pity! Some unfortunate man is missing out."

She smiled and closed the door of the room, after peeping back at Sue to ensure the girl was asleep. He kept at her side as she walked to her own door.

" Will you have lunch with me?" he demanded. " You had breakfast with David."

" I won't eat until Sue awakes. I'll have a meal when she does."

He glanced at his watch. " Well I'm sorry but I can't wait until then. I have to run out soon after lunch. But I'll be back around three. Be ready with Sue and I'll take you both on the lake."

She didn't know how to answer him, but evidently he didn't need a reply, and he went off towards his own room, obviously very pleased with himself. Clare went into her room and closed the door, a little bit mystified by Owen's change of manner. She looked at the bolt on the inside of the door and wondered what it was there for. Against whom was it intended? David had warned her to use it, so it couldn't be against himself! That left Owen and Adam!

There was a tap on the door, and she stiffened a little as she lifted a hand to open it. She didn't know if she liked this new Owen or preferred the first character he had presented. When he had been bad tempered he had kept his distance. But now anything could happen. She opened the door with something like a sigh on her lips.

But it was David standing there, and she lost her fears instantly.

" I'd like to talk to you if I may," he said.

" Certainly. Won't you come in?" She opened the door wider and stepped back to admit him.

" I'd rather stand out here in the corridor," he said. " If I enter your room then others might think they have the right to do so."

She shook her head as she joined him in the corridor.

His face seemed intent, as if he was trying to conceal a host of worries.

"Doctor Laverne had a few words with me this morning," he went on. "I assured him there is no danger here for you."

"Then why the bolt on the door and the command not to forget to use it?" Clare asked.

"I told you it was just a precaution."

"I'm not satisfied with that!"

"You're not going with me into town this afternoon!"

"You've just spoken with Owen?" she demanded.

"He just spoke to me." She heard him sigh as he spoke. "I wouldn't get too friendly with Owen if I were you!"

"I don't intend to!"

"Good. Why won't you go into town with me this afternoon?"

"Because I think Sue has done enough for today. She's asleep in her room now, and a heavy afternoon might overtax her."

"Then I'll put off my trip to town until tomorrow, and you can go with me then." His tones were quiet and firm, and Clare nodded.

"Very well, if your business in town isn't pressing. I'd like the opportunity to look over your town."

"And you won't go on the lake with Owen this afternoon?"

"He seemed certain that I would, and he's a forceful character. Apart from that I'm relieved that he's being friendly now."

"He hasn't changed his opinion. I can assure you of that. He bitterly opposed your coming, and he hated you before you arrived. Not you personally, but what you represent."

" What do I represent?"

" Woman!"

" Like Eve!" She smiled, and was a little surprised at the feeling which came over her. But he had made her feel afraid for no apparent reason, and she was beginning to think that he had done that intentionally, wanting to scare her off for some reason known only to himself.

" I can imagine your thoughts now," he said slowly. " But I assure you that I'm acting only in your best interests. You're here to help Sue, and I'm whole-heartedly in your favour.

" That's nice to know. But I have to come into contact with your brothers, and unless I treat them equally there may be some trouble."

" Only from Owen!" His dark eyes seemed to glow as he studied her face.

" I'm not going to ask you in what way I could expect trouble from Owen," she said. " I've had a lot of concern over what you said yesterday. I'm not going to let any-thing worry me."

" There's no need for worry, now," he told her.

She regarded him silently, and wondered why he seemed so sure after the warning he'd given her the day before. He seemed less grave, too, unless it was her imagination. But he seemed as if he were a man who had suddenly lost a great burden from his shoulders, and suddenly she felt a strange and compelling sympathy for him. He seemed to be the hardest working of the brothers, although she hadn't come into contact with Adam. But she took to him in an instant.

It was as if a page in her mind had been turned, and there were new and strange impressions inside her, all clamouring for recognition and expression. It seemed to her then that she was standing on the brink of a great, unknown adventure.

EIGHT

In the days that followed, Clare found herself settling down in a routine that was both satisfying and uneventful as far as her patient was concerned. Sue didn't attempt to speak, but she made good progress, and soon attached herself to Clare to such an extent that Clare was unable to leave her at any time during the child's waking moments. Grant Laverne called in each day, but there was nothing he could do, and he came really to talk to Clare.

After that first frightening night when David had warned her to lock the door the situation seemed to wane until it left nothing but a faint impression in the background of her mind. But she did bolt her door every night without fail, and always awakened in the morning feeling slightly guilty because she did not share the same measure of security with Sue.

Owen Harley maintained his friendliness that was born the morning he had driven them into the village, but Clare would not permit herself to become friendly with him. She maintained a gulf between them that was not spanned by any attempt at friendliness which he made. She liked him a little better, but the last thing she wanted was to become involved with him. He was not the man she could begin to feel emotional about.

But David was another matter, and she felt herself being drawn even closer to him as the days went by. He made more progress in her heart than any man since Tim Millard, but she kept a tight rein on her emotions and maintained an even manner whenever she was in his company, which was often.

Soon it seemed to Clare that she had known no other life or group of people. In one short month she became a part of the daily circle at Oakapple Farm. Betty Smithers declared that Sue clung to Clare tighter than she had ever yearned for her own mother, and Clare had great hopes of bringing about the child's complete recovery.

They went out together a great deal, for both Clare and Grant Laverne believed that the mental scars on the child's mind would only be healed by a great deal of happy experience, and David was usually on hand to drive them wherever they wished to go. Owen gave up trying to date Clare when he found no response from her, to her great relief, and she rarely saw Adam at all so he didn't enter into any calculations.

As still more days went by without any outward change showing in Sue's mental condition, Clare slowly became aware that David was getting more attentive. From the outset he had been on hand at all times, ready with advice and support, but now he seemed to be finding great pleasure in her company, and she found her own feelings regarding him swelling into larger proportions because of his seeming interest in her.

She was in the garden with Sue one Sunday morning when David came out of the house. Clare saw him immediately because she had been watching for him for some time, hoping against hope that he would appear. Her heart seemed to give a great leap when she spotted him, and she saw his smile of welcome when he saw her. Her blue eyes gleamed and she felt great joy begin to well up inside. He came across the lawn, tall, dark and handsome, his face gentle with pleasure, and somewhere inside her a pulse began a rapid beating.

" Hello," he greeted, sitting down at her side. Sue was

chasing butterflies among the nearby flower beds, and Clare had been watching the girl. " What plans have you made for today?"

" None at all, except to keep Sue occupied."

" On such a beautiful day as this you ought to get away from the house. No matter how peaceful it is here, the day will seem to drag unless you get a change of scenery. Apart from that, I want to talk to you about your duties."

His dark eyes met hers for a moment, and Clare felt a sudden pang of alarm.

" Is something wrong?" she demanded.

" Nothing at all, so don't start flapping like an old crow." He smiled, his teeth glinting in the brilliant sunlight. " You're just like a mother hen when I talk about Sue. The child is all right. But what I want to talk about is your off-duty periods. You don't have any. In five weeks you haven't taken a day off. It isn't right to tie yourself to the girl like that. Surely you have friends somewhere whom you'd like to visit once in a while. I could have Sue one day while you went off."

" Are you trying to get rid of me?" she demanded.

" Certainly not. I shall be sorry to see you go even for a day. You've become very much a part of my way of life, Clare. I know it's a wicked thing for me to say, but I wish Sue would never get better if it meant you staying on here."

" The case will come to an end one day," she retorted, feeling moved by his words. " What's going to happen to Sue when she has recovered completely?"

" We haven't decided yet. Father and I were talking last evening, as a matter of fact, and we've decided it would be better if we made no decision until she is better."

" That's a difficult period you'll have to face when the

time comes. But I rather fancy she will have to see a specialist before she recovers her speech. I'm sure the shock of the accident is wearing off now."

"It must be." He nodded briefly. "Even I'm beginning to lose the sharpness of grief. Father seems to be recovering. We're all getting back to normal. All of us except poor Sue, that is."

"She's happy enough now!" Clare narrowed her eyes against the glare of the sun and studied the girl, who was sitting on the lawn and pulling a dandelion to pieces.

"You've made a great difference to all our lives," he added.

"Have I?" She looked up into his dark face and saw emotion there. "In what way?"

"I don't know what you've done to me, but it feels good. I can see the changes in Sue, but my own are not apparent. It's hard to explain, but before you came here this house was like a monastery. It had a bleak atmosphere and no hope of a reprieve."

Clare nodded, recalling the heavy atmosphere that had greeted her arrival. But that seemed to have changed, she told herself, and could only agree with David. But she didn't think she was the cause, and told him so.

"It must be Sue's presence in the house," she said.

"A little of it is Sue, but you're to account for the rest."

"I'm sure Owen wouldn't agree to that." There was a smile on her lips as she spoke, and their eyes met for a moment.

"Owen has mellowed a great deal since your arrival. You've had some great effect upon him, too, although he wouldn't be the first to admit it."

"And what about Adam?" She kept her pale gaze upon his face, and saw his lips tighten. "Why is it I never see

anything of Adam? I don't believe I've seen him more than
half a dozen times in the past five weeks.

"He likes to keep to himself."

"But he's never around the house in the evenings.
Surely he doesn't work day and night!"

"No!" David suddenly seemed awkward and uneasy,
and he refused to meet her eyes.

"Is there something wrong with Adam?" she demanded.

"What could be wrong with him? He puts in a hard
day's work every day."

"I know he's all right physically, but what about his
mental condition?"

"Why should you say that?" He moistened his lips,
his eyes dark and steady as he looked at her. "Has someone been saying things to you about Adam?"

"Certainly not. But I am a trained nurse, remember,
and although I haven't seen much of Adam since I've been
here, I have had the opportunity of noticing him."

"Adam had a bad time of it when he was jilted."

"That's understandable when a man loves a girl. It
must have been a bad shock."

"It was one that affected him permanently. He had a
nervous breakdown, and since his recovery he's stayed
away from women. It affected all our lives because we had
to watch him a great deal. I think I ought to tell you that
there was an incident soon after his recovery which
involved a girl, and it might have had serious reper-
cussions if Owen hadn't been on the spot. Since then we've
kept a close watch on him, and he's given us no trouble
whatever."

"Is he the reason why you warned me to lock my door
at night?" she asked.

"That's right. But since your arrival Adam hasn't been
sleeping in the house. He's living in a farm cottage about
two miles from here!"

" Because of my presence in the house?" Clare was astounded and dismayed. " But this is too bad, David. He shouldn't be pushed out because of me. Such a situation could only make him feel more keenly the trouble he's had."

" It's better to be safe than sorry. I wouldn't be able to sleep nights if Adam were in the house. In fact Owen and I took it in turns to sit up and watch over you those first nights you were here."

" Really?" Clare could not control her surprise. " Poor Adam! But hasn't he had treatment for this condition?"

" He wouldn't have treatment. After his recovery he refused to consult a doctor."

" But it isn't fair to him, and you or your father should have insisted that something was done for him."

" We discussed it, but we decided that if it was discovered that Adam was incurable then he might have to be locked away. He leads a hard but simple life here on the farm, but he's happy in it, and if he had to go away then his life would become a complete misery."

" I can see your point of view, but I do think you should have taken a chance with him. He could be helped back to a normal life." Clare watched his intent face with pity in her heart. She felt for Adam, and she felt for David himself. " So you and Owen sacrificed your own chances of leading normal lives because of Adam!"

" That's about the size of it." He sighed heavily. " How could either of us get married and leave here? When anything happens to Father Adam would be here alone."

" All the more reason why something should be done about Adam," she insisted. " Supposing you or Owen meet a woman who becomes important to you? When love strikes there's not much you can do about it."

"We ensured that we didn't come into contact with women, so that was never likely to happen." He paused and looked away, his dark eyes taking on a distant expression, and he seemed to tense. His voice became harsh and he clasped his hands. " That was before you came, Clare. You made all the difference. Now life seems intolerable."

" Because of me?" She was surprised. " I know that I can't please everyone, and that some people have taken an instant dislike to me, but I didn't think I'd made such a bad impression on you, or Owen for that matter."

" You didn't make a bad impression. Quite the opposite, in fact. I've fallen for you in a big way, Clare, and life is sheer hell now."

He looked at her then, and she stared into his dark eyes, held immobile by his words. All that he'd said had seemed to drag veils from her eyes and her mind. A number of questions had been answered by his words, and she could understand perfectly the atmosphere that had seemed to exist at her arrival. But his declaration of love seemed to go right through her, unfastening flood gates in her mind, and her own feelings came coursing sweet and clear like a mountain stream, swirling and eddying inside her, filling her with intense hope and desire. She reached out a hand and touched his forearm, and her face showed some of her feelings.

" David!" His name tremored on her lips. " I'm sorry if my presence has created problems for you. But problems are there to be solved, you know."

" Does that mean you have some feelings for me?" There was sudden eagerness in his tones, and hope in his eyes. He reached across for her hand, and clasped it tightly. " But what's the use?" he demanded. " Everything is against me! Apart from this domestic situation which can't be changed anyway, there's your future to be considered. You're a private nurse and accustomed to working anywhere in the country. How can we get over that?"

" Perhaps you're looking too far ahead," she suggested.

He nodded slowly, his eyes still bright. " Let's go out in the car," he said. " I want to get away from here for the day. Sue is all right to travel, isn't she?"

" Yes. She'd like a day out."

" Then go and get her ready and I'll tell Betty to prepare a picnic basket for us." His tones had a boyish ring to them, and Clare got immediately to her feet.

" Doctor Laverne won't be calling today," she said. " There's nothing to prevent us leaving right away. I shan't be two minutes getting Sue ready."

Clare seemed to be in a whirl as she took Sue into the house, explaining to the girl that they were going out for the day. David's words had seemed to open up her mind and jolt her feelings. Her hands trembled as she put Sue in a clean dress, and when they were ready they went down to the hall, to find David waiting there for them, talking to Betty. The housekeeper gave Clare a friendly smile of approval, and David turned to the door with a smile on his face.

" The hamper is in the boot and we have a full tank of petrol," he said cheerfully. " I don't know what time we'll be back, Betty, so you can expect us when you see us!"

" Have a nice time," the woman said happily. She studied Clare's face and seemed to read something there which she liked. " Sue will enjoy herself, no doubt."

" And Sue isn't the only one," David retorted.

It wasn't until they were seated in the car and driving away from the farm that Clare felt completely relieved and certain that they would have the day to themselves. She frowned a little as she looked over her shoulder to glance at the house and saw Owen standing at the library window. His dark face was set in brooding lines, and he gave no indication of seeing her. She faced the front again feeling a little dampened in spirit, for the problems David said were facing him seemed insurmountable in that moment. But she soon cheered when they turned into the road and the farm was lost in the background.

" Where would you like to go?" David asked.

" I'm a stranger in these parts, remember," she replied. "Since I'm easy to please you drive on and find somewhere that suits you." She glanced down at Sue, on her lap, and the child looked up and smiled happily. " You like being out in the car, don't you, Sue?" she demanded.

Sue nodded emphatically, and Clare hugged the child. She had the feeling that this was going to be one of those days that stick in the memory for a lifetime afterwards. When she thought of the words David had spoken about his feelings for her she could hardly think of the future and what it might contain. She could not even decide what it was she wanted from life, but there were unuttered hopes in her heart and she felt certain that something would come of this.

From time to time she glanced at David, who was intent upon his driving, and she wondered what it was exactly that she felt for him. She was still a little surprised to find any emotion at all inside her. But her innate loneliness had slackened its grip upon her and she didn't want it ever to return.

David took them to a local beauty spot and they spread a car rug upon the grass and sat by a river bank. There were some pleasure craft on the river, and they watched the progress of the boats while they relaxed. Sue curled up beside Clare and promptly fell asleep, and Clare leaned back and closed her eyes against the glare of the sun. She was lulled by the heat, and felt pleasantly comfortable. David stretched out at her side and lay on his back with his hands behind his head, and when she looked at him she saw that he was staring thoughtfully at the bright sky.

"What thoughts are passing through your mind right now?" she asked softly, glancing at Sue to ensure that she didn't disturb the girl.

" I was thinking of you, and the situation that encompasses me. I don't like it much, but there's little I can do about it. However my hopes and fears don't enter into it. I've known you five weeks now, and I've resolved to wait and see what happens."

" That's rather a negative attitude, isn't it?" she challenged, and was only too aware of the sudden and rapid pounding of her heart.

" It has to be," he replied simply, and pushed himself up on one elbow. He looked down into her face, taking in all the details of her, and Clare tensed a little against her will. She was still trying to analyse her feelings when he leaned towards her and kissed her.

At first she could hardly feel the pressure of his lips, but she liked the sensation their contact provided. He seemed about to draw away from her, and blind panic flitted through her mind at the thought. Then she reached up and took hold of his shoulders, pulling him closer, and he gained confidence and encircled her with his strong arms.

Time seemed to stop and the world ceased to revolve as far as Clare was concerned. Nothing seemed real from the moment he kissed her. She closed her eyes and imagined that she was floating high and far on a fleecy cloud. The sensation swamping her mind was indescribable, and Clare could only hang on to David and hope that reality stayed far away.

When he released her she kept her eyes closed for a moment, and knew that he was studying her closely. Then she opened her eyes and looked up at him, and saw the tender expression on his face.

" I'm sorry if I did wrong," he said. " I wouldn't want to upset you in any way."

" Why should you think it was a wrong thing to do?"

" Well you're not the kind of girl to let any man kiss her!"

" You're not any man, as far as I'm concerned."

" That's nice to know." He smiled gravely. " But it has made matters more complicated, hasn't it?"

" In what way?"

" Nothing is simple any more. We can never go back to what we were early this morning, before I came out of the house to see you."

"That's true." She was aware that things would never be the same again. One kiss was all that was needed to make the change, and changes would keep on taking place. Love could never stand still, and love would never be satisfied with a vacuum.

" I've fallen in love with you, Clare, over the past five weeks." He spoke softly, almost reluctantly. " It was a process that started on the evening I saw you at the hospital. I've never had any trouble keeping my mind off girls. Owen was more the lady killer! But until I met you I didn't know the meaning of the word love. It's something you've taught me already. Now for the first time I can begin to understand some of the powerful feelings that were at work in Adam. Before this I couldn't really understand what had thrown him so badly. Poor Adam! If this was part of his suffering then I'm really sorry for him."

She watched his face and took in his fleeting expressions. She could hardly cope with the influx of emotion that had swamped her. She could feel her lips burning from their contact, and deep inside her was the desire to be kissed again.

"I'm relieved that my feelings have been expressed," he said quietly, still watching her. "But I expect you're astonished, aren't you?"

"I have been expecting it for days now," she replied slowly.

"Really?" He sounded surprised. "Have my feelings been showing to such an extent?"

"I had a feeling that you might be attracted to me," she said cautiously

"Attracted?" he repeated. "That's a poor word for what I'm feeling right now. But what about you, Clare? How has this found you?"

"I've been hoping you would lower your defences," she admitted.

"You wanted me to kiss you?" he persisted.

"Yes. I was hoping you would."

He leaned towards her again and kissed her once more, and she held his shoulders and closed her eyes, lost in a sweet world of pleasure. She couldn't understand what was happening to her, but she wanted it to go on, and she didn't dare look into the future, to the end of the case. That ending would probably bring other endings, and at this time and in this place she could not bear to think of them.

"I understand that it's a golden rule of yours never to become involved with the family of your patient," he said. "You've broken that rule, Clare."

"I hope I haven't made a mistake," she said.

"I hope you haven't. It would be dreadful if this wonderful feeling I have, brought you nothing but trouble."

"It wouldn't be the first time love brought trouble with it," she murmured.

"Have you been in love before, and found trouble?" he demanded.

" I wasn't in love, although I might have thought I was at the time. But I found trouble when I became friendly with a man." She shivered despite the heat when she thought of Tim Millard, and tried to get her thoughts moving.

" I'd never do anything to hurt you," he said tenderly. " I've been watching you over the weeks, and the way you handle Sue is a credit to you. You've got a way with her that's little short of miraculous. We were very worried about her before your arrival, but you've taken over perfectly, and we haven't a moment's worry about her future. You've solved all our problems concerning her, Clare."

" But I've saddled you with some fresh ones, haven't I?" she demanded.

" Personally, no. But with regard to the rest of my family I do see some difficulties arising. I don't know what Owen is going to say about this, or what Adam might do if he learned about it. I am afraid I'll have to ask you to remain silent about this for a bit, Clare."

" I wouldn't dream of saying anything, but if I recall the expression on Betty's face as we left the house together I wouldn't mind betting that she will have a thing or two to say."

" She knows enough about the situation to keep quiet in the house," he retorted.

" Then I really don't see where the problems come in," Clare told him.

He looked into her eyes with steady gaze, and she held on to his hands as if afraid that this was just a dream that would pass too quickly.

" I won't let any problems come between us," he said firmly. " It's the only attitude to take. I have a feeling that we are going to be important to one another before this case ends, Clare, and I'm not going to let anything change my mind."

NINE

CLARE'S LIFE seemed to change tempo from that day. It was the most memorable day she had ever spent, and when it was time to go home later she was regretful that it had ended. But she had come to learn a lot about David in the hours they'd spent together. In the previous five weeks she had learned only what he wanted her to know. She was happy with what she had discovered.

He was a tender man, with gentle ways, and a great sense of humour which had been suppressed for years. But by the end of the day he was chatting and joking with her as if they had known each other for very much longer than five weeks.

Sue enjoyed her day, Clare was certain, and the child's face was brown and healthy. The child had started to fill out a little, proof that she was making the progress they all desired, and as David drove them home that late afternoon, Clare felt that everything in her world was all right.

They were passing through the village when Sue spotted an ice-cream van, and the girl tugged at Clare's arm and pointed. David grinned as he brought the vehicle to a stop, and he glanced at Clare enquiringly as he opened the door.

" We'll all have one, shall we? I feel half baked, being out there in the sun all day. Would you like an ice, Clare?"

" Yes please!" She smiled at him, then looked down at Sue. " You like ice-cream, don't you, Sue?"

The child looked up at her and smiled, and David chuckled as he got out of the car. There was a small queue at the van, and David took his place in the line. Clare watched him for some moments. Her pulse was racing and she could feel her emotions churning up inside. Sue sighed and laid her head against Clare's shoulder.

" Are you too hot, Sue?" Clare demanded, and the girl nodded. " Never mind. We'll soon be home, and then we'll change you into something cooler. I expect you're ready for tea now, aren't you?"

Again the child nodded, and Clare hugged her tightly for a moment. She looked across the road to where the ice-cream van was parked, and saw David waiting patiently. Then she looked ahead, and saw a man getting out of a car about fifty yards from them. There was something familiar in the man's gait as he walked towards her on the pavement, and Clare frowned as she studied him. When he drew nearer she stared at his face, and for a moment she couldn't believe her eyes. It was the man she never wanted to see again—Tim Millard!

For some moments she stared at him uncomprehendingly. He came closer, looking at the houses as he passed, and slowly a sense of horror overcame the disbelief that had caught her. It was Tim Millard! She stiffened in her seat and tensed so much that Sue looked up into her face enquiringly.

Clare set her teeth and looked down at the child, pushing her face against Sue's cheek and watching Millard as he came ever closer. It was Tim Millard. Now she was certain, and dread filled her mind as she watched his progress. She felt as if he were stepping out of a bad dream, and her thoughts had frozen solid. She just could not think straight at all.

Then it dawned on her that he was looking for a certain house. She swallowed the lump that had risen in her throat. What was he doing here in Chippenbury?

Was it just a coincidence that he was in the same locality as she? She ducked her head as he came abreast of the car, but he was too intent upon the houses to glance in her direction. He went on, and she twisted in her seat to look at him.

When he paused at the doctor's house, Clare was overtaken by a great fear. Was he trying to track her down from London? Had he got as far as Grant in the line that led to her? She was in a fever of uncertainty as she watched him pausing outside the doctor's gate. If he went in and asked for her, Grant would reveal her whereabouts! She was horror stricken. If only she had thought to tell Grant that she didn't want to be traced. She wouldn't have had to give him any reasons for the request, and the way to her would have been blocked.

For some moments, Millard stood studying the outside of the doctor's house, and Clare watched him helplessly. He didn't look much different to the man she had thought she'd loved. But prison had taken some flesh off his frame. She wondered how long he had been free, and it hurt her to recall those early days after he had been convicted. It had taken her some considerable time to get over the shock he'd given her. But she didn't want to see him again, and she knew he would leave no stone unturned in order to find her. He had sent word to her by way of some of his friends, and she had worked hard at losing herself and that part of her painful past.

When Millard went to the door of the house and rang the bell, Clare felt as if she would faint. There was a buzzing sound in her ears and dark specks seemed to flash before her eyes. But there was no reply, and she heaved a long sigh of relief. Perhaps Grant and Amanda had gone out for a drive. He would be off duty on Sunday afternoon! She mentally crossed her fingers and prayed that it was so, and in that instant she saw David coming back to the car.

She kept watching Millard as long as possible, and nodded hopefully when she saw him turn away from the house and depart. She looked up at David as he got into the car, and kept one eye on Tim Millard as she attended to Sue.

" We deserve this after all the time we've spent getting baked today," David said cheerfully. He looked at Clare as he gave her a large wafer. " Is something wrong?" he demanded. " You look as if you've just seen a ghost!"

" I'm all right. Perhaps it's a case of too much sun today. I do feel the glare a bit, but I'm quite all right."

" Let's hurry and get you home," he said.

" No. Let's sit here and eat our ices," she said quickly. " I'm all right, David, really I am!"

" All right." He smiled as he looked at Sue, who was tucking into her ice-cream cornet. " Sue doesn't like ice-cream, by the looks of her."

Clare didn't answer. She was watching Tim Millard, who was getting back into his car. She was telling herself that she had to get in touch with Grant as soon as possible in order to warn him not to divulge her whereabouts. It couldn't be coincidence that Millard was here in Chippenbury and visiting Grant Laverne on some other matter. He was after Clare and she knew it.

Clare was on thorns until they returned to Oakapple Farm, and her mind was filled with fearful speculation as she thanked David for their trip and then started up the stairs with Sue. She wanted to telephone Grant. She had to get in touch with him before Millard did. She could think of nothing else as she freshened Sue with a wash and changed the girl's clothes. When she had changed herself they went down to see David again, and tea was ready for them. Clare left the girl in David's care and went into the hall to call Grant.

There was no reply to her call, and she could feel a fever of anxiety enveloping her as she went back to have tea. She had to contact Grant!

"You're still looking apprehensive, Clare," David observed during the meal. "Are you sure there's nothing wrong?"

For a moment she was tempted to tell him, but thought better of it and shook her head.

"I'm all right," she said. "It must have been the sun."

"I hope you're not going to be ill!" His tones were serious, and he studied her closely. "Perhaps we'd better get the doctor to check you over when he calls next time."

"It could be the excitement of the day," she said, forcing a smile, and although she looked into his face endearingly, it was Tim Millard she was seeing. A shiver ran through her when she pictured his harsh face, and she knew he would cause a great deal of trouble for her if he ever saw her, although she could not understand why he wanted to see her again! She had made it quite clear to him when his real character was exposed that she wanted nothing more to do with him, and he had seemed to accept it at the time of his trial. Then she thought of the visits she had received from some of Millard's friends just before she made the decision to disappear from his particular area. They had told her Millard was displeased with her, and she never discovered the reason.

"I'm sorry if my actions have caused you any discomfort," he said, his eyes dark and intent. " Perhaps I've been too impatient, Clare."

The door of the room opened then and Clare looked up to see Owen standing in the doorway. He looked around for a moment, hesitated, and then came in, moving to a seat opposite Clare. He stared at her with cool brown eyes, and then glanced at his younger brother.

" You've made a day of it," he remarked harshly.

" Why not?" David replied, smiling faintly. But he glanced at Clare as if afraid that too much might be said.

" You deserve a break now and again, David." Owen's tones softened quickly. " You work much too hard, you know."

" Well that's a change from your usual tune," David retorted. " What's brought this on, Owen?"

Owen shrugged, and Clare was glad when the door opened at that moment to admit Betty with Owen's tea. When the housekeeper had gone again, Owen looked at Sue. The girl was seated at Clare's side, tucking into her meal with all the signs of hunger.

" And what about you, Sue?" Owen demanded, leaning forward to stare into the girl's face. " Have you enjoyed yourself?"

Sue nodded, but did not pause in her eating, and Owen smiled his satisfaction and began his own tea. But Clare felt an awkwardness coming upon her, and she could not keep her eyes from Owen's set features. She tried looking at David, but he was so obviously full of elation that she was afraid he might say something of the developing situation between them to his brother.

" I've spent a lonely sort of a day," Owen commented at length. " It wouldn't be so bad for me if Adam came to the house on Sundays, but because he's not here during the week he won't come when he's not working."

" It's none of my business," Clare said impulsively, " but perhaps we ought to talk about Adam." She saw David frowning as she glanced at him, but she did feel strongly about his eldest brother. Owen glanced at David, too, and his face was beginning to set more harshly.

" Have you told her about Adam?" he demanded.

" I told her today," David replied easily. " I felt she ought to know what the situation is."

Owen stared at Clare, and she could tell there was conflict inside him. His dark eyes were stormy, passionate, almost wild, and she could see how intense a person he was. Then he sighed heavily and shook his head.

" It's a burden we all share," he said. " It's affected my life to a greater extent than David's, but you're going to get your share of the load, David. Make no mistake of that."

" I've never tried to do less than my share," David retorted. " I always seem to be the one to get the heaviest share."

" In some things, but not in others," Owen said sharply. " I think it all balances out evenly, taking everything into consideration."

" You're alluding to your romantic life!" There was a trace of bitterness in David's tones, and Clare saw his lips twist a little as he spoke. " So you had to give up the woman you loved for Adam's sake, but are you forgetting that she was Adam's future wife? Will you ever be able to forget that it was you who pushed Adam into his particular hell?"

Owen pulled a face, and his lips tightened. Clare listened intently, realising that she was learning more of the situation that existed here, and each little scrap of information helped to complete the picture she was building up in her mind. She recalled that she had seen Owen with a woman in the village, and Amanda had told her it was the woman

Adam had wanted to marry! So Owen had fallen in love with the same woman, and she had turned from Adam, causing him to suffer his nervous breakdown. And Owen was paying now for what he had done. He had to remain at home to help take care of his brother.

They finished the meal in near silence, and Clare was relieved when Sue intimated that she wanted to leave the table. She got to her feet with an excuse on her lips, and left the room with the girl, heaving a long sigh of relief as she closed the door at her back. She could foresee some of the problems facing David, and she didn't think there were any simple solutions readily available.

She put through another call to Grant's house, and didn't know whether to feel relieved because there was no reply. At least Tim Millard couldn't contact him while he was away from home, she thought, and took Sue up the stairs. There was a niggling worry fighting for supremacy over the joyful state of mind which tried to take hold of her because of the day's events. She sighed deeply when she pictured David's face and recalled the worry in his dark eyes.

When she had put Sue to bed and settled the child for the night, Clare went down into the hall again, and called Grant's number once more. She waited while the dialling clicked out the message at the automatic exchange, and then the ringing tone sounded. She tried to will someone to answer, and when she heard the receiver being lifted at the other end of the line her relief was immeasurable. It was Amanda who answered, and for a moment Clare could not reply. Then she moistened her lips.

"Amanda, this is Clare," she said stiffly. "Is Grant there? I would like to talk to him!"

"Clare! Is anything wrong?"

" Not here at the Farm," Clare hastened to reassure. " But I happened to be in the village just before tea and I saw someone calling at your house."

" Really? Someone you know?" Amanda sounded surprised. " We went out for a drive, and it was such a lovely afternoon that we decided to have tea out. We've only just got back."

" I know. I called several times." Clare tried to keep her concern out of her tones. " I hope you had a nice time!"

" It was wonderful, but let me get Grant for you. I must say you do sound worried, Clare."

" I think it will be all right if I can just talk to Grant," Clare said.

" Hang on a moment and I'll fetch him for you." The phone crackled as the receiver at the other end was put down, and Clare waited anxiously for Grant.

" Hello, Clare, what's the trouble?" Grant demanded as he lifted the receiver.

" Grant!" For a moment Clare couldn't think straight, and she hesitated while she tried to recollect herself.

" Yes?" he prompted. " You're all right, aren't you, Clare? Has anything happened at the Farm?"

" No, it isn't that! Do you remember just before you left the hospital to take up general practice here that I had become friendly with a man?"

" Yes, I do. It was such an event, and I was most pleased for your sake. What was his name now? Don't tell me! I'm sure I can guess! It was Tim something-or-other!"

" Tim Millard!" Clare moistened her lips. " I saw him at your door this afternoon, Grant!"

" Why should he be here, Clare? Look, you sound as if you're in a flat spin. Just take it easy and tell me what it's all about."

" It's obvious from what you say that he hasn't been back to see you," she said hastily. " I don't want him to know my whereabouts, Grant. I left the hospital and took this present job because I wanted to get away from him. If he does come asking for me, would you tell him you don't know where I am?"

" Well he must be coming to see me because he's learned I sent for you, Clare, so I'll have to tell him that you came here about a job but didn't take it, shall I? Would that do?"

" I'll be eternally grateful if you would put him off, Grant," she said.

" All right. It's none of my business, but if there's anything I can do to help then just let me know. I am responsible for you being here, and I wouldn't want to be the cause of any trouble for you."

" Thank you. If you'd just put him off when he calls to see you I think it will be all right."

" He must have got on to me through your Bureau. They wouldn't divulge your present whereabouts, would they?"

" No. The Bureau wouldn't do that. The most they'd do would be to forward his address to me in case I wanted to get in touch with him."

" Well then, you have nothing to worry about. I won't let him know where you are, but you'll have to be very careful if he knows you're in this area. He'll only have to bide his time and he's sure to see you."

" Then perhaps you'll tell him I've gone back to London," she suggested.

" I'll do that! Don't worry, Clare. He won't find you through me."

" He's a nasty type, Grant. I didn't find that out until almost too late."

" I'll be able to handle him if he comes here!" He chuckled. " I'll call in and see you in the morning, Clare. We'll have a chat about this!"

" Thank you, Grant. I feel much easier now I've spoken to you."

" See you tomorrow then. Good-bye for now, Clare."

" Good-bye, and thanks!" She sighed deeply as she hung up, and when she turned around she started nervously, for Owen was standing in the doorway of the library, watching her with a grim expression on his dark face.

" What was that all about?" he demanded.

" You were listening?" she countered.

" Certainly! Why shouldn't I try to learn a little about your previous background?"

" It is no concern of yours."

" I'm making it my concern. You're here nursing my niece, and my youngest brother is becoming much too interested in you."

Clare held her breath for a moment, and she could feel her pulses racing and her heart pounding.

" You'd better come into the library so we can have a talk," Owen went on. " I think it's time we got together."

" I can think of nothing we could discuss," she replied calmly.

" If you want to stay on here in your present capacity then you'd do well not to go against me," he retorted.

" Where is David?"

" In the office, doing some of the work he left today in order to take you out."

Clare walked towards him, determined not to be bullied in any way, but she felt that he held her at a disadvantage, and he knew it. She walked past him into the library and continued to the tall window. He shut the door and followed her, pausing at her shoulder. They both looked out into the gardens. The sky was still a deep blue, and bright sunlight bathed the lawns and flower beds.

" I'm not jealous of David and you," Owen said at length. " You can get that idea out of your head immediately. I've been interested in only one woman in my entire life."

" And that's the girl your brother Adam wanted to marry!" Clare turned and looked at him. " I saw you with her that day you drove Sue and I into the village."

" It's nobody's business!" he burst out. " I'm single and so is she!"

" But it wouldn't do for Adam to learn that you're seeing her, would it?"

" You wouldn't tell him. You're not a girl like that!"

" You've soon characterised me! But you're not so easy to put into a category. What's on your mind about me?"

" Why should there be something on my mind about you?" he challenged.

" You're not happy because David and I are becoming friends."

" I think you've both gone past that stage, well past it."

" And so?" She looked defiantly into his eyes, knowing that he didn't like the situation that was developing. But she couldn't worry about him now. She was only concerned about keeping out of Tim Millard's way.

" So I think I've found something to use against you." His face didn't change. He was harsh and determined, and his dark eyes were gleaming with triumph.

" I don't know what you mean."

" You know! Who is the man you're trying to keep away from?"

" I don't think that's any of your business." Clare faced him out, determined not to give anything away. " What is it you want from me? What do you hope for the future regarding my presence here?"

" I want you to do the job you came here for and then leave. There's nothing more than that."

" Why don't you like the idea of David and me becoming friendly?"

"Because he's the youngest of us, and will expect to be able to marry and go away from here!"

"You'd like to do that yourself, wouldn't you?"

"That's right, but it's impossible. While Adam is like he is then the both of us must remain here. We agreed to do this from the outset in order to keep it all away from our father, and no woman is coming in here to change the set-up."

"Your father doesn't know about Adam?" Clare demanded.

"Not all of it."

"But why haven't you spoken to the doctor about this? You must want Adam to get better."

"I imagine David had spoken to you about this. There's not much we can do with Adam. It takes us all our time to keep him here working on the farm."

"If he were my brother I would want him cured. He needs medical help and ought to get it. Supposing you can't control him one day? What happens then?"

"Just hope that you're not here if it happens," he retorted.

Clare turned and walked towards the door. "I think we ought to leave this situation just as it is," she said over her shoulder. "I expect Sue will regain her speech before long, and then I'll be leaving here for good."

"And what about David?" Owen demanded.

"I can't speak for him." Clare paused as she opened the door. "He's a man and can speak for himself. I don't know what he'll do about this situation."

"You can depend that I shall do everything in my power to control it," he said carefully.

Clare did not reply, but she was most thoughtful as she departed. She was beginning to realise that there were a lot of things she didn't know.

TEN

UNTIL CLARE saw Grant Laverne next morning she could not settle to anything, and felt that her impatience would cause her to burst. How she slept through the night she did not know, but she was awake very early in the morning and eagerly awaiting the doctor's visit long before he was due to arrive.

When Sue was awake, Clare prepared the child for the day, and they went down to breakfast in the kitchen. There was no sign of David, and Clare felt relieved when she didn't see Owen. She was very thoughtful, and had to make an effort to show a smiling face to Betty when they entered the kitchen.

"Hello, dear," the housekeeper greeted Sue. "What would you like for breakfast?" She looked up at Clare and smiled. "How are you today? Did you have a nice time yesterday?"

"We thoroughly enjoyed ourselves," Clare replied. "It was beautiful! I was sorry when the time came to an end."

"It did David a lot of good, too," Betty said slowly. She was watching Clare closely. "He was up very early this morning and had breakfast and went out. I don't know when he'll be back, but he said for me to give you his kindest regards."

Clare smiled. "I have the feeling that David has led a very lonely life here in the past," she said.

"They all have!" Betty set about preparing breakfast

for them. " Do you want to eat in the breakfast room or will you sit here with me?"

" We'll sit with you!" Clare was intent upon learning as much as she could from the housekeeper. Betty should know just about everything there was to know, considering the time she had been here.

" I've noticed a great change in Owen in the past few days," Betty said as she cut some bread. Clare was seating Sue at the table, and she glanced up at the woman. " I wouldn't swear to it, but I wouldn't be surprised if he's courting at last."

" Who's the girl?" Clare demanded.

" I don't know, but I have heard that there is someone."

" What about Adam, Betty?"

" Adam?" The woman met Clare's eyes with uneasy gaze. " What about him?"

" What's going to happen to him if Owen or David thinks of getting married?"

" Neither of them will consider that until their father is dead."

" Because they can't leave Adam alone?"

" That's about the size of it. I presume you've been told a bit about Adam!"

" Yes. That story you gave me when I first arrived about the place being haunted wasn't true, was it? It was Adam you were meaning when you said it was better to lock the bedroom doors at night."

" It was Adam!" Betty heaved a long sigh. " Did David tell you about him? I'm relieved that you know now."

" David told me yesterday! I tried to get him to see that Adam should have medical treatment. He should be able to recover from this."

" They tried to get him to see that point of view, but Adam was in hospital for some time when he had that breakdown. He also tried to take his life, you know.

When he got over that and came out of hospital he vowed then never to have anything more to do with such places."

"I see. It sounds like a difficult case, but I'm sure he could be won round. I'm going to have another word with David about this when I get the opportunity." Clare shook her head slowly. "It's a dreadful situation, isn't it? Poor Adam can't live a normal life and neither can either of his brothers."

"That's why Owen has been as savage as he has!" Betty shook her head. "You can't blame him, and he had to fall in love with the girl who jilted Adam."

"Did she leave Adam because of Owen?" Clare asked.

"Yes! That's the hurtful thing about it. Owen is a decent enough man beneath that awful temper of his, and he suffered a great deal by what happened. But when two people fall in love to that extent there's nothing they can do about it. I knew that kind of love. That's why it hit me so hard when my husband was killed."

Clare was trying to examine her own feelings while she listened to the housekeeper, but she could not keep her mind upon her own love affair. She wanted to learn all that Betty could tell her. She sensed that a stalemate situation was going to develop, and when deadlock was reached there would be mounting tension and fury from some quarters. What did she really feel for David? She thought of the day before, and tremored at the recollection of his kisses. She had never been moved like that before. She held her breath for a moment, then released it in a long sigh, and she broke that particular thread in her mind and returned her attention to Sue.

"I was talking to the Brigadier yesterday," Betty said. "We discussed Sue. I think they're going to have her see a specialist. It's about time she began to use her tongue again. It will be very nice to hear her talking once more."

" Doctor Laverne was saying the same thing." Clare nodded. " She's had time to get over the shock of what happened. Psychiatric treatment will do much for her. It should unlock her mind."

" What really happened to her then? What actually caused this loss of speech?"

" It's quite simple, really! Sue suffered such an overwhelming shock at the time of the accident that her mental condition was in danger of destruction by the strain put upon it. Nature has built into all of us certain defensive mechanisms that come into play under real stress. Loss of memory is one form of this. Sue's affliction is another. A part of the mental circuit cuts out, much like a fuse blows when something goes wrong in one of the wires. Then something happens, like loss of speech or memory."

" So this is something similar to what happened to Adam!"

" I wouldn't have thought so!" Clare shook her head. " Adam took such a shock that he completely broke down, and when he recovered he felt the need to make someone else suffer for what had happened to him. As it was a woman who caused his trouble then he instinctively decided that women should suffer. So when pressures and strains became too much for him now he turns to women to get rid of his anger."

" I had the feeling that it was something like that. But do you think he could get really violent and hurt someone badly?" Betty moistened her lips as she spoke.

" I wouldn't like to comment on that. But I do feel that David and Owen are making a big mistake by keeping his condition concealed as they are doing."

" No wonder we've been told to lock our bedroom doors at night!" Betty suppressed a shiver.

" I wouldn't like to be around if he really blew his top," Clare said firmly.

"Let's change the subject!" The housekeeper reached for the teapot. "More tea?"

"No thank you!" Clare returned her attention to Sue, who had finished her breakfast. "Shall we get ready and go out into the garden? Doctor Laverne is coming to see us this morning." Her pale eyes darkened momentarily as she thought of the reason for Grant's visit. She hoped that was one problem that would not materialise.

"Well have a nice time. You're filling in Sue's life just right, Clare. No one could have done such a good job. That child thinks the world of you now."

"We get along all right together," Clare said with a smile. "We'll see you later, Betty. I want to get Sue out into the sunshine."

The housekeeper nodded and bent to kiss the child as she slid off her chair. Sue smiled at her and then turned to Clare, holding out a hand trustingly. They left the kitchen and walked through to the front of the house. Clare paused on the bottom step when she saw movement in the corridor where David had his office.

She knew David was out, so she imagined it was Owen wandering around. Then she saw the heavy figure coming towards her, and she realised it was neither Owen nor David, but Adam himself. Clare seemed to turn to ice at the sight of him, and he came forward as if he hadn't seen her.

"Good morning!"

She had to speak, and he was only feet away when she forced herself to utter the words.

Adam paused as if he had run into a wall, and he blinked as he looked at her. Clare found herself staring into eyes that seemed as black as coal. He hadn't shaved that morning, and his chin and cheeks were covered by a thick black stubble. His eyes narrowed as he stared at her, and she felt that his gaze went right through her.

"I'm looking for David, but he doesn't seem to be around," he said.

"I understand that he's gone out," she said. "I have no idea when he'll be back."

He continued walking, although his eyes stayed on her, and he didn't seem to notice Sue at Clare's side. He went to the front door and departed, and Clare uttered a sigh of relief.

She stood staring reflectively at the door, and there was cold shock inside her. It was obvious that Adam Harley was living under a great strain, and he needed medical help. Her trained instincts told her this without hesitation, and she knew it was wrong of David and Owen to keep their brother's condition quiet. She resolved to speak to Grant as soon as he arrived, and continued up the stairs to Sue's room to get the girl's dolls and other playthings which occupied her on the lawn.

When Grant arrived later that morning, Clare was nervous and apprehensive. His cheery wave as he spotted her gave her some hope that nothing had happened in the village to alarm her, but she could hardly control her nerves as she waited for him to come to the spot where she and Sue were seated.

"Hello, Clare," he greeted, walking across the grass, and he seemed to be in high spirits. "You and Sue look very comfortable. How are you?"

"A bit worried, Grant," she said truthfully.

"About this Tim Millard!" He nodded. "Well don't be. He caught me at the house this morning just as I was about to leave on my round."

"Was he after me?" she demanded in breathless tones.

"Of course! What other reason would he have for seeing me? He has friends everywhere, he told me, and someone had informed him that you had come here to see me about a month ago. He didn't know for certain that you were in this area, but it was a matter of life and death that he sees you. That's what he said, anyway, and I told him I couldn't help him. I said you came here to see about a job but that it didn't work out, and that you'd left almost immediately, promising to get in touch with me again. So far you haven't written or telephoned."

" Did he say why he wanted to see me?" she demanded.

" No. He was curiously silent on that fact. He asked me to contact him if you should get in touch with me at any time, and he left me a telephone number in London to call. Someone would take a message, he said, if he wasn't there at the time."

Clare released her pent up breath in a long sigh, and her eyes narrowed as she considered. What could Millard want with her? Why had he let her know that he was displeased with her? She had done nothing about him since she learned that he was a thief. She had put him completely out of her life. But now he was back like a dark thundercloud, and she was afraid that he might manage to influence her present circumstances. But she owed him nothing and could not understand why he wanted so badly to see her.

" Well that's all I can do for you," Grant said, dropping to one knee and chucking Sue gently under the chin. " Go on with your game, Sue," he told the child. " You're looking very well. We're going to get you to see a specialist very soon. It's about time you started making some noise around here. The place is too quiet."

Clare told herself that was how she liked it, and she took a deep breath as she tried to dismiss all thoughts of Tim Millard from her mind. If he had gone back to London then she had little to worry about.

" Grant, there's something else I'd like to talk to you about," she said.

He straightened and turned to her again. "What's on your mind?" he asked.

She told him about Adam Harley, and saw his brows knit together for a moment. She explained that she thought Adam would recover with treatment, and Grant shook his head slowly.

"I have heard rumours about Adam, of course," he said. "One can't avoid hearing such things in this small community. But the first thing I did when you arrived was have a talk with David about Adam, and he told me that nothing could be done without Adam's consent, which is definitely not forthcoming."

"Did you learn anything at all about Adam's condition?"

"David was fairly frank with me. I told him I didn't like this arrangement, that it would benefit everyone if Adam were to be taken in hand, but he was afraid that any approach to Adam might upset him and shock him into a worse state. I was satisfied that David and Owen had made all efforts possible to safeguard you, and I don't think you have anything to worry about."

"I wasn't thinking of myself," Clare said softly. "But Adam's condition is affecting not only his life but David's and Owen's as well. Owen would like to get married, but he daren't leave the Farm, and he certainly couldn't bring a wife into it."

"And what about David?" Grant studied her intent face for a moment. "You're in love with him, aren't you, Clare?"

"The situation is fluid," she retorted, smiling faintly. "But it is a fact that Adam is the key to everyone's future here."

"Then we must try and do something!" Grant nodded slowly. "I could have a word with Owen. I don't know what his views are in this matter. But if he has hopes of marrying one day then he'll certainly want to get this business cleared up."

" David has gone out, but Owen should be around somewhere. His car is still in the garage so he hasn't left the place."

" Then I'll go and see him now." Grant smiled as he turned away. He glanced back over his shoulder. " You deserve some happiness, Clare, and if there's anything I can do to help you then I'll leave no stone unturned."

" Thank you, Grant. I shall always be in your debt if you can succeed."

" See you again," he retorted, and she watched his stocky figure as he strode away towards the house.

When he had disappeared into the house Clare relaxed a little. She was hopeful that Tim Millard had been put off completely, and she wondered if she had done the right thing in starting this business with Adam. But someone had to take the initiative. If Adam wasn't capable of making a decision to help himself then it was the duty of those nearest to him to do something. She knew she was right. Adam was living a bare human existence, and he would thank anyone who could help him back to normal. She mentally crossed her fingers that all would come right, and she thought of David, wondering what he would have to say when he learned that she had gone over his head in this matter.

Later she saw Grant leaving, and he looked in her direction and waved before getting into his car and driving off. She waved in reply, and watched the car moving swiftly towards the road. When it had passed out of sight she sighed heavily, knowing that wheels had been set into motion and that there was no way of stopping what she had begun.

Owen appeared from the house, and Clare spotted him immediately. He started around the house towards the garage, and she guessed he was going out. But then he glanced across at her and changed direction, striding out towards her with a intentness about him that sent a pang through her. She watched him until he confronted her, and when she looked up into his face she. could not tell what kind of a mood he was in. For a moment he stared down at her, and his face was brooding, filled with shadow.

" I suppose you're responsible for Doctor Laverne knowing about Adam!" he said sharply.

" Someone had to bring Adam's condition to the doctor's notice," she replied. " The fact that I had to do it proves that someone is neglecting his brotherly duty."

" I see! Well there will be trouble over this, and I hope you will be satisfied with the outcome. But for a start I suggest you pack your things and prepare to leave here. Sue is in good health and a visit to a specialist will completely cure her. You'd better get away from here while the going is good."

" What do you mean?"

"Adam will be coming back to the Farm to live. I shall. see to it that he learns the identity of the person who told the doctor about him. What happens then will be on your own head."

" You wouldn't do that. If anything serious happened, Adam would be put away for a long time, and you wouldn't want that. You have to think of your father. He's getting old now and couldn't take any great shock."

She saw his face change expression, and she knew her words had struck home. He had some sense of responsibility because he had sacrificed a great deal in his own life in order to maintain appearances here at the Farm.

"I'm not going to get into an argument with you," he said angrily, his tones rising to such an extent that Sue left her playthings and came to Clare's side, grasping hold of her hand and gazing fearfully up into her uncle's im-

passioned face. " I'll have you know that I will have my
way around here. If you think David will stand up for
you then you'd better think again. He'll do as I tell him."

" I want to help the situation," she said in even tones.
" We must be on the same side, don't you see? We both
want the same things. When Adam recovers completely
then everyone will be free to do what he wants."

" You're thinking of yourself in this. Supposing Adam
doesn't get better? The treatment could make him worse,
you know. Then what happens? They'll probably keep him
locked away in some institution. David isn't going to thank
you for interfering, I can tell you. Just wait until he learns
what you've done."

" He ought to have taken the same step months ago." she
said firmly. " In any case, nothing can be done without
permission, and no doubt you and David will confer on
that."

" And what do we tell my father?" he demanded.

" Tell him there is a chance of helping Adam so you're
taking it."

" I'll repeat what I just said. Adam comes back into the
house where he belongs. I don't care what you do, but if
you stay then the risks are on your own head."

He turned away sharply and strode back the way he
had come. Clare watched him, her breath caught in her
throat, and she was filled with conflicting emotions. He
was wrong, dreadfully wrong about her. She hadn't acted
out of selfishness. She wanted Adam cured completely, and
she wanted them all to be able to live their lives as they
wanted, without fear of what might happen if Adam were
left to his own devices.

The rest of the morning seemed to drag, and she did
what she could to amuse Sue. She wanted dearly to see
David and explain to him why she had done what she did.
He would understand! He had to. He must be feeling the

same fears that engulfed her. Adam was like a millstone around all their necks, and nothing could be normal until Adam had been treated and cured.

When she thought of Adam and the manner he had presented to her that morning she could not help feeling the greatest sympathy for him, and she told herself that she would have acted as she did out of duty, even if she hadn't been in love with David.

She considered her feelings for David. It had to be love, she told herself. When she compared what she felt for David with how she had suffered with Tim Millard, she knew she didn't need further proof. If David loved her, as he admitted, then she could look forward to a fine future. But there were so many ifs to be taken care of that she hardly dared to look at that aspect of the situation.

When it was time for lunch she took Sue into the house and prepared the child for her meal. There was no sign of David, so she went into the kitchen to be with Betty Smithers, not wanting to risk being in Owen's black company. The housekeeper had their meal ready, and they sat down at the table. But before they could begin, the door opened and Cornelius Harley appeared in the doorway.

"Oh!" He stared at them for a moment, then nodded slowly. "I am sorry! I want to talk to you, Nurse, but it will wait until after you've had lunch. Would you come to the library in thirty minutes?"

"Yes, Mr. Harley," Clare replied, and felt a pang stab her as she wondered what he wanted her for.

He nodded. "Sorry to have disturbed you," he said again, and departed.

"He doesn't have lunch," Betty said, listening to the old man's receding footsteps. "He has a snack at ten thirty, and then nothing until tea-time. But what does he want to see you about, Clare? You haven't seen much of him since your arrival, have you?"

" I haven't. I don't know what he does with himself each day, but our paths seldom meet."

" You haven't been doing anything you shouldn't have?" Betty persisted.

" Not to my knowledge."Clare thought of Owen's anger, and believed he had spoken to his father.

Clare left Sue with Betty while she went to report to Cornelius. He got to his feet as she entered, and seemed to bow to her.

" Please come and sit down, Nurse," he said gently.

" Yes, Mr. Harley." Clare went forward to seat herself on the chair which had been placed beside the desk.

" I understand from Owen that you're not entirely happy about the situation we have here," he said thinly. " I'm very sorry about this, for Sue seems to have taken to you and it might upset the child now you have to leave us. However she will have to grow accustomed to the hardships of life, like the rest of us, and I would inform you that your duties here are terminated as of this moment. Perhaps you would pack and be ready to leave in an hour. I shall drive you into town myself and see that you catch your train back to London. Your termination pay and all things relating to your employment here will be settled by post with your Bureau. Thank you for what you have done for Sue in the time that you've been here. I have been most pleased with the way you handled the case, and I'll forward a good reference to your Bureau along with the rest of your things."

He paused for breath, but Clare had nothing to say. She could only sit and stare at him, shocked by this drastic and unexpected move.

ELEVEN

" I THINK perhaps Owen misunderstood me, Mr. Harley," Clare said slowly. " I wouldn't dream of leaving a case before its logical end, and if I went now it might do a great deal of harm to Sue."

" I'm sure it wouldn't help her to have a nurse who isn't happy in these surroundings," came the smooth reply. " I think Sue will be all right. I've already made enquiries about a replacement."

" Then let me stay until the replacement arrives," Clare said, trying to keep her tones even. " Betty can't take care of Sue and do her normal duties."

" I think it would be better to have you gone within the hour," he said.

" Perhaps you'd better consult Doctor Laverne before you proceed with this." Clare's heart leaped with sudden hope as she thought of Grant. " Sue is the only one to be concerned about in this, and as I have no desire to leave the case then surely you can reconsider your decision."

" My mind has been made up for me," he said, shaking his head.

" By Owen, I suspect," Clare said. " But you stood out against Owen when it was first decided that a nurse was needed here. Why have you gone back on your own decision, especially after Sue has had time to get to know and trust me. I would ask you to do some more thinking on this before you send me away, Mr. Harley. Sue is going to be greatly upset, and this shock might undo some of the good I've been able to do for her."

His wrinkled face showed some signs of indecision at her words, and Clare felt a rush of hope in her mind. She couldn't go away without first seeing and talking to David. She couldn't understand why Owen should be so keen to get rid of her. He had as much to gain as David from Adam's recovery. But Cornelius Harley slowly shook his head.

"My house has been divided for a long time. I don't really understand why there should have been so much trouble. But now my son Frank is dead and there seems to be no end to the problem. Sue is looking better, and I feel that she will do all right after you've gone."

"I must go if you order it," Clare said. "But won't you first talk with Doctor Laverne before you make any firm decision?"

"This is something that doesn't concern the doctor. If you would prepare to leave I'll see that you get to the station."

Clare looked into his eyes and saw firm resolution in their dark depths. She felt a wave of despair begin to envelop her. It was like a bad dream coming true. She would have to leave. She got slowly to her feet, watching the old man's face, hoping against hope that he would suddenly change his mind and tell her to stay. But his lips were compressed and she knew he wouldn't say anything. It seemed that his mind had been made up for him, and Owen was to blame for this.

"May I say good-bye to Sue?" she asked as she turned towards the door.

"I would rather you didn't. Betty will take care of her. Do not worry yourself about Sue. She'll be all right."

"I'd like to call Doctor Laverne before I leave," she said finally. "He must know about this."

" Of course. Use the telephone in the hall."

Clare nodded and departed, and a sigh escaped her as she left the library. She went to the telephone and dialled Grant's number, hoping against hope that he was at home. It was Amanda who answered, and Clare informed the woman of the situation.

" This is dreadful," Amanda said. " Grant isn't home yet, but he won't be long. When do you have to leave?"

" In an hour. Sue is with the housekeeper."

" And what does David have to say about this?"

" David is out and I have no idea when he'll be back."

" I see. Well hang on there, Clare, and if Grant doesn't come home in the meantime or telephone in, I'll come and collect you. You had better stay with us for a few days. Grant will be upset by this. He thinks Sue has made sufficient progress to visit a specialist shortly, and this shock could put her right back to the beginning again."

" That's what I told Mr. Harley, but he doesn't agree with me." Clare was frowning as she tried to get her mind to work normally. She was badly shocked by what had happened, and she knew Sue would be similarly affected.

" I think I can hear Grant coming in now," Amanda cut in. " Just a moment, Clare."

Clare mentally crossed her fingers as she waited, and then Grant spoke at the other end of the line.

" Clare, what's this all about?"

" I wish I knew," she replied. " But Owen is at the back of it. That much I did learn."

" I see. Well don't worry, and don't pack. I'll be right out there. Wait for me."

" I shan't be going anywhere," Clare retorted.

" See you shortly then." The line went dead and Clare replaced her receiver. She took a deep breath as she looked around the hall. In the past five weeks she had come to like this place, and the strange atmosphere which she had sensed upon her arrival had faded away completely during the ensuing weeks. She looked towards the kitchen, and wanted very much to talk to Betty, but she dared not let Sue see her. The child clung to her now, and if she learned that they were to be parted there would be no end to the trouble which would arise.

Going up to her room, Clare took out her suitcase and prepared to pack away her clothes. But she did not pack. Instead, she paced the room and tried to marshal her thoughts, to get some semblance of order in her mind. If only David were here! That thought kept hammering away at her consciousness, and she wondered if Owen had arranged this somehow. But why did he want to get rid of her?

When she saw Grant's car coming up to the house her first instinct was to rush down and greet him, but she remained where she was. He would have to talk to Cornelius Harley, and it would be better for all concerned if she were not present.

She watched Grant get out of his car, and then he hurried out of her sight. Going to the head of the stairs, she saw Betty, with Sue along, opening the front door to Grant, and the mumble of their voices came up to her. Then Betty went along to the library, and Grant stood in the hall. A few moments later, Betty reappeared, without Sue, and showed Grant into Cornelius Harley's presence.

"Betty!" Clare went down several stairs as she called to the housekeeper. The woman looked up at her, then half turned to glance around the hall. The next moment she was running up the stairs towards Clare, her face showing puzzlement and dismay.

"The doctor just told me, Clare. This is dreadful. You can't go. What's going to happen to poor Sue now? She idolises you. It will put her right back if you have to leave."

" Have you any idea where David went to?" Clare asked. " If I could get in touch with him it might help. But they want me to leave before he returns."

" I can't help you there, I'm afraid, but I'm sure the doctor will be able to mend matters, whatever it is that's gone wrong."

" Owen has talked to his father, but I haven't the slightest idea what his arguments were. They must have been very powerful for Mr. Harley to agree to this."

" It's to do with Adam, I'm sure," Betty said. " Perhaps Owen is afraid that Adam will want his girl back if he gets back to normal."

Clare shook her head, unable to think clearly. She looked at the housekeeper and could tell by the woman's expression that Betty was as upset about this as she herself.

" Sue is all I'm worried about," Clare said. " You've left her with her grandfather, have you?"

" Yes. He told me to. I didn't know what was going on until the doctor told me."

" I thought it better not to let Sue see me in case I have to go." Clare moistened her lips. Hearing the fact on her own lips did not give any reality to the situation, and she couldn't believe that events had turned so quickly and completely.

" This isn't good for you either, is it? What is David going to say when he comes home, especially if you've gone."

" I'll be staying at the doctor's house," Clare said. " If I have to leave here I shall be there for a few days. Perhaps you'll tell David so he can come and see me."

" I'll let him know, don't you worry," Betty said firmly. " I'm not afraid of Owen."

There was a noise in the hall and Betty started down the stairs again. She looked back at Clare. " They'll probably want you now," she said. " I'll call you if they do."

" Let me know if I have to pack," Clare said.

She watched the housekeeper hurry down the stairs, and she could see the library door, which was open. Grant was walking into the hall, and she heard him speak. His words sent a pang of dread through her.

" Very well, Mr. Harley. If that is your decision then I'll take Nurse Crawford back to the village with me. If there's nothing more to be said, if I cannot dissuade you from this action even for Sue's sake, then I'll abide by your decision."

Clare caught her breath, and there was a pain in her heart as she turned and walked to her room. She had to leave. There was no reprieve. Her duties here were at an end. She entered her room and began hastily to pack, and a moment later Betty appeared in the doorway.

" You heard?" the housekeeper demanded.

" I heard," Clare retorted. " Is the doctor going to wait for me?"

" He's waiting below. He said you have plenty of time. Don't worry, Clare. I'm sure David will come after you to bring you back when he learns of this."

Clare forced a smile. She looked into the housekeeper's pale eyes. " It's not myself I'm thinking of," she said. " Poor Sue! She was getting along so well. Look after her, Betty. See that she doesn't want for anything, won't you?"

" I can't take care of her like you did, but you can rest assured that she'll still get the best of everything," Betty promised. " I wish David was here so he could do something. Is there anything I can help with?"

" No thanks. But you can make sure that Sue doesn't see me leaving."

" I'll attend to that, and I'm certain you'll be back here by this evening." Betty held out her hand. Her blue eyes were hard and bright with suppressed emotion. " I hope this will work out all right, but in case it doesn't I want you to know that I'm very pleased you came here. You've done a lot for Sue, and they ought to appreciate that."

" Well that's what I came here for in the first place," Clare said, forcing a smile. " Sue is out of the wood now, and if she doesn't pine for me then there's no reason why she shouldn't continue to make progress. I'll leave my forwarding address with Doctor Laverne, Betty, and I'll be kept informed of the child's progress after I've gone." Clare felt a pang of emotion in her throat, and she blinked rapidly as tears sprang to her eyes. She bent her head over her packing, and when she looked up a moment later the housekeeper had departed.

When she was ready she heaved a great sigh and took up her case. She paused in the doorway of the room and looked around slowly. Time had passed quickly, but for all that she had found pleasure here and knew she would not easily forget Oakapple Farm. She drew a sharp breath and turned away, closing the door at her back and walking straight to the stairs, descending quickly, forcing a smile as she saw Grant looking up at her.

He hurried forward to take her case, and his face was grave. Clare looked around as he ushered her to the door, and she was thankful there was no sign of Sue. They went out to his car and the hot sunshine seemed to beat down upon her shoulders. The glare was too much for her eyes, and she blinked as tears came into them. But she wasn't crying and she didn't want Grant to think she was.

" I'm sorry I couldn't do anything about the situation, Clare," he commented as they got into the car. " I really don't understand Cornelius Harley's attitude. He was the one who insisted having a nurse in the first place."

" Owen has put pressure on him," she said. " It has to do with Adam, Grant. Of that I'm sure. It wasn't until you spoke to Owen this morning about Adam that this started. Owen came and spoke to me, and he was furious because you knew of Adam's condition."

"Well I'm taking steps about Adam, whether Owen likes it or not. It's a crime against humanity to keep the man in that state. We could have him better in a matter of weeks."

"That's what I told them, but they didn't seem to want to know. Betty seemed to think it was because Owen is seeing Adam's ex-girlfriend. Owen may be afraid that Adam will want her back when he gets well."

"Don't lose heart, Clare." Grant glanced at her, seeing her blue eyes bright with emotion. "I shall talk to David about this, and he's going to raise the roof, you can be sure. I wouldn't want to be in Owen's shoes when David does get home. Everyone says Owen has a bad temper, but David can get quite heated when he has to. You'll go back if they'll let you, won't you?"

"If it will be in Sue's best interests, yes," Clare said promptly.

"Good girl! I thought you'd say that. Sue is at a critical stage right now, you know. In a few weeks she could be completely normal, I'm certain. She'll need some specialist treatment, but I am arranging for that. But it is vital that she has no shocks now or in the immediate future."

Clare nodded, well aware of the situation, and she felt slightly hopeful in her heart as she thought about David. He would do all he could to put matters right, she was certain. If only Sue didn't miss her in the meantime! That was the only thing Clare was afraid of.

When they reached the village, Clare looked around nervously, half expecting to see Tim Millard's car somewhere along the road. Everything seemed to have happened at once, she thought grimly. It seemed that the promise of the past days had evaporated quickly, leaving her nothing but faint recollections of what might have been.

She hardly saw the beauty of the village as she went with Grant into his house, and even the sun seemed to have lost its heat upon her shoulders. The door was opened to them by a concerned Amanda, and Clare listened woodenly while Grant explained to his wife everything that had happened. It sounded unreal to her ears, and she had to force a smile when Amanda expressed her sympathy for the way events had turned.

" Of course you did the right thing in mentioning Adam Harley's condition to Grant," Amanda said. " I can't understand Owen wanting to keep it a secret any longer. There's no shame in it. And the sooner it is cleared up the better for everyone. But is Sue going to miss you today, Clare?"

" That depends on what Betty tells her! But I think she'll be all right."

" Personally, I wouldn't want to go back there after this, but you do have your patient to think of." Amanda shook her head slowly. " I don't think I'd want your job for all the money in the world, Clare. You don't get much appreciation from some people, do you?"

" There are a few like that, but on the whole people are very good. I wouldn't be in any other job, Amanda."

" Well let's get your case put in your room, so you won't feel as if you're really all alone," Grant said. "We don't know what David will do, but if he's a man at all he'll have you back at the Farm before the evening is out."

Clare uttered a silent prayer as she followed Grant up the stairs, and when he showed her into a bedroom she turned to him apologetically.

" I'm sorry this has happened , Grant," she said. " And you had just come in to lunch when you heard about it, hadn't you? I am sorry! You don't get much time as it is."

" Don't let it worry you!" He smiled as he put a friendly hand upon her shoulder. You did the right thing. The Harleys have made the mistake. I'm sure this will work out, but in the meantime you've got to keep your spirits up."

" Did they ask you to find them another nurse?"

" No. Cornelius said something about getting in touch with your Bureau himself."

" I suppose I'd better make a report about this," she said.

" I'd leave it until we know for certain what's going to happen," he replied. He sighed heavily. " I'd better go and get some lunch and start out on my round again. I'm going to be late for evening surgery if I'm not careful."

" It's all my fault!" Clare said regretfully.

He just grinned at her and turned away. " You've had lunch, haven't you?"

" Yes, thank you. I feel overfed at the moment."

He nodded consolingly. " I'm sorry this has happened, Clare. You deserve better than this. I hope it won't affect your future."

She followed him down the stairs, and Amanda called to them from the kitchen.

" It's not my future I'm worried about," she said. " It won't affect me in the least."

" I'm not talking about duty now," he retorted. " You're beginning to fall in love with David, aren't you?"

" Is it that noticeable?" Her cheeks coloured slightly as she felt his keen gaze upon her.

" I can see it. I wish you luck. No wonder you want to see Adam cured. But it's going to take a lot of persuasion to get him into a hospital, you know."

" I didn't act from selfish motives, Grant."

" I know that." He led her into the kitchen, where Amanda was setting out his meal. The woman looked up with a rueful expression on her face.

" I'm sorry this is a bit dried up, Grant," she said.

" I haven't much time for it, anyway," he replied, pulling out a chair. " I've got several calls to make this afternoon."

" You're making me feel very guilty," Clare said.

" Nonsense!" Amanda smiled at her.

" It's kind of you, and thanks for the offer of tea, but if you don't mind I'll take a walk around the village. I need to think this over."

Grant looked over at her. "Amanda will handle everything until you return. I'm sure David will call or come here as soon as he learns of the situation."

She thanked him for his kind words, and then departed. Out in the sunlight, she paused and looked around, feeling something of the weight lifting from her shoulders. But when she pictured Sue's face and imagined what the girl must be feeling by now. She felt quite tearful. She walked across the green to the pond, where she stood looking at the ducks upon the placid water.

Clare could see her reflection in the clear water, and she studied her face, her head bent and her body held motionless.

· She was lost in thought, and started nervously when another face appeared in the water just at her side. She straightened instantly and turned swiftly, gasping in shock and dismay when she found a man close to her, and that man, she quickly realised, was a grinning Tim Millard!

TWELVE

" I HAD the feeling that you were in this area, Clare," he said sharply, his pale eyes showing triumph. " It was only a matter of time before I caught up with you. It's been a long time!"

" What do you want with me?" she demanded as soon as she recovered her speech. She was trembling inside, and filled with dismay, but she was not as scared as she imagined many times that she might be. She had often dreamed of meeting him, and those dreams had been more like nightmares; but now they were face to face and she could feel a swift anger beginning to stab through her fear.

" What do you think I want?" He reached out strong hands and grasped her shoulders, and Clare struggled to break his grip but could not.

" I told you in no uncertain terms as soon as I found you out for what you are that I would never see you again," she panted, still trying to get away from him.

" Don't come that old innocence act with me," he snapped, and now his face was harsh, his eyes suddenly vicious. " Do you think I don't know why you vanished so completely when you knew it was getting near the time for my release? I had you watched all the time. Your every move was reported to me inside. You didn't think you could get away from me, did you?"

" I have my own life to lead, and you'll never mean anything to me," she replied sharply. " You're a thief, a parasite on society, and wild horses wouldn't drag me back to you."

She increased her struggles to get out of his grip, and Millard uttered an oath and exerted his strength until she squirmed at the pain in her shoulders. But she was fighting a losing battle, and she knew she could never get away from him. She had been fooling herself for years now, thinking that she had dropped out of circulation, when all the time he knew he could reach her when he wanted her.

But what did he want? Surely he didn't think he could force her to go back to him! She thought of David and bit her bottom lip in determination. Nothing could affect the love she was nursing for him. Millard couldn't reach her now, no matter what he did.

The next instant she felt another hand upon her shoulder and she was dragged roughly away from Millard. Her eyes widened when she looked around at the newcomer, for it was Owen Harley, and he was angry.

"What the devil is going on here?" Owen demanded, his dark face suffused with anger. "Keep your hands off her, whoever you are!"

"Who the devil are you?" Millard demanded in equally angry tones. "Is this someone you're running around with now, Clare?"

"No," she snapped.

"What's this all about, Clare?" Owen demanded. "I saw you struggling from the road. Half the village has seen it. I came to Doctor Laverne's to get you."

"To get me?" She looked at him with surprise on her face.

"That's right. I've got to admit that I made a mistake when I spoke to Father about you this morning. Sue started crying for you as soon as Betty told her you'd gone, and we can't stop her tears. She'll be in a screaming fit before the day is over if you don't come back to the Farm."

"Poor child!" Clare turned away immediately and started for the road, where she could see Owen's car. "Come on," she said. "We can pick up my case from the doctor's later. Get me to Sue!"

"You're not going anywhere," Millard said, reaching out a hand and grasping Clare's shoulder, almost pulling her off her feet with his strength and determination.

"Let go of her," Owen said in dangerously quiet tones. "I don't know you, friend, but you'd better beware. Nurse Crawford has a case to attend to, and I won't let anything come between them."

A part of Clare's mind was rejoicing at his words, but she knew there was danger here and she was afraid. She saw Millard's face harden, and she tried to call out a warning to Owen as she realised that Millard was going strike. But Millard's right hand lifted quickly and his fist flashed towards Owen's jaw. Clare cringed in sudden terror.

Owen uttered an oath and moved swiftly, and there was the sharp sound of knuckles striking flesh. Both men came together, and for a moment it was impossible to see what was happening. There was a huge sense of protest in Clare's mind as she watched. Then Owen struck sharply and Millard tottered backwards. Owen went after him, fists ready, and Clare reached out and grasped at his shoulder.

"Leave him alone, Owen! Get me back to the farm!"

His face was terrible to see. His teeth were set into his bottom lip, and he was beside himself with anger. But Millard was coming forward again and Owen had to defend himself. He put a strong hand upon Clare's shoulder and thrust her violently away. She went sprawling headlong in the grass, falling heavily and rolling clear of them. She heard the confused sounds of brawling, and then a body fell to the ground. When she pushed herself to her feet she was surprised to see Millard lying on his back and Owen standing over him with clenched fists.

Clare started away from the pond, afraid to look back, and she hurried to the road where Owen's car was waiting. When she looked back she saw Owen following her, and Millard was still stretched out on the grass.

Owen caught up with her, and there was a smear of blood on his left eyebrow. He was sucking the knuckles of his right hand, and Clare was nauseated by what she had witnessed. But there was an expression of savage pleasure on Owen's face.

" I don't know who your friend is, but he certainly thought he could get things all his own way. He's the one you were talking to the doctor about, wasn't he?"

" That's right. But he belongs in my past and I'm going to see that he remains there." Clare paused at his car and waited for him to open the door for her. " Sue is all that matters now. Get me to her as quickly as you can."

He nodded and they got into the car. Clare looked back across the green as he drove away from the verge, and her lips tightened when she saw Millard's tall figure stumbling in their direction. But the car moved fast and they sped out of the village.

Clare was silent, her thoughts with Sue, and Owen had nothing to say. Once she looked at him and studied his intent profile. When he looked at her she said:

" Has David returned home yet?"

" No! He isn't at the back of this change in my attitude. I don't like admitting that I made a mistake, but Sue's welfare must come first in my calculations, so I want you back where you were this morning."

" I'm ready to come back, with no questions asked," she retorted. " But why were you so intent upon getting rid of me as soon as you knew I'd spoken to Doctor Laverne about Adam. Don't you want Adam to get better?"

He did not look at her, and his tones were carefully modulated as he replied.

" Of course I want him to get better!"

" Are you sure you're not afraid that when he does get better he might want his ex-girlfriend back?"

He gave her a startled look, and she knew she had come quite close to the truth. But he shook his head vehemently.

" That's not so! She packed him up before I started seeing her. But she is afraid he might give her some trouble."

" In his present condition he might give her trouble if he met her, but once he's been cured then there will be little risk of anything happening."

" I'd like to believe that!"

They lapsed into silence and remained so until they reached the farm. Clare leaped out of the car as it halted before the big front door, which was opening to reveal Betty and Sue. The child tore herself free from the housekeeper and came running towards Clare, who knelt down and gathered the girl into her arms. Sue was sobbing bitterly, and her tiny arms found incredible strength as they clung around Clare's neck.

" Don't cry, Sue! Didn't you know I was coming back? I had to go into the village for something and couldn't take you with me. It's all right now. I'm back and I'm going to stay!"

Sue said nothing, and by degrees her sobbing eased. But she kept her arms tightly locked around Clare's neck. Clare stroked the child's hair, talking gently and in soothing tones. She was aware that Betty and Owen stood silently in the background, and they made no move to interfere or interrupt. Then Clare got slowly to her feet, lifting the child in her arms, and Sue laid her head against Clare's shoulder.

" Let's go in and wash your face," Clare said softly to the child. " It's all right now. I won't leave you again. Next time I have to go out I'll take you with me."

There were tears in Clare's eyes as she carried Sue into the house. The child's silent sobbing had sounded so strange, and Clare felt so deeply for the girl. Something would have to be done about this situation, she told herself, and she wouldn't spare herself in the efforts she intended making.

She took Sue up to her room, and a glance behind when she reached the top of the stairs showed her that neither Betty nor Owen had followed her. Clare sat down on the foot of Sue's bed and comforted the child in her arms, and slowly Sue relaxed and became quiescent.

" That's better," Clare said softly. " Don't cry any more, Sue. I shan't leave you again."

The child clutched at her with strong hands, and Clare sat silent, nursing her gently. After some considerable time, Sue fell asleep, and Clare laid her down and covered her over. But she didn't leave the room. Going over to the window, she stood staring out at the garden, and her thoughts were complex as she considered all that had happened this day.

She couldn't really believe that she had spoken to Tim Millard. After all the trouble she'd taken to avoid him upon his release, she had been found easily, and she knew she could expect more trouble from him. But she couldn't run away any longer. Sue would see to that. She would have to stay and try and sort it out.

Impatience gripped her and she silently paced the room. What would Millard do after what had happened? Would he attempt to get some kind of revenge for the quick beating he had taken? She wished David would come back. He would know how to handle the situation.

She dared not leave the room for fear that Sue would awaken during her absence and think she had gone again. Sitting down by the window, Clare let her mind rove over what had happened. Owen had changed his mind about her departure because Sue had shown her great need for the nurse who had taken her mother's place. But that didn't mean Owen had changed his mind about some of the other problems that faced this family.

Clare felt stifled. She felt that there was no need for all this trouble. A decisive person could have sorted out the problems of this family with a few simple decisions, but it seemed that Owen and David had different feelings about the situation, and she felt that they would never get together to sort out the troubles.

The door opened gently some time later and Clare turned instantly to see Grant standing there. She glanced towards the bed and saw that Sue was still sleeping soundly, and she tiptoed to the door, going outside to join Grant in the corridor.

"I see she's sleeping, Clare," he said quietly. "How is she?"

"All right now! I don't think this episode will affect her too much. Now I'm back with her she'll settle down again."

"Owen came back for your case. It's in your room. But I heard about the fight on the green. Was it Millard?"

"Yes. He saw me." She shook her head slowly, but she wasn't worried about Tim Millard any more. He didn't come into her calculations.

"I've had a word with Constable Idden about Millard," Grant said. He looked her squarely in the eyes. "You have enough trouble here without additional worries building up for you. I have the feeling I've done the right thing. You didn't want to see him any more, did you?"

"I certainly don't want to see him again!" Clare spoke

with great firmness. " I can't understand why he should bother about me after all this time, and I made it quite clear to him as soon as I discovered exactly what he was that I didn't want anything more to do with him."

" Poor Clare! You deserve better luck. I only hope that you are doing the right thing by pinning your faith on David Harley."

" He's all right, isn't he?" she demanded instantly.

" Certainly! There couldn't be anyone better. But he has a lot on his shoulders, you know."

" Other things don't matter. Adam can be helped, and surely there are no other problems beside Adam! Is there anything I don't know about?"

" Only family pressures! They could be quite strong, and perhaps too much for a man like David. He has a strong sense of family duty."

" Well that part of it is pure speculation, Grant. All I'm really concerned about is Sue. What happens after that will have to take its chances."

He nodded. " I feel responsible for you, Clare, and I'll do all I can to help. But don't pin too much faith on your feelings. I wouldn't want to see you get hurt. You've had your share of loneliness, and it seems that this man Millard hasn't helped you at all. Some people are born losers, and you're too nice a person to suffer."

" I'll get by!" She smiled, thinking of David. " I'm not thinking of the future. I'll take everything as it comes."

" Have you fallen in love with David?" he asked softly.

" I rather think I have!" She nodded slowly. " But then I'm always doing the wrong thing!"

" I don't think so!" He suppressed a sigh. " Look, remember that I'm always in the background. I'll do anything within my power to help you. But you'll have to let me know if you need any assistance."

" I think it will be all right, but thanks for the offer, Grant."

" I'll have to be running along now. My routines have been upset today."

" I'm sorry for all the trouble you've been caused."

" I'll come and see you in the morning as soon as I start my round, but in the meantime, remember that I'm on the telephone, and don't hesitate to call if you want advice or help."

" I'll remember," she promised.

He nodded and departed, and Clare waited until he had disappeared down the stairs before going back into Sue's room. She went to the foot of the bed and stared down at the sleeping child. She couldn't worry about her own future when this dear child had so much to overcome.

Time seemed to hang heavily on Clare's hands, but she would not leave the room until Sue awoke for fear that the child might think she had departed again. The child slept on, and Clare began to wonder where David had gone. This was the first time in five weeks that he had gone away from the farm all day, and it had to be the time when trouble came.

Eventually, Sue began to stir, and Clare went to the bedside and sat down gently, watching the child's face as consciousness returned to the young mind. Sue stretched and turned, her eyelids fluttering, and then the eyes opened and the girl looked up at Clare. For a moment she was motionless. Then she uttered a sibilant gasp and leaped up out of the bed, throwing her arms around Clare's neck and hugging her with all her young strength."

" I'm still here, Sue," Clare said in a whisper. " I won't go away again. Try to forget this afternoon. It was just a horrid dream. Everything is all right again."

The child nodded, and would not relax her grip around Clare's neck.

" I think it's time we washed you and took you down to tea," Clare said cheerfully. " Are you hungry?"

Sue eased back to look into her face, and Clare could see the ravages of the tears she had shed. She kissed the girl's cheek as she got up and carried her to the bathroom.

Uncle David will be home soon, Sue," she said. " We mustn't let him see that you've been crying."

After she had freshened the child, Clare changed her own dress. Then they went down to the kitchen, and Betty Smithers was there, her face showing great concern as she studied Sue. Clare nodded to the housekeeper, intimating that everything seemed to be all right, and Betty began to act as if nothing had happened. She had tea prepared, and Clare glanced at the woman as she seated Sue at the table.

" Has David come home yet?" she asked.

" I haven't seen him. But I can tell you that there has been an awful row in the library between Owen and his father."

" And no doubt I was the subject of it," Clare said. She sighed as she sat down.

" Half the tensions and problems existed here in the house before you arrived, Clare, so don't blame yourself too much for what is happening, You just brought matters to a head, that's all. It will blow over, and the place should be all the better for these passions."

" It's really Adam, isn't it?" Clare demanded, watching Betty's expressive face.

" Yes! Owen is bringing him back into the house to sleep. That means we've got to keep our doors locked at night. You haven't got out of the habit of doing that, have you?"

" No!" Clare shook her head. " I haven't left it unlocked a single night that I've been here."

" Well make sure you check it tonight. I expect there will be another row when David gets in."

" What is Mr. Harley's attitude now, do you know?"

" I couldn't help overhearing part of what was said in the library when they were really going at it. Mr. Harley was telling Owen that he'd caused enough trouble in the house. He said Owen had to take a greater share of the responsibility around here, that there would be changes made all round. Owen didn't like that, and he threatened to pack his bags and clear out."

Clare shook her head. Trouble was building up still higher instead of diminishing. How it would all end she didn't know, but she meant to ensure that nothing happened to upset Sue again. No matter what was happening in this family circle, the child had to be protected against more emotional strain.

They had almost finished tea when there was a tap at the kitchen door and Cornelius Harley appeared. Clare caught her breath at sight of the stern old man, and recalled that the day's trouble had started when he'd looked into the kitchen after lunch. For a moment there was silence, and Clare looked into his wrinkled face and ageless dark eyes. He nodded slowly, and let his gaze drift to Sue, who reached out and grasped Clare's hand.

" I'd like to talk to you, Nurse," the old man said. " When you finish your tea will do."

" Very well, Mr. Harley," she replied. " I'll come along to your study, shall I?"

" I'll be in the library," he said, and backed out of the doorway.

Clare found that she was holding her breath as the door closed, and she released it slowly. She looked down at Sue, and saw fear in the girl's dark eyes.

" Don't worry," she said. " I won't leave you again, Sue. It's nothing to fret about."."

They finished their tea in near silence, and afterwards Clare helped Betty wash the tea things. She was trying to put off until the last moment the ordeal of seeing Cornelius Harley again, but eventually there was nothing else to do and she turned reluctantly to the door.

" I'll keep Sue with me," she said, knowing they would have trouble with the girl if she tried to leave her again with the housekeeper.

" Come back and let me know what he has to say," Betty said.

Clare nodded and held Sue's hand tightly as they left the kitchen. They walked through to the front of the house and crossed the hall to the library door. Clare could feel her heart pounding heavily as she rapped at the heavy panel, and then Cornelius Harley was calling out an invitation for her to enter.

She felt that history was repeating itself as she entered the library. But this time Sue was with her, and the child seemed to sense the heaviness in the atmosphere for she pressed against Clare and held her hand tightly.

" Please sit down, Nurse," Cornelius Harley said pleasantly, and Clare did so, putting Sue on her lap. They both stared at the old man, and the silence that surrounded them was oppressive. " Firstly, I would like to say how sorry I am for what happened earlier today," he went on. " In a moment of weakness I gave in to my son Owen, and that was a mistake. I realise that now. I have done what I can to put matters right, and I hope you will overlook the whole episode. Sue seems to have suffered little harm because of what happened, and if you are willing to over-look this afternoon then I shall be pleased to retain you until such time as Doctor Grant tells me Sue is well enough to be sent to a boarding school."

" I shall be happy to stay on, Mr. Harley," Clare told him in firm tones. " I can understand that there is a great deal of emotion at work here in your family, and I hope I can remain outside the sphere of its influence. Sue has suffered no setback for what happened this afternoon, and I think she'll forget it completely in a few days."

"Thank you, Nurse! I'm deeply indebted to you. I hope the future will be pleasant now. Owen is leaving the farm for a spell, and I hope his absence will enable us all to get to grips with our problems. Adam will be staying in the house again, and he is to see Doctor Laverne tomorrow. David will be home shortly, and he will see to it that you can do your duties without interference or hindrance."

"Thank you, Mr. Harley." Clare felt relief begin to seep into her mind. She got to her feet when she realised that the old man had finished, and there was relief inside her as she led Sue to the door. Pausing in the doorway, she glanced back at the spare figure of Sue's grandfather, but the old man was looking through the window, his shoulders slumped, his whole manner indicating unhappiness.

It came to Clare then that this was not the end of the trouble that seemed to be dogging this family, and she could only feel pleased that her part in it seemed to be settled. Everyone wanted to do what was best for Sue, and that was all Clare could ask for.

THIRTEEN

IT WASN'T until after Sue had been put to bed that David returned home, and Clare looked from the window when she heard a car below. When she saw it was David her first instinct was to rush to him, but she controlled her impatience and let him enter the house. No doubt Betty would inform him of the events of the day, and she waited in her own room in a fever of mounting anticipation. Presently there was a tap at the door and she hurried in answer. When she opened the door David was standing outside, and his face showed great emotion as he stared at her.

"Betty has just told me what's been going on here today," he said. "Is everything all right now?"

"Yes, David." She nodded. "I think it's all been settled."

"I've had a dreadful day myself," he said, sighing heavily. "It isn't often I have to go into town. I leave all the jobs that need attending to until there are almost too many to be handled in one day. Then this had to happen while I was away. But I shall have a lot to say to Owen about this."

"I wouldn't say anything if I were you," she told him. "I think you should talk to your father before doing anything else."

"Have you seen Adam around today?"

"I saw him this morning." She suppressed a shiver as she recalled the way Adam had stared at her. "Do you know that he will be sleeping in the house tonight?"

"Betty mentioned it. This is Owen all over. But if Father has put his foot down at last then perhaps we'll see some changes around here. Don't take any chances though, Clare. Make sure your door is locked, won't you?"

She nodded, and he glanced along the passage before coming closer to her, lifting his hands to place them upon her shoulders.

"I'm thankful that you did come back when Owen came for you," he said. "Poor Sue! She's made such good progress! It would be a great pity if anything happened to throw her back now! I'm glad Owen had the sense to come for you again."

She thought of the scene on the green at Chippenbury, when Owen had struck Tim Millard, and she knew she had Owen to thank for his intervention.

"Owen isn't all bad, you know," she said. "I can understand his point of view."

"I've been holding back for a long time because I can understand him too!" David said. There was a trembling eagerness in his tones. "I've missed you all day, Clare. I wish I could have taken you and Sue with me. The next time I go into town you will accompany me."

"I'd like that," she told him in soft tones.

"But if Owen is going away then there'll be nothing to worry about. I expect he'll get married now. He's been wanting to get away from here for a long time."

"And Adam?" she asked.

"Adam will be all right. When he's had treatment he'll be a different man, and a greater help than he is now. Don't worry about Adam."

"I hope he will get better," she said.

"You care about everyone except yourself," he told her gently. "I've never met a girl like you before, Clare. I hope nothing has happened today to make you change your mind about me and what might be in the future."

" I haven't changed my mind about anything," she said, and smiled gently. " I'm sure it will all work out right."

He drew her into his arms and held her close, and Clare felt some of the coldness packed around her heart begin to crack and melt. She had waited all day for his return, and for a few hours during the afternoon she had imagined all her dreams for the future had been broken. Now he had reassured her, and she pressed her head against his shoulder and relaxed for the very first time that day.

David put a gentle hand beneath her chin and tilted her face upwards. Then he kissed her lightly, and she clung to him with all her strength.

" Clare," he whispered. " I love you. I don't know why there should have been all this trouble. Everything seems straightforward to me! But I think you'll find a great improvement after this. I shall be keeping a closer eye on events, you can bet."

" I'm satisfied with the way everything is working out," she said, and he kissed her again.

" Perhaps you're too easily satisfied," he retorted. " But I know you won't be worried after this."

Drawing her even closer into his embrace, he held her tightly for long, blissful moments, and Clare felt the tensions and the worries of the day slipping away from her. She didn't care what happened so long as he was here to put his arms about her and whisper encouragement. She sensed that this was the turning point, and she wanted so much for everything to go right.

There were footsteps in the hall, echoing up the stairs, and David drew quickly away from her and went along the passage to the top of the stairs. Clare stood watching him, telling herself how much she loved him. But a frown touched her face when she heard the footsteps on the stairs, then saw the heavy figure of Adam Harley arriving beside David. She heard the sound of their voices, and Adam glanced once in her direction, his face dark and expressionless. Then he went in the opposite direction to his room and disappeared through the doorway. David came back to her, his face serious.

"Adam has moved back," he said, "Owen has already gone, and he's been telling Adam that the situation here isn't good. Adam wants to know what the trouble is, and feels that you ought to go. I've never known him to be so belligerent. I'm going to have to watch him, Clare. But Owen has deliberately aroused him in order to give us something else to think about."

" Perhaps I ought to leave the Farm until Adam starts his treatment," she suggested, and her tones were filled with apprehension.

" What about Sue? And where would you go?" David showed his concern by the way he considered her words.

" I could probably stay at the doctor's for a few days, and have Sue with me there. I certainly won't be able to leave her."

" No. That's the last thing we should consider. From what Betty told me about Sue while you were away this afternoon, I'm surprised the child didn't suffer a serious setback."

" In any case she's asleep now, and I doubt if she'll awaken before the morning. We can discuss the matter again then, if you like."

" Yes. Let's wait and see what's going to happen about Adam, shall we? If he has to go into hospital then we'll have a breathing space."

" I expect he'll need some intensive treatment at the outset," Clare said, her eyes narrowing. " Will he go into hospital without trouble?"

" Father can do anything with him, and Father has said Adam must have whatever treatment is necessary. I don't anticipate any trouble on that score, but we must be ready for anything."

Clare relaxed into his embrace once more, and he held her for long moments. But she heard him sigh, and she drew away from him and looked up into his dark face.

"You've been out all day," she said. "Have you eaten recently?"

"Not since lunch. Betty is getting me something now. I shall go down to the kitchen in a moment." He tightened his grip about her, and Clare felt so comfortable in his embrace that she began to lose her subconscious fear that something would go seriously wrong.

When he eventually released her she looked up into his face, happy to see that his expression was gentle and loving. He smiled at her, taking her hands.

"I'll see you later in the evening, shall I?" he asked.

"I'll come down to see you after you've had your meal," she replied. "I'll stay near Sue for a bit longer just in case she wakes up. But I think she's in her night's sleep now and she won't awaken until morning."

"I'll go down and look for you later. Come along to my office in about half an hour. We shall be able to talk there, and find plenty of privacy."

"All right!" She nodded her agreement, and he kissed her lightly before leaving her. She watched him until he descended the stairs and was lost to view, and then she went into her room and closed the door.

She paced the room for some time, her thoughts fast and furious. But there was no anxiety in her mind now. She sensed that all was well. Sue would go to see a specialist, and would probably have treatment to help her. There seemed to be no reason why the girl shouldn't recover her speech, and Clare was longing for the day when she would hear Sue's voice.

But there was another side to her future which she dared not consider too closely. What would happen when Sue was cured? Would she go on her lonely way as she had done in past cases? This was the first time she had broken her golden rule and let herself become involved with a member of her patient's family. No good ever came of such a situation those people at the Bureau who should know had led her to believe. But she was involved, and the how and wherefore did not matter.

She was in love with David! She pictured his face as she stood at her window and looked out into the sunny evening. Her feelings made all the difference to her outlook. He had become important to her and she had to consider him in a way she had never before considered any man. But she was helpless in the face of what was happening. There was nothing she could do to influence any decision. She was just a useless bystander, and could only hope that events would shape the way she wanted them.

Before going down to join David in his office, Clare went along to Sue's room and looked in at the girl. Sue was fast asleep, her breathing heavy and regular, and Clare smiled gently as she looked down into the child's sleep-flushed face. She turned when she heard footsteps in the passage, and saw the door opening slowly. Expecting the newcomer to be either David or Betty, Clare smiled a welcome, but it was Adam who came into the room.

Clare froze at the sight of him, and he paused to look at her. He said nothing, and she felt too nervous to speak. She glanced towards the bed, and he followed her gaze and looked at the sleeping child. Moving swiftly, he came across to Clare's side, and she tried hard not to flinch from him. But he was looking down into Sue's face, and she could not tell what was passing through his mind.

There was none of the sullen arrogance in his face which had usually marred Owen's features, and Clare took the opportunity to study him for a moment. One could tell he was a Harley, she decided, although he was rather more fleshy than either Owen or David. He looked round at her suddenly, surprising her, and for a moment their eyes met. She saw him moisten his lips, but his dark eyes remained dull. He glanced once more at Sue, then turned to the door, and Clare felt a pang of relief stab through her. He was leaving.

But he stopped at the door and turned to look at her, jerking his head in an unmistakable invitation for her to join him outside. She didn't dare antagonise him by refusing, and after a glance at Sue she walked slowly towards him.

When she joined him in the passage he closed the door of the room and stood with his back to it. Clare stood facing him, unable to take her eyes off his heavy face. He moistened his lips again, and his dark eyes narrowed.

" Is she all right again?" he suddenly demanded.

" She will be all right soon," she told him.

He nodded, and lifted his big hands and clenched them in front of him. Clare froze because she thought he was going to seize hold of her. He looked down at his hands as if he hadn't seen them before, and shook his head.

" Her father was my brother Frank. I liked him better than anyone. Now he's dead and she has to rely on people like Owen. I suppose they told you to be careful around me!"

Clare did not answer, and he nodded his head more emphatically.

" A lot of people have to be careful around me," he said sharply.

The next instant he walked away from her, and she felt her relief mounting as he disappeared into his own room. She sighed heavily, walked to the stairs and descended quickly, going along to David's office and rapping at the door. She was relieved when his voice sounded, and she opened the door.

The time she spent with David did much to soothe her nerves, and she didn't tell him of her encounter with Adam. When it was time for her to go to bed she felt nervous again, picturing Adam's dark, intent face, but she knew she could lock her door, and David would be on his guard.

" I'll see you to your room and wait outside until you've locked the door," he said when she stifled a yawn. " Don't worry about anything, Clare. It's going to be all right."

" I'm not worried," she told him as she slipped into his arms. His kisses reassured her still further, but when they left the office she had to take a deep breath to steady herself.

" I'm worried about a lot of things," he confided as they ascended the stairs.

" Not to do with me, I hope!"

" No." He smiled at her. " You're the one certain thing in all of this. I'm glad you're here. You add a touch of sense to everything; sense and hope."

" I'm glad." She smiled at him, certain that time would see them even closer together.

David waited while she checked Sue, and when she closed the door of the girl's room Clare looked into his face.

" I feel awfully guilty," she said, " bolting myself into my room and leaving Sue unguarded in her room."

" Sue will be all right." He smiled and touched her shoulder with a gentle hand. " Don't worry about a thing, Clare. Now if you're ready for bed then into your room with you and let me hear the bolt shoot home."

" Goodnight then!" She kissed him and went into her room, but she could not help glancing along the corridor as she did so, and she wondered about Adam as she closed her door and shot home the bolt with unnecessary noise.

" Goodnight, Clare, see you in the morning," David said through the panels, and she replied softly, standing by the door and listening to his receding footsteps.

She sighed heavily when silence descended, and tried the bolt once more, ensuring that it was firmly applied. Then she tried to relax, to get her mind to settle down and prepare for sleep. She got ready for bed, and went to the window, peering out into the gathering darkness, her mind trying to encompass many things. But it had been an exhausting day and she was very tired, both mentally and physically. She got into bed and settled down, closing her eyes and inviting slumber to visit her. But as she lay, her tiredness began to seep away, until she was wide eyed and staring into the shadows of the room. Then she realised that going to sleep was not going to be an easy thing.

How long she lay, Clare did not know, but the big house was silent and still. She heard many slight sounds that sent chills through her as her imagination went to work on them, but by slow degrees she began to drift into a troubled sleep. Then she heard footsteps, and was instantly on the alert.

The footsteps were slow and careful, and they paused outside her door. Clare half sat up in the bed, forgetting herself as she listened. There was tension inside her, a throbbing worry, and when she heard the doorknob rattle gently she caught her breath and clenched her teeth. But the door was securely bolted, and she heard the footsteps passing on again. Tension began to flee from her, and she told herself it was only David checking up. She lay down again and closed her eyes resolutely.

She didn't know when she drifted back to sleep, but she was asleep when a thin scream ripped through her slumbers and startled her awake. She lay listening intently, wondering if she had been dreaming, and she heard a thin, girlish voice calling her name.

"Clare! Clare!"

The voice was ghostly in the darkness, and Clare was tense, still half asleep. She could not move for a few vital moments, and she thought of the ghosts there were supposed to be in the house. Then her mind cleared and she told herself that the stories of ghosts had been told her to hide the real reason why she had been warned to lock her door. That voice was Sue's.

Sue! Clare leaped out of bed without thought and hurriedly pulled on her dressing gown. She heard a scream coming from the next room, and there were hurried footsteps in the passage outside. Clare's feet found her slippers without trouble and she ran across to the door and snapped on the light. Sue was still calling in a frenzy, and Clare gave no thought to herself as she pushed at the heavy bolt on the door and freed it. Without hesitation she opened the door and peered out into the darkness of the passage. There was a light on at the far end, and she saw two figures struggling in silhouette. Her heart seemed to miss a beat as she recognised one of the figures as Adam Harley, but she did not pause. She ran along to Sue's room and thrust open the door, switching on the light and staring wide eyed at the girl's bed.

Sue was crouching on the bed, shaking uncontrollably, and she was calling Clare's name over and over again. Clare was without fear as she hurried to the bedside and sat down, gathering the child to her breast.

"Don't cry," Clare said, patting the child soothingly.

"There was a man in here," the child said in thin tones. "I woke up and saw him bending over me. He put a hand over my mouth."

Clare hugged the girl to her, kissing her flushed face.

" You're talking, Sue!" She looked into the girl's eyes, and saw confusion there.

" I was so frightened I just screamed," Sue said. " I know your name. It's a nice name."

" Keep talking," Clare said. " Don't ever stop again, will you?"

" I couldn't talk before," came the steady reply. " I tried a lot to talk to you but nothing would come."

There were footsteps in the passage, and Clare tensed as she looked towards the door. The next instant Adam stood there, breathless and dishevelled, and there was blood on his face. He stared at them with wide, ferocious eyes, and Clare hugged Sue to her and stared at him in mounting horror.

Even Sue fell silent, and Clare felt as if she were living some nightmare as Adam came through the doorway and walked slowly towards them.

" Where's David?" Clare demanded harshly, and Adam started as if her words had slashed across his nerves. He took a deep breath, and his powerful hands were clenching and unclenching. " Were you fighting with David?" There was sudden fear in her tones because she recalled that he had been struggling with someone along the passage. It could only have been David. " Were you in here just a moment ago?" she continued. " Did you scare Sue?"

" I heard her talking," he said. " She's got her voice back!"

" Did you come in here and scare her?" Clare repeated.

He shook his head and came forward, and Clare tried hard not to cringe away from him. She faced him steadily, her pale eyes narrowed and expressionless, but her teeth were clenched and she knew she was afraid. When he stood over her she took a deep breath. He bent suddenly, and put a gentle hand against Sue's cheek.

" It wasn't me," he said huskily. " There's a burglar in the passage. David is telephoning for the police."

He stared at her a moment longer, then turned and went out of the room. Clare stared at him, unable to accept what he had said, and she pushed herself to her feet and hurried to the door, carrying Sue in her arms. When she looked along the passage she saw a man sprawled on the floor, and Adam was standing over him.

Was it David? Sudden fear was clutching at her heart, and Clare forced herself to go forward until she stood at Adam's side. Sue was looking down at the unconscious man, and her thin voice echoed in the stillness that surrounded them.

" That's the man who frightened me," she said loudly. " He made me scream."

" It's Tim Millard!" Clare said faintly, and for a moment the whole world seemed to whirl around her.

" You know him, Clare?" David came up the stairs and hurried to her side.

" I'll tell you about him," she said. " Owen fought with him this afternoon in the village."

" He scared me," Sue said. " I screamed and screamed!"

David stared at the child with astonishment on his face, and Clare hugged the child closer.

" The fright did it," she said. " Millard scared Sue back into her voice."

" Sue!" David's voice was husky with emotion. " You scared all of us when you screamed. I thought it was something else that caused the disturbance." He glanced at Adam, who was stolidly watching the unconscious Millard. " But when I came out of my room I found Adam struggling with this man. You did a good job, Adam. The police will be here for him shortly."

" He's not a burglar," Clare said. " He came to the village to see me. When Owen fought him I suppose he found out I was staying here, and he probably came into the house to talk to me."

" What does he want with you?" David asked.

" He's coming round," Adam said sharply.

They looked down at Millard, who groaned as he regained his senses. When he opened his eyes and found them looking down at him he stiffened and his face turned sullen.

" I've sent for the police," David said. " I thought you were a burglar. What are you doing in this house?"

" I had to talk to Clare!" same the sullen reply.

Betty appeared at the end of the passage, and the housekeeper stared uncertainly towards them, then came forward.

" Did I hear Sue's voice or was I dreaming?" Betty demanded.

" I can talk again, Betty," the child said, and Betty came to Clare's side and put her arms around both of them.

" Perhaps you'd take Sue down to the kitchen and give her some warm milk," Clare said. She looked at the girl, who tightened her grip around Clare's neck at her words. " Go with Betty and I'll be down shortly."

Sue nodded and went into the housekeeper's arms. Betty looked down at Millard, then glanced questioningly at Clare, but she said nothing and hurried away to the stairs. Clare listened to Sue's voice as the girl explained to the housekeeper what had happened.

" Why did you want to see me, Tim?" Clare demanded.

" I can't talk in front of these two," came the surly reply.

" You're not seeing her alone," David said fiercely.

Millard got slowly to his feet, and Adam closed on him in menacing silence.

" I'm not a burglar," he said. " I came to talk to Clare."

" What's so important that you have to take such risks, and you only just out of prison?" Clare demanded.

She saw David glance sharply at her, and she knew she would have some explaining to do.

" There was some money missing when the police caught up with me," Millard said slowly. " They never recovered it. I gave it to a friend to pass on to you, for safe keeping until I came out of prison. He told me he gave it to you."

" I've never seen any money," Clare said quietly. " If it had been given to me I would have passed it on immediately to the police."

There was silence for a moment, and Millard stared at her, his eyes calculating.

" So you would," he said at length, and there was a strange note in his voice. " So I've been double-crossed! I half suspected it! Look, I don't want to get mixed up with the police again. I'm not a burglar. Let me go and I'll disappear quietly and you'll never see or hear about me again."

David looked at Clare. " Is that what you want?" he asked.

" Perhaps it would be better for all concerned," she replied. " We have one thing to thank him for. He scared Sue into speaking again."

" All right!" David nodded slowly. " See him off the farm, Adam," he said sharply. " Don't ever come back, Millard, or you won't get off so lightly in future."

Tim Millard looked at Clare as he nodded slowly, and then he turned away and departed, with Adam following him closely. Clare watched until both men had disappeared on the stairs and then she faced David, who was watching her closely.

" I have some explaining to do," she said shakily.

" Not at all!" He smiled. " I can tell by your manner that he means nothing to you. What happened in your life before you came here is no concern of mine. All I'm interested in is the future that's awaiting us."

" Us?" she demanded. " I think my time here has come to an end. Sue has recovered her speech and she's back to normal. I can't do anything more for her, David."

" You can do a lot for her yet, and for me," he said softly. " Will you let me be the judge in this case? I'll tell you when I think Sue can be left." He smiled gently, his dark eyes showing pleasure. " There's a lot to be discussed all round, isn't there? But all that can wait. We can sort out one important fact now and let everything else come right in its own time. I love you, Clare! To me that's all that matters. I believe you feel the same way about me, but I'm not sure, so just tell me yes or no. If you say yes, then I can wait. If the answer is no, then I won't do anything to keep you here against your will."

He fell silent and watched her, and Clare looked into his face and knew that all her deepest dreams were coming true. This was better than a dream! It was real! At last it was real.

" The answer is yes," she said quietly.

She didn't get the chance to say more for he took her into his arms and kissed her passionately. But there was nothing else to be said. They both knew instinctively that this was the start of a life together, and they would go on from here with no regrets and a heartful of love and hope . . .

A Heart
of Shadows

Ruth Bovee

CHAPTER ONE

BANNFORD, MAINE

THE sea was there, as it had always been, but neglected now, with Bannford's wharves gently decaying. Back a hundred years, the same prosperity which had made Bedford and Salem and other coastal New England towns among the richest on earth, per capita, had reached Bannford. What was now the Bannford Cordage Company had once been the warehouse for the ladings brought into Bannford Bay in the holds of Ingraham sailing ships.

There hadn't been a sailing vessel, excluding yachts, of course, in the Bannford roadstead in no one remembered how long. Fifty years, perhaps; at least, that was what George Ingraham told John Harding when they were tallying the warehouse receipts against the invoices, upstairs in the dingy old offices. At least, George Ingraham could not remember having seen a genuine sailing vessel of the commercial variety in Bannford harbour in his lifetime, and was just far enough into his fifties to be reluctant to say just *how* far.

Not that it made much difference. Bannford hadn't grown much, if any, since the middle of the previous century. Actually though, it was in the town's favour because it had reached that size during the affluent, bustling, earlier days, and while most New England coastal towns whose mainstay had been the old-time sailing ships had dwindled, and while some had actually died altogether, Bannford had held its own.

The way it had managed this was by turning its back

7

on the sea almost before the last of the big ships had returned from the Baltic with news that German warships were making it uncomfortable over there. When the First World War broke out, Bannford sprang to the challenge, and the Ingraham Shipping & Import Company became the Ingraham Cordage Company, involved in the importation, refining, and ultimately the re-sale of cordage of every conceivable kind. The war had helped, no question of that. Ingraham Cordage got contracts to supply the naval fleets. That was exactly the kind of an impetus a new venture needed. By the time the war ended, Ingraham Cordage already had salesmen crisscrossing the country.

Captain Josiah would probably have sneered, as Elizabeth's father told John Harding one autumn day when they were having trouble making the ancient stove provide adequate heat for the upstairs offices, but Captain Josiah's day had come and gone, as had Captain Josiah, and this was another time with different rules and different players in the game.

John had agreed. He usually agreed, but about half the time George Ingraham had a very small, but very real, feeling that John Harding didn't actually agree. About how wonderful the old days must have been, John agreed. How old Captain Josiah would have stamped round in disgust if he could return and see his immense old warehouse now, so many decades after he'd had it erected, John agreed would be something to behold; but there had been a number of times over the past couple of years that John had performed his clerical duties as punctiliously as ever, with a face flattened with smouldering disagreement.

George Ingraham, unlike Captain Josiah, had always been quite willing to be corrected; he had never assumed an attitude of omnipotence. But, after all, he had been in cordage, running a good business now, for about twice as long as John was old. Not really, but fairly close to it. Once, when George mentioned this to his daughter, Elizabeth had come up with an answer her father probably should have anticipated.

"Dad, he's so much younger; of course his views differ. They have to, don't they? Would you want a clerk who at twenty-three thought as you do, at fifty? Anyway, I don't suppose any two people would ever run the same business the same way, would they? No two women run a house the same way."

George Ingraham never brought that topic up again. There really was no need to do so, in any case. John was a good worker, had a fine head for figures—which was very fortunate because that was all the cordage business was, an exercise in mathematics from eight to five everyday excepting Sunday—and could run the men downstairs in the warehouse as easily as he kept the books upstairs.

In fact, John Harding had been a fortunate find for George Ingraham . He had been employing young men in one capacity or another round the warehouse for many years, and frankly admitted that in all that time, among all those other men, he had not found one who could keep the books, boss the warehousemen, and muscle-up a load, when he had to, anywhere nearly as well as could John Harding.

It was ironic, too, because when John Harding had walked in looking for work two years back, George Ingraham had come within an ace of not hiring him at all. John had appeared at nine o'clock in the morning with liquor on his breath. It wasn't that George Ingraham was a teetotaller; no Ingraham had ever been that. And it wasn't that John had come applying for work smelling of liquor. It was the fear every employer whose warehoused products are stacked high, and which can weigh several tons per individual unit, has, that someone new at the business and who might drink a little to boot could get killed through negligence. The Ingraham Cordage Company needed some things, true enough, but a wrongful-injury lawsuit was not one of them.

But he had gone ahead and hired Harding, and it had turned out to be a very satisfactory arrangement.

Maybe John did not like all George Ingraham's decisions, and maybe he, as Elizabeth had said, thought he knew a better, or quicker, or more profitable way to do something. Thus far John had never argued, but when the day arrived that he *did* argue, George would explain once, and the second time he would fire John Harding.

A couple of times, when Elizabeth had gone to local dances with John Harding, her father, simply because he *was* her father, and all fathers reacted pretty much in the same way, had thought a little about, well, possibly having John in the family.

That was how many of the old-time family companies did it, kept the companies in the family and at the same time brought in new blood. But the last time Elizabeth had returned from a dinner-date she had come up where her father had been sitting on the front porch in the late evening, had dropped down upon the porch-swing, and had said, "Why is it that attractive men are always so dull?"

George hadn't had any answer then, and he still did not have one.

Ingraham's sold to hardware stores round the country and, individually, the orders were relatively small. But at the end of the year, the totals were usually gratifying.

One winter evening when John and George Ingraham were preparing to close up for the night John made a suggestion. He affected facetiousness while making the suggestion, but he was not joking at all. "Mr Ingraham, have you ever thought much about diversification? Maybe taking on another line besides cordage."

George pocketed his pipe and studied the younger man. "For example," he said. "What's on your mind, John?"

The tall younger man went with elaborate casualness and sat upon the corner of a desk. "Oh, possibly something that could be handled right here in the Bannford warehouse. Maybe something that'd be accessible here in New England." John shot his employer a narrow look, then went on speaking. "Possibly something we could capitalise on by using the same warehouse we're using now, and possibly even the same men."

George was agreeable; at least, he gave Harding that impression as he said, "All right. And what exactly might this mysterious inventory consist of?"

"Antiques," said Harding, and his dangling foot stopped swinging; in fact, his entire body seemed to grow taller and stiffer, as though he might be about to lean into a high wind.

George continued to gaze at the younger man. "Antiques . . . John, every town between here and San Francisco has antique pedlars by the score."

John did not yield. Not right then. He said, "Mr Ingraham, antiques from New England sell fast out on the West Coast. Any heritage stuff."

"All right, John, now tell me where we get all these

11

treasures, because you can't get into mass advertising until you know without any doubt that you'll also have the inventory."

John spread his hands. "We pass the word right here in Bannford. We advertise for heirlooms. And they don't really have to go all the way back to Independence. They don't have to go back any farther than our Civil War." John paused to try and read his employer's face. Evidently he thought the signs were propitious because he brought forth a folded illustrated brochure of antiques of the early Americana style, and went over a trifle anxiously and handed the list to George. "I've been thinking about this for several months," he explained as George Ingraham ploughed through the brochure.

George spoke without taking his eyes off some of the illustrations. "Why, John; aren't you happy here?"

Harding bit back an impatient retort, waited, then said, "I've never been happier, but the point is, Mister Ingraham, we're only pushing cordage."

This time George raised his eyes. He also passed back the folder. "John, it's getting dark out and I don't like to keep Liz waiting for supper. Antiques . . .?" George went across to the stair-well, and hiked downward. He did not shake his head until he had let himself out of the little postern gate which had been built into one of the mammoth sliding doors of the warehouse. Antiques! No wonder Liz gave up on him. How in the hell could you make a decent letterhead out of Ingraham & Company, Cordage and Antiques?

The night was crisp with a light, scattering little wind starting and stopping. To George, there was a scent of either sleet or plain rain before morning.

Not that he cared. The distance between office and home was not so great.

Antiques? All of a sudden anything people had made thirty or forty years ago was an antique. Now *real* antiques . . . upstairs in the attic at home there were old round-top trunks that would drive antique collectors right out of their minds.

He reached home, shed his scarf, coat and hat, went to look into the fireplace, where Elizabeth had kindled a nice little fire, then he drew forth his pipe and stoked it.

Antiques!

He puffed, let the heat soak in from behind, listened to that intermittent rough little wind worry the great old house, and eventually went to his favourite chair to sit and read the evening paper before supper was ready.

Antiques indeed! That was utterly ridiculous. Antiques did not go with cordage.

CHAPTER TWO

SOME SUBJECTS FOR THOUGHT

ROBERT WHITING was a handsome, bold-eyed, tanned and well-dressed man. He travelled for Gold Bond Incorporated, a large conglomerate which bought finished objects in enormous quantities in order to get the best price, then re-sold everything at a very healthy mark-up through hundreds of retail outlets country-wide.

Whiting was one of those confident individuals who would have managed, without actually ingratiating himself, to avoid being stabbed by Lucifer's pitchfork by simply offering a contract for mass-produced pitchforks. That was how he struck George Ingraham when they went up the street to the hotel dining-room for a cup of coffee on a blustery, wintry morning.

Whiting was likeable. Even John had to admit that. John, unlike his employer, had not known enough Robert Whitings, yet, to be able to tolerantly accept their flattery, the suave unctiousness, and their completely effortless capability. But later, after Whiting had departed and George called John to his office, George tried to explain. Not that he had to; John was his foreman, true, but he was still no more than an employee. But they had got to be fairly close friends over the last couple of years. That always made a difference among men.

"When you're my age," said George Ingraham, "you'll know the type the minute they walk through the door and climb the steps. We're here to sell cordage,

14

though, so we don't let personalities or prejudices interfere." George smiled upwards from behind his desk.
"He'll do a volume business with us. He brought the
contracts." George tapped some papers atop the desk.
"What I wanted to explain to you, John, is that unless
it's a government contract, volume business means
whittling down our net to the bone. In other words,
while we'll sell him carload lots, the company's net
won't be much more for, say, a hundred tons of
Philippine hemp than it would be for probably about
twenty tons of the same rope sold in small lots."

John started to protest. George held aloft a hand as
he rose from behind the desk. "Wait a moment. We
have to look at this kind of a tight deal two ways.
One, we will be selling our goods, which is why we're
here. Two, we will probably get more orders from
Whiting's company. Those things should make up the
difference. And what's the difference downstairs whether
they load out a hundred or twenty tons? We are keeping
the men busy, keeping our overhead down, and—"

"Mr Ingraham," Harding said, almost impatiently.
"I wasn't going to protest. After all, it's your company.
I'm just an employee. What I was going to say was that
hemp is getting to be a novelty item."

George Ingraham, whose belief in stout Manilla rope
was lifelong, stopped what he was doing over at the
coffee urn and looked around. "Hemp a novelty?"

"Mr Ingraham, the synthetics are coming on strong.
It'll only be a matter of time, five years maybe, ten years
at the most, and people will only be buying hemp rope
for a narrow list of purposes, and my guess is that it'll
become nothing more than a novelty. As for Whiting
and the Gold Bond corporation, I wouldn't object to
their penny-profit techniques since they're strictly a mass-

outlet, but why couldn't Ingraham Cordage sound them out on other items?"

George finally understood, and finished drawing off his coffee, which he took back to the desk with him. "I see. Maybe Gold Bond would be interested in antiques?"

George sipped coffee and watched John Harding nod his head. "Exactly, Mr Harding. Gold Bond is a conglomerate. They are diversified as all hell. Their outlet-stores across the country peddle anything that happens to be high on the social priority lists from year to year."

George put the cup down. "They sell antiques through their outlets?"

Harding did not know. "They sell *anything*. I've wandered through some of their retail stores. When people were enthusiastic about Chinese items, Gold Bond specialised in everything from Chinese kimonos to dinner-ware with bamboo handles. When there was a big demand for medieval artifacts from Europe, Gold Bond had men scouring old manor-houses and villages and castles from Sweden to the Isle of Man. They even had simulated artifacts made for the limited-income trade. Mr Ingraham, right now Americans are buying Americana like they have just discovered it."

George sighed and leaned back. "Americana antiques?"

John nodded briskly. "Yes. And right here in New England we're centrally located. Sure, Mr Whiting should have his cordage, but it seems to me that Ingraham Company ought not to be hoping for more penny-profit orders from Whiting; they should be obliging him so that we can have a foot in the door with Gold Bond when we've built up a decent inventory of the other things."

George ranged a slow glance round the dark old

ceiling. John's theory was correct; in business the true *entrepreneur* did, in fact, strive to make of each deal a means for working up additional transactions. But antique Americana . . .?

Someone entered the outer office and John went to look after them. George went back to the coffee urn.

There was another aspect of business, too; when an employee began to assume prerogatives which were not rightly his concern. . . . George refilled the cup and stood gazing at three side-by-side portraits of proud sailing vessels, all sails to the wind, riding low upon the greeny sea. They had been flagships of the Ingraham company over a hundred years ago.

He turned only when a light step and a faint flurry of cloth crossed the threshold. It was Elizabeth. She looked especially beautiful. She was one of those women who would look nice even down on her knees in the garden, because she was so obviously and abundantly female. As her father turned around, probably because the old office was dark with age, masculine in décor, and not too well lighted by the roadway windows, he was struck by the fact that she was exceptionally graceful. Her taffy hair came from the Hansen line; the Ingrahams had invariably had very dark hair. But her steel-blue eyes were from *his* side. People who had had occasion to know the Ingrahams had for generations called that shade of blue Ingraham-blue.

He smiled at her, and saw her gaze jump from him to the old portraits he'd been gazing at, then back to him again, as she said, "I met your Robert Whiting a few minutes ago out front of the hotel." She moved into the office, her gaze darkening with doubt. "He has charm, Dad."

George considered. He had mentioned Whiting the

17

previous evening at dinner. Now, he knew how his daughter's thoughts were running, because he knew that sceptical attitude of hers. She had never, to his knowledge anyway, been in love, but she had never lacked for young men either. Over the last year or so he'd begun to have an uneasy idea that she might end up as one of his aunts had, a lifelong, autocratic spinster. Whenever she mentioned a man in that tone of voice, and wearing that suspicious expression, the thought of her being an old maid returned. For no particular reason, except that she had mentioned Robert Whiting in that tone, and because he'd just had that other thought, he now said, "He's different, of course, but then he's from New York."

Elizabeth stopped by his desk, near to smiling. She was amused by his remark, which implied that New Yorkers might have three legs or an extra arm. What she had not liked very much in Robert Whiting had been the sudden showing of smouldering interest in his eyes when they had met. She knew that much about men; in some ways they weren't a whole lot different from other male animals. It seemed to her, at least within her own experience, that the ones who came to Maine from other places, from large cities and populous states, were more aggressively male than the local men.

Whiting was a handsome man, very well dressed. She knew instinctively that a dinner-date with him would involve more than eating and talking. A woman did not have to be worldly or experienced to understand the ground-rules of the game played between single women and men.

She said, "He mentioned doing business with you," and her father, remembering his recent conversation with John, stood by the coffee urn looking thoughtful.

"*Volume* business," he said. "We'll sell them tons of cordage, but the net won't be much more than we'd make on a hatful of small orders." He smiled at her. "But it's business, and that's what we're here for."

She turned and leaned upon his desk, looking directly at him. "Dad, are you and John still backing and filling?"

He affected innocence. "What about, Liz?"

"Well, about *any*thing." She knew, because she and John had spoken for ten minutes before she'd come to her father's office, what John wanted to do, but she also knew her father. He was not exactly a male chauvinist, but he skirted very close to it by being resentful of her interference in the business; he had very definite and set ideas about things.

He said, "I listen to John's notions, Liz. But what he seems to forget is that this is a cordage company. That's what we've been making our living at for a long time, and if we haven't got rich, we've managed to be quite comfortable."

"He doesn't want to change that, does he?" she asked, knowing the answer in advance.

"Well—not change it exactly, but he wants to take on a new line." George Ingraham cleared his throat. "Antiques."

He watched his daughter closely for the curl of lip, the slowly rising, sceptical eyebrow. None of this happened. "Antiques," she murmured, and straightened up off the desk to go get herself a cup of the coffee. With her back to him she said, "That's really very interesting, isn't it?"

He couldn't see her face, so there was no way to get a clue as to how he should respond, so he responded the way he had been thinking. "It's tommyrot, that's what it is, Liz." He went to the desk, sifted through some papers, then sat down as she turned towards him and spoke again.

"Dad, every summer lately tourists have been pouring into New England as though it were the Promised Land. They're buying up anything that isn't nailed down and which is at least fifty years old."

George said, "Sweetheart, this is *not* a seasonal business. We have never catered to the public, and have no interest in public whims. I've seen these fads come and go since I was a child."

She did not descend to his level of argument. In fact, she did not argue with him at all; she merely said, "The warehouse would be an ideal place to gather everything together, to sort and store things. I'm really pleased that you're giving it some thought. I've never thought of you as one of those hard-headed men of another generation." She smiled over the rim of her cup. "And your ability to make coffee is improving, too. This is quite good."

Her father picked up the Gold Bond papers and glared at them as he said, "John makes the coffee." He rattled the paper, and Elizabeth took this as her cue. On her way to the door she passed close to his desk, stooped and kissed his cheek.

George put down the papers. She used a very distinctive perfume. He looked at her, really and truly wondering why no young man had as yet asked his girl to become a wife.

She was beautiful, actually. Her figure was flawless; a bit on the abundant side, but since when did *that* ever discourage men? She was a good cook, a fine housekeeper. . . . He knew what it was, and sighed as she turned at the door to smile back at him: her tongue.

Elizabeth was not tactful. She never had been, not even as a small child. She had a very strongly developed sense of ethics, as well. She thought nothing at all of berating someone who did something she did not think was entirely forthright and honest.

Well, a hundred years ago those attributes had been prized and sought after in a wife. Of course, the trouble was simply that *this* was *now*, it was *not* a hundred years ago.

He smiled back, Elizabeth passed out of the room, closed the office door, and he could faintly discern her footfalls. He did not think they got as far as the stair-well before they halted, but he was already reaching for the Gold Bond papers again, so he did not pay much attention.

He was correct. Elizabeth only went as far as John Harding's desk. There she said, "I probably didn't help you at all, John, but I tried."

John's dark head came up, he tossed aside his pencil and made a sweeping, wide gesture with his arms. "Liz, there is no reason under the sun why we can't do it."

She said, "Go ahead, finish it. No reason at all, except that my father is a bull-headed man."

He leaned back, gazing up at her. It was difficult to concentrate the way she was standing there, full, round breasts noticeable, golden throat showing a faint, dull pulse, her attractive full mouth relaxed, without pressure.

No one had ever asked why he had been willing to stay at Ingraham Cordage for several years in a job any older man could have done, and it was just as well they hadn't asked because he'd have cut them off at the water-line. But there it was, six feet away, the reason he had stayed, and the reason he would go right on staying.

She said, "John, don't give up."

He smiled very slowly and wisely. "I never do that, Liz." He leaned forward upon the desk. "You're the first person who hasn't thought it wasn't a crazy scheme. I don't need any more encouragement than that."

There was one thing, and it bothered her a little. "If you harass him about it, he'll fire you."

John knew that, too. "I'm not going to harass him. I sounded him out and he didn't like the idea at all. I won't talk to him about it again. It was simply that this warehouse, the offices and all, would have been so perfect. Everything is already established. Even the name, Liz: Ingraham Cordage Company. That's right out of Pickwick." He cocked a grey eye at her. "Am I going too far; can you see what I mean? It doesn't have a thing to do with being derogatory to your father. I think he's one of the finest men I've ever known. Do you understand?"

She did. At least she *thought* she did. And when he'd first poured out his idea to her, she had been captivated at once. It troubled her now that she thought she saw a rift coming. She knew how highly her father prized John, but she also knew how uncompromising her father could be.

She said, "Good Luck."

John sat looking at the place where she had gone down the stairs for a full minute after her departure.

CHAPTER THREE

AN INTERESTING EVENING

IN BIG cities, salesmen often took clients to dinner on expense accounts. In small towns the process was very often reversed, as it was when Robert Whiting returned in mid-afternoon to discuss the agreements between his company and Ingraham Cordage. George invited him to have supper at the Ingraham home that evening, and Whiting had accepted without even a hint of a demur, although as a matter of fact it meant lying over at Bannford, because there were only two south-bound trains that passed through, one about eight o'clock in the morning, the other one about eight o'clock in the evening. Perhaps George should have marvelled at the acceptance, since Robert Whiting could have bought his dinner at the hotel and still made the eight o'clock nightly train, a procedure bound to be much less expensive than keeping his hotel room overnight simply in order to have dinner with the Ingrahams. But George was not that much of an analyst of human motives.

He went home early, leaving the closing-up to John Harding. When he told Elizabeth who was coming for dinner she accepted it almost stoically, and went to set another place and to shift the location from the kitchen table, where she and her father usually ate, to the formal dining-room, which was used only very rarely any more.

For Elizabeth, being told there would be another person at the dinner table caused no difficulties. She was not, in any case, one of those women who went into shock at not being given at least ten hours' advance notice. The only interest she evinced at all was when her father came to the kitchen to help, which he did almost every night, and first made both of them a mild highball. As she accepted the drink she said, "Did you sign the agreement with Gold Bond today?"

Her father nodded. "This afternoon. That was when I asked him to dinner."

Elizabeth bent to look into the oven where the roast was simmering. "Then he must like Bannford very much", she said, straightening up, "to stay over another day just to have dinner with us tonight."

George turned that round and round inside his head while he clinked ice on the side of his glass, and went to see if the table were set. When he returned from the other room his daughter smiled at him.

"That was one of my nasty asides, wasn't it?"

He smiled back, but vaguely. He had not known what she had meant when she'd made the remark, had not particularly cared what she had meant, and now he did not know, or even care again, whether she was being intentionally nasty or not. He said, "You don't like Robert Whiting." He sipped his weak highball. "All right. He will survive it, I'm sure, and so will you and I, but . . ." He looked down into the glass where the ice chunks were floating.

Elizabeth said, "I know, Dad. I'm getting crowsfeet, and soon now I'll be thickening up a bit. So wouldn't it

24

be nice if I stopped being so critical and accepted someone?" She brushed past with the salad bowl, and from just beyond the swinging door she called back, "Yes, it would be nice. I'd *like* to do this for you, too. But we can't really manufacture what we want in other people, can we?"

George Ingraham did not answer. He quite often did not answer when his daughter made remarks like this. He was not really sure he'd know *how* to answer, and all his life George Ingraham had made a practice of never allowing himself to be drawn off the deep end into things he could not properly handle.

Elizabeth had the meal almost completely finished, so her father ambled out to the parlour to finish his highball, and from there he went out to the front porch.

The night was not windy, for a change, but there was a feeling of change in the air, and although George Ingraham could not see the sea, far out through the trees and the darkness, he could imagine its uneasy roll. Like many former seafarers, George Ingraham never failed to take the sea's pulse when he wanted some idea what the weather would be like over the next day or two.

The sky was brilliant, clear, and cold. Elsewhere round the neighbourhood there were lights, and now and then a vagrant fragrance came from someone's fireplace chimney. Altogether, it was an exceptionally fine night for this time of year. Spring would be coming soon now, but in New England it never was allowed to appear until winter had turned in all fury to lash the land at least one more time.

Robert Whiting arrived, and briskly came up to the front porch where George Ingraham was standing.

25

They shook hands and George took his guest inside. Whiting shed his coat and hat, then breathed deeply and rolled up his eyes. "I knew she would be a good cook," he said, and jovially winked. "That's the most wonderful fragrance, coming from your kitchen, I've smelled in months."

George took Robert Whiting to the parlour fireplace, then went to make a couple more highballs. Elizabeth was shedding her apron, ready to go down the rear hallway to her room to powder her shiny nose. She watched her father a moment, then went over and wordlessly tipped up the whisky bottle, held it a moment, then set it back down.

Her father said, "Liz, there's enough whisky in that highball to make him fall down!" He was aghast.

Liz looked guilelessly up into her father's face. "I don't think so. Wasn't it you who said they were different? My personal guess is that Robert Whiting can drink two or three of those and still not fall down." She turned. "I'll join you in the parlour in a few minutes."

George made his own highball, as weak as before, which was the only way he drank liquor, and returned to the parlour. Whiting accepted his glass, sipped, then beamed. "You make a man's drink, Mr Ingraham. By the way, do you mind if I call you George?"

By the time Elizabeth arrived, fresh and smiling, and in her father's view, unusually pretty and alluring, Robert Whiting had almost finished his fortified highball. The only thing she thought was any different about him when she entered the room was that, although his eyes did not kindle any quicker, they showed more fire.

They went to the dining-room and when Whiting

26

held Elizabeth's chair, he afterwards managed somehow to gently and briefly let his hand brush along her shoulders as he was moving away.

Whiting was an easy and experienced conversationalist. He had an ability Elizabeth had never seen in anyone before, or, if she had seen it before, she had not recognised it. Whiting monopolised the dinner-table talk without once appearing to do so; he brought her out, brought her father out, kept the talk tight, informal and bubbly, and he did it all without appearing to do so.

Elizabeth did not appreciate this until near the end of the meal, and her father did not discover it at all. He thoroughly enjoyed himself and his guest. Nor did Elizabeth begrudge her father any of this; he was a man who needed laughter and levity.

What Elizabeth's discovery meant in personal terms, to her, was that she had better respect Robert Whiting, because a man this clever at dinner would certainly be equally as clever under other circumstances.

What lulled her was the fact that Robert Whiting would only be lying over until the morning train arrived, then he would go back southward to New York. At least, that was her assumption.

After dinner they went out into the parlour again where a glowing fire burned. Elizabeth's father brought forth a cedar box of Habana fillers, then held the light for Robert Whiting, and afterwards for himself. Elizabeth enjoyed this special fragrance. She always had, but her father actually smoked very seldom, so her opportunities to enjoy it had been few.

Robert Whiting talked of Habana. He also mentioned Puerto Rico, El Salvador, Cartagena. It seemed there were few places where he had not been. He asked

Elizabeth if she enjoyed travelling. About all she could say was that she did not know because she had never travelled.

He described some exotic places to her, his eyes speaking a personal and separate language to her, signalling a man's desires even though her father was right there in the room with them.

Elizabeth was intrigued; Robert Whiting was quite a new species to her, and even though her inherent scepticism kept her forewarned, she was perfectly willing to concede that Robert Whiting was a vastly experienced, cleverly articulate, totally willing, women's man.

Later, when it was time for Whiting to leave and Elizabeth accompanied him to the doorway, along with her father, it could of course have been purest accident, but Whiting managed to be in the middle, with Elizabeth at his right side. As they paused briefly at the door he felt for her hand, squeezed it, then as he released her hand he looked directly down into her face and thanked her for the meal, for the delightful hospitality—and signalled an unmistakable message with his eyes that her father never saw at all.

It did not matter. In the morning Robert Whiting would be on his way back to New York. They might meet again if he returned to Maine on business and specifically visited Bannford, but the chances were infinitely greater that they would never meet again.

CHAPTER FOUR

THREE MEN AND A GIRL

ELIZABETH had once worked briefly for Charles Ormond, who owned and operated the largest mercantile establishment in Bannford. Since that time Charles Ormond had died and his only child, a daughter named Lilith, had inherited the business. She and her husband had lived in Ohio, in commercial and industrial Cincinnati to be exact, since they were married. Their decision to return to Bannford had not been an easy one, especially for Lilith's husband, Will—William Spencer —who had never been out of a large city and who had all kinds of preconceptions concerning life in a small town, most of which were entirely justified.

Elizabeth was down at the store the day following Robert Whiting's visit talking about nothing in particular with Lilith Spencer, when she got quite a shock. A tall, handsome, well-dressed man came strolling along, turned to gaze in the roadside window, and Elizabeth found herself looking directly into Robert Whiting's bold and very self-assured eyes.

He entered the store at once, nodded pleasantly to Lilith, then, when Elizabeth asked if he'd accidentally missed the morning train, Robert Whiting threw Lilith a broad wink and said, "I missed it, but not by accident. Every time I'd start in that direction I'd think of you, and my legs just simply would not take another step."

Lilith smiled, her eyes full of lively interest. Elizabeth knew what thoughts were passing through Lilith's mind, and she blushed about that. Also, although Lilith was not a gossip, she would certainly pass the fruits of this little meeting along to her husband, and perhaps a close friend or two, which would amount to the same thing in a place like Bannford.

She decided to get Robert Whiting out of there before he said something else that would be even more devastating, and managed it by saying she thought she would go down to her father's warehouse. The moment she started away, Robert Whiting followed. Behind them, Lilith Spencer made the little clucking sounds of a woman who has just discovered something very worthwhile.

Elizabeth did not take Robert Whiting down to the Ingraham warehouse at all. She walked him out to the village green, which was now on the westernmost outskirts of town.

He was perfectly at ease. As they walked through the changling day with occasional flashes of chill sunshine alternating with impenetrable grey cloud masses, he told her he had decided to remain in Bannford for another day or two. He asked her to dinner that evening. He also asked her to have luncheon with him

He was an exasperatingly bland man. She could not really dislike him even though she were entirely satisfied that he was not sincere with her. Each time she looked up, he was warmly smiling. Each comment she made, he had exactly the right answer.

At the green, they watched a pair of white swans. It was too early yet, but soon there would be cygnets trailing after the big birds, minature in every way. She explained this to Robert Whiting and he duly smiled, then took her fingers in his hand as they strolled, and held them.

"Why don't you visit New York some time?" he asked, drawing her closer to his side on the path beside the pond. "Elizabeth, why don't you come down next week?" He said this as though it had just come to him, like a bolt from the blue. He even stopped in the middle of the pathway and pulled her round with him, showing his frank and lively interest in the idea.

She did not believe it had just come to him; she believed he was quite capable of being this good an actor. She thought he had used this same approach to many girls, and had probably been successful with some of them—perhaps even most of them.

She looked up, then stepped past and pulled him along as she kept on strolling. No question about it, she would like to see New York City, but not at his price. "Some day, perhaps," she conceded. "Perhaps the next time my father goes down on business I'll traipse along."

He was immediately interested. "When will that be?"

She laughed around at him. "He usually goes down once a year. This year it was in January. But I have no idea when it'll be next year."

He neither gave up easily nor became noticeably aggravated, but by the time they had got to the far end of the common where the old bronze cannon stood, with its pyramid of ancient cannonballs, he had told her why he was still in Bannford.

"The first time I saw you, Elizabeth," he laughed softly as he said this, "it was like watching the first sunrise; like seeing the first moonset. I couldn't leave until I knew you better."

She was certain that she knew what he was doing, but

that did not prevent her from liking it. Robert Whiting had a way of complimenting women no one around Bannford could equal.

"I thought possibly it was something endemic, so I went out looking around. Believe me, it's not endemic at all; it is simply you." He pulled her gently closer as they turned to stroll back. She did not actually resist, but when his hand groped its way to her waist she managed to handily avoid the encircling arm. "I can't quite make myself go back, Elizabeth."

She said, "I hope your company is very understanding."

He brushed that aside. "Gold Bond is headed up by an uncle of mine. My father is secretary of the entire corporate structure. Another uncle and a cousin control my particular end of it, which is purchasing." He raised her hand and patted it, then leaned closer. "Don't ever worry about the conglomerate eating us up; we're individuals, and that's what we'll remain."

She hadn't even thought of the conglomerate, either as a threat or as anything else. She freed her hand when they approached the end of the walkway where giant shade trees ended and cement began, then looked around. They were beyond the commercial district, and since Bannford had no industrial sector, they were standing upon the edge of the westerly residential area.

She saw children at play. She also saw several curious residents of the area looking her way. Some she knew, perhaps two-thirds of them she knew; after all, Bannford was actually nothing more than an oversized village. Everybody knew everybody else there. She thought of Lilith Spencer as a means for spreading information, and decided that dear Lilith would not have to work very hard, not if the stares coming her way as she and

Robert Whiting left the common, heading back towards the heart of town, were any indication of how news-worthy those women considered Elizabeth's park stroll with the handsome, well-dressed stranger.

She was right. Later that day, in the middle of the afternoon, long after she had left Robert Whiting out front of the hotel without ever really promising to go to dinner with him that evening, she encountered John Harding out front of the family warehouse directing some draymen. He nodded without smiling, and continued at his work until the draymen were safely inside the warehouse, then he turned and gazed at Elizabeth as though he really were surprised to find her still standing there.

He walked over, still without smiling, and said, "You broke off your stroll on the common early, didn't you?" He made it sound so elaborately casual she would have smiled at his exaggerated indifference, except that she was surprised that anyone could have got the word this far in so short a length of time.

She answered with decorous slowness. "No, we didn't end the stroll early, John." She did not lower her eyes. "I wanted to talk to him about the chances of selling his company some New England antiques."

John nodded. "But you didn't."

His tone implied something that made faint colour reach her face. "No, I didn't get round to that," she replied, annoyance building up in her. "But I will. Mr Whiting isn't going back to New York just yet."

John went over and leaned upon the rough old weathered boards along the front of the warehouse, and stood gazing at her. She thought his face looked a little paler, that his eyes were slightly darker, but there were shadows this late in the afternoon—they could be responsible.

Finally he said, "This afternoon I searched around for some answers, Liz, and maybe I've come up with one. I'll give your father two weeks' notice in the morning."

That did not exactly stun her. She had never really thought he would have stayed as long as he had; she had never been able to guess why he had stayed. She said, "Well, and what will you do after you quit my father?"

He leaned a foot up against the wall at his back, and looked slightly past her as he answered. "I don't have that decision made yet, but I think I'll borrow some money from the bank and start out around the country-side on a buying trip." He looked back at her, his wide, pleasant mouth drawn slightly flat. "Everyone has to do it sooner or later, don't they? I mean, try their wings."

She smiled and puzzled over him a little. She'd gone out with him a time or two, and he'd been dull and almost taciturn; yet at other times, as now, when they talked together, he was anything but dull and taciturn. She did not understand him. That was about the size of it.

He said, "It may all be a pipe-dream anyway. Maybe at the bank, if they know I've quit your dad, they won't loan me any money."

She had the obvious answer to that. "Then don't quit, John."

"I have to, Liz. . . . For one thing, I can't get into the antique business on a part-time basis. For another thing . . . never mind that." He straightened away from the wall and looked at his watch. "Better get upstairs or your father'll be poking his head out the window and yelling at me."

She instinctively glanced up. There was no face at the window. She said, "John, I'll mention the antiques to Robert Whiting. But honestly, today I just didn't really have a good chance."

He suddenly looked very intense. "Liz, you could make me a whole lot more at ease in m' mind if you'd just not go anywhere near that drummer from the city." John swung and disappeared inside the great, cavernous old warehouse.

She stood for a moment looking after him. Jealousy. That was what his trouble was; John Harding was jealous of Robert Whiting. Elizabeth repressed a great sigh of resignation and turned to walk home. There was nothing actually very simple about men, although as a matter of fact she had always considered most of their motives elemental enough.

She bathed when she got home, changed her dress, went out back to see what the sky looked like because the wind seemed to be rising, then she returned indoors and got to work. She had to stir a fire in the parlour hearth, and she also had to start on dinner. Although it seemed to have prematurely darkened outdoors, the clock said her father would not be home for another couple of hours, which allowed her plenty of time.

She had her private thoughts exactly as every other woman in Bannford had. She wondered about John, and came up with half a notion how she could help him. She also thought about Robert Whiting—who had wanted her to call him Bob instead of Robert—and smiled in spite of herself because he was so gallant, so uncompromisingly dedicated to her even though she had given him practically no encouragement at all.

By the time she had supper ready the world beyond her windows was black, that rising wind had become an intermittent squall bearing beads of rain, and when her father stamped in and leaned to close the door, she decided that regardless of whatever else happened in the world tonight, Bannford—probably the entire New England coast, was going to be storm-lashed before morning.

Her father came to the kitchen, eventually, to mix their traditional pair of weak drinks. He said it was going to blow up a storm, and when he handed her the glass he also said Bob Whiting had come by late this afternoon to announce that he would not actually be starting back to New York for another couple of days.

She kept waiting for her father to announce that John had quit. They had their drinks, had their usual small sessions of talking, and finally sat down to eat, all without her father even once mentioning John Harding. Finally, near the end of the meal when she could stand it no longer she said, "How was John today?"

Her father considered that stoically before replying. "Fine. He said he wanted to see me in the morning. Can't imagine what for, unless it's another crack-brained scheme to make us rich, like the antique scheme."

That had to be her answer; John hadn't gone to her father this afternoon; he intended to go to him in the morning.

CHAPTER FIVE

A MATTER OF JUDGEMENT

THREE things happened the following day. None of them actually had any right to surprise her, and probably being surprised was not what troubled her. She went to see Morgan Hendershot at the local bank, and almost had an actual argument with him; then from there she went over to the warehouse, and upstairs while she was having coffee with her father during John's absence—he was out back somewhere supervising a shipment—her father informed her of John's decision to quit, and she almost had a second argument.

When her father shook his head dolorously she said, "Well, if you didn't want it to happen, why did you let him do it, Father?"

George had looked up at once. "*Let* him. Sweetheart, I didn't let him; I couldn't prevent him from doing it. He was very formal and all. He even knocked on my door and—"

"You most certainly could have prevented it," said Elizabeth, and her father, caught unprepared, sat at his desk, coffee cup in hand, staring up at her. He probably had already guessed what she meant, but she said it anyway.

"You could have at least given him a little encouragement."

George wrinkled his forehead. "In the antique business? Sweetheart, that is utterly ridiculous."

She smiled coldly. "All right. Then you've lost him and that ends it."

George studied his daughter for a while. Eventually

37

he eased back gently in his chair, still eyeing her, but a little caustically, a little sceptically, this time. Then he said, "I don't understand you, Liz. You think John Harding is dull and boring—and here you are, standing before me, defending him."

She rolled her eyes before answering. "Dad, a man can be dull and boring and still be entirely agreeable in other ways, can't he? John is good with figures. He is energetic and intelligent and willing. You've said those things about him yourself. Well, I see those things in him too, and that has nothing to do with—anything else. As a matter of fact, John Harding just isn't my kind of a man—in other ways. Is that so impossible to accept?"

"No," her father came right back, "it's not impossible at all, but I'd be even more pleased if you would tell me just what exactly *is* your type of a man."

She sighed and went to the door before replying. "I don't know. Anyway, what good would it do you to know? There isn't one in Bannford, I'm quite sure of that." She smiled back towards his desk. "I'm sorry you're probably stuck with me."

George Ingraham rose to that at once. He got to his feet protesting. "I'm thankful every day of my life I'm stuck with you, sweetheart. I'm not trying to marry you off for *my* benefit. I only want to see you started out right." His face subtly changed. He strolled from behind the desk and headed towards her at the doorway. "You'd probably never be very happy with one of the locals. By the way, I'm going to stop by the hotel this evening for a highball with Bob Whiting. Would you like to join us?"

She looked at her father a moment, then laughed aloud, leaned to peck his cheek, and, without answering, went out into the big old draughty main office. John was still absent from his desk. She shrugged, started down the stairs without really thinking of anything, and without any warning John hove into sight down below, head down, brow creased in fierce concentration. He grabbed one side of the railing and started bolting up the stairs two at a time. Elizabeth did not have a chance to cry a warning. He was perhaps justified, because those steps were so rarely used, in his headlong haste, but almost anyone rushing up like that would have raised his head.

He didn't. They met hard about two-thirds of the way from the top. Elizabeth threw out both hands, but at the last moment dropped one to grab hold of the balustrade. He bowled into her.

She saw his head fling upwards at the first brushing of bodies, saw the look of astonishment, mingled with a look of annoyance, all in a fleeting second. Then he was lunging past, seeking something to hold to before falling. One arm went round her waist, the other arm grabbed higher, caught her just below the shoulders. She clung desperately to the railing and braced to keep them both from falling.

It only took seconds; everything happened as though it were a kaleidoscope. The first thing Elizabeth realised, after their initial headlong ploughing into one another, was that he had her in an embrace that was tight enough to force the breath from her body.

Then he kissed her.

She was still bracing, still fighting with all her power to keep them both from falling. She did not even see his head come down, did not realise her own face was tipped up until she felt the warm, firm pressure of his lips across her mouth.

He bore down almost savagely. It was no accident. When she began struggling, he released his hold of her, lifted his lips for a moment, then very gently, very tenderly, lowered his head, brushed her bruised mouth again, and whispered something. One moment later he had released her and was on up the stairs into the upper office.

She stood with a free hand exploring her injured mouth, looking back up where he had gone. Then she continued on down.

She remembered very distinctly what he had whispered. "Liz, there's no hope for me to ever love another woman the way I've been in love with you for years."

She went all the way home repeating that over and over. It was a little like being in shock, like being the survivor of some kind of unexpected trauma, but when she reached the front porch with shadows descending, and sat down out there for a moment, she began to be disgusted with herself.

She should have known; should have guessed long ago. She should have been able to guess why he had always been so taciturn and—well—clumsy and awkwards, on their dates.

But she hadn't guessed, and that meant she wasn't very perceptive after all.

Finally, then, the third event of this day occurred. She did not see him at once, but when he turned up the walkway she heard the grinding sounds of leather over stone. Bob Whiting was approaching carrying a white, rather long box.

She turned towards the porch steps, and when he was close enough she called a soft greeting in response to his soft greeting.

He came up beside her, pressed the box into her hands, then said, "You wouldn't have dinner with me, and I just couldn't keep you out of my thoughts. I had some idea that if I brought you roses you'd at least smile, and I could go on back to the hotel with that much to keep me going."

She said, "Thank you so much, Bob." As a matter of fact she *was* thrilled, because she had never before been given a box of roses. At the same time as she was thanking him she was also thinking in a recess of her mind that what he had just said rang false. He usually was too wary or discreet to let the rhetoric get out of hand, but he had this time.

He stood. She knew what he was waiting for—an invitation to come inside with her. She did not extend it, but for a little while she invited him to sit outside with her. That lasted until the chill became more pronounced, then he insisted that she meet him at the hotel dining-room for luncheon the following day, and left. He had not been gone a full ten minutes when her father arrived home. She was out in the kitchen arranging her roses in a long-necked vase, and her father eyed her endeavours and the beautiful roses with bright curiosity and interest.

"I'll guess," he said, in the doorway. "You won them at the grocery store raffle."

She finished arranging the roses and, still with her back to him, moved off a short distance to admire them. She did not answer until he had teased her again.

"You were discovered by a New York City dramatics producer, and those red roses are tokens of appreciation."

She turned. "Mr Whiting." Looking him squarely in the eye, she slowly shook her head. "And *he* is not my type *either*. Sorry, Dad." Then she reached for the apron and got to work making dinner.

He lingered a bit, making a pair of weak highballs, which he usually did not do until after he had cleaned up after arriving home. He did not have any specific reason, at least none she could discern, although he did act as though he wanted to talk about something, while being underfoot in her kitchen.

She guessed he had John Harding on his mind. For a moment or two she thought of bringing that up, but in the end she allowed sleeping dogs to lie. When she was thoroughly mystified, her father finished his drink and went wordlessly on his way through the house to prepare himself for dinner.

Elizabeth had an idea about what her father could have said about John Harding. She was particularly curious about what he *might* have had to say about John getting a loan from the bank. That was what she and Morgan Hendershot had had their furious argument about. She had told Morgan Hendershot that she knew exactly what she was doing, she was of the age of legal consent, and whatever she wanted to do with her personal funds was her own blessed business—and if Mr Hendershot called her father and told him what she was doing, *she* would hire a lawyer and make Hendershot and everyone connected with his bank wish they had never heard her name!

It was, in a way, the most violent outburst of her lifetime. She had raised a figurative fist at other times, but this was the first time she'd done it against an adult —and an adult, in fact, she had known all her life, and had feared for his great size, his forbidding banker's face, and his enormous prestige.

She had won, obviously. If Morgan Hendershot had said anything to her father, he would have most certainly said something to her. George Ingraham was not a man who avoided an argument, or a fight, if he felt one or both were justified.

While she worked, she reflected, and by the time her father returned for dinner she had almost decided to tell him what she had done. Almost. The moment he sat down and said, "Well, Bob Whiting and I had a very pleasant discussion at the hotel bar this afternoon," her curiosity was sufficiently aroused to prevent her from intruding her own affairs, for a time yet anyway.

"What kind of a discussion?" she enquired.

"Business," her father replied, beginning to eat. "Everything, you might say, from cordage to general trade. He's very interesting to talk to; there hardly seems a single field he's not capable of talking about. We even discussed John's favourite topic, antiques."

She looked up quickly. "How did that come up?"

Her father paused, squinted, then shrugged and went back to his meal. "I'm not sure how it came up, sweetheart. He had the facts and figures, anyway."

Making her voice very casual, Elizabeth said, "I'd be interested, Dad."

He drank some coffee. "According to Whiting, there isn't any real demand; there's only a sort of seasonal need for antiques along the eastern seashore. He said you couldn't give Americana away down in New York. Down there, they want only the best European stuff." Her father replaced the coffee cup upon its saucer. "I'd put faith in what he says, Liz. He's not only a very

43

clever businessman, he also knows what is selling and what isn't."

It was a blow, in a way, to Elizabeth's judgement, but, as she told herself, no matter how it came out ultimately, and even granting that Bob Whiting's judgement was excellent, no one was ever infallible. Bob Whiting might not be entirely right about anything he had told her father.

But that kind of thinking did not buoy up her spirits very much, even though she tried hard to keep 'positive' thoughts. Even later, when dinner was finished and they were doing the dishes, and her father casually said, "John will be back within a fortnight begging me to take him back," she still struggled to keep her spirits up.

She thought she was learning a very valuable lesson : how to see oneself as being quite capable of making bad judgements.

She would have been just as pleased if she could have learned this lesson without having it cost her her savings to do it.

But there was still the possibility that Bob Whiting and her father were wrong, and that John Harding was right. However, when she fell to comparing them, she very soberly decided John Harding probably could not have the kind of mature judgement the other two older men had, and *that* meant . . . she preferred not to think about it.

CHAPTER SIX

MOONLIGHT ON THE COMMON

BECAUSE she wanted to hear it first-hand from Bob Whiting that there was no demand for early-American artifacts, she consented to have supper with him at the hotel. She knew that because her father really did not have a genuine interest in Americana, he would not have pressed the topic. But she *did* have such an interest. Well, she at least had a financial reason to be interested.

She had no illusions, either, about what to expect on her date with Bob Whiting, but that prospect did not trouble her very much, and, initially at any rate, when she and Bob were in the hotel dining-room, it seemed that her caution and wariness were probably excessive. He was not only very pleasant, very self-assured even in surroundings that did not actually do him justice, but he was also very compatible.

When she brought up the subject of antiques, he smiled a little indulgently and said, "Liz, in my business we keep a hand on the buying public's pulse. We keep in touch with all our outlets across the country. When they indicate a specific demand, we take it from there."

She could feel her heart sinking. "And there has been no demand for . . .?"

"None," he replied, smiling down into her eyes. He beckoned a waiter and had their wine glasses refilled. "Once in a blue moon," he went on, "some particular novelty will catch on, and for a while, perhaps as long as a couple of years, there will be a strong demand. Our company is so organised that whatever it is people want,

45

we can immediately tap the source and supply the demand. That was originally how Gold Bond got its start. Of course, since then we've branched out. We are so diversified now we're in shipping, in coffee, even in book publishing." He leaned and stroked her hand where it lay atop the table. "Believe me, lovely lady, Gold Bond owes much to its early, rather humble beginning, and we've never abandoned the policies we used in those days. If anything, we use the same ones, but with much more finesse now."

She slid her hand from beneath his and reached for her cup of coffee. Well, as her father had said, Bob Whiting was worth listening to, and she had just listened to him sounding the knell on her hopes.

She was philosophical. Primarily because money, losing it or acquiring it, had never actually meant all that much to her. She finished dinner thinking what a blow this would be to poor John. He had been so *sure*, so absolutely and unshakeably positive that he had detected a burgeoning demand for Americana. She guessed that a man whose judgement was proven faulty in his own eyes, suffered a massive blow to his confidence. No man lacking in confidence was ever successful at anything.

She did not want this to happen to John. She was willing to believe that success was not inevitable but it hurt her to think that John's first real effort at testing himself, his judgment and his acumen against the world, would end disastrously, because she realized that the first effort was the most critical one.

She said, "Can Gold Bond anticipate demands, Bob?"
He sipped wine as he answered, sitting complacently

across the table watching her. "Sometimes, sweetheart, but that's risky. Gold Bond can gamble a lot of capital and come a cropper trying to anticipate. We like to take a conservative approach. I mean, let the demand show up first, then we rush out and supply it. You see?"

She 'saw'. She also saw something else. "But isn't Gold Bond in a position to perhaps nudge the demand a little? I mean, if Gold Bond suddenly started pushing some particular kind of items, wouldn't people across the nation think there *was* a demand?"

He laughed, finished his wine, put the glass aside and leaned towards her across the table. "I've never met a woman with a mind quite like yours before, Liz. You'd be a tremendous success down in the city."

She had no illusions about that; mainly because she did not like 'the city' which was always, to New Yorkers, only that one city. All other cities were towns or villages, and all but New Yorkers were rustics of one degree or another. But she smiled at him, which was her way of giving thanks for his compliment.

Then he said, "It's a beautiful night. Let's walk off our dinner by going out to the common."

She was agreeable. As they left the dining-room and strolled forth into the pleasant night, she caught a fleeting sight of John Harding. He was across the road out front of the local furniture store, talking very earnestly to the proprietor of the store, Claude Hopkins, who was also, among other things, president of the local chapter of the Maine Historical Society. She did not think John saw her, saw *them*, as Bob Whiting came up and smoothly took her arm as they turned to walk away.

She was wrong.

Occasionally, at the tag-end of winter, a bland night came as a sort of precursor of spring and summertime.

This was such a night. There was a discernible edge to the air, which would be increasingly noticeable as the hours passed, but for as long as they strolled along, it was indeed very pleasant.

Bob, apparently interested in her earlier relentlessness on the subject of antiques, finally said, "Are you interested in starting a business?"

She smiled. "No; I was just curious."

He still had her arm. "I could help, if you had some idea in mind along that direction." He moved closer, brushing against her slightly as they walked. "Do you know what macramé is?"

She had no idea. In fact, she was certain she had never heard the word before. "No."

"It's a form of plaiting, or braiding, using heavy yarn," he explained. "Right now it's very popular. In fact, that's why I wanted that hemp cordage from your father's company. He is one of the few large-scale cordage dealers who still handles old-fashioned kinds of rope. People desiring to achieve a look of rusticity in macramé want the old-time varieties of hemp rope." He released her arm and slid his hand round her waist as they walked. "If you wanted to start a business here in Bannford, you could begin with hemp macramé. It wouldn't require much capital. You could hire a few women to make the slings, or to plait and tie the macramé hangers, and Gold Bond would buy the finished products from you." His arm tightened slightly round her middle. "You probably wouldn't get rich; these fads come and go, but you'd get a start, and whatever the next fad was, you'd be able to swing over to it without much trouble." He gave her a hard squeeze, then removed his arm as they stepped off the curb and crossed the road in front of the common. As they walked across the way he said, "I can be good for you, Liz, and you could depend upon me."

She had no interest in macramé. Even if she'd known something about it she would not, right then, have felt much interest in it. As they stepped from the pavement on to the grass of the common, she began to suspect why he had suggested they walk there. The place was indifferently lighted. There were great trees set in almost complete darkness. No other people were in sight, at least not right then as they entered the greensward. His arm around her waist, as well as his increasingly personal conversation, did not leave much reason to doubt her suspicions of him.

Of course, there was another reason why she wouldn't have been interested in macramé. John Harding's current thrust towards finding himself, towards trying to find what he could do as an independent individual in order to make an independent living, had to do with Americana, not some kind of braiding of rope or yarn.

Bob took her hand as they trod the grass. He led her towards the large clearing mid-way across the common where an old-fashioned band-stand, round in shape, with an elegant little white-painted cupola stood. Sometimes the local firehouse crew put on band concerts here, always on Independence Day, and at other times as well. They did not have as many concerts now as they had when she'd been small. They also used to have veterans' parades when she'd been a child, but that was something else that people seemed no longer to care much about. Lately, the band-stand had been a point of local discussion; some people, mostly the younger ones, wanted to tear it down and put a small duck-pond where it stood. The older people, such as her father, who cherished memories of sitting round upon the grass years back, listening to the stirring marches, were dead set against seeing the band-stand removed.

When they crossed from the tree-shadows to the open ground out front of the little round stand, Elizabeth was relieved. She really did not actually fear Bob Whiting, but she had no illusions, by now, concerning his purpose in wishing to walk her out here. Nor did she have any doubts about his expertise at the things she strongly suspected he had in mind tonight. She was not experienced at all, but still she was an attractive woman with all the wariness that all attractive women inherently had.

She started to tell him about the local feeling towards the band-stand. He leaned patiently upon the side of the little structure, wearing a soft half-smile, listening to her, his face half in starlight, half in shadow. He was a good-looking man. The only thing that might have been said to constitute a blemish was his complete self-assurance. While she spoke, and he kept looking at her, she could sense his anticipation of triumph. He was looking at her the way a man would look at any desirable woman of whom he was confident.

Finally, when she ended her tale, he said, "Liz, come down to the city with me. I've got to be back next Monday for business, but after that I'll show you the sights. The latest plays, the stores, the night-spots. We can go to the parties people give this time of year." He hauled up rather lazily off the band-stand, facing her. "I can show you more of life in a week down there than you'd see in Bannford all the rest of your years."

It piqued her. Not what he had said, but what he left *un*said, but she hid that behind a small smile. "I'm sure it would be exciting," she murmured, "but I'm satisfied in Bannford."

He moved ahead, towards her, a couple of steps, and she eluded him easily by turning towards the band-stand, by climbing the half-dozen steps to the little circular decking up above where the band members sat when they played. From up there she had an excellent view all round the starlighted common. He halted at the bottom step gazing upwards.

"You *think* you're satisfied in Bannford," he told her. "You can't really know until you've compared this kind of an existence with real living." He leaned upon the railing. "One week, and if you don't like it I'll bring you back."

She looked down. His face was softly lighted, his eyes looked darker than usual. She knew he was a man women would want to marry, and yet he wasn't married although he was at the age, past it a little, actually, when most men got married. There would be a reason; she was sure she knew what it was. He did not want to be married. She said, "I'm flattered, Bob, but—no, thanks."

For a moment they continued to look at one another, then he changed his tactics. He loosened his hold of the railing, smiled easily, and said, "Let's walk around a bit."

She hesitated, sensing the change in him, instinctively aware that he was a subtle, knowledgeable man at this game they were playing. He climbed three steps and held out a hand to her.

Someone whistling a ragged little lilting tune came ambling out of the distant shadows, northward. She was so relieved that when she raised her head she did not even recognise John Harding, although as he came forth from the tree-gloom he was in plain sight.

Bob Whiting dropped his arm, twisted on the step to glower in the direction of the intruder, and finally stepped back down to the grass.

John ambled over, greeted Elizabeth with a tough little smile, and when she introduced him to Bob Whiting, John shoved out a strong hand. "Just passing through," he told Bob, making it sound almost too casual. For the first time, Elizabeth looked sideways at John with a feeling in her heart that John hadn't just happened along at all, and now, with her relief past and gone, she began to feel a new emotion : indignation. If John hadn't happened along as inadvertently as he had said, then he had to have been spying on them.

John stood and forced a conversation. He acted as though he were unaware of Bob Whiting's cold, hostile attitude. He also acted as though he would stand there all night, if he had to, until the three of them headed back towards the lighted parts of town.

CHAPTER SEVEN

THE BIG BATTLE

In the years that Elizabeth had known John Harding she had seen him in just about every mood possible. But the morning after her visit to the town common with Bob Whiting, when she went to answer the front-door bell during her house-cleaning work, she saw a John Harding standing out there who was almost a complete stranger. He was furious.

But her fascination was with the control he exhibited. He barely allowed her a moment to step forth upon the porch when he levelled a finger at her and said, "If you went out there with that man last night on purpose you deserve anything he had in mind. If you let him waltz you out there because he's suave and you're not, then I'll say you are just plain stupid, Elizabeth!"

She was aghast. During their entire acquaintanceship he had never spoken to her like this before, and he had never used this same double-edged tone of voice. But she did not remain aghast for long. She put both hands on her hips, quite forgetting she had a light towel wrapped round her head, something she invariably did whenever she got involved in spring house-cleaning, and almost let him have an equally as hostile blast right back. But he cut across her thoughts first, scattering them like wind.

"When a woman starts running round with men that old, and that—that experienced—what are folks supposed to think? I'll tell you what they *do* think, Eliza-

53

beth: that the woman's fair game, that she's probably cheap and willing."

She was left gasping. He dropped his arm and peered at her. "And suppose I hadn't happened along? Do you know what that slimy type is capable of? If I hadn't—"

"*Happened* along!" she exclaimed. "John Harding, you no more happened along last night than you happened along this morning. You were spying on us. I saw you out front of the furniture store last night. You were talking to Mr Hopkins. You saw us, too, didn't you?"

"Of course I saw you, Elizabeth, and so did two-thirds of the town. You brazenly walking off with that—!"

"Spying!" she hurled at him. "A man your age sneaking around spying on people! And what makes you think you have that right, anyway?"

He swallowed, hard.

Now, finally, she could reach her stride, and she was angry all the way through. "You ought to be ashamed of yourself."

"Yeah? And suppose I hadn't come along in the park when I did?"

"You idiot, John Harding. I could have handled him."

"Like hell you could have," he snarled. "You're a hick, Liz. You only *think* you know Whiting's kind. You could no more handle him than—"

"A *hick*!" that struck deep down into her like the worst of all insults. "I'm a hick, am I? And what are you?"

"At least I've been through a few cities," he shot back. "I've seen men like Whiting from New York to Boston, and even over in Philadelphia. I know how they operate."

She was almost rigid with anger. "You'll *never* know how a man like Bob Whiting operates. You're even more of a hick than I am! At least I *know* my limitations, and right this minute you're putting on airs that make you look downright ridiculous." She drew back a fresh breath. "And I *could* handle him!"

"You could not! For one thing, you can't think fast enough."

She was on the verge of balling up a fist and trying to knock him off the porch. Then he said something that cracked her armour just a little.

"When I kissed you on the steps down at the warehouse, you stood there looking stunned, hanging on to the railing like your life depended upon it—and you didn't even see what I was going to do until I did it. You couldn't think fast enough, Liz. You still can't."

This time, when the insult was uttered, she swung. He saw it coming, turned with the blow, caught her right wrist and easily forced her arm down before her knuckles connected. His grip on her wrist was surprisingly strong. She had never thought of John Harding as being particularly quick or strong, or well co-ordinated. But he had to be the latter, otherwise her blow would have connected.

He turned her arm loose with a short, angry thrust. "Liz, if Whiting had grabbed you last night, you'd never have had a chance. Believe me."

Her fury had lost its fire and was now cold, rational anger. "If I needed a chaperon, John Harding, or a protector, believe me when I tell you I can imagine almost anyone on earth helping me but you."

"Okay. But last night it *was* me, wasn't is? I don't know who'll be around next time. Probably nobody at all. Whiting'll add your scalp to all the others his kind

brags of taking when he sits at the bar down in the city.
. . . But, so help me, not as long as I'm around he
won't!"

"You mind your own business!" she exclaimed. "How
do you know I don't *want* Bob Whiting to kiss me?"

His mouth twisted slightly with pain just before he
said, "Kiss you? Elizabeth, you damned fool, Bob
Whiting doesn't just want to *kiss* you!"

She was shocked. "Get off this porch," she snapped.
"I'm glad I finally found out what kind of a mind you
have, John Harding! You leave now and I don't ever
want to see you around here again. And—I'm glad you
quit down at my father's office. You could do us both
an immense favour just by leaving Bannford. You don't
belong here, anyway; you didn't grow up here. For all
we know around town you could be a—fugitive from
justice, or something." She stopped because she was
beginning to sound, even to herself, as though fury was
making her say ridiculous things.

She was breathing hard, and although she no longer
had her hands on her hips, she was still standing stiffly
and adamantly.

He, unlike Elizabeth, seemed to lose a lot of his anger,
seemed to soften towards her or loosen a little, as he
remained standing there. She had hurt him; she knew
it, too, and right at this moment she'd have hurt him
worse if she'd been able to devise a way to do it.

He shifted his eyes for the first time now, letting them
range up the street along the fronts of the neighbouring
residences. He saw two elderly women on the porch next
door, sitting very erect in their rocking-chairs, clearly
straining to hear.

Elizabeth, with her back to the house next door, knew

nothing of their small audience, and right then she was so mad she might not have cared.

Finally, after the interval of silence had lasted long enough for her fury to burn down a little, she said, "John, what you did was adolescent and dishonest, and I'm glad I found out that you're capable of doing such a thing. Now please leave, and don't come back. I mean it. If you don't leave, I'll call the constable."

His eyes came back and settled upon her face, but they had hardness in their depths along with the shifting little patterns of pain. He said, "I'll come back, Elizabeth," and kept his voice down so low the small audience next door could not hear it, "when I'm damned good and ready." Then he reached with both hands, pinned her to the front of the house by the shoulders and kissed her. This time he deliberately bruised her.

She felt the pain and the revulsion in about equal parts. She raised a hand and struck him in the side. He did not even flinch. He held her pinioned by the lips. She tried squeezing her head sideways, but that did not work either. Then he suddenly softened, suddenly shifted his weight and pressure to make the kiss gentler. For a mindless second, she responded. He pulled her off the wall into his arms, held her tenderly, and when he was finally finished he released her without a word, turned and left the porch, walked away without even once looking back.

Finally, now, she saw the two elderly ladies next door. But they were no longer sitting very erect listening; now they were leaning forward in their chairs, eyes perfectly round, staring over at her.

She flung around, went indoors, leaned upon the closed door and flushed hotly enough to be conscious of it. He must have seen those women over there, and yet he hadn't said a word to her; hadn't even had the decency to warn her not to speak so loudly.

She could have killed him.

But it was over and done with. There was no going back. Something deep inside had made her respond so fervently to his savage kiss. Only the future would determine the strength of the feelings he had aroused.

She only knew that he had humiliated her; not once, with the audience on the porch next door, but again when he certainly had felt her respond to his lips.

She returned to the parlour where she had been washing picture-glass and windows, and resumed her work with a burst of furious energy. She did not want to think about any of it; not about what he had said about Bob Whiting, which was also in some degree what she already knew about him, nor about anything else John had said—or had done.

She worked until she had to go lie on the sofa for a short rest. While she was lying there the picture of old Captain Josiah looked slightly over her head—and she could almost have sworn that the bold, weathered, reckless features held the hint of a very faint masculine smile.

She sat up and looked in a different direction. John Harding was without any doubt the most hateful person she had ever known. He was despicable!

The front door opened, her father walked into the entry hall, stepped to the parlour doorway, looked in, and blinked owlishly at her.

He said, "Elizabeth? Are you feeling all right?"

She sprang up and ran out of the room, down the hallway to her bedroom, and stopped short before the dressing-table mirror. Her hair-covering was askew, her eyes were almost black with a sense of humiliation and outrage, and her face was still flushed.

"... *you are just plain stupid, Elizabeth!* ... *brazenly walking off with that* ... *You're a hick, Liz* ...!"

She tore off the hair-covering, shed her dress and went into the next room to bathe. The water and the solitude helped, and when she returned a little later to re-dress and to sit a moment brushing her taffy hair, although she was still very upset, it did not show as much. Finally, she went to stand by the window looking out into the wintry garden beyond. She told herself to be honest; she was very severe with herself. She *was* a hick. That was exactly what Bob Whiting had been telling her, too, but in a more suave and polished way, out at the band-stand, when he'd said she'd see more life in a week in the city than she'd experience all the rest of her days in Bannford.

Be honest!

She leaned beside the window, looking out. John had been right about something else, too, probably; she might not have been able to handle Bob Whiting. She had actually been just beginning to wonder about that when John had appeared.

She straightened up and, as though perhaps there *was* something beneficial about confessing things, she felt better after this short interval of soul-searching. She turned and went to the door, cast a final glance at herself, saw that she looked composed enough to pass muster when she returned to the parlour, and went slowly back up the hallway to the front of her house.

CHAPTER EIGHT

A MEMORABLE EVENING

THE house was immaculate, which it would have been in any case when her father brought Bob Whiting home for dinner the next night, because she had worked off the last of her anger and frustration completing her spring house-cleaning, beginning about eight in the morning and finishing shortly after three in the afternoon.

She had been sore all over, too, from the needless exertion she subjected herself to, so she had soaked in a hot tub for almost a full hour. It helped more than she thought it would have; even her usual mental serenity had returned to a great extent by the time she was dressed and ready for the evening.

She looked very pink and lovely when her father walked in, with Bob Whiting at his heels. She knew how she looked because it showed in the eyes of both men, the older one and the younger one.

Her father went to make highballs, leaving Elizabeth in the parlour with Bob; it seemed the proper thing to do, except that she knew her father as well as he thought he knew her. But she was equal to it. She invited Bob to have a seat, which he did. She sat near by and encouraged a little light conversation by mentioning that the weather seemed to be breaking up, seemed to be making the customary springtime, unpredictable changes from day to day.

Bob was a perfect gentleman. He was also as suave as ever. About the weather, he said that until someone had seen the East River, or the Hudson, or New York City's great cement skyline against the newly arrived springtime skies and stars, they really couldn't claim to have watched a real natural marvel.

She could have argued, of course, that the arrival of springtime was particularly the property of rural localities, which it was, but she simply conceded to him, and cut off any propositions by repeating what she had once told him before.

"Some day, when my father's going down on business, I'll come along."

Her father arrived with the highballs, and Liz sat only a moment longer. At least that was as long as she had intended to stay before returning to the kitchen to get dinner on the table, but suddenly Bob Whiting stopped speaking. Liz followed his glance and felt her heart sink. "The English gentleman" was there, upon the lower section of Captain Josiah's portrait above the mantel. The other pale glow was absent, the one she and her father had noticed shortly after the passing of Elizabeth's mother.

She heard herself pushing out words to draw Bob's attention away from Captain Josiah's likeness. Finally, then, her father saw "the English gentleman", too, and rolled his eyes round to her, sighed with resignation, and downed his drink.

Whiting turned his head slowly, gazing completely around the room. Liz knew exactly what he was seeking —the source of light that would be reflected upon the glass of the portrait; she had seen people react in this way since she'd been a small child.

She rose. "I'll call you when dinner is served," she said, shot her father a frowning look, and departed. In the kitchen, as she rinsed her highball glass, she was

61

tempted to demand aloud why "the English gentleman" had to pick this particular moment to appear, and why he'd felt impelled to do it before a sophisticated city-dweller to whom the only explanation of the affair would sound positively asinine.

She knew that by now, out in the parlour, her father was well launched into his quiet, matter-of-fact recitation about the Ingraham house's confounded ghost. She could visualise the expression upon Bob Whiting's un-believing face.

But she could become resigned to this much easier than she could become resigned to most of the other things which had occurred this day, so she got busy with dinner, and when it was ready she called them from the parlour.

Her father was no different than he usually was, but she thought Bob Whiting was slightly less exuberant than usual, slightly more subdued. She did not want the topic of "the English gentleman" to come up at dinner, but that, too, was beyond her control. It came up, finally, when Bob said, "Has anyone ever actually done any research into this English ship-captain, or has any-one ever removed the portrait above the mantel to see whether or not the glow persists?"

Elizabeth sighed.

Her father paused only briefly at his meal to answer. "The ship-captain was real enough, and I can show you his coat and cap upstairs in the room where he died, Bob. As for the portrait—yes—the year after I was married my wife and I took down Captain Josiah's portrait."

Elizabeth had never heard this before, so she looked at her father with the same alert interest Bob Whiting was showing. Her father made a small apologetic smile to them both.

"The glow came back, as always, only it was larger, more—well—more aggravated, and it was also more noticeable upon the bare wall. But that was a long time ago. Since then, in fact just recently, I've considered putting the blasted portrait up in the third-floor attic; maybe now, so much later, 'the English gentleman' would go up there and quietly glow out of everyone's sight. My mother used to claim it was 'the English gentleman's' gratitude to Captain Josiah that made him appear only upon the glass of the portrait."

Bob Whiting was mostly silent for the remainder of the meal, and although Elizabeth did not really object to seeing him diverted, at least from her, she felt embarrassed. She could guess about how Whiting's thoughts were running now: he had chosen a most bizarre family to become involved with in Bannford.

It was true, of course.

After dinner Elizabeth's father did something he had rarely ever done before within her memory; he asked to be excused while he went to his study and tried to find some invoices they had been unable to find down at the warehouse earlier in the day. Bob Whiting did not appear to mind in the least. He suggested that he and Liz return to the parlour. She went, not altogether willingly, but as soon as she stepped through the archway and glanced towards the mantel she was relieved to discover that "the English gentleman" had departed.

Bob was intrigued. He even lifted a corner of Captain Josiah's portrait and peeked behind it. She smiled at this.

"You won't find anything back there. When I was a little girl I must have done that at least fifty times. And

63

later, when I wasn't such a little girl, I still tried to find the source of the glow."

Whiting eased the heavy frame back into place. "And you never did?"

She shook her head. "I never did."

Bob stepped back and faced the mantle, gazing upwards. Whatever his thoughts concerning the bold, challenging, strong face above, he kept them to himself. But she thought he was impressed. Most people were; Captain Josiah Ingraham, in death as in life, had been a man worth a second glance. The passage of time could outmode a lot of things, his ship-master's coat, his cap, his New England merchantman's insignias, even the length of his hair, but it could never make that powerful, almost combative face appear out of style.

Bob crossed to a chair and sat. His conversation was desultory, and what Elizabeth expected—personal talk between them—did not materialise, at least not at once. She decided that Captain Josiah and "the English gentleman" were her allies.

Bob Whiting's reaction was actually not unusual. Most people never encountered anything supernatural, if that was how you could describe 'the English gentleman". Most people never encountered anything that could not be explained away with reason and logic. It was only to be expected, then, that an encounter with, "the English gentleman" left them apprehensive and uncertain.

Only later in the evening, when Bob rose to depart and took Elizabeth with him out to the entry-hall, well beyond the influence of Captain Josiah's portrait, did he finally appear to abandon his earlier inhibitions and anxieties.

He took both her hands. "It's been an evening I'll never forget, Elizabeth."

She almost laughed; she was quite certain he would never forget it. But that had nothing to do with the meal she'd prepared, nor the Ingraham hospitality.

"I wonder," he began, and hesitated before going on. "Liz, I wonder if you'd do something for me: would you ask your father how much money he would take for that portrait of Captain Josiah Ingraham?"

She felt no urge to laugh now. She stared at him, thinking that he wasn't asking about the portrait for himself, he wanted it for someone else; probably, he wanted it to exhibit, or sell through Gold Bond, because the portrait was haunted.

The trouble with that, of course, was not only that no Ingraham would ever sell the Captain Josiah portrait, but furthermore, it wasn't the portrait that was haunted, it was the house. But she said she would ask her father, then they stepped outside upon the porch, and a noticeable chill was in the night.

He took her hand to draw her closer. "Now I owe you another dinner," he murmured, and when she did not yield to his gentle tugging, he yielded to her obduracy by stepping over beside her. "Is tomorrow night too soon? I really don't want it to be any longer, Elizabeth. I wish you'd go down to the city with me, then we'd be together all the time."

She did not smile, but neither did she scowl. "I'm sorry about 'the English gentleman' arriving to spoil your evening," she told him. "He hasn't been around lately. Or at least I haven't noticed him lately. As for the city, when you're back down there, Bob, you'll forget all about Bannford and me."

He reached and lightly turned her. Their faces were

only inches apart. "I won't ever forget you, Liz; in fact, I can't even imagine meeting a new day without knowing you're part of it." He leaned, slid one hand up her back, slid the other hand down her back, and kissed her.

She did not resist. Neither did she respond. At the conclusion of every date it was customary for the man to kiss the girl on her porch before saying good night. Liz chose to interpret this particular kiss in this manner. It was his combination kiss-of-gratitude and good-night kiss.

But it changed to another kind of kiss, his hands and lips moving upon her. She was surprised. Bob Whiting was supposed to be the suave big city sophisticate. Right now, in the chilly, clear, dark night, he was acting the same as any of the country lads would have acted.

She pushed clear, coldly angry but in perfect control of herself. "It's getting late," she murmured, and took a couple of steps closer to the edge of the porch near the steps. "I wouldn't want to keep you up. Thanks awfully for coming, Bob. Good night."

He accepted the dismissal and smiled at her in his most unperturbed manner, then he went down as far as the lowest step and turned back to say, "Tomorrow night at the hotel at seven, Liz?"

She smiled sweetly. "Let's not make it so soon, Bob. Let's wait a bit. But I do appreciate the offer. Good night."

They stood as they had at the band-stand, she a few feet higher looking down; Bob on the steps below looking up. He nodded. "In a day or two then, lover." He raised one hand in a gallant little salute and walked away.

She did not waste another moment outside. As she closed the door behind herself and stood appreciatively in the warmth of the big old house, her father peered around from the parlour. "Well . . .?" he said.

She had her answer ready for him. "You didn't have to run off so we wouldn't have any interruptions. I already told you, he's not my type." Remembering his activity out on the porch, she added, "I'm not too sure he's really any self-respecting woman's type. Good night, Dad."

"Good night, sweetheart."

She was passing the parlour archway when she turned and threw a look towards the mantel. Captain Josiah was gazing over everyone's head, as always, and the lower part of his portrait was dark. She sighed and went on down the hallway to her room, and got ready for bed.

CHAPTER NINE

JOHN HARDING'S PROPOSITION

AT BREAKFAST Elizabeth asked her father when he thought Bob Whiting would be leaving town. Her father had no idea. "The last time we discussed our business deal he said something about it being in a few days."

It had already been more than a week. She did not say so, but it occurred to her that the Gold Bond company must give its executives, if that was what Bob Whiting was, very healthy expense accounts.

Of course, she did not mention the interlude of the pawing the previous night; she was quite willing to ban the thought, and after her father's departure, she was busy cleaning up in the kitchen for a while, which further kept her mind off that.

It was about ten o'clock when she completed her shopping list, changed, and was ready to leave the house. The day was warm with a pre-springtime fitful little wind. The air was as clear as glass, and all the sounds of a bustling town seemed closer and slightly louder than usual. She reached the main thoroughfare and turned north on her way towards the central shopping area, but as she passed the furniture store someone spoke her name. She turned back, recognising the voice, her figurative hackles up. She had said in no uncertain terms she did not ever want to speak to John Harding again.

As though nothing had happened between them, John

walked over and said, "Can you spare a minute, Liz?"

He looked slightly tousled, slightly flushed, as though he had very recently been engaged in some kind of manual labour. She was unrelenting. "Why?"

"I want to show you something." His eyes were direct and ready to smile at her, as always. "It'll only take a minute."

She did not relent. At least, she told herself she was not relenting as she said, "Only a minute," and went with him back down the side of the furniture store to the back-alley where there was a large old weathered warehouse which had at one time been the firehouse.

There was a solitary light bulb suspended from a dark and lofty ceiling. The old warehouse was about as dismal a place as Elizabeth had ever been in. She stayed close and when John stopped she almost bumped him. He made a gesture towards some shelves and tables up ahead; they were laden with old lamps, some with the original cut-crystal mantles. Some were soldered copper, some were coach lanterns; all had been cleaned and polished and shone now with a sombre brightness.

There were old hand-painted plates, pitchers, bone-china wash-bowls with elegant scalloped edges. There was a large old Concord coach and, beyond it, a small bronze cannon mounted upon a strong oak block, with metal-bound skids beneath it. The assortment was not only unbelievably varied, it also ran far back towards the rear of the warehouse. Elizabeth moved closer for a better look. If someone had told her John had helped the town clean out its cellars and attics, she would have believed them.

He said nothing until she turned back. Even then he

was quiet for as long as it took her to see the expression on his face. He wanted her approval; she read that in his eyes. She could not be angry with him still. She'd never been able to stay angry at people very long. And there was something else: regardless of what he thought, all this endless assortment of cast-offs had been bought with her money.

She searched for the right words, and finally said, "You've been busy, John," which was a non-committal statement. She was thinking of the dusty old coach and the thick, little old cannon. When he had originally confided in her she had felt enthused, but now she was having serious doubts. Her idea of antiques did not include things like old cannons and old coaches.

He said, "I need help, Liz."

She started mentally backing off even before he had finished his statement.

"All this stuff has to be catalogued. It's a lot of work, doing the buying, the selling and the cataloguing and corresponding, too. Liz . . .?"

She moved back closer to the light. He was acting as though they hadn't had that furious battle on her front porch. Right now she was willing not to mention that, but she hadn't forgotten some of the things he'd said.

He followed her almost to the doorway. When she started to turn, he reached for her arm. He evidently thought she was going to leave the building without speaking.

He released her at once. "I can guess what you're thinking : that I owe you a mile-high apology. All right, if that's what it'll take, Liz, but I still feel the same way about Whiting."

She waivered between agreeing to his conversation and avoiding what she was almost certain would result in another furious exchange. She decided to avoid the argument, and said, "John, wouldn't it be better to sell what you have in here before buying any more?"

He shocked her. "Most of it *is* sold Liz. That's why I need someone to keep the inventory straight and do the letter-writing."

She turned slightly. "That old Concord coach?"

"Sold to a tavern down in Pennsylvania called the 'Way Station'."

"The cannon?"

"Sold to an antique arms dealer who owns an island off New York where he stores old weapons and re-sells them."

She looked back. "But you've only been doing this for a couple of weeks, John."

He smiled at her. "Liz, I *told* you it would work out. I knew it would. I had the confidence."

"But Bob Whiting said—"

"Liz, Bob Whiting's judgement isn't very good in anything, as far as I'm concerned . . . Except that he appreciates beautiful women. Well, at least *one* beautiful woman."

She accepted the compliment without acknowledging it. This other thing took a little getting accustomed to. "What else is sold, John?"

He pointed out items, then he took her arm and returned with her to a cluttered old table. He pointed to the litter. "Letters, orders, enquiries. Liz, I work about fifteen hours a day as it is."

She moved to the table and looked down. There were envelopes there which had not even been opened yet.

71

Her astonishment passed gradually, and just as gradually it was replaced by a feeling of pleasant satisfaction. She had wanted very much for John Harding to succeed; she had wanted him to prove her father wrong. But most of all, she hadn't wanted his confidence in himself shaken by a serious failure. She smiled at him. "This is wonderful."

He smiled back. "I've got to go over to Shelbyville first thing in the morning, and this afternoon I've got a call to make east of town." He pointed to the littered table again. "If that correspondence isn't taken care of, Liz, I'm going to lose as much money as I'll make."

They stood looking at one another. She could do it. She had the time; at least, she could certainly make the time. She had no doubts at all concerning her ability, and some of his infectious enthusiasm was reaching her.

He seemed to think her hesitation was caused by something else, by their battle, because he suddenly said, "Liz, I didn't want to fight with you. Really. But you don't know men like Whiting."

She could have answered that; *now* she knew about men like Bob Whiting, and even before the interlude on the porch she had suspected almost as much as she now knew. She had got her initial introduction at the common, over by the little band-stand.

She also knew that the thought of Bob Whiting was aggravating John, so she said, "Let's just talk about this antique business, John." She did not realise that he would interpret her statement to mean she did not want him discussing Bob with her, because he thought she liked Whiting.

He acquiesced by nodding, a little slowly and bleakly, then by reverting to the other topic. "You can be a partner, if you'd like. Otherwise, I'll pay you a salary and you'll be an employee. As a partner you'd share in the profits."

Partners did not just walk in and go to work; they invested money, and she had already directed the bank to loan him as much as she had in her savings account, and her savings would be his collateral. But there was another way. She said, "If you want me for a partner, I'll expect to put some money into the business, John. A thousand dollars?"

He laughed. "You don't have to put any money in, Liz. I borrowed a thousand from the bank. That ought to tide us over until some of the collections and profits roll in. Within a month we ought to be operating free and clear on our own capital."

She was adamant. "A thousand dollars, John. I'll bring it round in the morning."

He kept looking at her as though he would laugh. Instead, he walked her back out into the bright morning sunlight, and just before they reached the street he said, "Liz, with you helping, we can't possibly lose."

She smiled at him. The second smile since he'd called to her an hour or so earlier. She wanted to say something personal, something he would want her to say, but she was cautious. Lately, she'd had reason to be cautious with men, even with John Harding, the man she had never really thought of in any way except as the clerk in her father's upstairs offices.

The smile had to suffice. As she turned away she said, "What time do we start work in the mornings?"

His eyes lingered on her. "Nine o'clock."

She nodded and stepped back upon the sidewalk.

The day seemed different now; she began to feel

pushed for time, as though her days might not be long enough for keeping house, preparing meals, and also working in the old warehouse out back of Claude Hopkins' furniture store. In fact, she hurried through her shopping and returned home before noon in order to do a few little odd jobs she'd neglected during her spring house-cleaning labours.

Finally, shortly before it was time to start supper, she went to bathe and change, and while she was alone and thinking about the future, she began feeling elated, somehow free and needed. It had not bothered her very often in the past that as her father's housekeeper she did not really have much of a life of her own. Now that thought came to her, and as she re-dressed before the mirror in her bedroom she felt almost as unsure of herself as a young girl. But in a way that thrilled her. For the first time in her life she would be making decisions that mattered; she would be challenging the male-dominated business world.

It did not occur to her to be fearful. In her own way she was just as self-confident as John Harding was. She sat brushing her hair, and smiled at the thought of helping make their business grow. She even permitted herself a flight of wild fancy and envisioned them in a large building of their own, with employees, with offices and order-clerks and shipping personnel. It would probably never come to that, but she was thrilled with the possibilities.

Finally, when she went to the kitchen to complete her lifelong routine of getting dinner, she remembered her promise of a thousand dollars. Her heart sank a little, not because she anticipated a refusal from her father—

although that was, of course, a possibility—but because she instinctively realised that not all businesses were huge successes, even when they started out as though they might be.

Her father arrived home punctually, as usual, greeted her in the kitchen, also as usual, and went to potter around making their pair of weak evening highballs. She waited until he was handing her the glass, then she said, "Would you loan me one thousand dollars?"

Her father blinked several times. He was not a man who could be taken by surprise very often, but clearly this time it had happened. He did not speak until he had strolled to the doorway and was leaning there, in his usual relaxed manner, then he said, "Whatever for?"

"John Harding's business is starting out wonderfully," she replied. "He offered me a partnership if I'd help him with the correspondence and clerking."

Her father's wise eyes were grave. "For a thousand dollars?"

She shook her head. "No. He offered me the partnership with no investment. The thousand dollars was my idea, Dad. I don't want to be a partner without an interest in the business. That's not fair, is it?"

"No," drawled her father, and drank half his highball. "No, a partner is supposed to take the risks right along with everyone else." He kept gazing thoughtfully at her. "When do you need this thousand dollars?"

"Tomorrow morning."

His tufted brows crawled up slightly. "Well, when you go into business you don't waste any time, do you?" He smiled. "All right, come round to my office after the bank opens. There'll be papers to sign."

CHAPTER TEN

SOUL-SEARCHING FOR LIZ

THE first misgiving hit her about mid-afternoon of the following day. She had replied to six letters of enquiry, one from as far away as California, before noon, and when the post arrived at two o'clock in the afternoon there were seven more letters. So what she had actually done was not gain ground, that morning, but had lost ground to the extent of one letter.

Also, when John returned just before five o'clock looking exhausted but happy, with a fresh load of what she had always before considered junk, she had to convince him that he should not only hand over the bills of sale with everything itemised, but he should also sit down with her and decide upon how much of a profit mark-up each item should have. Then, as she told him, she would have some idea what to tell the people who were writing.

He did not argue, he simply procrastinated on the grounds that he was dog-tired. He slouched in a chair, told her about his latest excursion in search of antiques, and when she finally relented he said, "I saw Whiting on my way back to town an hour or so ago."

She knew there must be more, but he did not seem inclined to tell her. Instead, he got up and went over among the shelves and tables. She rose and went over there too.

"John . . . ?"

He turned, holding a fragile little pink vase. His gaze was hard although his smile lingered around the lips.

"You're curious about Whiting," he said, making a statement of it.

She checked her annoyance. "I am curious about how long I'm supposed to go round carrying one thousand dollars in cash. It makes me nervous." She had got the money hours earlier from her father, and had also brought back the promissory note she had signed, but that was in her purse.

His hard gaze wavered. "I'm sorry," he murmured, putting the little vase down.

She had a small triumph, but did not want to take advantage of it. They returned to the table where she had created a measure of order from the untidy chaos, and she handed him the thick envelope without a word. He took it, hefted it lightly, and said, "Liz, if the business gets a little better, would you consider some other kind of arrangement between us?"

She got the table between them. "Yes, of course, John; you do all the buying and I'll hire a girl or two and operate the warehouse and sales end of things." She smiled sweetly at him. "Now please take this pencil and go among the things over on the shelves and put prices on them."

He took the pencil, pocketed the thick envelope, and went obediently to do as she had said. He worked in silence for about a half-hour. She watched, and was impressed by his memory. He seemed to recall everything over there and, as near as she knew now, there had to be at least two hundred and fifty small items.

When he finally returned and tossed down the pencil he said, "That's enough for tonight. By the way, what did your father think of you working with me?"

Her father hadn't said what he thought of this arrangement between them, and she had not pressed the issue by asking. "He didn't object," she told him, which was the truth.

John pointed to her purse. "Do you have the note you signed at the bank in there?"

She pondered her answer. She could, of course, have said she didn't have, and not technically be lying to him, since she hadn't signed any note at the bank. Instead, she answered frankly. "I borrowed the money from my father. And, yes, I have the note there. But I'm to give it back to him tonight at home."

He dropped his arm. "I wish you hadn't done that, Liz. We really don't need the money."

"And I don't need charity, either," she retorted. "Partners take part of the risk."

They stood looking at one another across the table. She sighed, finally. "John, let's not fight."

He laughed softly, his grey eyes twinkling at her.

"Lately, we only seem to be able to do one of two things."

She did not take that up. She was certain she knew what the *other* thing was. She was also certain she knew why he looked at her the way he did every now and then. She said, "I'll lock up. You're tired, and for me it's been a slightly hectic day."

She moved from behind the table. He did not take a step until she returned from putting some papers in an improvised file cabinet. Then he held out a hand to her. She knew better than to respond by offering her hand, but she did it anyway. He pulled her closer and squeezed her fingers, but when she was bracing for the embrace he simply said, "Be sure and lock the outer door," and dropped her hand to turn and stride past. He did not even say good night, and that upset her more than anything else.

She made doubly certain the outer door was locked when she departed a little later. Old Claude Hopkins who owned the warehouse they were using, as well as the building which housed his furniture store, came out back and ambled over to say, "Elizabeth, I like that young man, but I sure don't have much faith in his business ability. I've seen that stuff he fetches back here, and if he gives good money for it he's going to end up bankrupt. You can't sell folks junk they've been throwing out for years."

She had known Claude Hopkins since early childhood. He and her father were lifelong friends. She also knew that Claude Hopkins would hold the same views of the antique business her father—and probably, two-thirds of all the other older people in Bannford—held. She could, of course, have set Claude Hopkins straight by giving him examples of the sales they had made thus far, but she knew better than to do that. She simply smiled upwards at the older man and said, "But we all have to try our wings sometimes, don't we, Uncle Claude?"

He gave her an affectionate look. "We sure do, Liz. And anyway, it's not a bad thing for these young men to get a little taste of failure now and then. It sort of leavens them, as my father used to say. But mind you, now, don't let him get all his cash tied up in that stuff; take my advice and talk him into laying a little aside."

She understood the philosophy behind this remark, and could nod in agreement with it because although she was certain John would not fail—*they* would not fail—it was nonetheless good financial advice. "I'll do what I can," she promised, then excused herself and headed for home.

She was thrilled at the idea that soon, now, John

would be able to prove her father, Claude Hopkins, and everyone else who foresaw financial disaster, wrong. It was not a vindictive thrill; rather, it was the kind of a thrill a woman might feel when her man's judgement was being proven as good, and even better, than that of other people.

That evening at dinner, which was an hour late but her father chose not to comment on this, she mentioned a little of what they were doing down at the old warehouse.

Her father ate his supper as impassively and quietly as he usually did. Later, though, when they were in the parlour, he said, "John isn't going to plunge with that thousand dollars, is he, sweetheart? Because as a partner you've got equal say about how the finances are to be handled."

She knew the answer to that. "Dad, this was his idea, not mine. He's the one with the imagination and the courage."

Her father rattled his newspaper. "All right; you're correct enough in that respect. And also, being a woman, you wouldn't be expected to face a man down, not even John Harding who's still pretty young. But still and all, you could exert a little influence, couldn't you?"

She looked steadily at her father. "How much influence do you think I have with him?"

Her father coloured faintly. "You are a partner. That's all I had in mind."

She kept looking at him. That *wasn't* all he'd had in mind. She felt irritation with him, something she had rarely ever felt towards her father before. A few nights back he had disappeared, ostensibly to seek some invoices, while Bob Whiting had been in the parlour with her. Now he was suggesting that he thought her business arrangement with John Harding might extend beyond business. She was beginning to consider her father in a fresh light.

Of course he would want to see her happy, which in a father's eyes meant happily married and settled. But she'd thought lately, at least over the past year or so, that he was not very worried about her marrying.

He knew, because she'd told him, that John Harding was not her kind of a man. Then how had he rationalised to himself that, suddenly, John *was* her kind of a man?

She took the bull by the horns. "Dad, I'm not going to try and limit John in any way, in this business we're involved with, and that would be the only way I could influence him." She faltered, remembering his kiss, remembering his muscular arms, and his eyes that were sometimes masterful, dominating, very possessive. She had been furious with him—but that had passed, and afterwards she couldn't think of him in the same way again. He had ceased being just another of her father's employees when he'd kissed her on the stairs, and now, being master of his own business, he had ceased to be "just" John Harding.

She fidgeted in her chair. Her father, assuming the discussion was finished because she seemed not to wish it to continue, went back to reading his newspaper.

How did she *really* feel? She did not make an attempt to analyse her feelings at this moment, except to believe that, somehow, somewhere along the line recently, a subtle change had occurred in her thinking, in her *feelings* towards John Harding.

A light roll of knuckles echoed through the entry-hall. She gave a little start and her father lowered the newspaper enquiringly. He made no move to rise, so Elizabeth got up and went to answer the door. It did not occur to her who the caller might be until a second or two before she opened the door. Then she half-thought it might be John.

It wasn't, it was Bob Whiting. He smiled easily at her and held out a square, rather heavy package. "Guaranteed to make you sweeter," he said, entering the house.

She knew it was a box of candy. Her father appeared back in the parlour archway and called out. "Come in, Bob."

Whiting winked at her, stepped past, and headed for the parlour, leaving Elizabeth standing there like a dunce, still holding the candy. She hadn't thanked him. In fact, she'd hardly more than murmured a greeting.

She knew the reason, and that was what troubled her : she had been disappointed that it hadn't been John Harding, and *that* had to be an answer to what she hadn't been able to define before, while she had been sitting thoughtfully in the parlour.

She roused herself and went along to the parlour. There, forcing a pleasantness she did not feel towards Bob Whiting, she thanked him for the candy, and opened it to offer it around.

Bob was at his scintillating best; he was affable and expansive. He had made a couple of excursions into the countryside, he told them, and had discovered that this particular part of Maine was not at all as forbiddingly rocky and inhospitable as other parts he had seen were.

He had her father smiling, and eventually he even made her father laugh. She felt a little mean for not being able to open up to him as she probably should have done.

It wasn't just that slightly unpleasant interlude on the porch that kept her restrained, either; it was the fresh discovery out in the entry-hall. But she made a brave effort after a while,, and, as though this had been what Bob had been waiting for, he asked her to have dinner with him the next night at the hotel.

She could have refused, of course, but she felt her father's interested glance, and accepted after a moment of hesitation. It did not occur to her right then, but it did later, when she was alone in her bedroom, that if John happened to see her with Bob Whiting again there would very probably be another of those fierce battles.

She climbed into bed feeling tired; more tired in fact that she had felt in days, even though, actually, she hadn't done all that much work at the warehouse.

She lay awake wondering if she shouldn't manage to casually mention her dinner-date with Bob the next morning when she and John met at the warehouse. She completely forgot that John had already told her he wouldn't be in town tomorrow, that he had to get over to Shelbyville again, which would probably take the entire day.

CHAPTER ELEVEN

ELIZABETH'S TRAP

THE morning was slightly overcast and unusually warm for the time of year. During summertime Maine had its share of muggy days, usually followed by thunder showers, but this was still early spring.

Elizabeth arrived early at the warehouse and went to work with an almost grim determination. She did not keep track of time, which was probably just as well since there was so much that had to be done. Hunger drove her up the street to the cafe at two o'clock. She thought it was only mid-day, but the clock over the counter at the cafe corrected her on this score.

Something that particularly troubled her was the problem of shipping the things they were selling. She knew no more about wrapping packages than did most other women her age who only wrapped things at Christmastime and perhaps now and then through the year for birthdays.

She decided to ask her father for advice that night at dinner, then worked quite strenuously segregating the things to be wrapped and sent off. By four o'clock she was ready to let down a little, which was just as well because John returned a little after four.

He'd had more adventures. She was refreshed by his humour; he did not seem to do very many things in the course of the day that were not either humorous or at least interesting. It dawned on her, as she sat listening, that John Harding was one of those rare individuals to whom everything that happened during the course of an average day was an adventure. People who loved life were like this.

She smiled at him, completely forgetting to manoeuvre the subject around somehow so she could casually mention her dinner-date with Bob Whiting. Later, when they were discussing the business of shipments, she became too absorbed in their conversation to give Bob Whiting even a fleeting thought.

She did remember to tell John what Claude Hopkins had said. John's reaction was to lean across her table and sombrely wink at her. "Before we're through, Liz, we're going to have them all eating out of our hands."

She liked the idea and said so. "If work will do it, I think we might do it fairly soon."

Without a word of warning he said, "Liz, marry me."

Her smile congealed and deep down she felt a sudden warmth, along with a quick instinctive aversion. One was as strong as the other, and that made her confused until the astonishment had passed. Then she did not answer him at all; she simply rose from the table. It was time to lock up, anyway.

The silence stretched between them. She tidied up the table, avoiding his eyes, and he stood there watching, without making a move or a sound.

In the end, she raised cool eyes. "I don't believe we can afford it yet, John, but soon now we're going to have to hire someone to help round here. Every time I sit here to answer letters, that's more time lost in shipments." She suddenly remembered something, searched across the desk for it, and when she finally found the paper she held it up for him to see. "Did you write this advertisement?"

He nodded, still gazing steadily at her, still saying nothing.

She looked down at the paper when she returned it to the desktop. "It's surprisingly good. Did you put more than just this one advertisement in the newspapers?"

He nodded again, unchanged in stance and expression.

She became exasperated; for a moment or two she returned his stare, then she said, "John, it's just not going to work unless we remember we're struggling to start a business."

He seemed about to concede. "Maybe you're right, Liz."

She knew she was right.

He suddenly said, "I'd better get your thousand dollars back." His eyes were solemn. "Liz, I can't help it. I'm very much in love with you. I know, that doesn't come as any great surprise to you. And I don't think you really care, anyway. So maybe you're right, maybe we can't run a business this way."

He straightened up, still gazing at her.

She was shocked. She had expected almost any reply but the one she got. It caught her entirely unprepared; she had been thinking such positive thoughts, had been imagining how they would make the best uses of their growing success. In one sentence he was destroying something she had come to feel as part of her life after only a couple of days.

It not only did not seem fair, it seemed cruel and somehow dishonest, or at least unethical. She could feel the colour draining from her face. No man excepting her father had ever really hurt her before, but now John Harding had.

With stiff lips she said, "If that's the way you want it."

His steady stare and unmoving position underwent a

quick, sudden change. "The way I *want* it!" he exclaimed. "You know damned well that's not the way
I want it. I'll give you back the thousand dollars tomorrow, then I'll leave the keys to the warehouse on your
desk—and I'll finally do what you told me I should have
done a couple of weeks ago. I'll leave Bannford."

She couldn't help but screw up her face in slow baffle-
ment. He hadn't been talking about *her* leaving the
business; he'd been talking about *him* leaving, not just
their business but her town as well.

"No," she said throatily. "You can't do that, John.
This was yours right from the start; your idea, your
foresight, your initiative."

"You just said it's not going to work, didn't you?" he
demanded, with a quick rise to his voice.

She stifled a hot retort, waited, then said, "What I
said was that it isn't going to work if we're—being
diverted."

He slumped at the shoulders. "You're dead wrong,
Liz. Why do you think I got back here early today?
Because I wanted to at least see you before you left.
Why do you think I always rush to return? For the same
reason. Diverted? Why, hell's bells, Liz, I've been
diverted by you for the past year and more. And I'm still
functioning. I even started this business because you
made me want to strain hard enough to be a success—
not just a damned clerk for your father. I wanted you
to see me differently. Now that's about all the diversion
a person can live with, isn't it?"

Elizabeth realized that John's proposal had made
an irrevocable change in their relationship. John had
confronted her with an issue that she

did not want to have to face, and was not even sure she *could* face.

She hadn't any answer for him. She did not even have an answer for *herself*. She fell back lamely on the fact that it was quitting time.

"We can lock up and talk again tomorrow, John."

He did not yield. "Talk about what? What good does talking do?"

She pleaded with him, almost unconsciously. "We need time to think, to rationalise." She got her purse and turned as though to depart, but while she was still able to see him she said, "You're different."

"I am not," he stated flatly.

"You're different than I thought you were, I mean. You're a lot different." She left him after saying that, and whatever he thought she meant, however he chose to interpret it, was up to him.

She walked home without haste, troubled, of course, but as time passed, less troubled than she was anxious. She would not be false to herself, would not try and deceive herself, that she did not want to lose him. Also, she did not want the business to falter.

It was hard to have to make a forced decision, but that was basically where she thought she was now, in a position where she had to make some judgements, and to afterwards be loyal to them.

She almost forgot about her dinner-date. She was, in fact, bathing when her father came home a little early, and his arrival brought her back to the present with a solid thump of reality.

She got dressed and went to the kitchen to make his dinner. He was already at work out there, with his usual highball upon the table, and his usual serene expression upon his face.

He looked at her, then looked again, his second glance guardedly analytical. She understood and said, "Trouble at the warehouse," and went over to supervise his cooking, although as a matter of fact there were some dishes he could prepare very well.

He digested her comment without changing expression; as a lifelong businessman there were few difficulties he had not encountered. For most of them he had also evolved suitable defences. "What kind of trouble?" he eventually asked, and went to drain his highball glass while he awaited her reply.

She did not really wish to discuss it, but she was at least in part committed, so she said, "I suppose you could call it a personality difference."

Her father showed interest. "Last night you left me with the impression that whatever John did, you would approve of."

That remark drove her squarely into a corner. She took over cooking his dinner at the stove and answered while her back was to him. "It's a personal matter. Maybe I should have said that, instead of just saying it had to do with personalities."

Her father thought a moment, then went to stand by the back-wall window gazing out into the dying day. "Liz, a woman as beautiful as you are, and as mature and as—well—everything else, can't possibly work at close quarters with a young man like John Harding and not have something personal evolve out of it."

"It didn't just evolve," she said. "It's been there since about the time he first went to work for you."

Her father, who had never been blind to the caprices of others, got philosophical. "Well now, sweetheart, a man my age and a girl your age look at a lot of things differently; life, for instance, and success, and love, and alliances. But I can tell you right now, you could do a whole lot worse than John Harding."

She started to put his meal upon the plate. "Bob Whiting, for instance, Dad?"

He backed away from that. "That wouldn't be my decision, sweetheart, that would be up to you. But I know John much better than Bob, and for someone who wants to remain here in Bannford, John might be the better choice."

She sighed, put his food upon the table, poured his coffee, and when he crossed the room to sit down she looked squarely at him for the first time and smiled.

"Don't you wish you'd had a son instead of a daughter? A son would just go shopping around, find the woman he wanted, and marry her."

He laughed up at her. "It would be simpler, for a fact, Liz, but not nearly as interesting." He drew forth his watch. "It's almost six o'clock."

She had plenty of time, so she ignored that, got herself a half-cup of coffee, took it to the table and sat with him while he ate. Nothing ever really upset him; he felt secure and had no reason not to. She decided then and there that age had advantages. Peace was certainly one of those advantages.

He considered her and her pensive silence for a moment, then spoke as he returned to eating. "You can skirt round the bush, or you can face this personal thing with John head-on. Those are the only two choices you really have. They aren't so complicated, are they? All right, then think about them tonight, and tomorrow when you go down to the warehouse, have your strategy all worked out."

She rose. It was finally time to go. She went round

and kissed him, and left the kitchen with its imperturbable serenity thinking that people her age really shouldn't pity people his age because he had vast reserves of what young people valued most and never seemed able to find — contentment.

As for his advice, it was nothing more than she had already known. John had himself made it clear before she'd left the warehouse that she had two alternatives : stay with him under altered circumstances, or try and keep things going without him.

She thought she could do the latter. She had that much confidence in herself. The question she could not answer was whether she *wanted* to do it without him or not.

CHAPTER TWELVE

TURMOIL

Bob Whiting was especially suave when he picked her up that evening, but it seemed to reach her less tonight than it ever had before. She probably could have rationalised that this was the result of the pawing he'd given her on the porch, but as a matter of fact she did not analyse it, did not care one way or another.

At supper he was charming. She accepted that, too, as part of his act. He asked whether "the English gentleman" had reappeared and she had to admit that she did not know, that she hadn't made a point of looking for "him".

Evidently "the English gentleman" had made quite an impression. Bob said, "But I should think living in a house with a genuine ghost would be very unsettling."

Not, she explained, when one had lived in that house all one's life, and had known the ghost, or at least had seen it glow, since early childhood.

He wondered if she'd asked her father about selling the portrait of Captain Josiah. She hadn't asked him; she'd quite forgotten to. Not that asking would make any difference. She said, "No one in the family would part with Captain Josiah's picture, Bob."

He accepted that, but revealed his purpose by casually saying, "We have an exclusive department that deals only in rare and authentic items. We've never had a haunted portrait in it." He smiled at her, then shrugged as though the topic were closed.

She had told him, had explained at some length in fact, that it wasn't the portrait that was haunted. Now, she ate slowly, wondering whether he was dense or absent-minded. Then she decided that he was neither; that he would have sold Captain Josiah's portrait as a "haunted" picture, probably with an "authentic" phony legend attached, knowing very well the ghost did not go with the portrait, that the ghost went with the Ingraham house.

He may have sensed a change in her attitude towards him, or possibly he thought her silences and grave expression were due to something else. After, instead of suggesting a walk as he'd done on their previous date, he asked if she'd care to attend a stringed-instrument concert being presented at the fire-hall. She had not heard of any concert, but as soon as he mentioned that it was to be held at the fire-house and that it was a stringed-instrument group, she knew it was valid. Since she had been only about fourteen or fifteen the people of Bannford had been holding affairs of this kind to raise funds for a town clinic. Apparently raising money this way was a very slow process.

She was agreeable. She would have preferred to thank him for dinner and return home, but she couldn't really do that, so they left the hotel dining-room together and went out into the gusty night. She hadn't paid very much atention to the weather over the past half-dozen or so hours, so when the thick and heavy roll of wind soughed down the roadway with a damp breath, she quickly glanced upwards.

There was hardly a star to be seen.

Bob took her arm and led off, saying, "Rain before morning."

He was probably right, and if it did rain it would match her mood. At least, she told herself this as they headed for the fire-hall.

It did not occur to her until they were half-way along that she was being a very poor companion for him, which was rude. She attempted to brighten up a little, which seemed to encourage him. He told her a joke, then laughed with her. By the time they reached the fire-hall her forced pleasantness had fed upon itself, producing a small amount of genuine gaiety. It helped. She was able to smile at him, to augment his rising spirits with her own wit, until, as they entered the fire-house, she felt better than she had felt for most of the day.

As was usual around Bannford, benefit concerts were well attended. Elizabeth saw a number of people she knew, and a few paused to be introduced to Bob Whiting and to briefly chat.

The fire-hall had been decorated; there was a small raised platform at one end of the room, and all fire-fighting equipment had been temporarily hauled round back of the building.

It was a large room, actually, longer than it was wide. It had been built, so the story went, as a storage facility when the U.S. was establishing regional depots for the collection of supplies during the Spanish-American War. But Elizabeth's father and some of the other older men shook their heads about this; the building, they swore up and down, had been standing before '98.

Not that it mattered.

Elizabeth and Bob Whiting found benches about two-thirds of the way back, and when the concert started she was glad they hadn't tried getting any closer to the raised platform where the musicians were, because every sound in the old building seemed to strike off the walls and ceiling, making even the softest sounds boomerang.

Bob looked at her once and winked. She did not know whether that was meant to convey a feeling of good-natured derision, or whether it was meant to convey something more personal between them. In any case, she did not wink back, did not in fact offer any acknowledgement at all.

The musicians, several of whom were members of the local volunteer fire brigade, played very well, actually, but they seemed to have to feel their way through every bit of music that was not a march. However, when they launched forth into the marches, they opened up all stops, the sound welled up and outward, far beyond the fire-hall, and most of the men stamped their feet in time to the rousing music.

Elizabeth turned and said, "This is the kind of music they play on the common each Independence Day. It's really what they do best."

Bob smiled and nodded. He did not attempt to speak. It would have been useless anyway, because at this juncture the musicians opened up with the *Battle Hymn Of The Republic*, and played it as though the salvation of every person in the fire-hall depended upon their music reaching up as high as heaven.

Afterwards, they went to the other extreme, playing a sad old Confederate song entitled *Lorena*, and the difference in volume gave Bob a chance to bend and say, "They are really very good, aren't they?"

They actually were, but she thought he was being kind; she was sure this was not the kind of music people went to hear in New York City. She said, "I like them," and as the concert approached its end she nudged him. "If we don't leave ahead of the crowd we'll be trampled."

He took the suggestion to heart, rose, helped her up, and they headed for the exit.

They had almost reached it when Elizabeth felt something; felt a pull that seemed to come from the north side of the doorway, which was to her left. She raised her head, swung around—and met the impassive gaze of John Harding.

He was not sitting back there, he was standing, with some other young men who apparently had arrived late, along the rear wall. Her heart almost stopped. In fact, she faltered for a second and Whiting turned to look. Then she walked on.

She could actually *feel* the roiled atmosphere as she got closer to the door. She had forgotten to tell John about her supper-date, and now it was going to look to him as though she had deliberately neglected to tell him. He would realise that she had known about her date with Bob Whiting all day long and had chosen not to mention it to him.

Not that she was under any obligation to tell John Harding anything about her personal life. But she'd *wanted* to tell him about this particular date . . . But he would not believe any such thing now. Now, if she mentioned her date to him, it would sound as though she were trying to make an excuse, as though she were trying to justify something to him.

As they got almost to the doorway she saw him move, and her heart sank again. She was positive John was going to make a scene, was going to deliberately humiliate her.

She stiffened and her eyes, already holding hard to his, showed the slow-smouldering fire of the Ingraham temper.

But John was only moving slightly closer to the doorway in order to provide more space for a late-comer, a large, craggy, old greying farmer she had known since childhood : Franklyn Sexton.

Later, Elizabeth was convinced that walking the short distance from where they had been sitting, to the doorway leading from the fire-hall, was the longest walk she had ever taken in her entire life.

John never once showed any expression. She expected him to show fury or scorn, or perhaps pain, possibly even jealousy, but he showed nothing at all, even though he never once shifted his gaze all the while she was leaving, and when she passed beyond his sight she could still feel that blank, hard, cold stare.

Then she was outside in the gusty night, and Bob Whiting felt for her fingers and closed his hand around them as they turned southward, in the direction of her home.

She was hardly aware of the chill or of the scent of moisture; she thought instead of the certain confrontation that had to come in the morning when she entered the warehouse.

Bob tried to strike up a conversation with her. He slid an arm round her waist as they walked the empty roadway. He looked at her very closely several times, probably trying to puzzle out whether her lack of resistance to his advances, as well as her abruptly altered mood, was the result of something he might have said.

She was aware of his puzzlement but did not really care; nothing he would think of her would make one iota of difference. She was cold all the way through. But she still clung doggedly to the conviction that her personal life was her own. If she chose to go on a date with another man it was no one's business but her own. No one owned her, least of all John Harding.

Of course this was right, but being right did not necessarily have much to do with affection, and by the time she reached her front porch she realised that this was true.

Bob paused, looking at her, as she stopped by the front door. She did not drop her gaze as she said, "Thank you very much, Bob. It was a very pleasant dinner."

That much, at any rate, was the gospel truth. The *dinner* had been pleasant. Because he did not understand the rest of it, had not even noticed John Harding along the back-wall of the fire-house, he did not catch the innuendo.

He raised his arms to her, and instinctively she adopted a defensive posture. She had been through this with him once before, and, knowing about what to expect, this time she was prepared. She took both his hands down and held them with her hands, then she leaned to be kissed.

When he would have freed his hands, she tightened her hold on them. He kissed her, she stepped back, released his hands and smiled. *She* had held the initiative this time; it was a small consolation, but it *was* a small triumph for her, and right now she needed every one she could get.

He slowly shook his head. "Elizabeth, I can't stay much longer. I've already used just about every excuse I can think of to justify staying in Maine this long. Can't we have one more date before I have to leave? Maybe, the next time, I can coax you into coming back to the city with me."

She knew the answer to that: she wouldn't go to the

city with him under any circumstances, and she really did not want another date with him. But she said, "If you'd like to, Bob, come by tomorrow evening for dinner."

He looked a little cynical, as though that wasn't exactly the kind of date he'd had in mind—with her father present—but in the end he smiled and agreed, then he teetered a moment as though wondering whether to reach for her.

She saw it coming; at least, she recognised the look on his face and stepped up to lay a hand upon the doorknob. "Thanks again, Bob; we'll see you tomorrow evening. Good night."

He did not move except to turn his head towards her. "Good night, Liz," he murmured, and as she entered the house he turned, hands thrust deeply into trouserpockets, and went down off the porch, heading back towards the centre of town and probably for his room at the hotel.

CHAPTER THIRTEEN

FOOD FOR THOUGHT

She was awakened in the middle of the night by the sound of rainfall. It was a pleasant sound in springtime, much more pleasant than it was in winter, probably because people listening to an early spring rain knew instinctively that it would quicken new life, would warm the rich earth, and when the sun came afterwards, winter would be gone and summer would be close.

She dozed off again and did not open her eyes until morning at her usual wakening time. Because the world was grey and overcast and dismal with the soft, warm rain, she could have slept right on through if habit hadn't intervened because there was no daybreak.

She dreaded this day, but went through the normal routine as though it were simply another morning, another work-day. Her father did not say much at breakfast. He was probably curious about her date with Bob Whiting, but he had never been a particularly prying parent, even when she'd been younger and had first starting dating. Since she'd become a grown woman, unless she volunteered the subject, he did not bring it up.

This morning she did not feel like bringing up her date with Bob, or anything else that touched upon her personal life. They ate breakfast, talked a little about inconsequential things, then her father left, after giving her one long, pensive look from the doorway.

She also departed, but not for half or three-quarters of an hour afterwards, and each step that took her closer to the warehouse was a distinct effort.

She got a surprise when she walked in. Although the door was unlocked, and John had obviously been there, he was nowhere to be seen, so she went looking for him.

In a way, it was an enormous relief. In another way, now that she had screwed up all her courage for the confrontation, not finding him waiting, perhaps with arms folded across his chest and legs spread wide in a battling stance, was a big let-down.

She went through the warehouse, then went out back looking for him. He was nowhere around, and eventually this brought a sense of uneasiness to her. She really did not know him well enough to guess what this meant and that was unsettling.

She was wearing a cardigan, which was fortunate because the old warehouse was not only chilly, it was also draughty. As the rainfall began to diminish, a little breeze came up, making the old structure creak and groan, as well as leak air at every warped and cracked old length of siding that covered the four walls.

There was work to do, so she did it, but with an air of listening, of being ready to jump away from the table when he came in to confront her, except that he did not arrive. She accomplished quite a little before noon, which was slightly surprising since not for a single moment was she able to totally concentrate.

She did not go out to the café for the noon meal. She was not a big eater in any case, and under these circumstances had no appetite at all. And there was something else she began to feel as the day wore along : indignation.

In the first place, it was *still* none of his business with whom she went to the fire-house concert—or with whom she went anywhere else, for the matter of that. In the second place, she did not owe him anything, least of all an explanation or an apology, so, if he chose to go off sulking somewhere, that would ordinarily be fine with her, but right now there were mounds of work to be done round the warehouse, and although she would strive to do everything possible by herself, when she finally saw him she intended to give him a piece of her mind about loafing, or sulking, or whatever he was doing, when he should have been there with her working!

By two o'clock in the afternoon she was thoroughly annoyed. By three o'clock, if he'd entered the warehouse, she would have blasted him out through one of the rickety old walls with her anger. By four o'clock, when she paused to make a cup of coffee and savour it while leaning upon the old table that served as her desk, gazing around at what she had accomplished—which was quite a bit, as a matter of fact—she just wished he would walk in.

But he didn't.

She closed up a little past five, locked the front door, and as she reached the sidewalk out front, she encountered Claude Hopkins again. At sight of Elizabeth, the furniture-store proprietor snapped his fingers and gave a little start, then he called to her and went hastening down where she was, looking up at her with a screwed-up expression of what could have been chagrin.

"Elizabeth, for heaven's sake I was supposed to give you a note from John this morning, but I got all tied up with some deliveries and forgot all about it until just now when I saw you down here."

Hopkins rummaged his pockets, continuing to wear his look of distress, and when she was sure he never would find the note, he came up with it; it had somehow got wedged inside several heavily creased invoices evidently left over from recent deliveries. He handed it to her, and as she murmured an uneasy "Thank you," because she had a bad feeling about what John had written, Claude Hopkins said, "I'm really ashamed, Elizabeth. I only saw him for a minute before he left town this morning very early. He said something about an estate that was being liquidated up near Jefferson."

She felt the knot in her stomach loosen slightly. Without speaking, she slowly smoothed out the crumpled slip of paper and read that John had indeed got an early start to the village of Jefferson, which was a long day's journey north-eastward from Bannford. He explained about the estate liquidation and closed by saying he hoped to be back before quitting time this evening, but if he couldn't make it he'd be there bright and early in the morning, and if she could spare the time, perhaps they could tag the items he brought back with him.

There was not a hint of reproach, of anger, of disillusionment, of anything at all that she had been so positive would have been in the note. Even his choice of words left her with no feeling of something cold between them. The entire tenor of the little note was friendly, even more than friendly, actually; it was as though they were business partners, and perhaps even closer than that.

She thanked Claude Hopkins and walked on home through the grey, chilly early evening, not sure whether she should feel relieved or bewildered. She decided that bewilderment had to be the proper mood, and by the time she reached home—hurrying the last couple of hundred yards because it began sprinkling again—she really was baffled; the previous night, his stare at her from the back-wall of the fire-house could not have been interpreted in any other way than how she had interpreted it. He had been cold as ice towards her.

She went to her bedroom where she usually bathed and re-dressed before going to the kitchen to start dinner, and re-read the note twice. It still came over to her as something a friend would write to another friend. She had noticed long ago that when people wrote things, especially letters or notes, they unconsciously used words that were compatible with their moods. It was not a great discovery, it was certainly no original revelation, but to her it had been, and she still read letters in that light. This was what impressed her now: John hadn't been in a hostile nor antagonistic mood when he'd written the note.

She told herself it might have been because of the estate sale he was going to, up-country; perhaps he anticipated bargains up there. One second she thought this, and in another second she discarded the idea as ridiculous. She was no authority on men, but she knew enough about them to know that they did not allow small business triumphs to ameliorate personal sentiments.

Finally, she left the note flat upon her dressing-table and went to bathe, soak some of the aches from her muscles—there was quite a bit of lifting and pushing connected with the work at the warehouse. After when she returned to leisurely dressing and making herself presentable because she and her father were having a guest for dinner, she studied the note one more time, and gave up trying to fathom John Harding, who *should* have been readable enough; always before she'd thought him quite transparent, and went out to start dinner.

Her father arrived home and when she informed him

they were having company in for supper, he took his weak highball and retreated to his end of the house to make himself presentable. He did not ask her how she'd made out today at the warehouse, although he had to have been curious about that. Nor did he ask her anything else that could have been interpreted as being personal.

She almost wished that he would. She was getting a little weary of walking round with all manner of smoulderings bottled up inside her. Women, unlike men, could not contain their emotions indefinitely. She made this discovery, too, during this particular period in her life.

Finally, though, when her father returned with his empty glass, freshly scrubbed and re-dressed for the evening, he said, "By the way, did you know Hetty Hopkins and Robert Whiting have been taking drives into the country lately?"

It came as just enough of a surprise that she almost forgot her own problems. She turned from the stove. "Store-gossip?" she asked, and her father gravely shook his head.

"Right from the horse's mouth. Claude told me."

Elizabeth resumed her work at the stove. Hetty Hopkins was a buxom blonde girl, about Elizabeth's age, who had almost been married two or three times, and who had gone down to Philadelphia to work a year or so back, and had only recently returned. She now helped out at her father's furniture store. It had always been Elizabeth's opinion that Hetty could not concentrate. Liz remembered that since childhood Hetty had jumped unpredictably from one thing to another, from one toy to another toy, then, later, from one dress, one kind of hair-style, one boyfriend to another.

That was what had happened each of the several times Hetty had been on the verge of getting married; she had suddenly changed her mind.

Liz liked Hetty; they had always been friends, not especially close ones, but friends. But over the past two or three years Liz had just about given up on Hetty. It was too exhausting trying to keep up with Hetty's sudden and inexplicable changes.

So now it was Bob Whiting.

Liz finally said, "He'd better work fast," and her father's grizzled brows shot up. She saw, and smiled a little cynically. "Because if he doesn't, about the middle of next week, perhaps on Wednesday, he'll go up there and she'll have decided between breakfast and lunch that she can't stand the sight of him."

Her father's rebuttal was very dry. "Well, maybe so, sweetheart, but it's been going on hot and heavy now for about two weeks."

She wrinkled her brow in reflection. "Two weeks, Dad?"

"Yup." Her father was leaning in the doorway gazing over at her. She did not even have to turn around and look at him to know what he was thinking: two weeks back Bob Whiting had also been courting her very assiduously.

"Seems as though he's a pretty busy lad," said her father. "What was interesting to me was that he could do what he's up to in a place like Bannford and not get found out quicker."

Now she turned. "Do what he's doing . . .?"

Her father was blunt. "Well, he was courting both you and Hetty at the same time, wasn't he?"

It was the truth, but she did not choose to admit it, so she said, "Not *courting*, Dad. He's single, Hetty and I are single. There's nothing wrong with what he was doing."

Her father turned as Bob Whiting's distinctive knuckle-roll out front announced their guest's arrival, but just before he left the kitchen her father said, "Maybe not, Liz, maybe not. But the impression I got from Claude is that Bob's asked Hetty to marry him; at least, she told her father he'd asked her to go back down to the city with him."

Elizabeth stood looking at the empty doorway. *Marry* him? Hetty wasn't that naïve. She'd had more experience than Elizabeth had had; in fact, in listening to Hetty Hopkins, Elizabeth had got the impression that there was very little about men Hetty hadn't learned during her stay down in Philadelphia. Surely, then, Hetty did not really believe Bob Whiting meant to marry her. She may have said that to her father to keep him from worrying. Or—she may have told him that because Bob had told *her* that.

Liz removed her apron and started the final preparations for dinner. While she worked, something John had said about Bob came back to her: she only *thought* she knew men like Bob Whiting.

Maybe John had been correct. If so, Liz was certainly learning.

CHAPTER FOURTEEN

THE UNIQUENESS OF LOVE

THIS time Bob brought her a bottle of exotic perfume, and she was properly thrilled. She was not, actually, much of an actress though, but perhaps Bob Whiting's perceptivity was not the keenest, either, because he did not appear to realise that she was regarding him differently this evening than she had previously.

Her father did not allow either of them much of an opportunity to concentrate upon one another, though, and that undoubtedly helped. He was the perfect host, as always, and Elizabeth marvelled that this man she had always considered forthright, uncomplicated and simple, never for one moment allowed any of his dislike to show through.

At dinner Bob dropped a hint that he would shortly be leaving. Elizabeth was not too concerned; she had already heard this, but her father acted chagrined. Elizabeth watched her father's expression of concern, and wanted to laugh at the delightful hypocrisy of it. In fact, the more she watched, the more she was intrigued, and this amused irony helped her rise out of the solemn doldrums and eventually enter into the dinner-table discussions as though there were no reason for her not to enjoy Bob Whiting's company.

Later, when they were having coffee in the parlour, Elizabeth's father did not excuse himself and leave the younger people alone.

That tickled her, too. It probably did not amuse Bob at all, but Bob Whiting had by this time become an unsuspecting pawn between father and daughter. It was a little shameless, Elizabeth knew, but she excused it to herself on the grounds that Bob Whiting had it coming. He deserved what he was getting. Not all small-town people were as ignorant or as naïve as he believed they were.

Finally, then, the moment Elizabeth had been bracing for arrived. Bob had to leave, and her father said his good nights in the parlour, leaving Elizabeth to escort Bob out upon the porch.

There was a very light drizzle falling; the night had stars, though, which meant that by morning the sun would be back. She stopped out there, next to the porch railing, to take a deep-down breath of the fresh night air. He came over beside her and without a word slid an arm around her waist. She stiffened a little, but did not move clear. Not right then.

Bob looked up and around, as though only casually interested in her, and said, "The nights in New England are worth remembering." He dropped his eyes to her face. "And so are the women—especially one woman."

Elizabeth kept her face impassive.

He leaned closer, his grip round her middle tightening slightly. "Have you thought any more about coming down to the city with me?"

She had. "Yes. New York is like a huge zoo to me, Bob, except that the animals aren't all kept in cages." She turned her blue Ingraham eyes to him.

He laughed, but when he saw her eyes the sound dwindled. For several seconds he studied her. Finally he said, "How about Montreal? I have reason to go up there for a few days, on business."

She smiled very slowly and coldly. "Bob, you'll find a girl in Montreal, you don't have to take one from here." She paused, arranging her next sentence. She was going to mention Hetty Hopkins, but for some reason she couldn't fathom, when the name rose to her lips, she could not say it to him.

"Sure, there are always beautiful girls, Liz, but I've never seen one I wanted as much as I want you."

She sighed under her breath. Perhaps some day she and Hetty could sit down and compare notes.

His grip tightened slightly, his face moved closer, she could feel his ardour even through the chill of the drizzly night. "I'll make it a party from beginning to end, Elizabeth. Whatever you want, we'll get. Whatever you want to do, believe me, sweetheart, that's exactly what we'll do."

She turned her sweetest smile towards him. "Get married, Bob?"

He was a better actor than she had thought he would be, but even so she felt the flinch in his arm round her waist even though his smiling flushed face did not alter in expression. "Is that what you want?" he murmured.

She kept smiling. He'd countered her question with another question. He would not marry her. He would not marry Hetty.

"If I wanted to go to Montreal or New York with you, Bob, that would be the only way I'd do it." She let her smile fade but did not take her eyes off his face, and now, along with the weakening smile, she felt his arm around her loosening. She stepped free and turned towards the door. From over there, standing in the darkness, she said, "Good night, Bob. Have a good trip—wherever you go." She went inside, closed the door, listened to the quick, angry slap of his footsteps descending from the porch, and when they diminished she went, not to the parlour where her father was sitting by the fireplace, but out into the kitchen where she could let off some indignation and frustration by cleaning up the dinner mess.

Eventually, her father came ambling out, ostensibly to get a glass of water, but she knew better. Not that she objected to his unvoiced interest. Not his time. She said, "I don't think he'll be back."

Her father got his glass of water and sipped it, looking over at her. "I'll survive," he said.

She smiled at him, quickly, then resumed working. It was a relief to have something physical to do. Earlier, when she'd returned from the warehouse to soak in a hot tub, she'd felt wrung out. Now she felt just the opposite. She worked at setting things to rights in the kitchen as though her life hung in the balance.

Finally, she said, "It's still early, Dad. Maybe he can still make it down to the Hopkins house before they retire."

Her father put aside his half-emptied glass of water. "You're cynical for your age."

She turned. "You gave me the excuse to be, didn't you? I didn't know anything about him taking Hetty out until this evening."

He said, "Hetty couldn't make you like that, Liz. There's more depth to you than that. Some other girl might sound bitter over something like this, but you're not that narrow."

She reached for a towel to dry her hands and said, "Thank you for the compliment."

"That was no compliment," he retorted. "That was an indication of the faith I have in you. Not necessarily in your judgement—after all, you're a woman; not only

111

that, but you're a young and emotional one—but I have faith in your instinctive understanding of things. Even men, although I don't think you've known a hell of a lot about them until just recently."

That was very true. The last part of it, anyway, and she was not going to argue the other part with him because she had known his personal views of women for years, and whether she agreed with them or not—she didn't—she *did* agree that he was entitled to them. But about her recently acquired knowledge of men, he was absolutely right.

She went to a chair at the kitchen table, sank down, leaned with both arms atop the table and looked steadily over at him. "Dad, did Mother ever tell you, after you two had been married for a while, that before you got married she felt like braining you?"

He laughed, throwing back his head as he did so. She'd seen him do this before, but very rarely. Her father's New England sense of humour only responded when something shocked as well as amused him. When he looked down again, eyes bright with amusement, he said, "You're learning a hell of a lot more than I thought, Liz . . . As a matter of fact, she told me that several times, after we'd been married quite a few years. Why did you ask?"

Liz answered frankly. "Because I think I'm in love, and it's not the wonderful feeling of unlimited bliss and ecstasy I've always read that it is."

Her father stood a moment in pensive silence, looking over towards the table, then he raised his arms slightly, let them fall to his sides once more, and shrugged, in what could have been an indication of just about anything from resignation to pity, to sympathetic understanding, and afterwards said, "Good night," and marched out of the kitchen.

She perhaps had a right to feel abandoned in her hour of difficulty, but she did not feel that way; her parent had taught her very early in life that the surest defence against life's pitfalls was not reliance upon someone else, but rather reliance upon oneself.

The trouble with that was simply that there were too many uncertainties in her present dilemma. In short, she lacked experience.

As she arose to douse the light and head down the rear hall for her room, she told herself rather ironically that she was acquiring experience. Not necessarily pleasant or welcome experience, but experience nevertheless.

It was her custom to sit a moment at the dressing-table after she'd got ready for bed and cream her face. It was not a consistent ritual, but she did it whenever she could. It was her way of unwinding, especially after a day worth thinking about.

She did that tonight, massaged her face with the scented cream, gazed at herself in the mirror, and wondered why, among other things worth wondering about, she'd told her father she thought she was in love.

She did not find an answer, but in recollection she had to smile at her father's bewildered reaction. It must be very hard, she mused, for a man to raise a child alone; especially a *girl*-child.

Finally, she went back to her reasons for telling him that. They weren't easy to pin down, but the longer she dwelt upon them the more she discovered within herself a need to be dominated.

She was strong-willed. She had the Ingraham temperament. Bob Whiting's ingratiating way, his sly and covetous innuendos, his stealthy hands, gently and hungrily probing, set her teeth on edge. He left her with an odd feeling after that fondling episode upon the front porch. The only other time she'd ever felt quite the same way was when she'd encountered a snake while hiking in the hills.

But when John had seized her upon the stairs, when he had forcefully crushed down her will, she'd found in herself an almost eagerness to respond. And that other time when he'd pinned her shoulders to the wall out front, when he'd showed a quick, fierce temper, she'd been angered but she'd also felt just a little breathless; a little surge of passionate surrender.

Finally, finishing up at the dressing-table, she rose and went over to the bed, sat upon the edge of it for a few moments, and dryly decided that her basic trouble was that she was an Ingraham, which meant that she'd inherited some of the Ingraham forcefulness.

Her father had never demonstrated much of it, but then in his time he probably hadn't had much opportunity to express it. And, being a man during an era when masculinity was completely dominant, he'd probably been able to get by very well simply because he wore trousers. But with her, in changing times, and being a woman, things were different.

At least this was how her thoughts ran as she got into bed and lay back looking up where cold moonlight lay in an oblong, squarish patch across the ceiling. There was much she had to think about, had to make decisions about, had to try and understand about herself.

But of one thing she became convinced: when she had told her father John Harding was not her kind of a man, she'd been very wrong. Her excuse was simply that when she'd said that she hadn't really known John

Harding. Now she knew him better, and she was perfectly willing to concede that he *was* her kind of man.

It was almost a relief to close her eyes, with this decision made, and sleep. She did not even bother trying to imagine what would ensue, now that she'd made up her mind that she would yield to him.

Tomorrow they would meet at the old warehouse. Tomorrow could look out for itself. She was willing to be passive because she knew John would be as overwhelming as he always was whenever they struck sparks from one another's steel.

That high, squarish patch of moonlight grew narrower as the night advanced; Elizabeth slept without a dream or a tremor, totally relaxed for the first time in several weeks, and while she slept a lot of little things resolved themselves without her even being aware that this was happening.

CHAPTER FIFTEEN

FLINT ON STEEL—AGAIN!

THE day dawned beautifully. As invariably was the case after a storm, the air was glass-clear and winey to the taste and smell.

When Elizabeth got out to the kitchen she found her father already making their morning pot of coffee, which was unusual. About the only time in the past that she could remember him rising early had been when he'd had something troubling him, something perhaps at the office that bedevilled him into awakening early.

He greeted her with a quizzical little smile. "Good morning, my lovely personal cross of thorns," he said, and pointed. "Fetch some cups from the cupboard and we'll start the day the way all civilised people ought to start it—with hot, fresh coffee."

She got the cups, plus two saucers, then she went to tend the toaster and to start whipping up an omelet. Her father watched soberly, and as he had his first cup of coffee he sighed.

"How does it happen that you look radiant and fresh and sparkly-eyed this morning, when only last night the entire black heavens were poised to drop and smother you?"

She laughed at him. "Was I gloomy last night?"

"I don't recall any loud rejoicing," replied her father, finishing his first cup of coffee and going to the kitchen table with his refilled cup.

She shot him a sidelong glance. "If you're worrying about me, Dad, please don't. I'll make out just fine."

"Yeah," he said, studying his coffee. "Seems to me I remember my grandfather saying that's about what those farmers said on Boston Common just before the Redcoats marched up and opened fire."

She laughed, not so much at his remark as at his dry and dour mood. "Don't you have faith in me?" she asked. "You'd better have; you're the one who raised and trained me."

He rolled up his eyes. "Oh, Lord!" Then he dropped his stare to her face. "Some day you're going to have grown children of your own. You'll understand then a whole lot better what I'm going to tell you than I believe you'll understand it now." He paused, reflected a moment as though what he'd just said hadn't made much sense to him, then pushed on regardless of that. "The best any parent can do is instil a few ideas about ethics. All the pummeling and scolding and educating in the world can't begin to compete with natural instincts. Especially in a woman, and especially in a girl, when she reaches a certain stage in her life." He paused again, blushed slightly and looked meaningfully at the skillet. "How long does it take you to make an omelet? I've got a couple of fair-sized orders to get out this morning."

She fed him, and after he had left, in more haste than he usually did, she tidied up the kitchen, went after her purse and cardigan, and started for the warehouse.

Her feeling was different this morning than it had been the previous morning, which was unusual as she hadn't even seen John since the night at the fire-hall. She had only the implications hinted in the note to make her hope he wasn't still angry with her, but still and all, she did not have anywhere near the amount of trepidation this morning she'd had the previous morning.

The sunlight was wonderfully pleasant and warm. The entire day, no matter in which direction she looked, was superb. Everything, even the sooty old rooftops, had been scrubbed clean. It wasn't a new world, but it *was* a new day, and whatever it ended up being by its close, was up to her.

She saw Claude Hopkins opening the furniture store, but because he was bending over the door-lock, busy with a key, he did not see her. She turned down the side of the building anyway.

John hadn't arrived yet. When she entered the warehouse she discovered that although it was warm outside, inside it was still chilly. The old building was high-roofed, draughty, damp, and in fact, had much more in common with a barn than with anything else.

She left the door open to admit warmth, buttoned her cardigan, and went to the table. Everything was exactly as she'd left it the previous day. Some of her annoyance returned and, with hands on hips, she looked at the things she had wrapped yesterday which should have been posted. She was still pondering when she heard someone coming and turned.

John came in out of the brilliant sunlight, saw her standing, hands on hips, looking back at him, and hesitated a moment before approaching. Very suddenly, and for no discernible reason, she recalled the part of a discussion he had left unsaid when they'd discussed his seeing Bob Whiting in the countryside. When he halted, tentatively smiling, she said, "John, do you remember telling me you'd met Bob Whiting?"

He nodded. "Yeah. Is this a new way to tell someone good morning?"

She checked herself a moment, said, "Good morning, John," then went back to the other topic. "Do you remember that you wouldn't tell me any more than just that you'd seen him?"

He considered her lifted face. "Of course I remember. What about it?"

"He wasn't alone, was he?"

John shook his head. "No."

Elizabeth put it on the line. "He was with Hetty Hopkins, wasn't he?"

"Yes."

"And you didn't want to tell me?"

John cast a slow glance around, then back to her again. "Liz, you've been going out of your way to prove to me you're a big girl now; that your life is your own. You wanted to be seen with Whiting, and that was your business, not mine. Okay. That's how you wanted it, and I decided instead of taking you over my knee, and instead of knocking some tar out of him, I'd keep out of your life. That meant I wouldn't tell you any more about Whiting than I'd already told you. If he wanted to play the field, that wasn't any of my business, was it?"

She thought a moment. "John, being so liberal isn't like you."

His brows shot up. "It isn't? What the hell do you know about me, Liz?"

He was near anger and she knew it. Nevertheless she smiled as she replied. "More than I used to know about you, John." Then she eased off a little by gesturing to the work around them. "I got fairly well caught up on the correspondence yesterday, and all those packages over there are to be posted." She turned back towards him. "We've got to hire at least one more person, John."

He ignored all this. "I could cheerfully have killed him. You guessed that, didn't you?"

She smiled. "Yes. When you were standing along the

rear wall at the fire-house the other night I thought you might do it then."

"Not for fooling around with you, especially, but for making a chump out of you. Making you believe you were the only one, Liz, then going round and making Hetty think the same thing."

She coloured. "He wasn't making a chump out of me."

John's brows dropped a dark notch. "Like hell he wasn't. I don't know what else you could call it. He had you eating out of his hand, and Hetty eating out of his hand, and I heard last night at the hotel dining-room that he was making a play for Winifred Sexton whose father has that big farm out east of—"

"I know the Sextons!" she exclaimed, her annoyance with him making her voice husky. "I've known the Sextons all my life!" She paused to allow the annoyance to diminish, but it didn't lessen right away, and meanwhile she said, "Maybe I didn't know Bob Whiting at the start, John, but I certainly knew him eventually."

He blew out a little ragged breath. "I'll bet you did, Elizabeth. I'll bet you did."

She was stunned at the implication behind that statement. "John Harding, what exactly do you mean?"

They stood a couple of feet apart. She still had her hands on her hips. It wasn't at all a ladylike stance, but she wasn't concerned with looking much like a lady at the moment.

"I asked what you meant by that last remark," she repeated, when his silence drew out longer than was necessary.

Then he said, "Ask yourself, don't ask me, Liz. I've already told you, I'm turning over a new leaf. I'm not going to interfere in your life at all. You said it yourself

—I don't have that right. You also said that if we're going to make a success of this business we can't have diversions. All right, I'm willing to accept those things. I made up my mind about them night before last when I lay awake thinking about you being out with that New York City Romeo."

She was not going to settle for a statement of his new philosophy. "I want an answer to what you meant, John, when you said—that other thing, a minute ago."

He brushed her demand aside. "You aren't going to get an answer, Liz. Not from me. *You're* the only one who could really answer it anyway." He turned and went over where the things to be posted had been stacked, and began reading address labels. As though there had been no flare-up, and in his most maddeningly casual tone, he said, "There'll be a drayman arriving sometime this morning with the things I purchased at that estate sale yesterday. We'll have to tag the items, Liz."

He left her hanging in limbo with her anger. She'd never felt quite so helpless. She couldn't very well rush over, whirl him around by brute strength and demand that he explain himself—or else. She wouldn't have done that even if she'd been able to, but she wanted to do *something*.

Then he turned almost indifferently and gazed back at her. "Did you have anyone in mind to hire as your helper?"

She wanted to swear, and she knew some of the words, but instead she turned, went to the table, sat down and said, "No, I have no one in mind."

He strolled over and leaned upon the desk. "Liz?"

She glowered. "What?"

". . . Nothing," he murmured, and reached over to

121

pick up some folded papers. "These are the lists of the things I bought up at Jefferson yesterday." He unfolded the papers and spread them out on the table.

Her glare did not soften towards him. "What were you going to say, John?"

"I was going to tell you that Whiting left town this morning," he replied, glancing at the neat pile of mail, most of it orders and letters of inquiry.

She digested that, still angry with him, but now also curious about something. "Did you see him leave, John?"

"Yes."

"Did he leave—by himself?"

His grey eyes lifted. "Yes. Wasn't he supposed to?"

She lowered her eyes to the papers he'd spread on the table. "Well, I didn't know whether he would or not."

John's calm expression did not change. "You wouldn't go with him, Liz?"

"No."

"He asked you to?"

"Yes. And I think he may have also asked Hetty. For all I know he might have asked Winifred, too." She looked up again. "*That's* what I meant when I said I eventually got to know Bob Whiting."

He smiled slightly. "All right, Liz. And that's about what *I* meant when I said I bet you did learn about him. . . . If you interpreted it differently, that was your doing, not mine. I never lost faith in you. Not for a moment. But I'd have given about half the money I've got in my pocket this morning to have been able to walk over to Whiting and chop him down to size. Only that would have looked pretty childish, wouldn't it?"

The remaining embers of her anger died out then

and there. "Maybe it would have," she conceded, not entirely convinced. She hid her changed attitude by saying, "Was it a good sale, up at Jefferson yesterday?" And suddenly they were back where they had been earlier, when he'd first entered the warehouse.

"I wish you could have been up there with me, Liz. It came to me yesterday that we've got a pretty big inventory now; maybe what we ought to concentrate on from hereon out, for a while at any rate, is more quality. But, you see, a lot of that old stuff, like the vases and lace and marble-topped tables, the old bedsteads and paintings, are things a woman would be better at picking out than a man would be."

She felt herself relaxing. This was how she wanted it to be between them. She kept her voice calm as she said, "Maybe, when there's another sale, one of these days. . . ."

"There is another one, Liz. Down by Bangor in a couple of days."

They looked at one another, and she blushed, which annoyed her, so she got busy with the papers on the table until he said, "Well . . .?"

Without looking up she said, "All right. I'll go."

CHAPTER SIXTEEN

A WOMAN'S PREROGATIVE

THIS was something she had not anticipated, this going off with him. All she'd had in mind when she'd got out of bed this morning was meeting him, seeing him, being with him.

She hadn't meant to fight with him either. In fact, as he worked over in a far corner of the warehouse and she sat at her table ostensibly reading correspondence but actually thinking some private thoughts, she decided rather gradually that no matter what her plans had been, Fate—or something, anyway—had already established the ground-rules, and when she and John met a couple of hours earlier, it wasn't so much what either of them had had in mind, it was what Fate had already preordained for them both.

As for going over to Bangor with him, she was willing. She was willing in a way that she would have been shocked about in anyone else, or that she would have felt shocked about in herself even a couple of days earlier.

Of course, there were places where things like this did not cause a single eyebrow to lift, but New England, Maine in particular, was not one of them.

She thought of her father. She also thought of the gossip when people found out she had gone off for a day or two with John Harding. What the gossips said wasn't as critical to her as the hurt she might cause her father.

She rose from the table and went over where John was writing on tags which he then tied to things, and said, "If I told you I'd changed my mind, John, would you be angry?"

She didn't say what she might have changed her mind about; she didn't have to. He finished tying a tag to an ancient bell-mouthed, ugly little musket, and answered before he turned to face her.

"Angry, Liz? No. But I'd be disappointed." He turned. "What happened?"

She answered truthfully. "My conscience . . ."

"You don't trust me, Liz?"

She answered very frankly again. "I don't trust *me*."

He laughed and stepped over in front of her. She thought he had a wonderful laugh; she'd always felt a little slackening of her inhibitions when he'd smiled at her, but until lately she'd thought that was simply part of the problems of becoming a grown woman. Now she knew differently.

"The talk," she said softly. "The local gossip—and my father, John. Can you understand?"

He kept smiling down into her lifted face. "Yes. How are *you* at understanding things?"

She did not respond because she didn't comprehend. He did not leave her wondering long.

"Can you understand disappointment, Liz? For a little while I thought we were—well—working out our partnership."

She was in a squeeze. She'd been there before, but never under these same circumstances. Those other times she'd managed to resolve her difficulties by falling back upon training, by relying upon what she knew was right. She'd never before been in a position where she actually felt within herself a genuine wish *not* to do what was right.

He may have sensed her difficulty because he reached,

touched her shoulder, and turning her, led her back towards the table. "Don't worry about it, Liz. Anyway, it's probably not going to be much of a sale, and I'll be more particular when I buy." He removed his hand when they were by the table. "I'd better haul those bundles down and post them." He kept looking away from her as he spoke. "Maybe someone at the post office will have some suggestions about who we can hire."

He went over and started readying the packages to be taken away. She sat at her table feeling terrible, feeling as though she had betrayed him. As though she had betrayed them *both*.

When he left, finally, laden with bundles, she went as far as the door, which she held open for him, and she afterwards stood in the wonderfully warm sunlight watching until he was lost to sight.

She still stood in the doorway, bemused. She'd done one of those things her father was always using as a demonstration about the illogic and undependability of womenfolk; she'd agreed to do something, then, when she'd thought about it later, she'd reversed herself.

She went slowly back to the table and was sitting down with her thoughts in disarray when someone made a slight sound at the doorway. Her father was standing over there, looking in.

She was relieved, more so in fact than the simple matter of his appearance warranted. At the moment she did not think of this, she simply rose and smiled as she welcomed him.

He came in slowly, looking around. He looked longest at the little brass cannon on its thickly massive wooden mounting. Closer to her table, he paused to gaze with dispassionate curiosity at the old coach, then at the laden shelves, the other items scattered all around the back section of the warehouse. Finally, as he turned towards the chair she offered him, he said, "You mean you people are actually *buying* this kind of stuff?"

Elizabeth laughed. "Dad, if you know where there's some we can get free," she made a gesture with both arms, "we'll make room for it." She pointed to the coach. "That is sold. So is about half of the rest of the . . ." she started to say 'junk', but caught herself and changed it to ". . . inventory."

He sat down wagging his head. "It's a changing world," he muttered. "What possible use can anyone have for that old coach?"

The buyers own a tavern. They plan to display the coach out front," she explained, and her eye fell upon the cannon, but she chose not to say anything about that. "Those old lanterns," she went on, "are collectors' items."

Her father squinted. "You don't say. Personally, I like to just flick a switch." He settled back in the chair. "Where's John?"

"At the post office. He'll be back shortly." She remained standing. "Can I get you a cup of coffee?"

Her father declined. "No, thanks. I wanted to see him about a cordage sale we made a couple of months ago. I can't seem to find the order and I thought he might remember it."

Elizabeth spoke up before thinking. "He'll remember it, Dad. John's got a phenomenal memory."

Her father gazed thoughtfully at her. "Is that a fact?"

She blushed and sat down. While she was recovering, her father craned around again, then, as he straightened up, he pulled thoughtfully at his chin. "Are you really selling this stuff, Liz?"

"Almost as fast as John can bring it in, Dad." She

had a little sense of triumph about being able to say that. "There is more coming that John bought up near Jefferson yesterday. In fact, we've got to hire someone to help with the handling and posting. John is going to try and find someone at the post office, or perhaps on his way back, this morning."

Her father finished his second survey and resumed his forward posture on the chair, his gaze a little pensive, a little warily interested. Liz guessed how his thoughts were running. John had tried to interest him in a side-line over across the road at the Ingraham building. He had been so positive John couldn't possibly be right. Even Bob Whiting had been sure, but then Bob Whiting's opinion may have slipped a few notches with her father over the past few days; it certainly had slipped with *her*.

She said, "I wanted John to be successful, Dad. I can't remember ever wanting success for anyone as badly as I wanted it for him."

Her father pondered a moment before commenting. "Even if he's dull, Liz?"

"He's not dull, Dad. I was wrong."

Her father nodded. "I think I may have been wrong about him, too. I think I should have let him use part of our warehouse to try his idea in. But—well—I had no idea anything like this would happen."

She was pleased at what she interpreted her father's admission to mean, but that wasn't how he'd meant his remark at all. He cleared this up when he said, "I had no idea you'd have a change of heart about him, sweetheart."

Now she understood, and as she adjusted to his true meaning it occurred to her to say something that was still troubling her. "He wants me to go over near Bangor with him to a sale within the next few days."

Her father did not even hesitate. "Well, you're going, aren't you?"

She hung fire a moment before answering. "Dad, I was thinking of what people would say. Your daughter going off for a day or two with a man."

He raised his eyes to a near-by shelf of old-fashioned cut-glass carriage vases, and kept looking at them as he said, "I'll tell you one thing, Liz: they hadn't better say it within my hearing." He ranged a slow look along the shelf. "And what difference would it make anyway; you're here with him every day in this old barn of a warehouse, aren't you? If people want something to talk about, that ought to suffice." His eyes dropped to her face. "Are you going?"

She did not flinch from his look as she answered. "I'd like to."

He rose from the chair. "Then by all means go." He looked around again. "And while you're at it, Liz, you might bring up the fact that if he needs working capital . . ."

She rose too. "He says we have enough, and that he wants to get it all paid back so we can operate on our own money."

"Sound sense," assented her father, and sighed. "I should have listened." He grinned. "Oh, well; a man my age probably wouldn't be able to adjust to something like this anyway." He pointed. "You see that butter churn? I'd never get accustomed to calling something like that an antique; I had to work one of those things too many years in my lifetime to ever think of them as antiques." He grinned at her. "Tell him I was around, and that I'll come back another time when he's here." They looked at one another a long moment. "Go," he said softly. "Will I worry? Of course I'll worry. But then, I'm a parent, and parents just naturally worry all the time, anyway. One thing I'm no longer worrying about : Whiting left this morning."

She accompanied him to the door and went out into the sunshine part way towards the roadway with him. When he trudged onward she looked left and right for John but did not see him, so she went back to her table inside the warehouse.

Thirty minutes later John arrived looking pleased about something. She smiled as he came over and dropped down upon the chair her father had so recently vacated. "You found someone to help out in here," she said.

He laughed. "You're pretty perceptive, for a girl. He'll show up for work in the morning. His name is Carl Anderson."

She knew Carl Anderson; he was a man a little younger than her father who had been a local carpenter. He was a large, good-natured man, clever with his hands. He had bought a few acres at the edge of town several years back and had been spending most of his time out there lately. He was an old bachelor, highly thought of throughout Bannford.

She was pleased, and showed it. Then she told John of her father's visit and why he had walked over. She also said she was of the opinion that her father regretted not having listened to John, but she did not tell John *why* her father regretted it : because of her involvement with John Harding.

He promised to go over and make a search of the old record cabinets at the cordage offices for the misplaced order, for her father, as soon as he got a few free minutes. Then he dug the post out of a jacket pocket and scattered it across her table as he said, "We've got to write bigger and better ads, Liz."

She looked at the amount of post he'd brought along. "Whatever for? We've got all the business we can handle now."

He laughed and rose. "Walk up to the café with me for lunch."

She rose at once. "John, when are you leaving for the sale over near Bangor?"

"Day after tomorrow. Why?"

She turned towards the door so her face was averted when she replied. "I'll be ready."

He stood watching her walk towards the doorway. Finally he said, "You changed your mind, Liz?"

"Yes."

"*Again?*"

She turned and glared. "Do you want me to change it back, and stay home?"

He threw up both hands and went forward to join her. "No. Not at all. Forget I said anything."

CHAPTER SEVENTEEN

"I LOVE YOU, JOHN"

BANGOR was sixty miles up the navigable Penobscot River. It was a large city and because it had both railroad terminals and extensive wharves to accommodate sea-going ships, it was a cosmopolitan community. At one time, prior to the decline of the Yankee Clippers, the world's fastest and most far-ranging merchantmen, Bangor, in fact all the New England shipping communities, had been both very wealthy and very colourful. But the clipper ships were gone, or nearly so, the sea trade had gone elsewhere, most notably down south around New York City, and now the New England ports and inland communities were only beginning to reach their former affluent status as a result of industrialisation.

But almost every residence, warehouse, and store, all the way from Long Island up to Canada, had items left over from those far distant days. There were even a few rotting old hulks, still sleek as greyhounds, dying slow deaths in the abandoned and neglected old shipyards, the last of the Yankee Clippers.

It was, as John told Elizabeth, a treasure trove for people like themselves who were seeking early-day Americana, and by the time they reached the Penobscot River she was convinced he was correct.

The village they were bound for, called Madison, lay thirty miles below Bangor, even closer to the mouth of the Penobscot. At one time it had been a flourishing town with great, ramshackle old warehouses filled with the ladings brought back from every corner of the earth. But Madison, making its primary living now from local fishing fleets, had been unable to sustain itself and had gradually withered back to drowsy village status.

Several of those old warehouses were still standing, but a fire which had swept the town a generation earlier had destroyed other warehouses as well as a number of stores and homes. When Elizabeth got her first view of Madison, from a slight rise in the river-road, it looked like almost any other small Maine village, except that it had the wide, deep Penobscot at its doorstep; but when she got close enough to make out the overgrown ruins where the fire had burned, she could see that at one time the place had been at least twice as large as it now was.

They registered at the hotel, a half-stone, half-board building opposite the old stone river-wharf, and because it was late in the day by the time they arrived in Madison, Elizabeth was willing to stroll the town when John suggested it, while there was still enough daylight to see well.

She was not in the least uneasy about registering at the hotel with him, and when they went forth to explore, it seemed the most natural thing in the world to be with him in this alien place.

Elizabeth had been to Bangor once in her lifetime, as a half-grown, self-conscious girl. She'd accompanied her father that time, and since it had been a business trip her father wasted no time in getting over there and back to Bannford. But to tell the truth she had not been to very many places, and never before to Madison, so when she went down to the worn old stone wharf in the early evening with John, to gaze at the rather ugly but durable fishing boats, and to smell the

133

sea-scent, it was a distinct thrill. If they had been in Bangor itself, or even up at Portland, which was another hundred miles and more beyond Bangor, she couldn't have felt herself any more of a traveller.

John smiled at her restrained excitement. He had never been to Madison before, either, but he had seen the length and breadth of New England in his lifetime, so the act of travelling, of arriving in a strange place, did not hold the same fascination for him.

While they stood on the smooth-worn old granite sea-wall, holding hands, he pointed out one of the huge old rusted iron rings which was embedded into the mortar and stone where the great sailing ships had tied up back a number of decades. He also showed her a set of stairs leading up from the water which had been hewed from local New England stone. They were abraded in the centre of each step by sailors who had probably been dead many years. It was, he said, an indication of how much activity had once taken place around Madison; granite was the hardest of stone, and to wear it down with foot-leather would not only require a lot of foot-leather, it would take a great many years of that kind of abrasion.

They went over to one of the remaining old slatternly warehouses and peeked in. The place still, after a century or more, had a unique fragrance of dried spices, tobacco, and rum. There were other smells that were more easily identifiable; tar, for example, and pitch, items much used by the men who sailed all the seas in wooden ships.

Then, as the light began to fail, they went over towards the lower end of town where a vast old community dock had been at one time, the most prominent feature of Madison's sea-going existence. There they

134

saw lobstermen still at work, some by lantern-light, and John said that if there was a way to capture this scene in a picture it ought to bring them a lot of money.

Elizabeth shook her head. "Money, pictures that would make money." She pointed out where the water was running in a long-spending ebb of tide. "Doesn't all this *do* something to you, John; doesn't it make you conscious of a heritage, of the past, of the wonderful innocence and honest labour of another time?"

He looked, then he looked back. "Yeah, it does all that too, but when I've got all that out of my system, I start thinking about *now*, and that means money." He laughed at her disgusted expression, slid an arm round her waist, almost lifted her bodily as he turned her, then started back up towards the hotel, still holding her round the middle.

"It was all right for Henry Thoreau, he could sit round Walden Pond and philosophise a lot of nonsense —and personally I think that's about what two-thirds of his philosophising was—but for you and me, Liz, it's got to be buying and selling." He leaned and looked at her profile in the gathering dusk.

She knew he was right, of course, but she still liked to view their world as a romanticist would, and with his arm around her she more than ever felt a leaning towards softer, warmer emotions. But she smiled at him when he looked searchingly at her, quite willing not to dissent. In fact, she was beginning to feel less and less able to disagree.

She was conscious of an insidious lassitude as they walked slowly towards the hotel and she was well aware of the peril of this mood. However she put aside these vagrant warnings.

This was completely different than when Bob Whiting had touched her. Then, she had felt an inner stiffening, an inner revulsion. She hadn't been aware of warnings when she had been with Bob because she felt no letting-down within herself when they had been together.

They got almost to the hotel when her emotional tumult urged her to confess her feelings. Of course she said nothing, not even when he halted outside, where they could see the merry glow of orange light up ahead, and removed his arm from round her waist as he said, "This is torture."

Then, before she could respond, he blew out a great ragged breath and, without looking at her, felt for her hand and led off towards the lighted lobby, and beyond that to the lighted dining-room.

It was too early for the tourist season which annually inundated the New England coast, so the dining-room was anything but crowded as they sought a table and sat down.

He handed her a menu and did not select one for himself. She thought she knew how he felt because she had no appetite, now, herself. But she went through the motions and ordered a lobster dinner. When the waitress asked John, without taking his eyes off Elizabeth he said, "The same, please." Then, as the waitress departed, he laid his hand on the table, palm up, and smiled without speaking. She smiled back and put one of her hands across his palm.

There was nothing really to say. Or else there was so much to say she couldn't have said it all in one night. As his hands closed strongly round her fingers, she returned the grip, briefly.

Somewhere beyond the lobby someone had a wireless set switched on. The music was nothing Elizabeth would have selected for this very special, magical moment, but it had to suffice.

Their food came. John suddenly snapped his fingers. "I forgot to ask, Liz. Would you care for a highball first?"

It was too late, but even if it hadn't been she still would have declined. If there was one thing she did *not* need this evening, it was a highball. Not even one of those exceptionally weak ones her father usually mixed back home, about this time.

"No, thanks." She freed her hand and reached for a fork. The silence endured. She wished there was a way to break it, but words wouldn't come, not the kind that would be appropriate; any other kind would have sounded silly. She knew what he was thinking. It was the same thing *she* was thinking. Under those circumstances saying something about the weather, or about their trip to Madison, or perhaps about the people they might meet the following day at the sale, would have sounded ridiculous.

Once, when she raised her eyes, she saw him stab without interest at his food. He glanced up and caught her watching him, and leaned back as he said, "You were dead right when we had our argument at the warehouse, these damned diversions are murder. I'm supposed to be shrewdly concentrating on that sale tomorrow, and do you know what I'm thinking about instead?"

She did not ask; she did not *dare* ask.

"I'm thinking about you; about two years of thinking about you, and being alone with you in this village tonight."

When he paused she decided it might be a good idea

to intervene, so she said, "Shouldn't you perhaps go look up someone about the sale tomorrow?"

His mouth lifted in a crooked small smile. "I don't give a damn about the sale tomorrow, Liz."

She went silent. There was nothing more she could say. There was nothing she could do to change this mood or the situation. No way at all.

It was an effort for her to even try. And she really didn't want to try. She looked squarely at him and said, "The diversion is winning, isn't it?"

That pleased him. He laughed a little. "I think it's been winning for some time now. You were right. Does that please you, Liz?"

What she had meant was that *she* had also become diverted. She did not know exactly how to answer him, so she procrastinated. "Eat your dinner, and maybe afterwards we can go back down by the dock and watch the tide run in the moonlight."

He shrugged, but he started eating. They did not say much more until the meal was finished. She had actually eaten more than she'd have believed possible under the circumstances; she had been very hungry without being actually aware of it. Travelling affected some people that way.

He ate about half his meal, too, and afterwards, in a somewhat altered frame of mind, he joked about that. "I thought being in love destroyed one's appetite." His eyes twinkled across at her. "Maybe my only trouble was simple indigestion, not love."

They left the dining-room, were intercepted near the doorway by the manager who handed them separate keys, then they returned to the sea-scented night, only now there was a hint of coolness abroad.

She knew, before this night was over, she would confess to him that she loved him, but she had no idea when this moment would be, nor how it would arrive. She only knew that she *wanted* to tell him.

Madison went to bed early, especially if the night was a little raw as it became this particular night. There were a few lights along Main Street, in store windows, and off on the residential side-streets there were other lights, but they began diminishing gradually as time passed. When Liz walked beside John back down towards the old seawall she did not see another couple strolling, not even an individual. She told John they had the entire town to themselves, and his answer cut across that with a purposeful observation.

"Not the town, Liz. We have the whole *night* to ourselves."

They halted where the water brushed at the seawall making a soft lapping sound, and watched a boatman hoist a glass-enclosed old-fashioned lantern aloft his stubby mains'l mast. She laughed softly. "That looks like a very old seaman's lantern."

He looked, then grinned down into her lifted face. "What would you offer him for it?"

She looked deep into his eyes. "Tonight, I wouldn't make him any kind of an offer. Tonight . . . I can't make myself think of business. Can you?"

He turned her gently by the shoulders and kept each hand up there. He did not answer the question. For a couple of seconds he watched moonlight across her tilted face, then very gently he lowered his head. She saw his shoulders block out a big segment of sky, saw his face come steadily downward, and she moved up closer to him, reaching high with both hands, and when his mouth touched her lips she reached farther around and drew him closer with a quick rush of fire that even surprised her it was so wanton.

Somewhere, a clock struck ten times. She heard each ring of the chimes, they touched down through her as though they were originating somewhere within her own being.

She felt his unexpected response to her fire, and by twisting her face away until one burning cheek was against his chest she was able to say what had now to be said, before anything else happened. It had to be said.

She clung close and kept her face down as she said, "I love you, John."

CHAPTER EIGHTEEN

A TIME FOR FEELING

IT WAS a long night, a longer morning, and when Liz finally awakened she could hear the village on all sides as the sun stood well above the horizon filling as much of the world as she could see through her bedroom window with fresh, brilliant promise.

She did not move for a long time. For a long time she did not want to think or to remember, she simply wanted to lie there re-*feeling* her experience. There were words to be recalled too, but they came right along with the rest of it, and now, lying there in peace, she wondered how she had ever *not* been in love with him.

Now, afterwards, it was as though she had stepped through into another, very different world, as though whatever had been awakened in her couldn't possibly have existed anywhere, prior to last night.

She eventually stirred a little, then rose. The day was going to be perfect, she could tell, and that had very little to do with the sunshine or the fragrant warmth.

She did not hasten in making herself presentable for the day. They had promised to meet in the dining-room for breakfast, and she knew without a shred of doubt that when she got down there, John would be waiting.

He was. When she entered the dining-room, which was nearly empty of others who had breakfasted earlier, he rose, his smile tender, his eyes dark with moving feeling. Ordinarily when he moved to kiss her she would have eluded him in a public place, but this morning she didn't. She wanted the kiss and met it head-on with a

141

kiss of her own. Then they sat and without a word passing between them, locked a hand across the tabletop. Even when the waitress appeared and they ordered, they did not loosen the hand-grip.

Eventually she made an effort and said, "What time does the sale begin?"

He answered as though it did not matter when it began, or even if it ever began. "Ten o'clock."

Their food arrived, they broke the grip, and Liz reached first for her coffee. It always had the ability to bring the world down into proper focus. It did this now, too, but not as clearly as it usually did.

He finally concentrated on eating. As he did so he said, "I've already reconnoitred the place. It's at an old sea-captain's estate south of town a mile or so. He died a few years back, but until now no one went through the place. They wouldn't have now, except that his married son wants to sell out and move to Philadelphia." John looked up briefly. "There's a list of items nailed to a tree down there. If we're going to be selective, there are only a few items we ought to bid on."

She nodded. Their inventory was amply large, back in Bannford. Her father had probably been right when he had implied that they ought to sell down a little. She thought so too, but all she said was, "If we buy very much how will we get it home?"

He smiled. "That's no problem. But we either have to buy enough to make a full load, or pay the same rate for sending along half a load."

Gradually, she was able to concentrate on what they had arrived in Madison for, but even so she was unable to concentrate as hard on that as she ordinarily would have been able to.

They could have hired transportation to the sale site,

but she wanted to walk, so they enjoyed the morning, and one another's company, by following the southern post-road.

They arrived late; the sale was already well under way by the time they reached the spacious, shaded gardens around the big old house, but that did not bother either of them very much.

They parted out front. John went over to examine the articles displayed on tables under the huge old shade trees, while Elizabeth went inside to look through the opened house.

If she had been constituted differently, or if the circumstances had been different, she could have concentrated. As it now was, when she saw the old-fashioned child's rocker-crib, the faded portrait of a handsome woman with severely pulled-back dark hair and large expressive blue eyes, she could think only of the baby who had lain in that crib, and of the mother who had borne him.

Everything in the old mansion seemed to appeal to her as though she were somehow personally involved with it. Finally, she returned to the front porch and sat down out there.

The sale had a moderate attendance. People, mostly local couples, browsed. When they bought it seemed to Liz that they did so because they wanted something to take home with them as a memento. If the people of Madison were anything like the people of Bannford, a good many of them who attended the sale were in some way related to the family that had lived in the old sea-captain's house.

Finally, John came up on to the porch. He drew an old cane-bottomed chair over to her and as he eased into it he said. "My heart's not in it," and smiled.

She understood.

Far out across a large, square green field, past the trees and the post-road, lay the river, wide and moving. Undoubtedly the old sea-captain had often sat where they were sitting looking out there, possibly seeing in the running of the tide re-enactments of his long and active life.

She shook her head a little. It was impossible to put into mere words her feelings right now; it was as though she had known the old sea-captain, as though they had been somehow related, or had been at least kindred spirits.

She wondered if this depth of perceptive sentiment might not have arisen from the awakening she had only recently experienced. Everything seemed at least a little different; the air was purer, the vistas clearer, the day more vivid, and the man next to her seemed more handsome than ever.

Even the colours of the clothes the people wore who were strolling here and there beyond the porch were brighter-seeming.

She reached for his hand and held it tightly. If others noticed their preoccupation, she did not see it. Then John said something that hit home, and which also made her smile in understanding.

He said, "A regiment of cavalry could dash past right now and I wouldn't even hear them."

She gave his hand a hard little squeeze, then released it.

"What have you bought?"

He showed mild surprise. "Bought? Nothing. And I don't feel much like buying, either."

She rose. "Then why are we sitting here?"

Without another word passing between them, they left the grounds and turned back up towards the village in the mid-day warmth, with a hint of salt breeze preceding them most of the way. It got stronger when they crossed the post-road to stroll the riverbank, even though the sea was distant.

When they had the lower end of the village in sight he said, "There's a minister round here somewhere."

She did not ask the obvious question. She did not have to ask it; he had poured out his feelings towards her last night, had said he'd locate a preacher today if he had to scour the entire countryside to do it.

They did not head for the hotel, instead they kept to the riverbank, and where it changed from earth to stone and mortar they paused to watch a local lugger go heading downriver in the direction of the salt water. He said, "I'm the world's least talented poet—but sights like this usually make me think how little life changes from century to century. The *mechanics* of living change, but nothing else seems to change very much." He jutted his chin in the direction of the thick, durable little fishing boat. "How many generations of men have gone down to the sea as that man is doing? It doesn't make much difference that he's got an inboard motor and they had paddles or sails, they all went in the same direction for the same purpose, didn't they?"

She held his arm up high and leaned close to him. "And the women didn't change, either. Not in purpose, John."

The sun edged little thin waves with pure gold. The sky shook out its finest blue raiment for them, and the massive stonework underfoot throbbed with each surging lift of tide. Elizabeth closed her eyes for a moment, feeling herself being absorbed by all those different

145

things, feeling herself also absorbing them until she and the river, the sky and the ancient stone were one and the same.

Then he tugged gently and they went on up to the community wharf, but it was all but abandoned this time of day. It was too late to watch the fishermen head out and too early for them to be returning with their day's catch.

Here, Elizabeth knew, lay the pulse of the village. It no longer had any other kind of a pulse. She thought of home, of Bannford, and wondered how it had managed to survive when it did not even have a river.

John looked down at her. "I'll never forget this place. Sometimes, when I'm standing perfectly still, I can sort of feel things, like I've always lived here."

She understood, and marvelled that they could both feel the identical things and still be different.

Finally, they strolled back in the direction of the hotel. Out front, a little group of old men, some greying, some already grey and some with no more than a fringe of grey, were sitting in relaxed, shaded comfort. They looked with frank curiosity at John, and with an equally as frank admiration at Elizabeth. She smiled at them; not only were they as old as her father, but several appeared to be quite a bit older. Moreover, she wanted to smile at them.

The men smiled back. A dark-eyed, thick-set older man who was puffing a pipe, removed it and spoke to John. "Fine weather on the coast this spring, eh?"

John agreed that it was, indeed, fine weather they were having along the coast this season; then, encouraged by this display of friendship—which did not always exist among strangers in New England—he paused at the hotel entranceway and said, "Is there a preacher in Madison?"

Elizabeth did not blush despite the fact that she could feel those knowledgeable old eyes all move slowly to John, pondering, then move to her and linger there.

The pipe-smoker inclined his head very gravely. "Yes." He pointed with the stem of his pipe. "In that grey-painted house yonder. His name's Norman Anderson." The dark-eyed man put a thoughtful glance upwards at John. "He's a Methodist preacher," the man said, as though that might discourage John. New England's native families were either Catholic or Episcopalian, one or the other. Other denominations had come surreptitiously over the centuries, but the natives, true descendants of English, Irish and Scottish immigrants, and just as dogged in their convictions as those ancestors had been, still considered the other faiths interlopers.

Elizabeth smiled in spite of herself. Madison, then, was no different from Bannford. She squeezed John's arm and he replied to the thick-set man.

"Thank you." He started on through the doorway.

The pipe-smoker gazed after them a moment, then called forward. "Young man—and young lady—if you wanted to see Norm Anderson about a marryin' matter, if I were you I'd hustle on over. This is his day for heading out into the countryside, and he usually don't return until about three, maybe four, days later." The old men all began smiling. They knew what was coming next; it evidently was something they had been smiling over for a long while.

The pipe-smoker explained. "Norm Anderson is a real fisherman. Between Sundays he hits just about every creek between here and Bangor."

Elizabeth smiled back. She knew these older men; she also knew Preacher Anderson even though she'd never seen him in her life. The people of Madison really weren't any different from the people back home in Bannford. She pulled John around and headed him off across the wide roadway in the direction of the grey cottage. Behind them, the bench-sitters watched for a while in silence, then the pipe-smoker rekindled his tobacco, blew smoke, and said, "Sure would be pleasant to be their age again for a spell."

At the far end of the bench a craggy-faced man with clear blue eyes put it more plainly. "That ain't what you're thinking about, Frank."

They all laughed, the sun beat down, the little salt-scented breeze began to die as the heat increased, and an orange-and-white cat who had been sleeping in a corner of the porch, roused by the laughter of the old men, rose in disgust and disappeared round the side of the building, intent upon finding a place where he could resume his nap without interruptions.

CHAPTER NINETEEN

LIZ'S DISCOVERIES

ELIZABETH decided, after they had spent almost an hour with the Methodist preacher, that she and John Harding had not been united in matrimony as much because God required it as because the people around them required it.

Not that it was all that important. She was smiling about this an hour afterwards when the first thin shadows began appearing.

If people wanted something poignant to remember about a wedding, or if they wanted something amusing or hopeful to remember, it was always there. John did not have a wedding ring. Neither he nor she had thought of that. The Methodist minister had a small tray of rings. He sold them at a very fair price.

Back home folks would have thought her marriage to John Harding skirted very close to the edge of being scandalous. For witnesses the minister had stepped to his front porch, placed two fingers between his lips and had let loose a shrill whistle which summoned those old men over in front of the hotel. Elizabeth and John did not remember a single name of their witnesses.

Afterwards, when they were eating a belated noon-day meal at the hotel dining-room, Elizabeth laughed without giving her reason, and John joined in, wagging his head from side to side. "All I originally had in mind doing over here was perhaps picking up a few items for re-sale," he said. They were not amused by the same

things, but it did not matter. Right then, for Elizabeth
at least, not too many things *did* matter, including
another meal, but she pecked at it thinking that it was
downright incongruous, people going through their
established routines, eating, sleeping, sitting in the sunshine, doing business, discussing the weather, and within
her was unfolding a tableau that had the power to
blindly illuminate the entire perimeter around Madison.

She said, "John, we belong to another world. Can
you hear those people talking out in the kitchen, and
the wireless music coming from the lobby? None of it
makes any sense at all to me, does it to you?"

He grinned. "Not a bit." He touched his lips with
the napkin, dropped it, and rose from the table. "Do you
want to start back this afternoon, Liz? If we're not
going to buy anything at the sale. . . ."

She also rose. "If you like, John."

He kept staring at her. "But do you *want* to start
back?"

She didn't. "No."

He didn't either. "Good. We'd get too late a start
anyway."

They went out into a small fenced garden in which
was a huge old apple tree. Elizabeth went over to see
if the buds had come and gone yet. She couldn't really
tell because John intercepted her, turned her gently and
kissed her in the tree-shade with the orange-and-white cat
and one yellow-eyed woodpecker watching with clinical
interest.

She could no longer simply kiss him, and he seemed
to share that same problem as her hands encircled his
back, the fingers becoming gentle talons, someone
coughed and she gave a little start as though what they

had been doing was a crime. The dark-eyed, heavy-set pipe-smoking older man was standing near the corner of the building with a large bouquet of local flowers in one hand. He did not pretend he had not seen anything. He was past the age for things like that, and Elizabeth thought, when she returned his smile, that he had probably some wonderful memories of his own, too. He was old enough, and wise enough looking, to have them.

He brought the flowers over and handed them to her. "Seemed like," he said, "you folks being strangers in Madison and all, and getting hitched here, the village had some sort of responsibility. At least that's what some of us decided. The flowers aren't much; we scattered out a while back and each of us plucked what we could. But it's the feeling behind them they're supposed to represent, isn't it?"

Elizabeth stepped over and kissed the older man's cheek. He took that with aplomb, but when John offered his hand again, as he'd done over at the minister's place, the older man cleared his throat, finally showing slight embarrassment. He covered it up by saying, "Where you folks from?"

Elizabeth answered. "Bannford."

The dark eyes went thoughtfully to her face. "Bannford, eh? Now that's a coincidence. My father sailed with a shipmaster from over there. He was cabin-boy to Cap'n Josiah Ingraham a lot more years back than I like to reflect about."

Elizabeth was surprised, then pleased. "It must have been a long time ago," she agreed. "Captain Josiah's been dead for many years. I am . . . I *was*, Elizabeth Ingraham. My father is George Ingraham. We are descended from Captain Josiah."

The black-eyed man's furry brows shot upwards.

151

"You don't say! Well now, that makes me standin' up for you folks even more of an honour. It makes it a sort of family-like matter. Incidentally, did you ever hear the story of that Scot shipmaster Captain Josiah pulled out of the sea? Probably not; it was an old yarn when I was a lad, and those old-time tales sort of die out."

Elizabeth said, "I've heard the story since I was very small." She hesitated, thinking of the opaque glow on Captain Josiah's portrait over the mantel, wondering whether to mention it or not.

The dark-eyed man cut across her thoughts with a little self-conscious smile, and spoke again. "According to my father, Miz' Harding, he sat with the old Scot shipmaster two nights straight running, before they got back to land; sat up with him a candle on a fo'castle bench and a demijohn of Jamaica rum and a tin cup, nursing him along, just the pair of them."

This was an interesting bit of history concerning "the English gentleman" Liz had not heard before. She listened with the big bouquet of flowers cradled in one arm, and with her other hand held behind her, out of sight because she and John were standing very close and she was clinging to his fingers.

"The shipmaster told my father, who was a mere lad in those days, he'd known he'd never return from that trip, that he had a curse, and that when Captain Ingraham pulled him from the sea Captain Ingraham was only prolonging his miseries."

Elizabeth said, "What curse? My father never mentioned a curse. All we've ever known was that Captain Josiah brought the shipmaster home, and he died in an upstairs bedroom."

The dark-eyed older man simply shrugged thick shoulders. "That's all he told my father, Miz' Ingraham, that he had a curse. Well, there was one other thing he said. He told my father he didn't want to die aboard someone's ship or in their house because the curse might cause a haunt after he was gone. He said a woman in Aberdeen told him before he sailed he'd never come back, and that unless someone was right careful, the curse would torment them too."

Elizabeth, thinking of Captain Josiah's "English gentleman", had a cold thought: the opaque glow had never caused any harm in the Ingraham household or, if it had, she had never heard of any such harm. But it *did* always seem to haunt Captain Josiah's portrait. Did that mean Captain Josiah was now carrying the curse, wherever he was, or did it simply mean that his portrait was haunted?

She did not mention "the English gentleman", and after a while, when the dark-eyed man left the garden, she took John inside with her, to her room, and while she arranged the flowers she told him the entire story. He sat spellbound. When she finished he reacted as she might have expected.

He said, "It's very hard to believe, Liz. I know people believe in such things, but . . ." He threw up his hands.

She continued to arrange the flowers. Their fragrance spread throughout the room. What she was thinking had to do with the elderly, dark-eyed man; if they hadn't met him, or if he hadn't come into the garden with the flowers, the affair of "the English gentleman" wouldn't have intruded. Nothing had any right to intrude.

She finished with the flowers and turned slowly to smile at him. "Maybe we ought to go home tomorrow."

He rose and stepped to the window as he answered.

153

"I suppose so." He turned towards her. "What will your father say?"

He didn't mean what would her father say about the ghost. "He'll say—what took you so long, daughter? And I'll say—because I didn't know my own mind."

He smiled slightly. "If I were your father I'd be angry—probably."

"But you're not my father." She went over closer to him. "And he's known for some time."

"That we were in love?"

She nodded. "Yes. I think he suspected it some time ago. Then, too, I told him."

John was surprised; obviously he didn't think their love was a long time thing. At least, he didn't think *her* love was. He blew out a breath and leaned upon the sill. "I don't suppose I'll ever really understand women, Liz. I've always had the same trouble with horses. Just when I've thought I could handle them, they did something unexpected."

She laughed. "What a poetic comparison, my love." She decided then and there that she *liked* him as well as loved him. He was not a complicated person; he was honest enough to be very forthright.

She did not think, right then, how odd it was that although she had known him for several years, she had overlooked things in him that seemed, now, to be so worth while.

He moved away from the window, towards her. She did not retreat. When his hands touched her she had no defence, and wished for none. Whatever it was that love unlocked in a woman's psyche, he had unlocked in her. She thrilled to his touch, of course, but that was physical; what actually happened was something a lot deeper. She could feel herself subtly, insidiously becoming a different person when his arms slipped round her. There was the joy of belonging and the need to be held and loved by him, but there was also an indefinable spirituality that had to do with their blending; it was almost as though her identity blended with his, almost as though, instead of being separate people, they became one person. She was aware of him as belonging exclusively to her, and now that they were married she let her mind expand to include whatever he did, whatever he became involved with, as being part of her world, too. If he succeeded or failed, she would share; if he became ill or demoralised, her resistance added to his would be what would re-energise him.

She liked all this very much, and clung to him as she said, "Did you know how big love is, John?"

He would have lifted her face to look down into it, perhaps for a clue as to her meaning, but she resisted, keeping her head down. He gave up trying and answered in his own way.

"I think I'll find out. *We'll* find out. Right now it looks big enough to last for ever and to include a lot of things we haven't thought much about—like children."

She kept her head down. "How many children?"

His grip tightened. "Five or ten, maybe."

That made her raise her head. "Five or *ten*?"

He laughed at her. "You asked."

She studied him long enough to realise that he was teasing, then dropped her head and continued to cling close as she said, "Well, as long as we have them one at a time. . . ."

CHAPTER TWENTY

ALTHOUGH they left Madison early and the distance was not especially great, they did not arrive back in Bannford until well along in the afternoon, something Elizabeth did not object to in the least. She was quite content to be with her husband, and while she was beginning to accept his presence, she hadn't yet got accustomed to being a wife.

It was a natural feeling; after all, she had lived twenty years, first as a child, then as a girl, and finally as a young woman, and all of it with personal freedom.

She did not think of being married as a condition ensuring any loss of independence. She thought of it in terms of trading something she'd always had for the privileges of love and a new responsibility. It made her realise that, for ever after, she was a woman and could never again be a child or a young girl, could never again run to her father. From here on, whatever happened, she would have to resolve it through her own resources.

She was willing. As they rode along between Madison and Bannford, heading inland, she cast an occasional sidelong glance at John. Neither of them said much and she was curious about his thoughts. His expression was calm, relaxed, gently pensive as though he were inwardly quite at peace. She thought she could guess what he was thinking, but she'd have died before mentioning it. After all, they hadn't even been married two full days yet. Later, they would be able to smile and discuss those things, she was confident of that, but right now she was willing for him to think about them, exactly as she also did, but only in silence.

Bannford looked peaceful in the afternoon. The heat was a little more noticeable inland than over near the sea, but the landscape was prettier. Maine's extensive woodland areas, mostly mountainous, lay off a fair distance from Bannford, but they had always seemed to Elizabeth to be very beautiful, the way they held a blue-blurred haze in hot summertime, and the way they suggested dark warmth during Maine's frigid and sometimes prolonged wintertimes.

The village was quiet when they arrived. It was too early for the stores to be closed, but it was not too early for the customary summertime lethargy to be noticeable. It wasn't as if it was summertime yet, it was still springtime. But summer had its scouts out, bringing warm days now and then.

They went, first, to their warehouse. Everything was exactly as they had left it, which was not unusual since they had been gone only a couple of days, even if neither of them felt that their sojourn had been that short. They had good reason to feel as though they had just returned from a distant, lengthy journey; more things had been crowded into those two days of living than most people crowded into a year.

Elizabeth stood in the big old warehouse, where it was pleasantly cool, coming face to face with two important realities: her father, and where they would live. She said, "John, we're back, and we're married—and what do we do now?"

He laughed at her. "Do now? Well, get back to work and start anew. . . ."

She felt his comprehension. "That's my point, John.

First off—do we take up residence here in the warehouse?"

He pulled out a chair, sat, crossed one thick leg over the other leg, and showed her a twinkle. "I'd be satisfied living here, with you."

She felt herself melting towards him, and controlled it. "There are houses to rent. Not many, but some."

He slapped his legs and stood up again. "Then let's go rent one."

She was agreeable. "All right. But we're not going to be able to move in tonight."

He said, "Tonight. Yes, well, I'll go engage a room at the hotel."

She winced. "No, you won't. Tonight we'll stay at my house." She didn't try to explain how it would look if they spent the night at a hotel in her own home town.

"Someone had better inform your father," he said drily.

She crossed over, took his arm and headed for the door. They locked the warehouse, then went alongside the furniture store, across the roadway on a diagonal course to the Ingraham building, and at the rickety old stairway he made a mock low bow, and she preceded him to the upper offices.

There was an older man working at the desk John had once occupied over near the roadside window. He shoved glasses up his forehead as they appeared, and seemed to hesitate. Elizabeth did not know him, so it was a fair assumption that he did not recognise her either.

Her father called from the doorway of his office, coffee cup in hand. "What did you find over at Madison?" he said. "Come in here and . . . Oh, excuse me. Liz, this is Mr Hudspeth, my new clerk. Mr

Hudspeth, this is my daughter Elizabeth . . . and John Harding."

She didn't know what to say, so she said nothing as she turned to cross the room to her father's doorway.

John followed, silent, slightly distant, but seemingly entirely at ease, which he couldn't have been because no young man is ever entirely at ease the day he announces to a girl's father that he has married her.

But George Ingraham was not a subtle individual. He might have left that impression because he was normally quiet and somewhat reticent, but no one who knew him very well, which included his daughter, had ever thought of him as being dense. He proved it now by motioning towards the old coffee pot across his office.

"Help yourselves, folks."

He had never included Elizabeth in any such impersonal term as "folks" before. Perhaps, another time, she might not have noticed, but this afternoon she did.

Her father went behind his desk and sat down. "You are married," he said quietly.

From the corner of her eye Elizabeth saw John give a slight start. That didn't annoy her, but her father's usurpation of an initiative that should have belonged to her or to John did annoy her, so she said, "Yes. Over in Madison the day before yesterday."

Her father's placid face did not change. He gestured again. "That's a fresh pot of coffee, John." Then he leaned and dug into a low desk drawer, brought forth a bottle of rum and set it resoundingly on the desk. "Lace it, boy. Always lace your coffee on special occasions." He smiled at his daughter. "A wee dram wouldn't hurt you either—now that you're a woman."

Her father leaned back, regarding them. John finally went over, took down two cups from an overhead shelf

159

and filled them. While his back was to Liz and her father, the older man winked slowly at his daughter as though to say he approved, as though to imply that he was pleased.

She had said what she'd had to say. Beyond that she did not know what, exactly, was expected of her. But she went round the desk, leaned and kissed her father; then, as John brought the cups over and reached for the bottle of rum, she felt the sting of tears briefly.

These were the men in her life. These were the men she loved. She did not know what kind of procedure a young husband and a new father-in-law went through, but instinctively she felt aware that there would be *some* kind of ritual, man-like, to be performed, so she remained in the background, watching, as John filled her cup, then his, and passed over hers to her without a word or a smile.

Her father picked up the bottle, considered its faded old label briefly, then tipped some of the rum into his cup as he said, "There were eleven cases of this left over after Elizabeth's grandfather died. We carried it on the inventory because no one wanted to buy it, until about thirty years ago, then I started keeping a bottle up here." He smiled up at John Harding. "I wonder how long eleven cases last? There are five cases left. It is a very good brand of rum."

Elizabeth had a thought: If there could *be* such a thing as good rum!

John loosened as her father lifted his cup in a kind of gentle salute. "Congratulations, son, and good luck."

They drank. Elizabeth almost forgot to, but then she was not actually being included in this little ritual.

John put down his cup and offered his hand. He hadn't said a word. He didn't speak now until after he had pumped the older man's hand twice and then released it.

He said, "Thank you, Mr Ingraham. We—I—should have said something before we left. I apologise for that."

George Ingraham looked from one of them to the other. "Did you *know* before you left?"

John's gaze wavered. *He* had known, of course, because he had known he'd been in love with Elizabeth for at least two years, but *she* hadn't known, and that made a simple answer just about impossible to give.

"Well," John replied, speaking a little awkwardly, "maybe we didn't know, exactly, Mr Ingraham."

Elizabeth wanted to come to his aid, but her father did that for her. He drained his cup and stood up behind the desk. "Never apologise for something, John, that you can't help." His face brightened. "I'll tell you honestly, I'm glad." He was looking at Elizabeth when he said this. She thought she understood. Her father was glad she had chosen John Harding, not Bob Whiting. Maybe he had always had secret reservations about Bob Whiting, she would probably never know now. Her father was one of those individuals who seldom lost time worrying about what might have been or what could have happened. Elizabeth thought that was a good way to be; a person never developed the capacity for brooding.

She finally decided it was time to speak, and mentioned the fact that, as married people, they had to make some adjustments, some accomodation adjustments. Her father pondered that a moment before answering.

"You wouldn't want to live at home, I suppose. Married folks should have their privacy, their own separate lives."

She said, "Dad, maybe for a few days, until we can find a place of our own?"

He looked at her with a beaming expression. "For as long as you like."

Suddenly, she realised that he was going to be alone. It hurt her to think of this. Gradually, she began to understand that love and pain were not too distant from one another. Some day she and John would lose a child in this same fashion. Perhaps more than one child, and in the end they too would be alone; well, possibly not exactly alone. They'd have each other, if God was willing, but her father now would have no one.

She did not trust herself to speak, so she went over by the coffee pot, not with any intention of refilling the cup in her hand until her father chuckled and said, "It's a good brew. Just before you arrived I was telling Mr Hudspeth that sometimes I made a mighty good pot of the stuff, but as a rule it wasn't worth a tinker's damn."

She had that tearful sensation again, so she kept her back to them as she forced a lightness into her spirit to match the lightness in her father's voice. It was not an easy accomplishment. Usually, in her life, she'd been fairly successful at controlling herself, but for some inexplicable reason that was not true now, and hadn't been true for the last couple of days. Evidently being loved, and loving in turn, was a lot more complicated than she knew.

John sensed something and crossed over to her side, gravely refilled both their cups, and only looked into her eyes as he replaced the pot. She knew her eyes were shiny, and she also knew that he had the ability to plumb her thoughts, but she kept smiling anyway, and he smiled back, very gently. Then he took the pressure off her by resuming the masculine conversation with her father.

Finally, as though everything were settled, as though her father accepted completely the matter of their marriage, he said, "John, I came over a few days back to see if you knew where an old invoice is."

Liz heard her husband say, "It'll be in one of the old cases on the safe. If you'd like, we can go look for it."

They left her alone in the office. She knew perfectly well it was no accident, and that made the tears start up all over again. How many women deserved, and got, men who were this understanding, this tolerant and loving?

Finally, the tears broke through and she let them come, for a while anyway, because they were a needed release. They could have come at a better time; but then, emotions, and tears, were not nearly as susceptible to amenities, particularly in brides, as the brides might have thought, or hoped, they would be.

CHAPTER TWENTY-ONE

THE ENGLISH GENTLEMAN

THEIR first night in the old Ingraham house was an interlude she would remember to her dying day. They had a pleasant, congenial dinner in the kitchen. Her father and John had always got along well, and, of course, now that her husband was no longer an employee of her father, there was little reason for either of them to feel any kind of social disparity.

John had a good sense of humour. Her father, whose sense of humour was not as well developed, or at least was not as near the surface, managed quite well to respond, and to retaliate when either Elizabeth or John made an effort to keep things light.

Too, now that she was home again, in her customary environment, Elizabeth had no more emotional problems.

She did not delude herself that this condition was going to be permanent. She knew by instinct that from now on the chances were greater than ever that one of her biggest dilemmas would be emotional involvement, first with the man she loved, and, later, with the children he would give her. But that was different; she was ordained to have those emotional upheavals. They could be expected and she felt no fear of them.

In fact, as she fed her menfolk and enjoyed their company at dinner, she felt within herself a swelling sense of pride and gratitude for what had happened to her, and for what she felt certain would continue to be the mainstream of her existence for many years.

Later, they went out front on the porch to talk,

because it was one of those rare, warm springtime evenings, beautiful and tranquil. Her father recalled anecdotes from his first few months of marriage. Most of them Liz had never heard before, but that probably was because her father hadn't felt much compulsion to relate them to a single young girl.

John and her father discussed John's business venture. She noticed her father listening with a fresh intentness, and it occurred to her that if John were now to ask her father if he'd care to join the company, her father would very probably accept. But John did not mention anything like that, and in a way Elizabeth was glad. Maybe later; maybe after a few years when her father was getting older, and when John might have his business so organised that he might want to branch out.

But those were thoughts for the future. She sat out there, gently rocking, listening to the night, to the deep voices of her men, listening to the peace in her own heart, and almost dozed off. She hadn't been sleeping too well lately. Tonight none of the things which had kept her awake the previous few nights were likely to intervene.

Finally, along towards nine o'clock, her father thought it was getting a bit chilly out, so they all trooped back indoors and to the lobby. Liz sat down on the sofa, as she usually did, and her father took the overstuffed chair he'd been using for years. John, without a precedent, went over by Liz and sat within a couple of feet of her on the sofa. Her father dug around for a pipe, stoked it, and was in the act of lighting it when Liz saw the match freeze in mid-air six or eight inches from the pipe-bowl. She turned to follow the line of her father's stare—and there was "the English gentleman" along the lower one-third of Captain Josiah's portrait above the mantel.

Her first impulse was to excuse herself and go to her room. That had been her escape lately, but it wasn't tonight; she had a husband. Her next thought was to keep John averted. But that wouldn't have worked either for very long, so she took in a big breath and said, "John, remember what I told you about the haunt when we were over in Madison? Well, look at the portrait above the mantel."

She steeled herself as he turned to gaze towards the far wall. Every question he would ask, she had heard others ask before.

Her father got his pipe going; strong, pure tobacco-fragrance permeated the big old parlour. Her father leaned to put aside the match, and as he straightened back he looked at Liz. She said nothing, she simply shrugged. The two of them waited.

John rose, went slowly up to the portrait and stood, hands clasped behind his back, studying the faintly vibrating soft glow. Then he turned and said, "Reflection."

She shook her head, and John turned around very slowly to study the lighting in the room. When he seemed satisfied it was not a reflection, he stepped slightly closer, reached for a corner of Captain Josiah's picture, lifted and peeked behind it. Very gently he eased the picture back and removed his hand, but only temporarily. Very carefully, he put forth his fingers to touch the spot where the glow was. For several moments he did not move his hand, but when he finally did Elizabeth knew what he would say. And he said it.

"It's not cold. In fact, it doesn't feel any different than the glass over the portrait."

Elizabeth's father settled back in his chair, puffing up

166

little tufts of smoke. "Confounded nuisance, is what it is," he averred.

John turned. "Mr Ingraham, we met a man over in Madison whose father was a cabin-boy on Captain Ingraham's ship when he pulled a Scots shipmaster from the sea. He told us there was a curse on the shipmaster; that the shipmaster told his father that."

Elizabeth's father removed his pipe and looked at his daughter. She nodded. "That's exactly what he said, Dad. And furthermore, he told us that the Scot said that the curse could be transmitted, and that it would would work harm."

Her father plugged the pipe back between his teeth and sat a long while gazing at the glow of opaque light. Then he said, "Nonsense. There's never been any harm around here. At least, there's never been any more than families usually have."

John was not taking part in this exchange. He was back studying the quivering blob of pale light again. After what seemed an interminable length of time he said, "Liz, come over here and give me your hand."

She and her father exchanged a look, then she rose and went over to the fireplace. John turned, gravely, and she offered him a hand. He took it, still looking very solemn, drew her a little closer, then faced the orange-sized glow.

"It won't work. I'm sure it won't work," he said, as though addressing "the English gentleman", and gave her hand a convulsive little squeeze. "But once, up in Salem, an old woman was explaining how witchcraft used to work, and I remember now that she told me the surest way to rid a house of ghosts was for two new lovers to go, hand-in-hand, and touch the ghost. She said nothing worked but pure, strong love."

He did not look at Liz for a few seconds after he said this. Then he turned, and she saw the hint of a scoffing twinkle in his eyes. For some reason she was very relieved.

He pointed. "When I raise my hand and put it on the blob of light, Liz, you raise your free hand and do the same. Are you ready?"

She was ready, but she was also a bit hesitant. She looked over her shoulder at her father, who was leaving his chair to stroll over and watch. Her father said, "By all means try it, sweetheart. It may deprive Bannford of its own special ghost, but as far as I'm concerned I've detested 'the English gentleman' ever since I can remember."

She turned back. John was waiting. She raised a hand. So did he. Simultaneously they both touched the pulsating glow of opaque light. Just for a moment it seemed to writhe more brightly, then, although Elizabeth did not believe her eyes, it began to wither, to wane, to fade until there was nothing left but a dull brightness. Then that, too, faded and finally disappeared.

Elizabeth pulled back her hand and would also have freed the fingers John was holding, except that his grip tightened.

She could feel her heart beating solidly. She had never been superstitious, had never believed one way or another about ghosts in general, had never felt any fear, or at least not since she'd matured, of "the English gentleman". But this was something altogether different from watching him glow on Captain Josiah's portrait; this was a little like actually exorcising him, like being a witch with a full bag of *maleficia*.

John smiled and her father stepped past them to lean with his squinted eyes almost touching the portrait, examining the place where "the English gentleman" had been. Then he turned and said, "I'll be damned, it worked! Most preposterous thing I ever heard of, John. Downright unbelievable. I've never, in all my life, seen 'the English gentleman' disappear until he was damned good and ready to do so. Miraculous!"

John took Elizabeth to the sofa and sat down beside her, a heavy arm across the back of the sofa for her to lean her head against. "Too bad we can't patent it," he said, grinning at her. "The Harding Sure-fire Way To Tell If He Loves You. In the instruction sheet we could tell them to simply join hands and touch a ghost."

Elizabeth's unique feeling was passing, the coldness was giving way to her usual sense of energetic good health. She said, "That's enough for me. I never want to do anything like that again as long as I live."

Her father returned to his chair, looking sceptical. "Will he return tomorrow night?"

John, still smiling, said, "Not a chance, Mr Harding. My wife and I have got rid of him."

Elizabeth's father rose, laid aside his pipe and said, "Humph! We'll see, my boy, we'll see. If he never comes back it will suit me just fine. But I'm not going to believe he's been got rid of for a long time yet. Anyway, it's past my bedtime. Good night, you two. See you at breakfast."

After her father had departed, Elizabeth turned slowly on the sofa. She was completely recovered, but the memory was still vivid. "What old woman up in Salem told you about doing that, John?"

He hesitated briefly before replying. "My grand-mother. She died when I was about eight or nine. She told me quite a few weird tales she'd got from her grandmother. Some day we'll have to pull all the blinds, put out all the lights, and I'll tell you those stories."

Liz, watching how his face brightened and softened with humour, said, "No, thanks. You may pull the blinds and put out all the lights, lover, but no witch's tales. . . . Was your grandmother's grandmother one of the Salem witches, by any chance?"

He didn't know. "I never knew her, and I don't recall that ever being mentioned. And who cares, any-way?" He reached, and she very willingly came into his arms.

"I married a warlock," she murmured, as he tried to catch her moving lips beneath his mouth. "An exorcist. John, how do I know you didn't bewitch me into marrying you?"

"You don't know," he said, and stifled her rising laughter as he finally caught her, silenced her with a kiss that seared all the way down to her heart.

Afterwards, she was slightly breathless, but she clung to him, perfectly willing if he chose to kiss her like that again. He didn't, not right then at any rate. He leaned back with her and let his eyes roam the room, settle upon Captain Josiah's face, linger there a moment, then continue roaming until they returned to her.

"You actually resemble him a little," he told her. "At least, the same strength of character is in both faces." His eyes twinkled. He was teasing. "But your lips are ever so much softer and fuller, and your throat, and your shoulders, and your—"

"That's enough," she remonstrated, and rose, pulling

170

him up with her. "Is it written somewhere that new husbands can't help new wives clean up kitchens and do dishes?" She pulled, and he allowed himself to be led away, but he resisted briefly in the archway to look back once more at Captain Josiah's portrait. Then he went willingly enough to the kitchen, and when she handed him a dish-towel he shrugged.

"It's not a man's work, is it?" he asked.

She had an answer for that. "A *real* man is glad to help his wife. It's only the other kind that thinks it's beneath them." Right after saying that, she had a sudden, momentary vision of Bob Whiting, as though he somehow might have prompted what she'd said. Then the vision vanished, and she went to work at the sink.

It did not take long, with both of them working. When she took the dish-towel from him to hang it out on the pantry to dry, he whirled her by the shoulders, and kissed her the same way in the kitchen that he had kissed her in the parlour, only this time she was standing, so the rubbery sensation in her legs was more noticeable.

She did not want to lose the moment. Even after the kiss, when he was holding her close, she did not want to move. In fact, she did not even want to open her eyes, or to believe she couldn't spend eternity like this.

But of course she couldn't, so finally she left the unattended dish-towel where she had placed it and, taking him by the hand, led him down the starlighted back hallway to her room. It wasn't, actually, the kind of a room a man would have enjoyed living it. It was too pale and frilly and sweet-scented, but she was quite confident that in the dark he wouldn't notice the frilliness.

She was right. He didn't notice. There were other more important things to do.

171

THE HOUSE OF ROMANCE PUBLICATIONS INC.

Suite 400
562 Eglinton Ave. East
Toronto, Canada
M4P 1B9

Please send me the House of Romance Trio Volumes
I have indicated.

☐ **Trio 1 @ $2.50** per volume
Cupids and Coronets by Charles Stuart
Love's Treasure Trove by Julia Davis
The Heart's Own Sweet Music by
   Georgina Ferrand

☐ **Trio 2 @ $2.50** per volume
Topaz by Francis Hart
The Troubled Summer by Janet Roscoe
A Girl Called Debbie by
   Elizabeth Brennan

☐ **Trio 3 @ $2.50** per volume
Two Against the World by Harriet Smith
Love Dangerously by
   Peggy Loosemore Jones
No Eden for a Nurse by Marjorie Harte

☐ **Trio 4 @ $2.50** per volume
Nurse in Danger by Edna Murray
Man from the Vineyards by
   Marjorie Stockholm
Stranger in the Shadows by
   Angela Gordon

☐ **Trio 5 @ $2.50** per volume
Love Has a Hard Heart by
   Kathleen Bartlett
Springtime of Joy by Georgina Ferrand
Run Away from Love by Grace Richmond

☐ **Trio 6 @ $2.50** per volume
The Crystal Cage by Juliet Gray
Tomorrow's Promise by Iris Weigh
The Inconvenient Marriage by
   Winnifred Mantle

☐ **Trio 7 @ $2.50** per volume
Tessa Jane by Joan Warde
Victim of Love by Joan Marsh
Love is a New World by Helen Sharp

☐ **Trio 8 @ $2.50** per volume
Whispers of Fear by Brenda Castle
Love Has a Double by Beth Gorman
Angel in Abbey Road by June Mortimer

☐ **Trio 9 @ $2.50** per volume
Golden Care by Renee Farrington
The Happy Hostage by Charles Stuart
Flame of the Forest by Doris Rae

☐ **Trio 10 @ $2.50** per volume
Encounter in Athens by
   Georgina Ferrand
Ride to Romance by Joan Murray
Broken Vows by Christine Wilson

☐ **Trio 11 @ $2.50** per volume
Back to Sorrento by Jill Hoyle
Secretive Nurse by Valerie Scott
A Heart of Shadows by Ruth Bovee

☐ **Trio 12 @ $2.50** per volume
Awake to the Dawn by Doris Rae
Passport to Peril by Ann Hutton
A Labor of Love by Joan Warde

Name_____

Address_____

City/Town_____ Zip_____

State_____

I enclose $_____ for_____ books which includes
all postage and handling costs.
(No C.O.D's please)

volumex